DECEIVED

By

The Phantom

RJ Publications, LLC

Newark, New Jersey

The characters and events in this book are fictitious. Any resemblance to actual persons, living or dead is purely coincidental.

RJ Publications
Thephantom_8182@yahoo.com
www.rjpublications.com
Copyright © 2010 by RJ Publications
All Rights Reserved
ISBN 0981999832
978-0981999838

Printed in the Canada

January 2011

1 2 3 4 5 6 7 8 9 10

Chapter 1

<u>December 1989</u>

 I could definitely get use to this, Stink thought to himself, as he roamed from room to room in his grandparents' huge, luxurious home. It was surely a far cry from the cramped, two bedroom apartment that he shared with his mother in one of Greensboro, North Carolina's roughest housing projects.

 "Stink! Come on down these stairs!" His grandmother yelled, snapping him out of his thoughts.

 "O.K., Grandma, I'm coming!" he responded, amazed that there was a Jacuzzi in the bathroom.

 "Boy! Get down these stairs! I know you have finished unpacking your things by now!" She barked.

 Stink hurriedly went down the stairs to see what his grandmother wanted. As he walked into the kitchen, his grandmother glared at him evilly.

 "Boy, go and get washed up for dinner."

 Stink turned and headed off in the direction of the bathroom. After he washed his hands and came back into the kitchen, his grandmother was still over the stove, placing greasy fried chicken onto a platter.

 Stink bypassed the kitchen and went into the den where his grandfather lounged in his recliner watching television.

 "Wazup, Papa?" Stink asked, as he took a seat opposite his grandfather.

 "What's up? The rent... The sky," his grandfather replied sarcastically.

 Stink's grandfather was a very dear man to him. A college professor, he expressed the importance of education.

When Stink felt there was nobody to talk to, his grandfather was always there.

The grandchild of actual slaves, Stink's grandfather had experienced the brutality of racism first hand. He attended colleges and universities in southern states, such as Alabama and North Carolina, witnessing some of the most heinous crimes against Black folks.

"You, young folk, just don't know how to talk anymore," his grandfather stated, averting his attention from the television to Stink. "What ever happened to 'Hello' or 'Good evening'?" he asked incredulously.

"My fault, Papa. Good evening," Stink refashioned, half-heartedly.

Situations like this would prove to be life lessons for Stink, but at that moment, Stink felt he was being ridiculed.

Born in 1973, Rahsaan Abdul Jones was Rahnetta Jones's first and only child. It's said that if a father isn't present during the birth of his child, then it's likely he won't be there for the child's life either.

This rang true in Stink's short sixteen years of life. With an absentee father, he began to show his lack of fatherly love through anger and aggression. By the age of thirteen, it was well documented that the youngster would not hesitate to act that aggression out on anybody that ignited his fury.

Stink's mother finally had enough when he was implicated in a vicious attack that took a human life. His mother promptly sent him to live with his grandparents in Hampton, Virginia although he was never formally accused by any law enforcement agency.

So here he was. The only family he had in Virginia, besides his grandparents, was an aunt and her two kids. Paul, who everyone called PJ, and his sister Wanetta - named closely after Stink's mom.

PJ and Stink were roughly the same age; Wanetta was a few years older. They lived in the roughest section of Newport News - East End, often referred to as 'Downtown' or 'The Bottom', because of its geographical location on Newport News's peninsula. Newport News bordered Hampton so closely it almost seemed as if they were one city.

The two cousins clicked immediately, hanging out almost everyday. After being in Virginia a short time, Stink meshed with his new surroundings. He quickly became known as PJ's cousin and to some, even his brother.

Stink and PJ could definitely pass for brothers. Their light complexion and sharp features mirrored one another. PJ's scrawny figure and curly hair, however, contrasted Stink's naturally muscular build and coarse hair. Nonetheless, they could still pass for brothers.

They were inseparable - hanging out, cruising the city, hollering at girls and occasionally smoking weed. Stink had been experimenting with the exotic hemp since he was old enough to steal his mother's roaches out of the ashtray.

PJ's girlfriend, Sharon, hooked Stink up with Nikki, one of her friends. After getting to know one another and talking on the phone, they made plans to hang out with PJ and Sharon the following weekend.

Stink and PJ picked Sharon and Nikki up and followed their regular routine. After riding around half the night and smoking countless blunts, they all ended up at Sharon's house. As soon as they entered the house, PJ and Sharon disappeared leaving Stink and Nikki alone.

Getting girls was nothing new to Stink, however it was something he hadn't experienced since he'd been in Virginia.

"What's your real name?" Nikki asked, eyeing him appreciatively.

"Rahsaan."

"Oh, why they call you 'Stink', then?"

Stink hesitated, knowing it wouldn't be wise to divulge how he'd actually gotten the nickname. Then he thought, *Fuck it,*

"When I was a baby, I supposedly shit on my moms while she was changing my diaper so she called me Stink," he explained, judging her reaction closely.

Nikki began to laugh hysterically. "For real?" she asked, attempting to control her laughter.

"Oh, that's funny, huh?" Stink asked with a hint of attitude.

"Nah. It's cute," she replied sexually.

Stink took this as his cue, quickly closing the space that separated them. "So, you think it's cute, huh?" he inquired, eyeing her hungrily.

"Yeah, it's cute," she replied, biting on her pinky. "You're cute too."

Stink leaned in close and gently kissed Nikki's lips. Instantly, Nikki reciprocated, giving him all the tongue he could handle. While interlocked in the kiss, Stink reached up and fondled Nikki's pert titties. Her kisses became more intense, so he took things a step further and slipped his hand between her legs. Even though Nikki was fully clothed, Stink felt her breath quicken when his hand made contact with her jean-clad vagina. He fumbled with her buttons in an attempt to get her jeans off.

As he unbuttoned her jeans, Nikki placed her hand on top of his. "Hold on! Stop Stink!" She gasped heavily. "Do you have a rubber?"

"A rubber?" Stink asked in surprise.

"Yeah, a motherfucking rubber. A condom. You know, protection?" Nikki asked sarcastically.

Stink sat there for a moment in thought then stood up. "Hold on, I'll be right back."

Frantically searching the house for PJ, Stink found him as he heard Keith Sweat's *Make it Last Forever* playing loudly through a closed door. He knocked on the door impatiently. Not receiving a response quick enough, he knocked again.

"Yo, wasup?" PJ asked through the door.

"Yo, P, I need to holler at you for a minute."

"A'ight, just give me a minute," PJ replied, brushing Stink off.

"Yo, P, it will only be a second man!" Stink stated, expressing his urgency.

"A'ight, man, hold up," PJ retorted in a frustrated tone.

After a brief wait, PJ emerged wearing only his boxers. "What's up, man?" PJ asked, visibly irritated.

Stink looked to his cousin with pleading eyes and said, "Yo, man, I need a rubber."

"Shit, I ain't got one," PJ said and then turned to leave.

Stink grabbed his cousin's shoulder. "Hold up man! Nikki's in there waiting on me to come back with a rubber! What I'm-a do?"

PJ looked at his cousin in deep thought then said, "Come on, I've got an idea."

Stink followed him into the kitchen and watched confused as PJ began rambling through drawers until he found what he was looking for. PJ held up a roll of saran-wrap and said, "Use this."

Stink looked at him quizzically. "What am I supposed to do with that?"

"Just wrap it around your dick like a rubber and before you put it in, pull the plastic off," PJ advised.

This nigga must be crazy! Stink thought to himself. There was no way he was going to get away with that.

PJ noticed his hesitancy. "Look, man, just let her feel your jaunt then take it off," he instructed, pushing the roll of plastic toward Stink.

Willing to try anything at that point, Stink took the roll of plastic and tore off a piece. As soon as PJ saw him attempting to try the hoax, he left Stink in the kitchen to fend for himself. Stink quickly undid his pants and did as PJ had instructed, wrapping the plastic around his limp penis as a makeshift condom.

Once the plastic was in place, as best as he could attach it, Stink headed back into the den.

Nikki sat on the couch, watching television when Stink entered the room and took his place on the couch beside her.

"It took you long enough. Did you get one?" She asked frustrated.

"Yeah, I got one," Stink lied.

To his amazement, Nikki reached over and began kissing him. As he returned her kiss, he could sense the urgency in her tongue. Stink quickly picked up where he'd left off. Laying her down, he frantically began to undo her jeans. He moved from her mouth to her earlobe and began to gently suck.

She responded by reaching for his zipper.

Not wanting to be busted with the plastic wrapped around his dick, Stink quickly pulled away.

"Wha...What's wrong?" She asked breathlessly.

"Nothing," Stink replied, pulling his shirt over his head. He then leaned down and pulled Nikki's pants completely off. As she lay there, naked from the waist down, Stink dropped his jeans and boxers in one fluid motion, and then laid between Nikki's thighs.

Reaching for his manhood, she asked, "Is it on?"

"Yeah, yeah, it's on," Stink lied, gripping the base of his penis, making certain to cover the excess plastic that bunched up around his pubic hair.

Nikki gingerly reached down and touched the head of Stink's dick, then smiled in a seductive manner. Once she wrapped her arms around his neck and spread her legs invitingly, Stink knew he had her. Smoothly, he snatched the plastic off and dropped it to the floor.

"Put it in," Nikki huffed passionately.

Stink responded by rubbing the head of his penis between her vaginal lips. The warm juices oozed from her slit.

"Ooh, Stink, please put it in!" Nikki begged.

He obliged by pushing his entire length into her pussy. Nikki's back arched as she accepted the sweet intrusion.

"Oh, Yeah, Yeah! Stink!" She panted with each stroke.

Stink began to pump in and out of Nikki furiously, feeling the orgasm rise deep within his loins.

Unable to hold out any longer, his entire body convulsed as his seed shot deep into Nikki's pussy.

"Aww, shit," Stink grunted, collapsing on top of Nikki. He immediately felt her tightness pushing him out.

He pulled completely out of Nikki's pussy then stood up and retrieved the piece of balled up plastic and his jeans.

Feeling between her legs, Nikki asked, "Stink, why do it feel like you nutted in me?"

"I'ont know. Maybe the rubber bust," he offered cynically.

"Boy, you better not had come in me!" Nikki warned, pulling at her jeans as Stink stood on them. "Move!" she snapped.

After retrieving her clothes, she took off in the direction of the bathroom.

The rest of the night, Nikki didn't say one word to Stink; she only glared evilly at him occasionally. That was fine by him, he'd gotten what he wanted - his first piece of VA pussy. For a long time, Stink and PJ laughed about that saran-wrap incident.

At home, things were going smoothly for Stink; he was working and doing well in school. More importantly, he was staying out of trouble. His grandparents were proud of his transition, enabling them to give him more freedom.

Just before his seventeenth birthday, his grandfather bought him a car. It wasn't a flashy car like a lot of teenagers at Stink's high school were driving; it was what people in his age group called a "hoopty." Nevertheless, it was a car.

PJ, a year out of high school, had begun to sell marijuana. Stink also toyed with the idea but was never able to regain his initial investment due to his smoking habit, thus he learned a hustler's cardinal rule: Don't get high off your own supply.

It was unbelievable to him how PJ maintained his steady flow of money and still was able to smoke freely.

Stink gave up trying to sell weed and simply assisted PJ in his operations. The block where PJ sold his weed was right around the corner from his house. When they weren't hanging out, they would hit the block and post up.

Toward the end of the summer, PJ's weed business was booming. He had gone from buying ounces to buying pounds while Stink worked at a restaurant making minimum wage. On several occasions PJ attempted to give Stink his own package, but Stink continuously turned him down, knowing he'd always break that cardinal rule.

Chapter 2

It seemed as if every time Stink saw PJ, he sported a new article of clothing; whether it was the new Used jeans or a pair of sneakers, PJ stayed fresh. Stink attempted to keep up with his cousin when it came to his clothes but this proved to be disastrous because in no time, Stink's meager savings from his summer job had dwindled.

Stink used the upcoming school year as an excuse to quit his job.

The streets were calling and there was a new epidemic hitting the streets of America, hard. Even though Stink wasn't aware of it, he would soon be introduced to it. Crack was already running rampant through the major cities of the U.S. and was just about to land in VA.

On this particular day, a brand new white jeep with the custom flip-flop paint job pulled over in front of PJ's house. PJ and Stink eyed the jeep hard, trying to figure out who was driving the flashy car. As the door swung open, Dame stepped out.

Dame was a guy who occasionally bought weed from them. His partner, Lil Man, usually in tow, casually stepped out of the jeep's passenger side. The duo made their way up to PJ's porch and exchanged pleasantries.

Everybody in the 'hood knew Dame and Lil Man hustled, they just didn't know exactly what it was they hustled.

After kicking it for a few, Dame offered Stink and PJ a ride in his new jeep.

After making a few drop-offs and pick-ups, Dame and Lil Man shed some light on their hustle.

"Man, crack getting niggas paid for real. I know ya'll got the 'Lil' weed thang going," Dame explained, inhaling deeply on the blunt, "but I'm telling ya'll crack is where it's at," he stated, passing Lil Man the blunt.

Stink was intently listening to every word being spoken, responding with a barrage of questions. "How much it cost? How much you make? How do you get it? Where do you sell it? How do..." He grilled, firing questions in rapid succession.

Dame and Lil Man answered all of Stink's questions, giving him a brief Crack 101.

"If ya'll start with a 16th, you'll more than double your money," Dame advised.

"Yeah and ya'll could sell it on the same block ya'll selling weed on now. Ole boy's crib on 27th is a regular spot for crack heads," Lil Man said.

Stink was confused because all the time he'd spent on the block, the only drug he'd seen being bought was weed.

Dame quickly picked up on Stink's confusion. "I know ya'll know Darlene who lives on 26th street."

Stink and PJ nodded in unison.

"She be buying crack all the time. And she don't spend no less than thirty dollars when she come," Dame boasted.

This came as a surprise to PJ and Stink because they knew exactly who he was talking about and they weren't aware that she was on crack.

Stink began to feel apprehensive about Dame and Lil Man trying to shuffle their wonder drug off on them.

Knowing that the only way he would find out if they were gaming them or not, Stink cut through all the bullshit and blurted, "When can I get something then?"

"Shit, right now. I just gotta stop by my sister's crib and pick it up," Dame replied, detouring in the direction of his sister's house.

Stink only had thirty dollars on him. He needed an additional fifty dollars in order to buy what Dame explained as a 16th.

Stink looked at PJ and asked, "You trying to do this or what?"

PJ shot him a look as if to say, *Nigga is you out of yo' fucking mind?*

Stink ignored his expression and pressed on. "Man, I need to borrow," he paused to recount his money, "like fifty dollars. I'm-a give it back to you as soon as I make it," Stink promised.

"Yeah, I got you," PJ stated, reluctantly digging into his pockets.

Dame parked the jeep in front of the projects off of 12th street and hopped out.

Lil Man, PJ and Stink sat in the jeep waiting on Dame to return when someone tapped on the passenger window, startling the trio.

"Wha…What the fuck!" Lil Man exclaimed, instinctively grabbing at his waist. He quickly recognized the figure standing there. Rolling the window down, he warned, "Ladybug, I almost shot yo ass for creeping up on me like that. Whazup?"

"Hey, Lil. Ya'll holding?" She asked unable to hold still.

"Yeah. What you want?" Lil Man asked, reaching inside his jacket producing a bag full of dice-sized rocks.

"Umm, I got thirty. Can I get two for that?" She asked, eyeing the bag of rocks greedily.

Ladybug waited impatiently for Lil Man to give her the drugs continuously shifting her weight from one leg to the other.

Lil Man dug into the bag, handed her two small rocks and then snatched the money from her hand. Ladybug held the two rocks in her palm gently, inspecting them closely. Unexpectedly, she pulled a small metal tube from inside her mouth, stuffed one of the rocks in one end and placed her mouth on the other end. Lighting the end of the tube with the rock in it, she inhaled deeply. Instantly, a dazed look appeared on her face. She lifted her free hand to form the ok sign with her thumb and forefinger.

"This…shit…da bomb!" she proclaimed, while still holding the smoke in.

Stink and PJ looked on in awe. The sight of the woman smoking crack in broad daylight was both shocking and hilarious.

"Where ya'll gonna be at later?" she asked with a wide-eyed look on her face.

"Just beep me," Lil Man said, between chuckles.

As she walked away, they all burst out laughing. The sight of her giving Lil Man the 'o.k.' sign, while still holding the pipe in her lips was too much.

Witnessing the drug transaction, Stink was anxious to get his own package of rocks.

Dame came walking out of the apartment and hopped in the driver's seat. "What did Ladybug want?" he asked, tossing Stink a rectangular shaped rock, tightly wrapped in plastic.

"She got two for 30. But, yo, the bitch did some funny shit…" Lil Man went on to explain the spectacle that they'd just witnessed.

Inspecting the rectangular rock closely, Stink passed Dame the eighty dollars then asked Lil Man, "How much you give her for thirty dollars?"

Again, Lil Man pulled his bag of rocks from his jacket then poured three or four of them in his hand. "Each one of these goes for twenty dollars, but if they come with thirty, I just give 'em two," Lil Man explained.

Stink eyed the size of the rocks, taking a mental picture of their exact size and shape.

Dame headed back to PJ's crib where he dropped Stink and PJ off but not before giving Stink and PJ his and Lil Man's pager numbers. Impressed with the small electronic devices, Stink vowed to get him one real soon.

Stink followed PJ upstairs to his room then anxiously stated, "Yo, P, I need a razor or something."

PJ left the room and quickly returned with a razor.

Stink frantically tore the plastic and eyed the block of crack, remembering the size of the rocks Lil Man showed him. He took the razor and drew perfect little squares, similar to a Tic-Tac-Toe board. He made sure each square equaled the size of Lil Man's rocks. He then counted each square. Thinking that he must have messed up somewhere, he recounted them. Stink couldn't believe that he had counted twenty-one perfect squares. Lil Man had said, *double your money* not *quadruple your money*. Stink meticulously cut into each square, chipping off perfect little rocks.

PJ leaned over his shoulder, eyeing his every move. "Man, you crazy as hell for buying that bullshit. You don't even know nobody to sell it to," PJ scolded.

Stink ignored his cousin and continued to concentrate on cutting the rocks. As he finished, he counted the rocks again, just above a whisper, "1,2,3,4,5…17,18,19..." Stink was shocked at the total amount.

Intently watching Stink's every move, PJ asked, "What you say?"

"I just counted twenty-one rocks and I got some crumbs left," Stink replied, thinking that maybe Dame had given him the wrong bag or something.

"You better hope you can sell that shit."

Ignoring PJ once again, Stink put all the contents into a sandwich bag and headed out the door.

Once Stink hit the block, he went straight to Darlene's house on 26th Street. He casually walked up on her porch and knocked on the door.

"Who is it?" A man asked behind the closed door.

"It's Stink, PJ's cousin. Is Darlene home?"

After about two minutes, the door creaked open and a scraggly dressed Darlene appeared. "Uh, yes, may I help you?" She asked suspiciously.

"Yeah, um, I just wanted to let you know that we, um, got some rocks if you trying to buy some," Stink stammered, purposely using PJ as an accomplice.

Darlene stood there for a moment in contemplation, then said, "Well, I usually get a tester before I buy anything. Do you have something for me to test?"

"Yeah, I got something," Stink replied reaching for his bag of rocks.

"Naw, baby, not out here. Come in," she said motioning for him to come inside.

After what he'd witnessed earlier, Stink thought it was okay to pull his bags of rocks out on the porch.

As he entered the house, he immediately smelled the stench of old trash and smelly dishes. There were clothes thrown all over the living room and beer bottles littered the floor. Darlene's house was in total disarray.

She stood there waiting on Stink as he stood there eyeing the room in disbelief.

"Ahem!" She cleared her throat.

"Oh, my fault," Stink apologized, pulling out his bag of rocks. He pinched some of the crumbs from the bottom of the bag, and carefully placed them into Darlene's outstretched hand.

As soon as the crumbs hit her palm, she took off up the stairs without saying a word. The old man who had opened the door was in close pursuit of Darlene when she hit the stairs.

Standing there alone, Stink sighed in disbelief then quickly let himself out of the house. There was one more stop Stink had to make before he went back to PJ's crib.
Stink walked up on the porch and instantly noticed a pair of eyes staring at him through a tiny slit in a first story window. Before he could knock on the door, it was snatched open.

"What's up?" A man who looked like a monster asked in a threatening tone.

"Is Reggie home?" Stink asked, attempting to seem unintimidated.

"Ay, Reggie! Some young dude out here looking for you!" the monster yelled over his shoulder.

"What up, Young Blood? What can I do for you?" Reggie asked, taking the place of the monster in the doorway.

Stink looked at the tall man dressed as if it was dead winter when it was actually a warm, fall day.

It was a long shot, but Stink was willing to try anything to come up. "Yeah, I'm Stink, PJ's cousin. You know, we be out here with the weed," Stink paused, then continued, "Well now we got some rocks too if you know somebody trying to get some," Stink explained, using PJ as an accomplice once again.

Reggie looked at him suspiciously, then asked, "Oh yeah. What ya'll got?"

Stink shrugged his shoulders. "We got whatever."

"Well let me get a bump and if it's good, I've got some people that's trying to buy something."

Stink had no idea what a "bump" was but he wasn't about to make the same mistake that he'd made earlier and pull his bag out right there on the porch. "Can I come inside?"

"Yeah, yeah. Come on in," Reggie said, leading Stink into the house.

Compared to Reggie's house, Darlene's looked like a mansion. Reggie led Stink down a dark hallway into a room that looked to be the kitchen. The flickering light from candles burning gave the house a dungeon type of vibe. Two guys and a woman were seated at the table. Stink was unable to make out their faces, due to the poor lighting.

Reggie hovered over the table, waiting for Stink to produce what he'd called a "bump." Stink took this as his cue to pull his bag of rocks out. He pinched the remainder of the crumbs out and placed them in Reggie's hand. Reggie meticulously poured them onto the table in a small pile.

He instantly pulled out a replica of the pipe that the woman from earlier had used. Pushing the small pile of crumbs into the pipe, Reggie carefully placed the other end to his lips. Quickly producing a lighter, he put the fire to the pipe and inhaled deeply.

As soon as the fire made contact with the crack, Stink heard a crackling noise. Reggie dropped to one knee, while holding the smoke in. Everyone seated at the table focused their attention on Reggie, as he blew a cloud of the potent smoke into the air.

Reggie looked to Stink, with a look of disorientation on his face and said, "Don't go nowhere." He quickly rose and exited the room.

After a brief wait, he reappeared. "Give me a fifty," he stated demandingly, holding the money out to Stink.

He quickly did the math in his head. *If two cost thirty, then three must cost fifty*, Stink thought, digging three small rocks out of the bag.

Exchanging the drugs for the money, Stink quickly turned to leave.

"This the same shit?" Reggie asked.

"Yeah, it's the same," Stink threw over his shoulder.

Just as Stink grabbed the doorknob, Reggie yelled, "Don't go far!"

Relieved to be out of the house, Stink counted the bills Reggie had given him. Walking up the block, Stink heard someone call out to him. He looked up to see the old man from Darlene's trotting in his direction.

"You're just the man I'm looking for," the old man said, breathing heavily. He held out a handful of crumpled bills. "Darlene sent me to get a thirty."

Not wanting to break his new found rule, Stink ducked behind an abandoned house, retrieved two of the rocks for the old man and watched him briskly walk away, but not before turning to ask, "You gonna be around, aint'cha?"

Suppressing a smile, Stink replied, "Yeah. I'm-a be around." His first two transactions had netted his initial investment.

The remainder of that afternoon, Stink was being called from Darlene's house to Reggie's until he was completely out of rocks. He rushed to PJ's house with a pocket full of money and a new sense of pride.

Stink entered PJ's room and barked, "Yo, beep Dame an'em!"

Lying across his bed with the phone glued to his ear, PJ sat upright and asked, "What happened? You alright?"

Stink emptied his pockets, allowing the money to do the talking for him.

"Ay Yo, Sharon, I'm-a call you right back, a'ight," PJ blurted, eyeing the money hungrily.

PJ quickly paged Dame while Stink counted his money. Stink promptly gave PJ the fifty dollars he'd given him earlier, leaving him with nearly $350. In just a few hours, Stink had turned a thirty-dollar investment into almost $400. It was funny to Stink because at first PJ didn't want anything to do with the crack game, but after seeing the money Stink made, he was all for it.

Stink and PJ continued to buy drugs from Dame and Lil Man, building each of their stashes up to a few thousand. Now, Stink could buy all the things that he couldn't afford before.

School had begun for Stink and with the money he made from hustling, he was one of the flyest dressed guys at his high school. Donning Polo and Guess nearly everyday, Stink was definitely one of the elite.

It had begun to be hard for Stink to hide all of the new things he'd bought from his grandparents. He would have to tuck his gold link inside of his shirt before he came into the house and when he went shopping, he would have to hide his bags in the garage until they were asleep.

One of the first things that Stink and PJ bought with their drug proceeds was two matching Beretta 9mms. Since Stink had been in VA, he hadn't displayed that rage that lived deep within him. He simply bought the gun as a prop to signal he was a hustler.

One day Stink and Dame were cruising the streets of Newport News, smoking a blunt, when Dame abruptly pulled his jeep up behind a crowd of guys hanging out on the corner.

Stink lounged in the passenger seat, boppin' his head to the beat that played through the speaker box in the back of the jeep. He eyed Dame as he walked up to one of the guys in the crowd and began talking to him.

The longer their conversation persisted, the more menacing each man's face became. Before long, the entire crowd was focused on the exchange between Dame and the other man.

Once Stink saw Dame grab a hold of the man's collar, he bolted from the jeep, gripping his nine.

Stink approached the spectacle and cocked his gun back, quickly garnering the attention of everybody on the block.

"Dame, you a'ight?!" Stink asked, aiming his pistol directly at the man's head.

"Yeah, I'm straight man. This nigga gonna give me my money though!"

Stink eased closer to the pair and placed his free hand over Dame's hand. "Let him go, D," Stink advised calmly, then turned his attention to Dame's adversary and asked, "You got my man's money?"

Before the man could open his mouth, Stink swung the big black gun with tremendous force, landing crushingly against the man's head. The blow of the gun wasn't even heard, due to the accompanying shot from the Beretta.

The entire crowd, including Dame, stood in shock as the guy's body crashed to the ground. Dame peered down at the guy whom he just held in his grasp, noticing the trickle of blood coming from his head. "Oh, shit! He's dead!" Dame proclaimed in a hysterical tone.

Stink calmly walked away from the scene and hopped in Dame's jeep.

Dame jumped in the driver's seat, babbling non-stop. "Stink, he dead, man! What we gonna do? Aww shit, man! I don't believe this, man…"

"He ain't dead, man," Stink informed, cutting his rambling off.

"Wha…What?"

"He ain't dead, man. Trust me."

"How…How you know?"

Stink smiled at his man's inexperience with gunplay. He knew he hadn't shot the man, maybe grazed him, but not shot. He just smiled.

By far, Stink was the wildest member of his crew. The slight act of brutality that he'd displayed had separated him from the rest of his crew. Although PJ had a mean streak in him also, it just took a substantial amount of persuasion to bring it out.

After Dame was assured that the guy wouldn't die, he treated Stink as if he was the Maharajah.

Unlike PJ, Stink didn't have a steady girlfriend. He played the field, hitting what he could and moving when he should. That is until he met Trina.

Stink and PJ attended the annual football game which showcased the area's best high schools. During the half-time show, they walked around showing off their newly-purchased outfits, enjoying the attention they received from the girls.

Stink wore a pair of blue Polo jeans and a red and blue Polo rugby style shirt, along with a pair of white and blue Nike Airs. PJ had on a Tommy Hilfiger jumpsuit, a matching orange Tommy shirt and a pair of white Reebok Classics.

As they walked past a group of girls standing near the concession stand, one of the girls called out, "Hey, you, in the red and blue, come here!"

Stink looked himself up and down, as if to say, *you talking to me?*

"Yeah, you," she replied in a sexy tone.

Stink walked over to the group of young ladies, closely followed by PJ. "Yeah. Whazup?" he asked, attempting to seem debonair.

"What's your name?" A short brown-skinned girl asked.

Stink looked the girl over, liking what he saw, he replied, "Rahsaan."

This girl was definitely fine. Her hair was cut in a short bob style and definitely added to her sexiness. The way she allowed a lock of hair to partially cover her light brown eyes was alluring. Her nice round ass and shapely bowlegs complemented the package. Stink definitely liked what he saw.

"So, what's your name?" he asked.

"Trina," she replied, extending her hand toward Stink. "So what school do you go to?" Trina asked, tenderly gripping Stink's hand.

"I'm a senior at Bethel," he announced proudly.

With a slight giggle, she asked, "So you from Hampton?"

"Yeah, I'm from Hampton. Why you smiling?"

"Oh, nothing. You just don't seem like a guy from Hampton," she explained.

Stink took this as a compliment, because most guys from Hampton were considered soft and he was nowhere near soft. "So what school you go to?" he asked, allowing his eyes to rest upon Trina's smooth, beautiful face.

"I graduated from Denbeigh two years ago," she replied, instantly intimidating Stink.

He had never gone out with a girl older than himself so immediately he felt uncertain about their age difference. Nonetheless, they continued to talk throughout the second half of the game. Before they parted, Stink had Trina's number and a kiss on the cheek.

\-------------------------------------

In no time, Trina became Stink's girl. She showed him things that he hadn't experienced with the little flings he'd been involved in; she showed him love. He in turn, showered her with gifts - clothes, jewelry; you name it, Stink bought it.

Although Stink was happy with Trina being his girl, he still practiced his infidelities with other girls. Trina had never caught him cheating on her. It was rumored on a few occasions, yet Stink was never caught. That was until...

Stink's crew was basically at the forefront of hustlers at that time. A lot of girls were trying to get next to them just because of what they did and how they dressed. PJ and Stink, by far the better-looking of their crew, usually received most of the attention. PJ practiced more self-restraint when it came to his sexual indiscretions than Stink.

One night during a show held at the coliseum, this proved to be evident. Stink's entire crew rented a hotel suite near the event, as it was customary to do at the time. As the alcohol and marijuana flowed in abundance, girls flocked to their suites making their spot the place to be. With a couple of hours before the actual show began, they held their own party. One of the girls, a short, pecan-complexioned cutie with a nice round ass and sizeable titties, continuously gave Stink a lustful stare, beckoning him to her. Once Stink finally acknowledged her silent invitation, it was on.

Instead of attending the show with the rest of his crew, Stink decided to take his female companion into one of the other suites, unbeknownst to anybody in his group.

As soon as Stink and Kesha entered the empty hotel suite, their hands tore at each other's clothes. In a matter of seconds, Stink had stripped to his socks. There was no question of a condom nor were there any sentimental words spoken; there was only lust on each of their minds.

Their first round of sex was rough and to the point. "Oh Yess! Fuck me! Yess, Stink, fuck me!" Kesha hissed through clenched teeth.

Stink pounded away, until sweat dripped from his forehead onto Kesha's chest.

After round one, there was two and three. Totally destroying the suite from their vigorous sex, Stink decided to go to one of the other rooms to chill.

PJ, Lil Man and Dame strolled through the packed crowd of the nightclub. The after party was definitely the place to be. PJ eyed the ladies in attendance and thought about Stink. It was somewhat strange how he'd disappeared before the show, but PJ knew his cousin.

Dame, leading the trio, headed straight through the dance floor. Out of the sea of people, someone grabbed PJ's arm. "Hey, PJ. Where is my baby at? I know he's with ya'll," Trina stated, looking around for Stink.

"Uh, yeah. He got sick though," PJ lied.

"Forreal? Where he at?" she asked full of concern.

PJ thought for a second, then figured if he gave Trina the suite number where he knew for certain Stink wasn't located everything would be cool. "Uh, he should be at the Red Roof, room 212," PJ revealed, unaware of what was taking place in room 212 at that moment.

"Ah shit! Wha…What the fuck! Shit!" Stink gasped, as Kesha's mouth worked magic on his manhood. He could only throw his head back in ecstasy and enjoy the warmth of Kesha's mouth wrapped around his genitals. Stink had never experienced the sensation that he was feeling at that moment.

Facing the ceiling in a daze, he felt the familiar rumbling in his groin. He was on the verge of cumming in Kesha's mouth, when a loud knock at the door jarred him out of his euphoric state.

Kesha abruptly stopped, then looked up to Stink. The knocking persisted, urging Stink to ease from the bed and peek out of the curtains. What he saw instantly made his jaw drop to the floor.

Sounding naturally concerned, Trina whined, "Stink, open the door, baby."

Looking toward Kesha, he placed his finger to his lips signaling her to keep quiet while he paced the floor formulating a plan.

Quickly, he rushed Kesha into the bathroom, threw his jeans on and went to the door.

Stink eased the door open, only to be bombarded by Trina and her entire crew.

"You alright, baby?" Trina asked, placing her palm to his forehead.

"Yeah, I'm a'ight."

"You sure, baby?"

"Yeah, I threw up and shit, but I'm good now," Stink lied.

"Can I use the bathroom?" one of Trina's friends asked, making her way to the bathroom.

Stink shot past her, and stood in front of the door. "Um, um, nah.   You can't use this bathroom," he stammered.

"Why can't she use the bathroom?" Trina asked suspiciously.

"Uh, cause, ah, I got something in there."

One of Trina's girls snapped, "I bet you do."

Trina stepped up, and said, "Let me in the bathroom, Stink."

Stink stood there in a defiant stance, provoking the other four women to corral behind Trina.

Stink looked in the face of each woman and knew that he was busted. There was no way he would be able to prevent them from getting into that bathroom. Shocking the entire crew, Stink walked away from the door.

He grabbed the remainder of his clothes and exited the room. He stole a quick glance before leaving, only to see Kesha on the floor balled up in the fetal position, as stomps and kicks rained down onto her body.

\-

Being caught in the hotel room with Kesha caused Trina to keep close tabs on Stink from then on. If he wasn't handling some sort of drug business, Trina was sure to be in close proximity. Usually when Stink wasn't downtown hustling, he was in Denbeigh over Trina's house.

Denbeigh was a section of Newport News. Unlike downtown, Denbeigh was more of a suburban area. The slums were located downtown. Denbeigh had its projects but nothing like downtown.

Stink lounged on the couch in Trina's living room, eyeing her and her girlfriend Eyvette, through veiled eyes. The marijuana caused him to giggle with every move that the two young ladies attempted. They were reenacting a performance by the female rap duo, Salt-N-Pepa and the jiggling of their firm asses beneath the tight spandex shorts, caused a slight tingling in Stink's groin.

Just as he began to visualize digging Trina's girlfriend's back out, the doorbell rang loudly.

Trina rushed off to the door, leaving him and Eyvette alone. When Stink heard Trina conversing with a young man, he intuitively grabbed for his trusted Beretta.

As Trina led the guy into the living room, Stink clutched his nine beneath his sweatshirt.

"Stink, this is Jamal, Eyvette's boyfriend," Trina introduced.

Stink relaxed and threw his head up at the guy.

After sitting around holding small talk, Stink's pager went off. As he stood to go and use the phone, he could see Trina focusing her attention on him like a hawk. She quickly stood to follow him into the kitchen as he used the phone, still watching him closely. Stink shook his head in frustration at how jealous she had become. In some strange, twisted way, Stink actually confused her actions as love.

After talking to one of his customers from downtown, Stink hung up the phone and turned to Trina. "Baby, I gotta go make a run right quick."

"You coming back, ain't you?" she asked in a voice filled with hostility.

"Yeah, I'm coming back."

Trina stood there with her lips poked out, then blurted, "If you coming right back, take Jamal with you."

He looked to Trina in preparation to dispute her idea, however, upon seeing the defiance in her demeanor, he walked back into the living room. "Hey yo, you trying to roll with me real quick? I'm just gonna make a run downtown," Stink said to Jamal, interrupting a physical moment between him and Eyvette.

Jamal's eyes seemed to have gotten noticeably wilder at the mentioning of downtown. Stink was sure that he would refuse the invitation.

To Stink's surprise, Jamal replied, "Yeah. Yeah, I'll roll."

After Stink handled his business downtown, he and Jamal began to kick it on the drive back to Trina's house.

"I ain't know you were from downtown," Jamal inquired with a hint of skepticism.

"Nah, I ain't from down there, I just do my thing down there. I live in Hampton," Stink explained, full of self-confidence. Even though Stink had handled his business in an inconspicuous manner, he still wanted Jamal to know what it was he did.

"So you be slangin' downtown, huh?" Jamal asked, somewhat amazed.

Stink had never heard of hustling referred to as "slangin'," nonetheless he went with the flow. "Yeah, I do my thang down there," he replied boastfully.

Jamal was in awe that Stink sold drugs downtown. The notorious stories that he'd heard about that part of the city immediately made Jamal respect Stink.

"You know, I heard that the twenties downtown go for forties in Denbeigh," Jamal revealed casually.

Unable to mask the look on his face at the mention of *doubling* what he already made, Stink looked at Jamal in amazement.

"And the police don't be sweating niggas that much up here," he continued.

This was too much for Stink. His mind raced. Jamal's last statement had him sold. Stink could recall on numerous occasions where NNPD's Vice Squad had chased him and PJ for countless blocks. Things were getting hot downtown and Stink was looking for a way out. This was definitely his lucky day.

"So where you be at up here?" Stink asked, hiding his excitement.

"Oh, I live out at Aquaduct with my sister."

Aquaduct was by far Denbeigh's roughest project, however, it wasn't downtown.

Stink and Jamal continued to kick it the entire ride to Trina's house. By the time they arrived, plans had been made to check out 'The Duct,' as Jamal called it.

A few days later, Stink and Jamal met up and went to Aquaduct. Just as Jamal had said, the rocks that Stink sold for twenties downtown went for forty in Aquaduct. He couldn't believe how sweet the money was in Denbeigh.

After becoming known, Stink's business flourished. A few of the other hustlers began to get jealous of the clientele that he had built among the crack heads and petty hustlers. Stink used this popularity and a keen sense of business to lock the entire project down. So quite naturally, it wouldn't be long before someone tried to test him.

Stink and Jamal were chillin in Jamal's sister's apartment on a Friday night when someone knocked on the door frantically.

Instinctively, Stink reached for his gun. Nobody was supposed to come to the apartment. All of their runners knew to use the payphone and either he or Jamal would promptly appear. So for somebody to be knocking on the door was a violation - or an emergency.

"Who is it?!" Jamal barked.

"It's me, Von," one of Stink's young protégés replied through the door.

Stink motioned for Jamal to let him in, maintaining the grip on his Beretta just in case. As the youngster entered, Stink immediately noticed he was visibly shaken. "What's wrong, Von?" Stink asked in a concerned tone.

"Knowledge an'em just took my package," he paused to catch his breath, then continued, "I told'em it was yours, but they just…" his voice trailed off.

"They just, what?" Stink questioned emphatically.

"They said…you next," Von revealed.

"What?!" Stink yelled, his voice dripping with rage. "Oh yeah! They wanna play games, huh?" he stated to no one in particular with a menacing smile. He calmly turned to Von and asked, "Where they at now?"

With a gloomy look in the young boy's eyes, he said, "They, um, in the first parking lot."

"Stay here!" Stink commanded, pointing to Von. "Come on, Jamal. Let's take a ride," he said leading the way out of the door.

"What you gonna do?" Jamal asked, trying to keep up with Stink, who took the steps two at a time.

"Just watch, you'll see," Stink shot back. He had already formulated a plan, he just needed to get his cousin PJ. Then he would see what Knowledge and his crew had to say.

The entire ride downtown, Jamal was silent, making it evident that he was afraid.

Leaving Jamal in the car, Stink quickly made his way to PJ's room. Without knocking, he barged in the door.

"Damn, Stink!" PJ yelled clearly upset, quickly snatching the covers up to cover him and Sharon's nakedness.

"Man, I need to holla at you. Now!" Stink blurted, obviously distressed.

From the grimace on Stink's face, PJ knew it was serious. Quickly jumping up and putting his clothes on, he motioned for Stink to follow him out of the room. "Man, whazup, cuz?" PJ asked, eyeing Stink worriedly.

"Those punk-ass niggas just robbed my lil man then they had the balls to threaten me. Yo, cuz, I gotta go see these niggas. I just want you to watch my back and I'm-a handle my business."

PJ shook his head disagreeably. "Nah, cuz. If I'm rolling, I'm going all out wit'chu," he turned to go prepare. Turning back, he snapped, "I told you about them bitch-ass Denbeigh niggas. I told you!"

Stink sighed, then walked outside on the porch and watched the bustling ghetto traffic. *I'm-a show those niggas tonight, they ain't fucking wit no bitch*, he silently vowed.

PJ exited the house and threw Stink a black hooded sweatshirt matching the one he wore. With a treacherous glare, he said, "Let's roll, cuz."

The drive back to Denbeigh was tense. Stink silently concentrated on the task at hand, while PJ and Jamal wrestled with their own demons. When they got close to the apartment complex, Stink began to put is plan into motion.

"Jamal, ain't it a path or something behind the building in the first parking lot?"

"Yeah, but you gotta park on the street by the houses and go through their yard," Jamal advised.

Stink drove past the complex and into the residential area, located directly behind the apartments. "Where is the cut at?" Stink asked in a hushed tone.

"Pull up there, by the third house," Jamal instructed, pointing at the house. "Yeah, the cut is right behind this house."

Stink cut the lights off and turned toward PJ. "Just watch my back, cuz. I got the rest."

Tucking an exact replica of the gun that Stink carried, PJ snarled, "I got you, cuz. Let's go."

Stink turned his attention to Jamal. "Jamal, get in the driver's seat," he instructed, pulling the hooded sweatshirt over his head. "Be ready to jet when we get back." Stink took one last look at his cousin. "You ready, cuz?"

"I'm ready."

With that said, they made their way out of the car and through the backyard of the house that separated them from their prey. As the parking lot where Knowledge and his crew were supposed to be came into view, Stink took on a new demeanor. His eyes became evil slits as they scanned the parking lot. Initially, he didn't see Knowledge or any one of his crewmembers, causing his boiling blood to descend a few degrees.

Upon further inspection, Stink's heart rate kicked into high gear as he finally saw his target. He motioned his head in the direction of the group lollygagging around a parked car, letting PJ know that he had spotted his victim.

Stink casually began walking toward the unsuspecting group. With the hood of the sweatshirt over his head, he placed the gun in the sweatshirt pocket for easier access. PJ's strides matched Stink's step for step as they approached the group.

Oblivious to the imminent danger that approached, Knowledge and his boys continued to laugh and giggle, until Stink's voice cut through the air.

"You supposed to be looking for me, nigga!" Stink announced with a deceptive glare etched into his features.

All action ceased as everybody focused their attention on Stink who was gripping the Beretta tightly, aimed directly at Knowledge.

"I...I..., Stink, man, I ain't," Knowledge stammered, unable to find the correct words to defuse Stink's anger.

"You supposed to be robbing me, right?" Stink asked, in an almost mocking tone.

"Man, I swea-," was all Knowledge was able to get out, before Stink began to squeeze the trigger.

Bop-Bop-Bop-Bop-Bop-Bop!!! He fired the gun aimlessly, trying to hit every one of the fleeing men.

The scene was in absolute chaos as Stink continued to fire the weapon until it was empty.

In a murderous trance, Stink continued to pull the trigger on the empty gun until PJ grabbed his shoulder. "Come on! Let's go!" PJ yelled, dragging Stink in the direction from where they had come.

They quickly made it to the car and hopped in breathlessly. Jamal instinctively turned the ignition and floored Stink's car.

"Man, slow this muthafucka down before the police pull us over," Stink instructed, before turning to PJ. "Yo, P, I bet them niggas won't make no more threats at me."

PJ shook his head in astonishment. His cousin had proven he was truly demented.

Chapter 3

November 1990

It wasn't long before the streets were buzzing with the talk of who was responsible for the Aquaduct shootings. Quite naturally, it wouldn't be long before the police got word of who was responsible also.

One day in early November, Stink received a page from PJ's house, followed by '911-911'. This code was used strictly for emergencies, so Stink knew it was urgent. He quickly pulled over and returned the call.

"Hello," a woman answered, barely above a whisper.

"Yeah, PJ there."

"Oh my God! Stink, they got him!" Sharon yelled hysterically.

"Who got him, Sharon?" Stink asked confused.

"The police! They just took him to jail! Stink, please do something!" Sharon pleaded.

Stink's mind raced as he hung up, promising Sharon that he would do something. *What the fuck I'm-a do?* he thought as he drove to Trina's house.

Soon as he arrived at Trina's house, she knew something was terribly wrong with him.

"What's wrong, baby?" she asked in a concerned tone.

"I need you to call the jail and see why they got my cousin locked up," Stink commanded in a panic-stricken voice.

Trina instantly went to work. After being put on hold several times, she was finally given the information that Stink desired.

Paul Latrell Jones, aka PJ, was being charged with two counts of attempted murder and a host of other felonies that could land him in prison for the rest of his life.

As Trina relayed this information, Stink's heart dropped. He knew it was just a matter of time before they came for him, as more than likely, he was next on their list.

A week later, Stink turned himself in to the city jail, accompanied by his attorney. He was formally charged and booked on the same charges as PJ. After being strip-searched and degraded, Stink was then thrown into a cellblock with eleven other criminals. Stink had been through a lot in his life, but jail was something that he had managed to escape up until that point.

Jail conditions were horrific. The concrete floors were caked with mildew and dirt and sweated profusely causing a hair-raising stench. The food, which resembled pig slop, was even more disgusting than it looked, prompting Stink not to eat for days.

Due to the seriousness of the crime, neither Stink nor PJ were afforded the opportunity to invoke their Eighth Amendment Rights. Setting their bail at the excessively unreasonable amount of one million dollars each, the judge made sure they'd be jailed until trial.

After a week of moping around, Stink received a kite from PJ, given to him by a trustee. Immediately, Stink opened it and read PJ's words.

"Yo cuz, they trying to throw the book at us but don't worry, I've got something in the works for us. I hollered at Dame and Lil Man. They want you to call them at 555-5683. Call as soon as you get this!

Ps. Don't talk to none of them niggas in there.

Peace, PJ"

Stink sat on his bunk and sighed in frustration. He hadn't so much as looked at the phone since he'd been in jail. He pulled himself together and walked to the phone. There was somebody already on it, so Stink turned to walk away.

"Yo, son, you trying to use the jack?" the guy on the phone asked in a thick New York accent.

Stink nodded his head.

"Yo, ma, hit this number on the 3-way," the New Yorker instructed into the phone, then turned to Stink. "What's the number, B?"

Stink stared at the New Yorker with a confused look on his face.

"Oh, you ain't trying to use the 3-way, son?"

"Nah, nah, I'm good. I just needed to use it for a minute," Stink explained.

"Oh, ok," the New Yorker replied, then turned his attention back to whoever was on the phone. "Ma, I'm-a hit you back in a minute. Peace," he said hanging up and quickly handing Stink the phone. "Any time you need to use the 3-way, just holler at me, a'ight?"

Stink, surprised by the New Yorker's hospitality, simply nodded his head and dialed the number that PJ had given him. After the fourth ring, someone answered.

"This is a collect call from the Newport News City Jail. This call is from - caller, state your name," "Stink," he said in to the receiver. *"To accept this call press-"*

"Hello," a girl answered, bypassing the remainder of the automated phone system.

"Uh, yeah, is um, Dame or Lil Man there?" Stink stammered.

"No, they are not here. But Dame told me to call him as soon as you called. So hold on," she blurted, clicking over onto her other line.

After a brief silence, she clicked back over, accompanied by a phone ringing. "Yo whazup?" a voice answered that Stink instantly recognized.

"It's me, Dame, Stink!" Stink announced cheerfully.

"Oh shit! Whazup, Nigga! I've been waiting on you to call me. You must've seen P."

"Nah. He sent me a letter by some nigga."

"Oh, that's cool. So how you holding up in that bitch?"

"Shit, nigga, you know me. I'm good," Stink lied. He hadn't eaten in nearly a week.

"O.K., I hear you nigga, but did PJ tell you that me and Lil trying to get them niggas to drop the charges?" Dame inquired.

This was totally new to Stink. "Nah, nah. He ain't say nothing about that," Stink replied, confused.

"Oh, well just be cool. Lil and me gonna try and handle that for ya'll. But ya'll niggas gonna owe us when ya'll get out," Dame stated in a joking tone.

"Man, I'll do whatever. Just name it," Stink replied desperately.

"A'ight. Remember you said that," Dame chuckled then asked, "You need some money for commissary?"

Stink had no idea what "commissary" was, answering, "Um, I don't think I got no commissary."

Laughing at Stink's inexperience with jail, Dame replied, "I got you, man. Just keep your head up. Peace." Then he hung up.

Stink replaced the receiver and walked back to his cell, feeling better than he'd felt the entire time he'd been in jail.

"Yo, son, my name is Leaf," the New Yorker said, stepping into Stink's path with his hand extended.

Stink gripped the New Yorker's outstretched hand, and then replied, "My name is Rahsaan but everybody calls me Stink."

"Oh, word. You from VA, son?" Leaf asked.

"Yeah, but I'm originally from North Carolina."

"Say word, son! I was in Durham doing my thing," Leaf revealed animatedly, pronouncing Durham as it was spelled - Dur-ham.

The two continued to kick it until lockdown. Stink allowed the cool New Yorker to take his mind off the severe situation that he was facing. To Stink, Leaf seemed like a cool dude, minus the theatrics that seemed to come along with most New Yorkers.

Throughout the days, weeks, and even months, Leaf was the only person that Stink would talk to. He would sit and listen to Leaf's 'Big Willie' stories, never interrupting, nor questioning their authenticity.

Chapter 4

<u>April 1991</u>

Stink had been in jail for five months where he'd just about succumbed to its conditions. He began to devour the food they served and whatever knickknacks the commissary provided. The combination of the jail food and a rigorous regimen of push-ups and pull-ups had Stink's already naturally-muscular build reminiscent of a body builder. Leaf would still take up most of Stink's days with his stories, yet Stink loved to sit and listen to the New Yorker talk.

Stink and PJ had less than a month before they were to stand trial on the shootings. Dame and Lil Man had made contact with Knowledge and his boys, however nothing had been written in stone.

Less than a week before the trial was to begin, Stink called Dame at the number he'd always called. Over time, Stink had learned that the house he'd been calling was Natasha's, Dame's baby's mother.

"Hello," the familiar voice answered.

"You have a collect call from..." As always, she accepted the call before allowing the recording to go through.

"Hello, Stink," she said hurriedly, "Hold on! Damien and Lil Man just pulled up!"

Stink could hear her yelling Dame's name in the background. After a brief wait, someone picked up another extension in the house.

"Yo, what up, Stink?" Lil Man said full of energy.

"Ain't shit, just chillin'," Stink replied dryly.

"Come on, nigga, keep ya head up. You only got like a week and you'll be home," Lil Man assured him.

Stink didn't respond right away. He didn't know if Lil Man was insinuating that he and PJ would beat the case or if they had finally gotten into Knowledge's ear.

Lil Man quickly picked up on Stink's silence and boastfully stated, "Yeah, nigga, that's right, ya'll will be home next week so just be cool!"

Now Stink understood what Lil Man was saying. With a big smile plastered on his face, he asked mildly stunned, "So, everything is everything?"

"And then some, nigga! We just waiting on ya'll's arrival," Lil Man replied arrogantly.

Stink was sure now that they had paid Knowledge and his boys off. Without saying as much over the phone, Lil Man assured him that they'd be seeing him and PJ that following week. With that understood, Stink slept a lot better for the next week.

PJ and Stink sat in the holding cell, catching up on the events that had taken place for the last six months. They hadn't seen each other for a while and they were deeply engrossed in conversation when a deputy opened the door. "Paul L. Jones and Rahsaan A. Jones, let's go!" the deputy ordered.

Stink and PJ stood and began walking out of the small holding cell, where another deputy stood with handcuffs.

Handcuffing them, the deputies led them through an adjacent door where the courtroom was located.

As they entered the courtroom, Stink noticed his grandmother seated along with PJ's girlfriend, Sharon, who had begun to show considerably from her pregnancy. Stink and PJ smiled in their direction, as the deputies escorted them to their seats.

Inside, Stink was fuming. Trina had promised him that she would be there to support him. Even though Stink had been gone for six months, he still considered Trina to be his girl. They'd sometimes talked on the phone and in the six months he'd been in jail, she'd visited him a few times. Sitting at the defense table, Stink glanced back one final time to see if she'd shown up.

"Damn," Stink whispered to himself disappointedly.

"All rise! All rise! The Honorable Wesley Kerns…," the bailiff yelled.

Stink and PJ stood along with their lawyers. The judge, an old white man, walked in and took his seat at the bench.

"You may be seated," he instructed, then looked over towards the prosecutor and asked, "Mr. Denny, are you ready for trial?"

The prosecutor, who was quickly shuffling through papers, looked up and said, "Um, yes and no, Your Honor."

The judge looked at him inquisitively, then stated, "Mr. Denny, this isn't a 'yes' or a 'no' question. Now are you ready or not!"

Nervously, the prosecutor asked, "If it may please the court, may I approach the bench?"

"Yes you may, and all counsel present may approach also," the judge replied, looking toward Stink and PJ's lawyers.

Their lawyers, along with the prosecutor approached the bench and huddled in conference.

After about ten minutes of what looked like a feverish debate, they parted for their respective sides. Stink noticed his lawyer sported a smug look as he took his seat at the table.

"OK, Mr. Denny, call your first witness," the judge instructed.

The prosecutor threw his hands up in exasperation and said, "The prosecution moves to nolle prossed these changes until it has more evidence to go to trial."

Stink didn't understand any of the terms until the judge stated in a firm voice, "This case is dismissed!" He then banged his gavel.

Stink and PJ were released later that afternoon. Stink left with his grandmother while PJ left with Sharon.

During the ride home, Stink listened as his grandmother preached about the way he was living. "I'm telling you, Stink, if you don't straighten up and do right, you're going right back where you just left. Now let them six months you just spent in that jailhouse be a lesson. Me and your grandfather have tried all we can…," she preached on and on, until they arrived home.

The first thing Stink did when he got home, was rush upstairs to see if the $5,000 he'd hidden in his underwear drawer was still there. Frantically rambling through the drawer, Stink's heart rate descended once he felt the knot of bills.

"Yes!" He yelped joyously, seeing that his money was where he'd left it. He knew that he would have to part with some of it, if not all of it, for what Dame and Lil Man had done for him and PJ.

Just as Stink was contemplating his money woes, the phone rang, snapping him out of his thoughts. He quickly snatched the receiver up.

"Hello."

"Yo, what up, Stink? I see they let you go," Dame stated jokingly.

"Yeah, man, but whazup with you?"

"Same ole shit, you know. But when can I holla at you?"

"Shit! Whenever you want to. Even right now."

"A'ight, cause I need to holla at you about some shit," Dame revealed.

"OK, just come through."

"A'ight, give me about twenty minutes," Dame said, then hung up.

Stink walked downstairs into the kitchen and caught a menacing scowl from his grandmother. More than likely she'd eavesdropped on his conversation with Dame, Stink surmised, ignoring her grimace.

"Stink, you get caught back up in them streets and go back to jail, don't come calling me," she threatened.

"Grandma, I ain't done nothing; I keep telling you," he replied in an agitated tone.

His grandmother sighed, rolled her eyes and walked off.

Stink and Dame were rolling up Jefferson Avenue in Dame's new 735i BMW. Stink was under the impression that Dame wanted to talk to him about the money that he and Lil Man had coughed up in order to free him and PJ.

Stink pulled out his roll of money and began counting it. "How much I owe you, man? All I got is five Gs but you know I'm-a get more."

Dame waved him off, "Man, keep your money. We did that for ya'll. Besides, we got big plans."

"Man, I gotta give you something," Stink stated pleadingly.

"Nah, you ain't gotta give me shit! You and P are my niggas and I would expect the same from ya'll," Dame snapped sincerely.

Hearing that, Stink let it go and put his money back into his pocket, then asked, "So what you wanted to holla at me about?"

"Yeah, I do wanna holla at you about something," Dame stated in a serious tone, glancing at Stink before continuing, "Man, this shit really ain't that serious, but your girl, Trina, she ain't shit for real."

Stink sat in silence, waiting on Dame to finish.

"Man, I've been fucking with these Denbeigh niggas, and this lil nigga name Los was talking about some freak-bitch named 'Trina'. So I grilled the nigga about the bitch. Come to find out, it's your Trina. Man, the nigga been fucking her since you got locked up," Dame revealed, judging Stink's reaction closely. "Nigga say she gave him head and the whole nine," he finished, shaking his head in disgust.

Sitting back, Stink showed no emotion although deep down he was hurt. Masking his emotions, he tossed Dame a patronizing smirk and responded, "Man, fuck that bitch! I gotta trick for that ho anyway."

Dame immediately picked up on Stink's pain. "Man, that bitch ain't even worth you getting into no trouble for."

"Nah, D, I ain't gonna do no stupid shit. Just take me around there," Stink instructed, plotting his revenge that instant. Noticing the car phone that sat in the console, Stink asked, "Let me use the phone, real quick?"

Dame promptly took it out of its cradle and handed it to him. Stink punched the familiar number in and waited patiently for Trina to pick up.

"Hello," Trina answered.

"Hey, whazup, baby?" Stink asked cheerfully.

"OOOH! My baby home! My baby home! My baby home!" Trina sang joyously.

Her crooning made Stink sick to his stomach but he somehow managed to keep the act up. "Yeah, I'm home and I'm trying to see you," he announced sensuously.

"OK. Are you on your way?"

"Yeah, I'll be there in a few," Stink said, then hung up. With a devilish grin, Stink looked over at Dame who shook his head discouragingly.

As Dame pulled up to Trina's house, Stink looked over and asked, "What's dude's name again?"

"Los," Dame replied.

"A'ight. Don't go far; this is only going to take a minute," Stink informed, with a sly grin and then hopped out of the car.

As Stink walked up the driveway to Trina's door, she burst out of the house in a full sprint and jumped in his arms. "Baby, I missed you soooo much," she revealed earnestly, planting kisses all over his face.

Not wanting to blow his cover, Stink managed to dodge all of her kisses directed at his mouth. Her kisses were revolting enough, but the thought of her kissing him in the mouth would've been….

He carried Trina into the house and to her bedroom, with her legs tightly wrapped around his waist.

As he laid her back onto her bed, Stink noticed she only wore a pair of panties and a short t-shirt that barely covered her ass.

"You miss me, baby?" Stink asked, pulling his shirt off.

"Hell yeah!" she exclaimed, looking deep into Stink's eyes. Running her hands over his chiseled chest, she commented, "Damn baby. Your body is sexy as shit." She began to plant kisses over his rippled torso, leaving a hot trail down to his navel.

"Ah…Shit…." Stink moaned, as the kisses became sensitive to his skin.

Trina fumbled with his belt, allowing his pants to drop around his ankles, freeing his stiff erection that strained against the fabric of his boxers.

Trina pulled her t-shirt over her head, revealing her perfect 36C-sized breasts.

Stink leaned over and pulled the flimsy material on both sides of her panties down over her outstretched legs.

Once she was completely naked, Stink stood over her nearly perfect body and thought, *Damn, I'm-a miss this pussy.*

Trina reached out to him and guided him between her thighs. Once they were face to face, she tried again to kiss him in the mouth. Stink moved his head defensively, allowing her wet kisses to land on his cheek.

Stink quickly found Trina's already moistened pussy and pushed a finger into her. She instinctively grinded back onto his probing finger, making her juices trickle over his knuckles.

"Ummm, hmmm, baby, I'm sooo wet. Please put it in," Trina moaned, winding her hips onto his fingers.

Stink removed his fingers from her pussy, then grabbed his dick at the base and rubbed the head up and down her quivering pussy lips teasingly.

"Please, baby, oh fuck! Please give it to me," Trina begged.

Stink placed the head of his throbbing manhood just within the fold of her lips, interlocking her thighs with his forearms and thrust forward. Feeling the hot moistness of a woman for the first time in months immediately caused him to buck wildly.

"Oh, baby! You have no idea how long I've waited for you to fuck me," Trina hissed, grimacing in a lustful manner.

Stink peered down at her, as her titties flopped up and down with each thrust. "You like this dick?" he inquired harshly with an angry sneer on his face.

"Yess, Yess, baby!"

Stink pushed her knees against her chest and began to violently pound her pussy.

"Oh, baby! Yess! Give it to me!" she gasped, as her eyes rolled back into her head.

Stink felt himself on the verge of cumming. Between the lack of sex and the tightness of Trina's pussy, he knew he wouldn't last much longer.

"Oh, yes, baby! You feel so good! Please don't stop!" Trina urged.

Stink felt himself spasm, as his load of cum flooded Trina's pussy. He continued to pump his quickly deflating member in and out of Trina, savoring the moment. Narrowing his eyes into evil little slits, he asked, "Did you fuck *Los* the same way?"

"Wha…What are you talking about?" she stammered, then reiterated her question. "Baby, what are you talking about?"

Unable to look her in the eye, Trina held Stink's face, forcing him to look at her.

"Bitch, you know what the fuck I'm talking about!" Stink barked. Slowly pulling his limp penis from her pussy, he took a deep sniff and hock spit a glob of mucous right into Trina's face. "Now that's what I think about yo nasty ass, bitch!"

Trina laid there in shock with the mixture of spit and tears running down her cheeks. Stink hurriedly dressed, eyeing the hurt and pain on Trina's face.

"Baby, please. Let me explain!" she yelled between sobs.

Stink grabbed the doorknob then turned to look at Trina one last time.

Trina held her face in her hands and screamed hysterically, "Why…Why are you doing this to me??!"

Stink turned from the scene and exited the room without turning back. As soon as he walked out of Trina's front door, Dame's 735 was sitting exactly where it was when he'd entered the house, making his getaway that much smoother.

Chapter 5

<u>June 1991</u>

As summer kicked in full swing, Stink couldn't properly give the streets his undivided attention because he had to attend summer school in order to graduate with his class. No sooner than summer school was over did he begin to hustle at full throttle.

Dame and Lil Man had stepped their hustles up. Instead of buying their drugs in Virginia, they had begun to travel to New York. The prices in New York were a lot cheaper therefore making the profits a lot higher.

Since Stink and PJ had been released from jail, PJ wasn't the same. Having a baby on the way seemed to shift PJ's focus from the streets to fatherhood. This was never more evident than when Stink attempted to rally PJ to take part in one of their trips to New York.

"Yo, P, I know you trying to make this move," Stink said into the phone.

"Nah, cuz. I'm good."

"Come on, P. You got a baby on the way, you gotta get that money right, baby?" Stink asked emphatically.

"Nah, I don't need no money, cuz. I need to be there for my daughter," PJ snapped.

"Yo, you buggin', P."

"Nah, you buggin'! You out there running around like... like shit is a game! Yo, Stink, shit is not a game! We just spent six months in jail for some shit that could've gotten us life."

Stink was silent, allowing PJ to rant. After he felt that he'd heard enough, he retorted, "You do you, cuz. I'm-a do me." With that, he hung up.

Stink hustled from sun-up to sundown. Traveling to New York on just two occasions, he'd turned his $5,000 into nearly $20,000.

On his second trip to New York, Lil Man introduced Stink to his cousin, Cross. Upon first meeting Cross, Stink could tell he was a loose cannon. Lil Man had told Stink stories about his infamous cousin, however, nothing prepared him for the real deal.

Stink sat in the passenger seat of Lil Man's Mercedes Benz 300E parked in front of Cross's building on 139th and Lenox Avenue. Suddenly, Cross came from his building and hopped in the driver's seat and pulled off.

"What up, god?" Cross asked full of energy.

Stink nodded his head toward Cross, under the impression that Lil Man had given him permission to drive his prized car.

Flying down Lenox Avenue, Cross rolled down all of the windows and blasted the system up to ear shattering decibels. As they approached 135th, Cross attempted to maneuver Lil Man's Benz between two cars in order to make the right turn onto 135th. Edging dangerously close to the car, Cross gunned the engine in the Benz, scraping the left front fender as if the Benz was a bumper car.

Cross stuck his head out of the window. "Get the fuck out of the way!" he yelled to the other driver, then zoomed down 135th street.

Stink couldn't believe what had just taken place before his eyes. "Hey yo, Cross, be cool, man! We dirty," Stink warned, remembering the four kilos of crack that were hidden in the car.

"I got you, B. We in New York; ain't shit gonna happen to you in my city," Cross proclaimed boastfully.

After riding through a few other blocks, they finally returned to Cross's building where a frantic Lil Man paced back and forth on the sidewalk. No sooner than the car came to a complete stop did Lil Man begin inspecting it from front to back.

"Oh, hells no!" Lil Man yelled. "I know you ain't wreck my shit, Cross!"

Cross looked to Lil Man as if he was over-reacting, then retorted, "Come on, god, you know how these immigrant cab drivers are in New York." Walking toward the entrance of his building, he threw over his shoulder, slyly, "You got paper anyway."

Lil Man meticulously inspected the damage, then flopped down in the driver's seat. Furious, he glared over to Stink. "Why'd you let him take my car, Stink?" he asked accusingly.

"Shit, I ain't know what the fuck was going on! I thought you sent him out here!" Stink shot back defensively.

Lil Man sighed in frustration, turned the key in the ignition and headed back to VA.

Things were going lovely for Stink and his crew as the money began to roll in. Since the fiasco with Trina, Stink hadn't gotten involved with anyone. With all the traveling and constant hustling, he didn't have the time for anybody.

Dame and Stink pulled in front of the gigantic house, in the heart of Newport News. Dame had moved his children's mother along with two other girls into the house. All of the young ladies who lived there had at least one child, with the exception of Natasha, Dame's children's mother, who had two and one on the way.

The house was so big and welcoming, that they gave it the nickname, "The Friendship House." Their whole crew would hang out around the house in an upstairs bedroom that Dame had transformed into a makeshift office.

Stink had become extremely close to Dame's children's mother, Natasha. When he was locked up, she was the one who would always accept his calls, no matter what. And from that, they had formed a slight bond. Natasha had gone as far as to name Stink the godfather to her and Dame's unborn child.

Natasha's housemates, her cousin Bonni and her best friend Lee-Lee, were a sight for sore eyes. Although they were complete opposites of one another, they both were fine.

Bonni, with her golden banana complexion, creamy thighs and sashaying walk, always caught Stink's attention, but her defensive demeanor kept him at bay.

Lee-Lee on the other hand was a chocolate sister with a bubbling ass and a cute face who always let Stink know that if he chose to, he could have her. To put it simply, Lee-Lee was easy and Bonni wasn't.

Even though Stink garnered attention from most women, Bonni totally ignored him as she came and went with her little girl in tow.

Lil Man continued trying to proposition Bonni only to get cursed out or even swung on for some of his more extreme advances.

Bonni, whose real name was Bonita Labelle Lawson, played the hard role, however, she wasn't hard at all. The child of a single mother, Bonni had witnessed some of the struggles of a single mother firsthand. Her child's father had been sent to prison for killing a man over another woman. This had destroyed Bonni's will to ever love again. In her mind, it was she and her daughter; nothing else mattered.

Bonni had noticed Stink the first day she'd moved in. She had even asked her cousin about him, after observing the closeness he and Natasha shared.

"He's cute, ain't he?" Natasha asked.

"Yeah, he's cute but-," Bonni started.

"You like him!" Natasha blurted, attempting to play match maker.

"Tasha, girl, you know I ain't looking for no man."

"Well, cuz, I'm-a tell you, Stink's a good nigga and some bitch gonna snatch him up real quick."

"I wish them luck, 'cause I'm through," Bonni stated firmly. She couldn't allow herself to love or trust again, so for now she would just ignore him.

Stink pulled up in front of the Friendship House in his new Saab 9000 Turbo. As he exited the car, he noticed all of the kids jumping from the porch to the ground when he witnessed Bonni's daughter fall and hurt herself. He quickly ran over, cradled the little girl in his arms and carried her up the stairs to Bonni's bedroom.

"You gonna be OK," Stink consoled the little girl, as he knocked on Bonni's door.

"It hurt," she replied in obvious pain.

"Who is it?" Bonni yelled through the door.

"Um…It's um, Stink. I…Um, your daughter hurt herself," Stink finally said, getting tongue tied.

Bonni immediately snatched the door open in a panic. Wearing only a towel tightly wrapped around her otherwise naked body. "Wha…What happened?"

Stink looked Bonni up and down, noticing how the towel barely covered her heart-shaped ass and managed to reply, "I think she just scraped her knee."

Bonni began to reach for her daughter, only to quickly withdraw as the towel covering her came loose. She refastened the towel with a flushed look on her face.

"I'll just put her on the bed for you," Stink said, attempting to be a gentleman, while averting his gaze from her body. Bonni stepped to the side and allowed him to enter. Stink carried the little girl to the bed. Inspecting her scrape, he asked in a boyish voice, "What's your name, pretty girl?"

"Tay-via," she replied giggling.

Bonni quickly appeared over Stink's shoulder clothed in sweat pants and a t-shirt and asked, "Is it bad?"

"Nah, she should be OK. Can you get a washcloth with some soap on it?"

Bonni went into the adjoining bathroom and quickly returned with a washcloth. "Here you go and thank you so much. I was just getting out of the tub. Tayvia was supposed to be down the hall playing, not outside," she finished firmly, glaring at Tayvia accusingly.

Stink washed Tayvia's wound gingerly, relishing the mother/daughter interaction, with a smile. "Do you have a band-aid?"

Bonni went into the bathroom again and quickly returned with a band-aid. "Here you go." Turning her attention to her daughter, she said, "Tayvia, thank Mr...Um..."

"Rahsaan, but everybody calls me Stink."

"Well, I think I like Rahsaan better. I don't like to be like everybody else," Bonni insisted with a slight grin.

"Rahsaan is cool," Stink quickly agreed.

Tayvia looked up to Stink with a heart melting smile. "T'ank you, Mr. Wassaan."

"You're welcome, Tayvia. Just be careful, OK."

"OK," Tayvia giggled.

Bonni stood back and observed the way her daughter's eyes lit up as Stink tended to her. She knew that her daughter was starving for the attention of a man, something she herself was unable to give. "Well, thank you again, Rahsaan," Bonni said extending her hand, signaling it was time for him to exit.

Stink shook her hand delicately then made his way out of the door. As he trotted down the stairs, he knew that he had to have Bonni.

Dame waited patiently on Stink in the living room. "You still trying to roll over to Norfolk to get some rims for your whip?" Dame asked.

"Yeah, I'm ready whenever you are, man."

They promptly jumped in Stink's car and headed to Norfolk.

Stink smiled broadly, leaning hard in his car with the newly-acquired chrome, 3pc, BBS racing rims, mounted on 17- inch low- profiles. Stink and Dame were giving each avenue a glimpse of his new ride and even newer rims.

Just as Stink pulled behind Dame's BMW, he noticed Bonni and Tayvia coming down the steps. Soon as Stink exited the car, Tayvia acknowledged him. "Hey, Mr. Wassaan!" she yelled, waving her hand frantically.

He walked over to them, noticing the large duffle bag thrown over Bonni's shoulder. "Hi, Ms.Tayvia. Hello, Bonni. Where you headed?" he inquired.

"Oh, I'm taking Tayvia to my mom's house," she replied.

"You need a ride or something?"

"No. It's OK, my mom only lives a few blocks away," Bonni declined, noticing immediately that her refusal had bruised his ego as his facial expression changed.

"Oh, OK, be safe then. See you later, Tayvia," he said, turning and walking away.

Bonni stood there and watched him disappear into the house. She was beginning to warm up to the advice of her cousin, however, she just didn't want to be hurt again. Bonni glanced at the immense smile plastered on her daughter's tiny features and knew that Tayvia had fallen for

Stink. If the opportunity continued to present itself, she just might allow herself to fall for him, too.

Chapter 6

<u>August 1991</u>

Stink, Dame and Lil Man were flying up Interstate 95. Each in their respective cars - Stink in his Saab, Dame in his 735i, and Lil Man in his freshly-painted 300 Benz. As the money poured in, they each felt optimistic about their prospective futures. Between the three of them, they had over $100, 000 in cash. With the money, they planned to make at least $75,000 dollars a piece in drug proceeds.

Lil Man being the cautious one didn't want to chance transporting the drugs by car, therefore he'd entrusted Cross to get the drugs back. More than likely, he'd get a girlfriend to actually transport the drugs and he'd just accompany her on the trip.

Arriving in New York City, they all jumped on the Westside Highway and raced to the exit for 125th Street, the mecca of New York. Dame led the way, followed by Lil Man, while Stink brought up the rear. They each relished the attention that they received from the onlookers along 125th. Not only did they come to New York to buy drugs, they also came to shine.

As they approached 8th avenue, the stoplight impeded their progress. Bopping his head to the music, Stink noticed a guy who looked extremely familiar get out of an 850i BMW. As the light turned green, they started across 8th avenue, allowing Stink to further scrutinize the man. Stink got a clear view of him and knew exactly where he knew him from. It was Leaf. The same guy who used to tell Stink all of those 'Big Willie' stories while they were in jail.

Blowing his horn frantically to stop Lil Man and Dame, Stink pulled over up ahead of where Leaf casually strolled down the block.

Lil Man noticed Stink pull over then quickly got Dame's attention also. Double-parked on 125th, Stink hopped out and began walking in the direction of where he'd seen Leaf, but he no longer saw him.

"Ay yo, Stink, whazup, nigga?" Lil Man asked, walking toward him.

"I saw this dude I know today," Stink replied dumbfounded.

"Where?" Lil Man asked incredulously, holding his arms wide.

As soon as Stink shrugged his shoulders and turned to leave, he spotted Leaf exiting a store. "Yo, Leaf! Leaf!" Stink yelled.

Leaf looked toward them with an awkward glare until he noticed Stink. His expression immediately turned into a wide smile, as he yelled, "My nigga, Stink!"

Walking toward one another, they embraced with a thunderous handshake.

"What up, son? What brings you to the city?" Leaf asked, looking Stink up and down warmly.

The first thing Stink noticed was the blinding, diamond-encrusted medallion hanging from his neck that matched the same emblem as the car he drove.

"Man, you know me, I'm just chillin," Stink replied, hypnotized by the sparkling stones in his medallion.

"Yeah, so how long you gonna be up top?" Leaf asked, looking down to check his pager.

"Maybe a day or two," Stink surmised.

Leaf handed Stink a business card and said, "Here. Hit me in about an hour. A'ight, son." He then rushed off.

Before Stink reached his car, Leaf zoomed by in the burgundy 850. *"That nigga's Big Willie fo'real"*, Stink said to himself.

Sitting in Cross's small apartment on Lenox Avenue, Stink, Lil Man and Dame were silently contemplating their next move.

The old black gangster flick playing on the television caused Cross to abruptly jump up. "Yo, watch this part! Watch this!" Cross yelled animatedly, mimicking the actor on the screen. He continued, "Whadda ya know, the big nigga got some sense. Yo, god, that's that shit," he stated in apparent excitement.

Each man in the room looked at Cross as if he was crazy, yet only Lil Man commented. "Enough of this bullshit. Whazup with the girl that's supposed to be taking the shit back?"

"Shorty gonna be ready by 7 o'clock, plus you ain't even got the work yet," Cross snapped, momentarily ignoring the movie.

"I'm about to holla at the 'Ricans on Amsterdam in a minute. Just be ready when I get back," Lil Man instructed, then looked at Stink. "Ay yo, Stink, who was that nigga you holla'd at on 125th in the 850? The nigga had the crazy medallion," Lil Man said, putting on his best New York accent.

"I was in jail wit dude. He was doing a lot of braggin'; I guess he wasn't lying," Stink concluded presumptuously.

"You need to holla at dude, Stink," Dame advised.

"Yeah, I'm-a holla at him," Stink retorted assuredly.

Lil Man and Dame prepared to go uptown and handle the purchase of the drugs, while Stink stayed behind to page Leaf.

No sooner did Stink page the number than the phone rang.

"Yo, What up?" Cross answered, then quickly passed Stink the phone.

"Yo, whazup, Leaf?" Stink blurted, thinking, *Who else would be calling me?*

"What up, son? What you doing right now?" Leaf asked hastily.

"Uh…nothing. Why?"

"A'ight, meet me at 155th and 8th Avenue in let's say…thirty minutes," Leaf instructed, then hung up.

Little did Stink know he was on his way to meet a cocaine kingpin.

Arriving back in Virginia, one thing was certain: Stink and his crew would not be traveling to New York to obtain drugs anymore. Leaf had made it clear that whatever Stink needed, he would provide.

After selling all the drugs they'd bought in New York, Stink called Leaf. From the meeting he had with him in New York, Leaf would give him the same prices that they'd paid in New York, instantly making their crew a force in Virginia's drug market.

Stink's first plan was to find himself a place to live.His grandparents had become overly suspicious of his activities. Things had really hit the fan when his grandfather gave him a piece of mail, bearing the Virginia tax department's address.

Stink had told his grandparents that the Saab was a friend's car so consequently the piece of mail shattered his lie.

His grandfather held up an exact replica of his envelope, addressed to himself. "Looks like your friend *gave* you that car somewhere down the line," his grandfather stated sarcastically.

Unable to garner a reply that would validate his lie, Stink stood there in silence, with a stupid look on his face. He knew that he'd have to enlighten his grandfather about his actions sooner or later.

Stink managed to find a two-bedroom townhouse in Hampton. After spending nearly a couple of thousand dollars to furnish the place, all he ended up with was a black leather sectional couch with a matching bar, two big screen televisions, and a king-sized bedroom set.

His grandparents weren't happy to see him leave, but when they visited his townhouse, they were impressed knowing that he had become a man.

After Stink got settled into his crib, his sex life shot through the roof. He didn't have a main girl. However, if he chose to fuck, he had a willing partner for every night of the week. Trina had been trying desperately to get in contact with him but Stink managed to block all of her attempts. There was a rumor floating about her being pregnant that did catch his attention. Stink quickly dismissed it as just another ploy for him to talk to her.

He still hadn't been able to break Bonni's invisible wall down, mainly because he hadn't been around the Friendship House like he used to. Since he'd been dealing with Leaf, there was no need. Instead of him going to Lil Man and Dame, they now came to him. Although their friendship was the same, their business had shifted.

Stink was home, laid back on his plush, leather couch, watching football, when the phone rang.

"Hello," he answered.

"Stink, whazup?" Dame asked.

"Ain't shit, just chillin', watching the game."

"I got somebody wanna holla at you. Hold on."

After a brief pause, someone clumsily picked up the receiver. "Mr. Wassaan, I want you to come to my birf-day party," Bonni's daughter, Tayvia, stated shyly. "Can you please come? Pleease!" she begged innocently.

"Yeah, Tayvia, I can come. When is it?"

Tayvia dropped the phone and began yelling, "Mommy! Mommy! When is my party?"

After a few seconds, Bonni picked the phone up. "Yes, hello."

"Hey, whazup, Bonni? How you doing?"

"Oh, hi, Rahsaan. I'm just trying to get this girl's party together," Bonni explained, while still directing traffic in the background. "I haven't seen you in a while. Tayvia just had to invite you to her birthday party. The child nearly worried Dame to death," she said chuckling, then continued, "If I didn't know any better, I'd swear she had a crush on you."

Stink giggled at her remark, then replied, "Yeah, that's my lil girlfriend."

"If you can't make it, I'll explain it to her," Bonni offered.

"Oh, nah, nah, I can make it," he quickly replied, "I just wanted to know what time and is there anything I can bring?"

"I think she's getting enough presents as it is, soo…"

"Oh, ok. Put Tayvia back on the phone."

"All right. Hope to see you later then. Oh yeah, I almost forgot, the party is at 5 o'clock," she said then yelled for Tayvia.

"Heello," Tayvia sang into the receiver.

"Tayvia, if you could wish for anything for your birthday, what would you wish for?" Stink asked, knowing if she asked for a horse, he'd try to find one by 5 o'clock.

"Ummm…I wish for a Barbie car, so I can drive it."

"Is that all, Tayvia?" he asked hoping that she would change her request to something easier to find.

"Oh, and a Barbie doll, so I can play with it," she responded excitedly.

"Ok, Tayvia. I'm coming to your party, but I'm not telling you what I'm bringing, ok?" Stink said simultaneously wondering where he was going to find a Barbie car in two hours.

"Ok, bye-bye," she said in a disappointed tone.

Soon as the phone hung up, Stink grabbed the phone book and began to frantically search for toy stores.

After failing to locate the toy at several stores in Newport News and Hampton, he finally found a store in Chesapeake that carried a Barbie jeep - not the car.

Sensing Stink's frustration, the sales clerk explained, "The Barbie car was last year's model."

"Well, how much is it?" Stink asked impatiently.

"Umm, three hundred and sixty-nine dollars, plus tax."

"What?" Stink asked in disbelief.

"Yes sir, it's three hun…"

Cutting the clerk off, Stink blurted, "Just hold it, I'm on my way!"

The pink Barbie jeep that Tayvia wanted was securely strapped into Stink's trunk. He increased his speed to 70 mph trying to make it to the party on time. With only ten minutes before the party was to begin, Stink floored the Saab, prompting the turbo to kick in.

When he finally reached the 'Friendship House,' the party was in full swing. Pulling behind the line of cars, Stink jumped out and checked himself. After being absolutely sure that the combination of Polo shirt, Polo jeans and white-on-white Nikes completed his attire perfectly, he pulled the toy from the trunk. As Stink rolled the jeep toward the porch steps, Natasha stepped out onto the porch.

"Boy, what the hell are you doing?" She asked suspiciously.

"Come on, Tasha, help me with this shit, girl," Stink said in a frustrated tone.

"Boy, I know you ain't went and bought that damn jeep for Tayvia?" she asked in amazement.

Stink quickly retorted, "Yeah, I bought it for her! Now help me hide it somewhere."

"All right, all right. Bonni must really got you open," Natasha remarked sarcastically. "Put it on the back porch but watch out for the kids in the kitchen."

"Good looking out, Tasha," Stink said, as he carried the jeep around the side of the house.

Quietly placing the jeep on the porch, Stink noticed Natasha leading Bonni onto the porch. Bonni looked more beautiful than he'd ever seen before. Her hair flowed down her back as the sun reflected in her pretty brown eyes. Stink felt an incredibly strong need to touch her.

He was so caught up in her physical beauty, that he didn't hear the two women talking about him.

"Damn, girl. Did you even give him the pussy yet?" Natasha asked vulgarly.

"Shut up, Tasha!" Bonni snapped, giving her cousin an evil glare. She quickly changed her expression to a smile as she turned to Stink. "Hi, Rahsaan. Please excuse my nasty cousin but I'm glad you could make it," she said, opening her arms, inviting Stink into a friendly embrace.

Gently hugging Bonni, Stink could feel the curves of her body meshing into his.

Bonni swiftly broke their embrace then asked, "Rahsaan, did Tayvia ask you for this?" She had gone from sensuous to serious in seconds.

Stink looked from Bonni to the expensive toy, then back to Bonni. "Nah. I asked her," he smirked.

Grinning, Bonni soaked his lie up like a brick. "Mmm-hmm, I bet you did but I can't accept it," she concluded flatly.

"I bought this for Tayvia, not you. You're too big for it," Stink replied, jokingly.

Drawing a wide smile from Bonni, Stink knew he'd won their first disagreement.

"All right but I'm not taking her to drive it, you are."

This was music to Stink's ears. If he could have read Bonni's heart at that moment, he would've known that he had her then and there.

Bonni allowed her gaze to linger on Stink a little too long, prompting Natasha to blurt, "You just gonna stand here looking at the damn boy with stars in yo eyes or are we gonna have a PAR-TAY?!" Natasha rolled her hips and clapped her hands for emphasis, then led the way inside.

Stink, Lil Man, Dame and PJ were upstairs in the office blazing a blunt while the girls and the kids were downstairs enjoying the festivities.

"So, you trying to get wit Bonni, huh, Stink?" Lil Man asked, inhaling deeply on the blunt.

"Yeah, I heard about you, cuz," PJ added, smiling.

Dame, the one person Stink had actually divulged his true feelings about Bonni to, shot him a patronizing smirk.

"Man, ya'll niggas is buggin' and shit," Stink replied defensively.

"So what did you get Tayvia for her birthday?" Lil Man asked suspiciously.

"Ya'll niggas gonna get the fuck up off me!" Stink retorted, intentionally evading the question. In an attempt to shift the attention, he looked to PJ. "P, you that nigga on that 'lover boy' shit, not me."

"Nah, cuz, I'm on some fatherhood shit," PJ responded in a serious tone. "Just keep it up, you'll see," he finished sarcastically, managing to shift the focus back to Stink.

To Stink's relief, Bonni yelled up the stairs, interrupting their clowning session. They all shared one final laugh, before Stink stood to exit the room.

Standing at the bottom of the steps, Bonni said, "Come on, we're ready to open the presents."

Stink didn't feel up to being scrutinized by Bonni's family and friends, however, he strolled into the crowded room by Bonni's side anyway. Everybody quickly assembled around the table as Tayvia prepared to open her gifts.

Watching Bonni assist Tayvia in tearing through colorful, wrapped presents was amusing to Stink.

As they finished opening the last gift, Bonni turned to Tayvia. "Tayvia, Mr. Rahsaan bought you a present. Wanna see it?"

Wide-eyed with anticipation, she yelled, "Yess, Mommy! Yes!"

"Come on," Bonni said, leading Tayvia through the kitchen and onto the back porch with the rest of the children following closely behind.

When Tayvia saw the pink jeep with the ribbon on the hood, her eyes lit up bright as the sun. "Mommy, he got it! He got it, Mommy!" she screamed hysterically.

Tayvia jumped in the jeep, marveling at her present. Once inside, she looked over and saw the two neatly wrapped packages. Ripping them open, she screamed, "Barbie! Mommy, I got Barbies too! Can I drive, Mommy? Puh-lease, can I drive?"

Bonni looked at Stink and snickered, "You have to ask Rahsaan, but first you have to thank him."

Tayvia jumped out of the jeep and ran to where Stink stood. "T'ank you, Mr. Wassaan," she crooned sincerely, then looked up to Stink and asked, "Can I Puh-Lease drive? Puh-lease?"

The pretty little girl had Stink wrapped around her finger, yet he decided to play with her. "Yeah, you can drive but only if you can call me Rah-saan," he said, pronouncing his name slowly so Tayvia could catch on.

"Wah...Ra...Rah...Sun," Tayvia stammered.

"Ok, that's good. Come on," he said, lifting the jeep off the porch.

As Stink looked back toward Bonni, he could've sworn that he'd seen a tear escape her eye.

As the party wound down and everybody began to leave, Bonni walked Stink outside. "Rahsaan, I'm really glad you came," she stated, giving him a tender hug.

"Yeah, I had a nice time," Stink replied, enjoying the feel of Bonni's body once again.

Breaking their embrace, Bonni stepped back and said, "I would give you my number, but I'm pretty sure you've already got it."

"So, why don't I give you mine and you call me," Stink requested, then trotted off to his car to retrieve a pen. "Make sure you use this," he said handing Bonni his phone number.

Backing away slowly, Bonni bit down on her bottom lip sexually, then mouthed, 'Thank you.'

Chapter 7

<u>October 1991</u>

Stink and Bonni had talked on the phone a few times, yet they still hadn't been able to go out. They had made plans for the following weekend and Stink wasn't about to let anything or anybody stand in his way. Since his plan was to be serious with Bonni, he needed to clear up the persistent rumors that Trina was carrying his child.

He hadn't seen her since his infamous spitting incident which had been months before so if she was indeed pregnant, she would be showing by now. Stink wanted to just pop up at Trina's house, but thought better of it. Deciding a call would be more appropriate; Stink hesitantly picked up the phone and dialed her number.

"Hello," a very familiar voice answered on the first ring.

"May I speak to Trina?"

"This is she. Who is this?" she snapped. Before Stink could reply, she stated, "I know this ain't who I think it is?!" The tone of her voice was laced with attitude.

"Yeah, this Rahsaan," Stink replied, regretting that he'd called.

"Rahsaan, what do you want?"

"Look, Trina, I ain't call you to argue. I just wanted to know what was going on with this shit I hear about you being pregnant and the baby being mine."

"Well, for your information, I am pregnant...by you!"

Stink held the phone in shock, he couldn't believe his ears. "Trina, how do you know that I...I-."

"Cause you the only nigga I fucked without a rubber, that's how!" Trina barked angrily.

Her open admission to sleeping around enraged Stink. "Well, I want a blood test, bitch!" he declared.

"You gonna pay for it too, muthafucka!"

"Set the date, bitch!" he yelled, slamming the phone down. As Stink paced back and forth in his bedroom, he didn't even notice his pager dancing on his dresser.

Retrieving it from the dresser, he eyed the screen and noticed Leaf's code: '155-155-155'.

Stink picked the phone up after having just thrown it to the floor and called Leaf.

"Yo, what up?" Leaf answered full of energy.

"Whazup, Leaf?" Stink asked trying to mask his anger.

"Yo, Stink. What up, son? What's the science?" Leaf asked in his thickest New York accent.

Dumbfounded, Stink wondered why New Yorkers always tried to make up some new shit. He replied, "Man, I'm waiting on you."

"A'ight, B. I got something sweet for you. Can you meet me at the Applebees on Coliseum drive, let's say... 10 o'clock?"

"Yeah, I can be there."

"A'ight, 10 o'clock. Peace," Leaf confirmed, then hung up.

Stink immediately thought, *There goes some more shit these New York niggas be making up - 'Peace, Son, God, B.'* "Nigga's confusing me forreal, forreal," Stink said to himself.

With an hour to burn before his scheduled meeting with Leaf, Stink decided to go into the mall that was conveniently located near the Applebees.

After only going into two stores, Stink had spent nearly fifteen hundred dollars. He'd picked out a Guess jean outfit for himself and the newest Air Jordans available.

He'd also purchased a pair of Agna riding boots with a matching pocketbook for Bonni after a quick call to Natasha to find out her shoe size. As always, Natasha had something slick to say.

"Damn, boy! You gonna spoil the damn girl before you even get the pussy. Or have you already gotten the pussy and her ass just ain't told me? Let me find out," she stated impetuously.

"Tasha, you crazy as shit. Bye," Stink said, hanging up after getting the information he sought.

With thirty minutes left before he was to meet Leaf, Stink headed to Applebees.

As Stink drove to his grandparents' house, he went over the new arrangements that he and Leaf had come up with. Leaf was now going to give Stink fifteen kilos of crack for $275,000, which Stink had to give half of up front. He knew he had it and it wouldn't be a problem getting the remainder from Lil Man and Dame. The dilemma would be whether he was going to reveal to them the new prices Leaf was offering.

As Stink pulled into his grandparents' driveway, there were no lights on which wasn't uncommon given it was almost midnight.

Using his key, he quietly entered the house and crept upstairs to his old bedroom.

Since Stink had moved, he still kept his money at his grandparents' house in his new, secure stash spot. He had accidentally stumbled upon the compartment in the floor of the bedroom's closet and had been using it since.

A perfect square section of the carpet moved revealing a rectangular opening in the floor, roughly the size of a large shoe box.

Stink pulled his money out of the compartment and counted six stacks of $10,000 and a smaller stack of $4,000.

As he put all of the stacks except for the $4,000 back into the compartment a noise outside of the bedroom door slightly startled him, causing him to clutch the cold black steel of the four-fifth inside his coat.

"Rhasaan, is that you?" his grandfather asked cautiously.

Instantly relaxing, Stink replied, "Yeah, it's me Papa. I just came to get something."

"Boy, what the hell you doing this time of night? Couldn't it have waited until tomorrow?" he asked in a hushed tone.

"Yeah, yeah, I guess you're right," Stink agreed trying to slip past his grandfather, who stood in the doorway.

Defiantly standing in Stink's path, his grandfather looked him in the eyes. "Boy, before you go anywhere, I want you to know that I know everything that goes on in my house and what's hidden in it, so don't think I'm stupid, cause I'm not. I knew about that hole in that floor before you were born. You may fool your grandmomma, but not me," he stated firmly, pointing his finger close to Stink's face for emphasis. Stink stood there, electing not to respond. His grandfather continued, "I've been meaning to talk to you, you've got to start compensating for some of that money. Them white folks gonna come at you so fast you won't know what hit you. Boy, you'd better get a job or something. I'm telling you now!" he advised sincerely.

Immediately, Stink felt stupid for putting the Saab in his name. At least he was smart enough to put his townhouse in somebody else's name. He knew he had to get rid of the car sooner rather than later.

Before walking away, Stink turned to his grandfather. "Thanks, Papa. Oh, and if you need some money, you know where it is," he said, tossing his grandfather a secretive smirk, then exited.

As soon as Stink got home, he went upstairs to his bedroom to check his answering machine.

"Message one, 'Yo, this Leaf, son…'" Erase.

"Message two, 'Hello, Stink, this Kesha, I was…'" Erase.

"Message three, 'Hey Rahsaan, call me when you get this message. Oh, and if you get your females mixed up, this is Bonni. Bye.'" Stink replayed the message numerous times, allowing her seductively raspy voice to reverberate throughout the room.

Stink eyed the clock which read 12:48 a.m., then decided, "Fuck it." Grabbing the phone, he punched in the numbers while doing a double take at the clock.

After only one ring, a woman answered groggily, "Hello."

"Is Bonni home?"

"Who is this!" the woman snapped, sounding like Natasha.

"This Stink."

"Boy, what the hell are you doing calling here this time of night? I know you done lost your mind," Natasha stated in an irritated tone.

"Come on, Tasha, I know you gonna get her for your lil bro," Stink stated, attempting to butter her up.

"'Lil bro' my ass. Yo ass owe me big time for this. Hold on!" Natasha stated in a voice full of attitude, then dropped the phone.

Stink held the phone in silence for at least five minutes until he heard someone picking up an extension.

"Hell-o," Bonni said sleepily.

"I'm sorry if I woke you up, Bonni, but I just got in from out of town and checked my messages," Stink blurted apologetically. "I hope you ain't trying to back out on our date Friday?"

"Naw, boy. I was just calling, that's all," she replied just above a whisper, making her already sexy voice seem even sexier. Yawning, she asked him, "What time is it, anyway?"

"It's like a quarter to one, maybe one o'clock. I really am sorry for waking you up. If you want to, you can call me in the morning and wake me up," Stink joked.

A slight giggle escaped her as she replied, "I just might do that."

Bonni and Stink talked on the phone like two high school sweethearts until nearly three o'clock in the morning.

Before hanging up, Bonni asked, "Rahsaan, do you live alone?"

"Yeah, just me. Why you ask?"

"Just wondering. It's kind of hard imagining you not only living alone, but also being alone," Bonni admitted, incredulously.

"Well, believe it, because I'm definitely single and I do live alone. Although, I was thinking about getting a dog," he said humorously.

Bonni chuckled lightly, then said, "I don't mean to seem as if I'm prying, I was just-"

"Look, Bonni," Stink began, cutting her off, "if you want to know anything about me, just ask. I promise to tell the truth, the whole truth and nothing but the truth, so help-"

Laughing uncontrollably, Bonnie blurted, "Boy, stop! You are too funny. You got my side hurting and I'm about to wake my daughter up."

"Oh, my fault. But forreal, this weekend you can ask me whatever you want," Stink announced broadly, knowing that he'd lie in a heartbeat.

"Ok, we'll see about that. Goodnight, or should I say good morning."

Long after they hung up, Stink still had Bonni on his mind.

After Stink let his crew in on the new pricing arrangements, they quickly came up with their portion of the money. Stink picked up his part of the money from his grandparents' house, and headed to Norfolk to meet Leaf.

He parked in front of the car lot that Leaf had directed him to. There were exotic cars and trucks situated around the lot for sale.

Leaf strolled out of the small office, and embraced Stink. "What up, B?"

"Ain't shit, man," Stink replied. "Whose lot is this?"

"You looking at him, son," Leaf announced.

Immediately, Stink was reminded of his dilemma; he needed to get rid of the Saab. He briefly explained his situation to Leaf who quickly responded. "No problem, B. Pick out what you like and we'll talk."

After Stink browsed around the lot, a charcoal gray Nissan Pathfinder caught his eye. He had always wanted a jeep so he quickly made his choice.

As he entered the office, Leaf held up his finger, signaling for Stink to hold on while he finished up his conversation on the phone.

Hanging up the phone, Leaf asked, "Did you find something you like, son?"

"Yeah. I like that Pathfinder. What year is it?"

"Umm, a '90, I think," Leaf said, checking the board on the wall. "Yeah, it's a '90. You trying to trade the Saab, right?"

"Yeah, but umm, I ain't trying to, umm…" Stink stammered.

Leaf quickly picked up on Stink's hesitancy. "Don't worry, I got you. Look, the Path is almost new, but since you's my man, I'll do you an even trade. A'ight, B?" Leaf offered, holding his hand high in preparation to slap Stink up, sealing the deal.

When Stink finally pulled out of the lot, he was the proud new owner of a Pathfinder, already equipped with two fifteen-inch subwoofers and all the extras. With the fifteen kilos of crack that sat on the passenger seat, it was definitely a good day.

In preparation for his date with Bonni, Stink had his truck detailed, his hair cut and even toyed with the idea of getting a manicure but passed on the latter.

Exiting the shower, Stink laid his new Guess jean suit out and retrieved his new Air Jordans from the closet. Primping as if he was preparing to enter a beauty contest, he meticulously dressed then grabbed Bonni's gift and headed out the door.

When Stink pulled in front of the Friendship House and hopped out of his sparkling clean jeep, he knew he was fly.

Lee-Lee and two of her girls were sitting on the porch eyeing him hungrily as he made his way toward them.

"Whazup, Lee-Lee," Stink said casually, then threw his head in the direction of the other two girls.

"Damn, Stink, you rocking that shit!" Lee-Lee complimented, referring to his outfit.

"Oh, thanks," he replied nonchalantly, then walked in the house.

"Umph, umph, umph," they all huffed in unison.

Stink ignored their open display of seduction and called out for Bonni.

Without a response, Bonni slowly descended the stairs, revealing a piece of her at a time.

First, her perfectly pedicured toes appeared, then her slightly bowed legs and golden thighs. Next, her perfect hips, along with her tiny waist...

"Damn!" Stink gasped in amazement, once he had a full view.

Biting her bottom lip teasingly, she asked, "How do I look?"

"You're beautiful," he stated, openly gawking at her thick, creamy thighs.

"You like?" she asked, spinning around in an attempt at giving Stink her best modeling pose.

"Definitely!" Stink replied, taking her by the hand, leading her out the door.

As they walked past Lee-Lee and her friends, Lee-Lee said, "Stink, I like that bangin'- ass jeep."

Refusing to take part in the subliminal game of seduction Lee-Lee and her girls were playing, Stink nonchalantly replied, "Thanks," and led Bonni to the passenger side of his jeep.

Settling into the black leather seat, Bonni asked, "Is this yours?"

"Yeah," he replied, turning the ignition, causing Jodeci's *Forever My Lady* to come blaring out of the two 15s.

"Forever my lady, you mean so much to meeee. There's nothing more precious, than to..."

After eating a delicious meal at one of the area's most preeminent seafood restaurants, Stink and Bonni began to talk about their respective lives, past and present. Bonni explained how she had completed cosmetology school while she was pregnant and somehow managed to finish high school. She talked a little about Tayvia's father and the trials she had endured with him.

Hearing her story, Stink was filled with a deeper compassion for her as a person.

He elected not to tell Bonni about his childhood in North Carolina and how he grew up poor. Instead, he talked about some of his past relationships, especially Trina, but chose to leave out the part about her impending pregnancy.

Their evening ended with Stink walking her to her door. Just when they'd said their goodbyes and turned to leave, Bonni said, "Rahsaan."

Stink abruptly turned to face her. Their eyes locked in a brief silence until Bonni moved in close and slipped her tongue into his mouth.

Locked in an embrace, their tongues battled for position while Stink's hand gently palmed Bonni's ass.

Reluctantly breaking their embrace, Bonni wiped Stink's bottom lip with her thumb, removing traces of her sweet-tasting lip gloss.

"Rahsaan, I had a wonderful time and I hope we can do it again soon," she proposed before she turned to go inside.

Remembering the gifts, Stink blurted, "Hold on! I got something for you." He quickly trotted off to his jeep then returned to the porch with the bag. "Here, this is for you."

Bonni peeped in the bag, then replied, "Ooh, Rahsaan, thank you so much." She gave Stink a friendly hug, ending their evening.

Chapter 8

December 1991

Although Leaf had come down on the prices, he had asked that Stink take the money to New York. It was a lot easier than transporting drugs down Interstate 95, so Stink agreed.

Taxying down the runway, Stink looked out the window at the bright lights of New York, and quickly contemplated where his life was headed.

After retrieving his luggage, Stink went straight to the pick-up area where Cross was supposed to be waiting. Lil Man had appointed Cross to personally chaperone Stink while he was in New York. Lil Man didn't think it would be wise for Stink to be running around New York with nearly $150,000 alone so Cross was brought in to look out.

As Stink stood in the pick-up area looking around for any signs of Cross, he heard, "What up, god?"

Turning toward the voice, Stink observed Cross leaning against a wall casually, as if he'd been there the entire time.

"Ain't shit, man. I'm just glad to be on level ground. Them muthafuckin' planes scare me," Stink smiled, giving Cross a brotherly embrace.

"You ready to bounce, son?" Cross asked, grabbing Stink's bags.

As Stink and Cross rode across the Queensboro Bridge into Harlem, Cross began to talk, breaking the silence. "Yo, son, I'm trying to get the fuck up outta New York. A nigga can't get no paper wit niggas claiming blocks and shit. A nigga fuck around and gotta murder a nigga just to get money. Then you still might not get no paper. Shit's crazy, forreal, god," he surmised in a frustrating tone.

"Damn, it's like that up here?" Stink asked in astonishment.

"Hell yeah, son!" Cross retorted. "I know ya'll got a spot for a nigga down there. Any-fucking-thing! I don't give a fuck what it is, son. I will walk your fucking dog for you, just to get the fuck up outta N.Y.C!" he declared in despair.

"You ain't holla at Lil Man yet?"

"Yeah, I hollered at him, but Lil be on some bullshit sometimes. Nigga be dragging his feet on shit, feel me?" Cross explained. After a short contemplation, he continued, "I mean, Lil looks out and all, but I'm trying to eat, B. I'm trying to do shit too. Nigga got me on a leash or some shit."

Stink listened to Cross intently, envisioning how he would fit into their operations in Virginia. One thing was for certain, Cross was a lunatic, and Stink had learned first-hand that gun-play caused - jail.

Arriving in Virginia the following day, Stink went home and promptly checked his answering machine. Hoping to hear Bonni's voice replayed on the tiny machine, he was shocked to hear Trina's instead.

"I received this notice from your lawyer and you will get your precious little blood test but it's fucked up that you haven't seen your son yet. Oh, by the way, his name is Rahsaan Adrian Adams. Bye!"

Stink sat on the bed astounded. He couldn't believe that Trina had given the child his name without being assured that he was the father.

He quickly grabbed the phone and dialed Trina's number.

"Hello," Trina quickly answered.

Unable to mask his anger, Stink blurted, "Look, Trina, I'm trying to come see the baby."

"What you mean, 'the baby'? You'd better be saying 'your baby', nigga!" she spat. Pausing to catch her breath, she continued, "Matter of fact, since he's 'the baby', wait until the blood test results come back before you come and see 'your son'." *Click!*

Furious, Stink sat there gripping the phone. He contemplated calling back but decided against it. He now understood why so many black kids grow up without a father in the home.

The thought of being connected to such a hateful person for the rest of his life filled Stink with a sudden sense of hopelessness.

In order to clear his mind, he decided to call Bonni. It was a little after four o'clock, so he knew she'd still be at work.

"Hello, Honey's Hair Salon. May I help you?" a woman answered full of bright spirit.

Stink decided to have a little fun. "Yes, may I speak to a Ms. Bonita Lawson?"

"Yes, please hold."

After a brief wait, Bonni picked up. "Yes, hello."

Hearing Bonni's sexy voice, Stink almost gave up on his act, yet managed to keep his composure. "Yes, Ms. Lawson, I'm calling from Publisher's Clearing House. Are you sitting down?" Stink asked in his best prize-winning voice.

"Who is this? Stop playing!" Bonni said in a serious tone.

Incapable of continuing his act, Stink burst out laughing, "Girl, it's me, Rahsaan."

"I knew it was you the whole time! When did you get back?"

"A little while ago."

"Did you have a nice trip?"

"Yeah, it was okay but I'm trying to see you," Stink said with a sense of urgency.

"Well, I still have about thirty minutes before I'm finished with my last client. But yeah, you can-."

"Come pick you up!" Stink blurted, finishing her statement.

Allowing a slight giggle to escape her, Bonni replied, "Yeah, you can do that."

"Okay, I'll be there in thirty minutes."

Stink quickly jumped in the shower, threw on some jeans, his Timberland boots, a Pelle Pelle leather jacket, and was out the door.

When he arrived at Honey's, it was a little after 5 o'clock in the evening, yet the salon was still crowded. Stink casually strolled into the salon amid the 'umph, umph umph's' and openly gawking women. He walked straight to Bonni's station and gave her a peck on the cheek.

Working on what looked to be a perfectly finished hairdo, Bonni said, "I'll be finished in just a second."

Stink walked over and took a seat in the waiting area, watching the women who openly stared at him.

It only took Bonni a few minutes to finish with her client before she walked over to Stink with her coat and purse in hand. "Let's go," she announced, grabbing Stink's hand and leading him out the door.

When they got settled in the jeep, Stink turned to Bonni. "Are you hungry?"

"Nah, not really, but don't let me stop you. Maybe watching you eat will give me an appetite."

Stink and Bonni were in Applebee's, laughing and joking, when he asked, "Do you have to pick Tayvia up at a certain time?"

"Well, she's at my mom's for the rest of the weekend, but I usually go by there after work," she explained.

Stink dug into his pocket to retrieve some change. "Well, you'd better at least call," he said, handing her a quarter.

Bonni took the coin, slid from the booth, and walked off toward the payphone.

Stink sat there appreciating Bonni's sexy walk and the way her perfect heart-shaped ass jiggled with each step.

"Umph, umph, umph," was all he could say.

Right before she disappeared from his view, she turned and gave Stink a sexy wink that said, *I know you're watching my ass*.

Once Bonni made the call, she came back to their table with a sudden appetite. After devouring her entrée, she ordered a mixed drink while Stink was already on his third gin and tonic. The alcohol loosened their conversation up tremendously, allowing them both to talk more freely.

After a nice meal and a few drinks, things began to wind down. Stink eyed the clock which read 8:30, then asked, "You ready to go?"

"Yeah, I guess so," she replied gathering her coat and purse.

Stink dropped three twenty dollar bills on the table, then stood to lead the way outside.

The over-consumption of alcohol had Stink tipsy, barely making it to the jeep on wobbly legs.

Bonni, who'd only had two mixed drinks, promptly grabbed the keys and took the driver's seat.

After getting situated, Bonni looked to Stink, and asked, "So where to?"

He didn't have a plan, yet he didn't want the night to end. "Uh, how about you come check my crib out?" he proposed, then added, "I mean, you haven't been there yet, so…"

Bonni gave him a patronizing smirk, then asked, "Which way?"

Just as Stink finished showing Bonni his townhouse in its entirety, his pager began to vibrate on his hip. Looking down at the small screen, he sucked his teeth in exasperation. "Damn!" he said in a frustrated tone, seeing Leaf's number.

"What? Is something wrong?" Bonni asked with concern.

"Oh, nothing. I just gotta handle something real quick."

"Well, you can drop me off at home. I under-"

Stink began to shake his head disagreeably before she could finish. "Nah, you can stay here. I won't be that long."

Bonni shot him a look of skepticism, then asked, "You mean to tell me, that you'd leave me here, alone, to snoop through ALL your stuff?"

"Yeah, why not? I ain't got nothing to hide," he stated defiantly, holding his arms wide. Taking a deep breath, Stink's demeanor turned serious. "Look Bonni, I really, really like you and I want to get to know you better. I'm forreal, I-." His pager vibrated again interrupting him.

Bonni shook her head in disbelief, then said, "Go on, boy. I'll be fine, but if one of your women calls here-"

"Just tell'em you my girl and don't call no more," Stink chimed in, as he quickly dialed Leaf's number. He desperately wanted to put the pick-up off until the next day, however, he knew that he had to handle his business.

Hanging up the phone, Stink turned to Bonni. "Make yourself at home, Bonni. Whatever you want to do, do it;

take a shower, cook, clean, whatever," he advised, as he hurriedly made his way out the door.

As soon as Stink was gone, Bonni began to take notice of how neatly decorated the townhouse actually was. From the expensive-looking paintings that adorned the walls, to the colorful imitation floral arrangements, it seemed to be the work of a woman. Feeling that there was no way Stink could have decorated the place himself, Bonni concluded that a woman had definitely done it.

Walking up the stairs, Bonni smiled a devilish grin at what she was about to do. If a woman had lived there at any point in time, she knew exactly where to look.

After meeting with Leaf in Virginia Beach, dropping the drugs off at Lil Man's house, and making a quick stop to get gas, it was almost one o'clock in the morning when Stink returned to his townhouse.

Grabbing the stack of money he'd picked up from Lil Man, Stink made his way into the house.

As he walked through the house, he felt a slight sense of panic, after seeing no signs of Bonni. Quickly, he ran up the stairs to his bedroom and let out a sigh of relief. Bonni laid cuddled up in a thick comforter, with an angelic look on her sleeping face.

Grinning foolishly, Stink stepped out of his boots, took his jeans off and slid into a pair of gym shorts.

In an attempt not to disturb her, Stink cautiously sat on the bed.

As soon as Bonni felt the soft mattress move, she stirred. "What time is it?" she asked sleepily.

Eyeing the clock on the nightstand, Stink replied, "It's almost one."

"I must've been tired," Bonni said, yawning.

"It's ok, go back to sleep," Stink urged, rubbing her shoulders gently.

As Stink got up to retrieve the remote control, Bonni grabbed his arm. "Do you have a t-shirt or something that I can sleep in?"

"Yeah, I got something," he said, going to his dresser, pulling out a long polo shirt, and handed it to Bonni.

She sat up and pulled her shirt over her head, revealing her bra-covered breasts.

Stink stood there watching her every move, with a lustful look on his face. Bonni pulled his shirt over her head, then maneuvered her bra off.

"What's wrong? You've never seen a girl in her panties and a bra before?" she asked, handing him her discarded clothing.

"Nah, not as beautiful as you, though," Stink replied sincerely.

"I bet you say that to all the girls you have in your bed in their underwear," Bonni said, flashing a phony smile.

"Would you believe me if I told you that you're the first woman who's been in this bed?" he asked with a sly grin etched into his features.

Bonni gave him and incredulous look. "Mmm-hmm, I bet."

Shaking his head in defeat, Stink walked downstairs and poured two glasses of juice.

On his way back upstairs, he noticed the door to the laundry room slightly ajar, yet he thought nothing of it, even though he always kept the door that housed his dirty laundry closed.

"I thought you might be thirsty," Stink said, offering her one of the glasses.

"Thank you so much, Rahsaan. You're so sweet," she responded affectionately. "Your house is comfortable," she commented before placing her glass on the nightstand, then laying back snuggling into the comforter.

Stink gulped his juice down in what seemed like one swallow, then replied, "Thanks." Grabbing the remote, he laid across the bed and began to aimlessly flick through the channels.

After getting comfortable, Stink felt Bonni's hand gently rubbing the back of his head, causing a shiver to run down his spine.

"What's wrong? Are you feeling cold?" she asked affectionately.

Sliding up on the bed to give Bonni's hands easier access, Stink replied, "Nah, it…just, feels good."

Bonni continued to manipulate Stink's spots as if she had been there before. While her hands moved feather-like, sending chills up and down his spine, he squirmed under her touch.

Desperately wanting to return what he was feeling, he turned over slowly and maneuvered his body, until they were face to face.

Cunningly, Stink slipped his tongue into Bonni's mouth and they shared a long, lustful kiss, which became more intense as Stink began to grope her body through the thick comforter.

Breaking their embrace, Stink pulled the t-shirt that he'd just given Bonni over her head, revealing firm breasts with nipples the size of half dollars.

Choosing not to go straight for her breasts, he started at her neck, leaving a hot trail with his tongue and worked his way down to her nipples.

Suckling gingerly on her nipples, Stink felt Bonni's hand on his head, silently urging him on.

"I love the way your mouth feels on my nipples," Bonnie huffed sexually.

Stink pulled the comforter completely off her and moved his hand between her creamy thighs, feeling her moisture through the fabric of her panties.

Sliding her panties to the side, Stink pushed a finger into her opening, instantly feeling the tightness of her wet opening around his finger.

Bonnie began to gyrate her hips onto his probing finger. "Oh, oh, yess!" she moaned in her customary raspy voice.

Stink threw the covers back with his free hand and began to plant wet kisses down her stomach.

Arching her back in anticipation, Bonni announced through clenched teeth, "I'm sooo wet, Rahsaan."

Stink pulled his cum coated finger from Bonni's dripping center, then slipped her panties down around her ankles, giving him a clear view of her womanhood.

Eyeing her thick bush hungrily, Stink kissed her sensuously on the insides of each thigh. He had never tasted a woman before. However, at that moment he wanted nothing more than to savor her juices.

Once he was face to face with her hairy slit, he dove in, sampling her pussy hungrily.

"Oh...my...GOD! Rah...Rahsaan, what are you doing?!" Bonni exclaimed in ecstasy.

Her juices were sweet as candy and the aroma of her pussy made Stink's manhood defiantly hard.

Experimenting further with his new found craft, Stink placed his tongue on her clit and gently licked, instantly sending Bonni to heights of passion she'd never experienced.

"Ohh! Oh shit, God! Rahsaan, please! Please Rah...saan, stop!" she begged, gripping the back of his head. The act of actually having her vagina eaten had her in a frenzy. "Rahsaan, pleeeaase!" she cried.

This seemed to motivate Stink, as he vigorously sucked at her clit.

Bonni gripped Stink's head, holding him in place between her legs. "I'm cum...miing! Oh, shit, I'm cumming!" she yelled as her body began to spasm as if she was having a seizure.

Stink had never witnessed this from a woman. Instantly stopping, he eyed her with concern. "Are you all right?"

Unable to answer, Bonni bit down hard on her bottom lip as spasms racked her body.

"Are you ok?" he repeated.

"Rahsaan...I just had an orgasm," she responded, breathing heavily. "I've never had one before," she declared sincerely.

Grabbing Stink by the back of his head, Bonni kissed him with a sense of urgency, while tasting her own juices on his tongue.

"Do you have a condom?" she asked desperately.

Oh, not this shit again, Stink thought to himself. Disappointedly, shaking his head 'no,' he began, "Listen Bonni, I want you to know that whether we do anything or not, I'm trying to be your man." After a brief pause, he continued, "As a matter of fact, after tonight, I am your man," he announced with sincere eyes.

There was a brief stillness between them until Bonni reached for his throbbing manhood, releasing it from its confines.

Stink quickly shed the remainder of his clothing and positioned himself at her opening.

Bonni guided his manhood into her wanting core, while looking deep into his eyes.

Planting soft kisses on her forehead, Stink whispered, "Baby, you feel sooo good." Feeling the warmth of her pussy surrrounding his shaft made him want to scream.

Bonni gazed into his eyes, willing him to go deeper. "Give it to me! Please, Rahsaan!" she begged.

Stink was amazed at how good her sex felt. Thrusting into her deeper, he could see her juices glistening onto his manhood.

"Oh, my...God! Baby, you are so deep in me! Fuck me, baby! Fu...Fuck me, please!" Bonni commanded.

Feeling his own nut building, Stink pumped furiously, causing the sounds of their bodies clasping together to reverbatate throughout the room.

"Ah, Fuck! I...I'm..." Stink grunted, as he felt his seed shoot deep into her.

"Cum for me, baby. Cum for me," Bonni coaxed tenderly, wiping sweat from his face.

Stink collapsed on her, feeling the warmth of their juices mixing, wishing he could stay there forever.

Chapter 9

Things had become hectic for Stink. The results from the paternity test he'd taken were due any day and he'd taken a more active role in his crew's drug operation.

Leaf had started pressing Stink for the payment of the drugs almost immediately after delivering them. Although Lil Man and Dame were doing their part, it wasn't enough, prompting Stink to establish his own clientele.

Being away from the hands-on part of hustling for so long caused Stink to become extremely paranoid, treating every deal as if it would be his last.

The only bright spots in his life were Bonni and Tayvia. Stink had moved them into his townhouse a few weeks after he and Bonni had made love. He didn't think it was acceptable for his girl and her daughter to be living in the conditions that they were living in. Tayvia needed her own room and Bonni needed her own house. Being able to provide this filled Stink with a strong sense of pride; he felt responsible.

Stink had been invited to an album release party by Leaf, and was planning to take Bonni along with the rest of his crew. The rap group, Wrecks-N-Effect, had just released a single entitled *Rump-shaker* which was blowing the airwaves up. The group, originally from the same projects as Leaf in New York, had just filmed a video for their hit in Virginia Beach. Oddly, Trina had squirmed her way into the video so it was quite possible that she would be at the party as well.

As Stink drove through the slums of downtown Newport News, his pager vibrated on his hip. Seeing Bonni's code, followed by Honey's Hair Salon's phone number, Stink quickly pulled over at a pay phone on 25th and Wickham Avenue.

Exiting his jeep, he witnessed a drug deal in progress, a bum begging for change and a drunk woman selling herself. Punching the number in the phone, Stink thought, 'I gotta get me a carphone fast'.

"Honey's, may I help you?" a woman answered professionally.

"Yeah, can I speak to Bonni?" Stink asked, eyeing his surroundings cautiously.

"This is me, baby. Damn, you don't even know my voice," she replied, disappointed.

"Girl, I knew it was you. I was just playing. Whazup?" Stink lied.

"Look, I'm running a little late. Can you pick Tayvia up from my mom's?"

"Yeah, I could do that, but does your moms know I'm coming?"

"I'll call her right now."

"A'ight, I'm on my way," Stink replied, preparing to hang up.

"Oh, and Rahsaan."

"Yeah."

"I love you," Bonni stated affectionately.

Intentionally avoiding the sentiment, Stink responded, "Me too," then hung up. Walking back to his jeep, Stink eyed the hustlers, peddlers and prostitutes that loitered the streets of downtown Newport News and shook his head.

As Stink pulled up in front of Bonni's mother's house, he noticed Tayvia jumping up and down in the doorway.

Hopping out of the jeep, he heard her tiny voice yelling, "Grandma! Grandma! Wassaan's here!"

Tayvia was still unable to pronounce Stink's name properly, yet he loved her the same.

Ms. Lawson, Bonni's mother, met Stink at the door. "Come on in, Rahsaan. It's nice to see you," she said, directing him to a seat on the sofa, while she went to the back to assist Tayvia in gathering her things.

Stink had never been in Ms. Lawson's company without Bonni, causing him to be slightly nervous. The short, stout woman's demeanor demanded respect. Stink could tell she had endured a lot of hardship in her life, somehow survived it all.

When Ms. Lawson re-entered the room, she rested her hands on her wide hips and took a deep breath, then said, "I'll tell ya, that lil girl loves you." Resting her eyes on Stink accusingly, she continued, "I hope this ain't some type of game for you."

Stink started to respond to her comment, but was abruptly stopped by Ms. Lawson holding her palms up.

"My daughter has been through hell and I haven't seen her this happy since she was that girl in there's age," she said, pointing in the direction that Tayvia had gone. "Now, I'm-a give you the benefit of the doubt because you have helped my daughter by moving her and buying her a car and all. But the minute you hurt her, I'm-a hunt'cha down and kill you myself," she vowed, pointing her finger at him threateningly.

Stink sat there, comforted only by the 9mm in his waistline and nodded understandably.

"Bonni and that lil girl in there is all I got," she concluded.

As soon as Tayvia appeared with her little Barbie book bag, Ms. Lawson's attitude changed immediately. "Here's my little princess. Grandma's gonna miss you," she said, hugging Tayvia, lovingly.

As Stink placed Tayvia in the back of his jeep, Ms. Lawson stood in the doorway waving. Just as he was about to pull off, she mouthed, 'Remember what I said', and winked her eye.

"Rahsaan, I need you to check the car out," Bonni said as she entered the house.

Stink and Tayvia were sitting on the couch eating McDonalds and watching one of Tayvia's favorite animated movies.

"Mommy! Mommy! Look what Wassaan got me!" Tayvia yelled, running to greet her mother, showing her the toy that accompanied her Happy Meal.

"Why? What's wrong with it?" Stink asked.

"While I'm driving, this bell keeps ringing," she explained.

Stink had purchased the Honda from Lil Man, who had taken it from a guy that owed him money. To Stink's knowledge, the car was in good shape.

He grabbed Bonni's keys and headed outside. As he drove the car up the block, just as Bonni had said, suddenly a bell began to sound. Immediately, Stink found the source of the bell. Shaking his head in despair, he headed toward the gas station.

Walking through the door, Stink arrogantly stated, "I can tell you ain't never owned a car."

Defensively, Bonni replied, "Why you say that?"

"The bell was telling you that the car needed gas. What? You thought it ran off air?" he asked sarcastically.

"Fuck you!"

"Why you talking like that and there's a child in the house?"

"Boy, Tayvia's upstairs and I doubt she can hear me," Bonni replied, then said, "Oh, tomorrow I'm going to the mall to find something to wear to the party, so I'm-a be late again. Can you pick up Tayvia?"

Just the mentioning of the party filled Stink with a sense of trepidation. He knew that Trina was going to be there. He'd contemplated telling Bonni about Trina and the baby, however, he just couldn't find the courage.

Friday, the night of the party, after making a few moves, Stink called Lil Man.

"Whazup?" Lil Man answered cockily.

"Yo, Lil, whazup nigga?"

"Ain't shit, just about to go to the airport to pick Cross up."

Slightly shocked at hearing that, Stink replied, "Oh, yeah. How long is he gonna be in town?"

"Just for the party this weekend, then his ass is on the first thing smoking back to New York."

When Stink had returned from New York, after he and Cross had their conversation about him coming to Virginia, Stink ran the idea by Lil Man.

Lil Man was adamantly against Cross coming to Virginia, simply saying, "Virginia ain't big enough for that nigga! He'll have all of us locked up forever for some crazy shit."

With that said, Stink didn't bring the issue up anymore.

"So y'all trying to hit the mall later?" Stink asked.

"Yeah, I'll be back on that side in about an hour. Where you trying to meet at?"

"Umm, meet me at Peddler's Village. I'm-a go holla at Peady about one of them mobile phones."

"A'ight, peace," Lil Man said, ending the call.

Stink parked in front of the Peddler's Village and went straight to see Peady. Peady was an African guy who owned a pager/phone business located in the back of Peddler's Village. He offered good rates without credit checks and contract signings, making Peady's a favorite for hustlers.

Peddler's Village was actually an old supermarket located downtown that had been gutted and sectioned off, giving each merchant their own small shop. There were clothing shops, shoe shops and jewelry shops; you name it, and Peddler's Village had it.

After paying nearly $500.00 for the newest, sleekest phone that Peady offered, Stink browsed through some of the other shops.

Glancing through a jewelry shop that a Chinese couple owned, Stink heard someone outside yell, "Yo! Stink, what up, god?"

Stink knew it could only be one person using that lingo. Turning, he saw Cross bouncing in his direction.

"Whazup, Cross?" Stink said as he and Cross embraced. As always, Cross's hair and dress were immaculate.

"I know you ain't up in here buying this bullshit, B," Cross stated loud enough to receive menacing frowns from both the shop owners. "I could take you to a spot uptown and get that fly shit," Cross boasted, oblivious to the Chinese couple's glare.

"Nah, nah, I'm good, but where Lil at?" Stink asked, leading Cross out of the store.

"He outside, talking to some shorty," Cross replied, then led the way to the parking lot where Lil Man was.

Stink heard the loud music coming from Lil Man's Jeep Wrangler, before he even saw him. Leaning against the jeep's door, talking to an attractive light-skinned girl, Lil Man was the epitome of a drug dealer.

This nigga thinks he's Nino Brown forreal, Stink thought, referring to the drug kingpin played by Wesley

Snipes in the movie *New Jack City*. As Lil Man turned to dap him up, Stink noticed the extravagant piece of jewelry that hung from Lil Man's neck. The Gucci link chain, at least an inch-and-a-half thick, was adorned with a diamond-encrusted charm that read 'RICH LITTLE'.

Shaking his head in disbelief, Stink said, "Whazup, Nino Brown?"

"Aww, nigga, go on with the bullshit," Lil Man responded, smiling from ear to ear.

Lil Man quickly diverted his attention back to the light-skinned cutie, while Stink and Cross indulged in their own conversation.

After getting the young girl's phone number, Lil Man dismissed her, then asked, "So whazup, Stink? Which mall you trying to hit?"

"Shit, it don't matter to me; Military or Coliseum will work."

"Well, let me hit Dame so he can meet us there," Lil Man said, pulling out his phone.

Stink pulled out his own, newly purchased phone and casually stated, "Nah, I'll call him."

"Oh, shit! You got the new joint!" Lil Man exclaimed, reaching for Stink's phone.

"Nah, nigga. I...gots...this," Stink said, dialing Dame's number.

Stink, Lil Man, Dame and Cross were strolling through the mall, laughing and joking among themselves. They were leaving the trendy store Merry-Go-Round, where they had spent nearly $3,000 between the four of them.

Standing near a kiosk situated in the middle of the mall was a strikingly beautiful young woman. Lil Man, the smoothest of the bunch, eased up to the lady and attempted to put his rap game down. Just as Lil Man began to kick his game, an older guy with an intimidating glare walked up.

"Felicia, who the fuck is this?!" the guy asked, clearly agitated.

Lil Man looked at the guy as if he was crazy, then back to the woman who had an I-told-you-my-man-was-crazy look on her face.

Instantly, the exchanged prompted Stink, Dame and Cross to approach.

"Whazup, Lil? You a'ight?" Stink asked, eyeing the dude with an unblinking stare.

"Yeah, I'm good," Lil Man replied, then focused his attention back to the woman. "Damn, baby, this the best you could do?" he exclaimed, turning to walk away.

Unbeknownst to Lil Man, he had just invited the wrath of a real live fool.

Marco Jenkins, a one-time baller and full-time lunatic, shot daggers at Lil Man's back as he walked away. Their crew represented what Marco no longer was – a hustler. It was by the grace of God that his children's mother, Felicia, stuck by his side through his uproarious down slide into oblivion. The young hustler with the shiny jewelry had sparked Marco's quest for the three things that every hustler yearned for - money, power and respect; things Marco felt he no longer had.

Stink struggled to open the door with the shopping bags in hand. Entering the house, he was greeted with, "Wassaan! Wassaan! I drew you a picture today at school," Tayvia yelled excitedly, waving the colorful drawing in his direction.

Stink sat his bags down and eyed the drawing conspicuously. It was a picture of a man, a woman and a little girl.

"Is this for me, Tayvia?" Stink asked in amazement.

"Yess…It's me, you, and mommy."

"Thank you, Tayvia," Stink responded animatedly, kneeling to give her a hug.

"You   welcome."

"I'm going to hang this on the refrigerator, right now."

"Yippee!" Tayvia yelled.

"Hey baby," Bonni said as Stink entered their bedroom.

"Damn! I see you went all out!" Stink declared, eyeing the sparkling dress hanging from the door.

"Boy, it's Donna Karan, and I got it on sale," Bonni stated, pushing Stink's hand away from the dress. Turning him around to face her, Bonni teasingly asked, "You want me to look good for you, don't you?"

Her seductive tone immediately caused Stink to slip his hands around her waist and pull her body close to his.

Hugging him tightly, Bonni whispered, "Rahsaan, I love you."

The prolonged silence without a response caused Bonni to look deep into his eyes questionably.

Giving an exasperated sigh, Stink faced Bonni's unyielding stare. "Bonni, I want to say 'I love you too', but I've never experienced love. I don't know what love is. But what I do know is that if love means never wanting to be without a person, then I love you," Stink surmised sincerely.

As they stood there looking into each other's eyes, a single tear rolled down Bonni's cheek as she planted a soft kiss on Stink's lips, then led him into the shower. While making love under the hot spray of water, Bonni's tears were shielded along with her gasps of ecstasy.

Bonni rummaged through Stink's cassettes until she found what she was looking for. Popping in Mary J. Blige's cassette, she sat back and sang along with the newly crowned Queen of Hip-Hop and R&B.

Stink looked over at Bonni, marveling at how beautiful she was. To him, she looked as if she was a super model or a superstar. Eyeing her thick yellow thighs, Stink nearly missed their exit, which would've made them later than they already were.

As they pulled in front of the Friendship House, there was a line of luxury automobiles, confirming that his entire crew had arrived.

Stink and Bonni quickly went inside only to find all of the women in Natasha's bedroom primping and all the fellas in the makeshift office puffing on some of the most potent-smelling weed Stink had ever encountered.

Stink gave everyone daps and hugs as Lil Man passed him one of the blunts that was in circulation. He hit the powerful herb, while checking out his crew's attire appreciatively.

Lil Man, the flashiest of the crew, wore a deep green silk suit with matching green suede Ballys. Dame, with his short, stocky build and dark complexion, wore all things black - from his black Timberland boots to his Polo pullover. Cross, being the New York nigga he was, kept it strictly uptown. He wore a Guess jean suit, white Air Force 1s with the blue check and a matching blue Champion hooded sweatshirt.

Stink had chosen a Nautica jean suit, a pair of wheat construction Timberlands and his butter soft, beige Andrew Mark leather jacket.

Each one of them were draped in their jewelry and of course, Lil Man's 'RICH LITTLE' piece was the most extravagant. Stink, usually the most conservative, even pulled out his Cuban link with the half dollar medallion that was surrounded by flawless diamonds.

"So y'all ready to bounce?" Stink asked, eyeing the clock.

"Nah, nigga, we ain't finished getting smoked yet," Lil Man snapped, emptying the contents of another Philly blunt into the trashcan.

Cross tossed Lil Man a small bag of marijuana and said, "That's that New 'Yoke' smoke right there, so be careful," Cross warned, pronouncing New York as if he was a southerner.

Lil Man rolled the blunt, lit it up and hit it a few times before passing it to Stink. Ignoring Cross's warning, Stink pulled deeply on the blunt, only to be choked by the potent smoke.

Cross promptly began smacking him on his back. "I told you, god, be careful," he said mockingly.

Once the blunt made it around to Stink again, he inhaled it with precaution, being careful not to get choked again.

Stink was too high from the weed that Cross had brought from New York. In fact, he was so high he headed to the passenger side of his jeep, prompting Bonni to drive. Once Lil Man and Dame saw this, they followed suit. Nicole, Lil Man's girl took the wheel of his Benz, while Natasha jumped in the driver's seat of Dame's newly-acquired 750i BMW. Cross, who drove alone, decided to ride with Lil Man.

The girls took advantage of the wide open interstate on their way to Virginia Beach, racing each other furiously until they pulled in the parking lot of the Bridge nightclub.

Stink instructed Bonni to pull directly in front of the packed club.

Looking at him quizzically, she asked, "Are you serious?"

"Yeah, I'm serious," he retorted.

"But I can't, those things are blocking the entrance," Bonni whined, pointing at the orange cones that sat in the parking lot.

"Girl, you're in a four-wheel drive. Run that shit over!"

As Bonni cautiously drove over the cones, Stink pulled out his phone and dialed Leaf's number. Just as Leaf answered the phone, Stink noticed two burly security guards headed his way. "Yo Leaf, I'm out front," he announced.

"A'ight, playboy, I'm on my way out to get you."

"Yo, hurry up, 'cause two bodyguard-looking niggas is coming at me as we speak," Stink informed, sliding the P89 from under the front seat.

"Don't sweat it. I'm on my way right now," Leaf assured, then hung up.

One of the security guards walked up to Stink's window, sporting a serious grit. "Those cones were there for a reason. You can't park in front-,"

Abruptly cutting the big man off in mid-sentence, Leaf appeared, "They wit me! Let 'em through," he commanded.

Both the big men turned and walked back toward the entrance of the club, with defeated looks on their faces.

Leaf dapped Stink up through the open window, then said, "I'll be in front waiting on you."

Bonni began to apply a fresh coat of lipstick, while Stink looked around the packed parking lot for the rest of their squad.

Unable to locate them, he blurted, "Where the fuck they at?"

"Who, baby?" Bonni asked oblivious to whom Stink was referring to.

"Fuck it!" Stink concluded, stepping from the jeep, only to notice Lil Man and Leaf standing in front of the club talking.

"Come on, girl! Everybody's waiting on us!" he barked.

"I'm coming, boy!"

Meeting up with the rest of their crew, the girls instantly clicked together, reenacting their race while Leaf ushered all of them into the club.

The onlookers, stuck in the long line, looked at them as if to say, *Who the fuck they supposed to be?*

The bright lights and pulsating music immediately amplified Stink's high. As Leaf led them into the VIP, Stink noticed a large table with four bottles of ice cold Moët reserved for them. Stink could only smile at the hospitality that Leaf was extending.

The girls took their seats after a brief miscommunication over who was sitting where and with whom.

Cross took a seat at the small bar located inside the VIP. Leaf left them to entertain some of his other guests, throwing over his shoulder, "Order whatever you like, it's on the house." He then disappeared.

Stink grabbed a bottle of Moët and popped the cork, filling two flutes for Bonni and him. Dame quickly followed suit doing the same for Natasha. Lil Man had stepped into the bathroom, so Bonni grabbed Nicole a glass.

Exiting the restroom, Lil Man yelled, "Oh, y'all couldn't wait for a nigga?" He grabbed one of the bottles of champagne and popped the cork. "Fuck it, I got my own bottle," he said, turning the bottle up.

Bonni was beaming at how the night had begun; her smile seemed to be a permanent fixture on her face.

They all sat back and enjoyed a few rounds of champagne while enjoying the DJ's mixture of hip-hop and R&B. That is, until the DJ began to mix in the thunderous sounds of reggae music. Bonni, who loved reggae music, looked at Stink while winding her body sexually and said, "Baby, I want to go dance."

Stink, not known to be much of a dancer, yet feeling good from the synergistic effect of the marijuana and alcohol, obliged.

"Come on, let's go," he said allowing Bonni to lead him to the dance floor.

"Baby, this is my shit," Bonni yelled over Nado Rankin's *Woman if Ya Love Me*. Bonni grinded her shapely backside against Stink's manhood as if they were simulating sex. He gripped her waist and allowed her to do as she pleased, while he swayed to the music.

The DJ played several reggae hits before switching the music back to hip-hop, prompting their exit.

Just as they were leaving the dance floor, Bonni said, "Baby, I've got to go to the bathroom."

Stink hesitated, wanting Bonni to wait and use the restroom in the VIP, but he was urgently pulled toward the ladies' restroom.

Standing in front of the restroom, Stink eyed some of the sexy women in attendance until Bonni appeared.

They walked hand in hand back to the VIP section, where the bouncer removed the velvet rope, allowing them to enter.

Stink, being the observant person he was, noticed a group of females eyeing him evilly. Upon further inspection, a grimace appeared across his face at the sight of Trina and her crew.

Trina caught Stink's piercing glare with one of her own, as their eyes locked in a silent battle. Apparently, this long range confrontation was enough for Trina, because she didn't make an attempt to approach him.

As Bonni took her seat, Stink asked, "You want something to eat, baby?"

"Um, maybe some wings or something."

Stink walked over to the small bar where Cross sat, nursing a bottle of Moët.

"What's up, B? Why you screw-facing like that?" Cross asked, eyeing Stink suspiciously.

Releasing a sigh, Stink explained, "Man, I just saw this stupid bitch I used to fuck wit and I know she gonna trip."

"Yo, son, don't sweat that shit! Bitch get outta line, I'll knock the bitch out myself," Cross stated seriously.

His statement caused Stink to laugh uncontrollably.

"Yo, word is bond, son!" Cross vowed, holding his hand high.

"Nah, nah, I'm-a handle it if the bitch get outta line," Stink assured through chuckles.

Stink ordered a tray of buffalo wings, then took his seat beside Bonni, continuously giggling at Cross's remark.

The packed crowd began to scream, which meant only one thing: the guest of honor had arrived. The club's security team rallied around the rap trio then bullied their way through the crowd. They ushered the rap group toward the VIP section where Stink and his crew stood at attention, eyeing the mayhem.

Once the members of Wrecks-N-Effect were safely in VIP, screaming ladies attempted to gain entrance by any means. The scene was on the verge of chaos, causing the bouncers to push the women back forcefully.

After the madness was brought under control, two of the group's members began to hand pick girls that they wanted to be allowed to enter the restricted area.

"Oh, yeah, give me her, and her. Yeah, I gotta have her. Damn, she phat as shit!" one of the rappers said, pointing out women he wanted to join them.

Stink watched the spectacle, somewhat amused, until he noticed Trina being ushered in. His first reaction was to protest her admittance, but quickly decided against it, knowing the attention that he'd bring to the situation.

Dame and Lil Man, who were witnessing the spectacle as well, shot Stink looks that summed the situation up.

As Stink turned his attention back toward the scene that was playing out before him, he witnessed Trina heading straight for their table, sashaying her hips seductively with every step.

Stopping directly in front of their table, Trina placed her hands on her hips and said, "Hey, Dame. Hey, Lil Man. Hello, Rahsaan." Expressing every syllable in Stink's name, she continued," I wanted to speak to you earlier, but you seemed to be in such a hurry," she said a little too seductively for Stink's taste.

With an inferno in his eyes, Stink chose to remain silent.

Bonni looked from Stink to Trina, with an amused look on her face.

Trina extended her hand toward Bonni and said, "Hi, I'm Trina, Rahsaan's baby's mother."

Bonni looked to Trina's outstretched hand as if it was leprous, then turned to Stink for some type of explanation.

Stink's eyes became demonic slits, as he vehemently spat, "Bitch! That ain't been proven yet! So until it has, stay the fuck outta my face!"

Trina stood there, with a look of shock on her face. Before she could raise a reply, Stink shot her a murderous glare that instantly silenced her.

Quickly, Stink grabbed Bonni by the hand and exited the club.

Bonni sat in the passenger seat with her palms covering her face as Stink rambled.

"Rahsaan, why didn't you just tell me?" Bonni asked on the verge of tears.

"I wanted to. I swear, but I thought…I just felt…" at a loss for words, his voice trailed off.

Bonni knew she couldn't be mad forever, especially about a situation that transpired before they were together.

Sighing deeply, she asked, "Rahsaan, how do you know that the child is not yours?"

"I…I don't know," he confessed, then continued, "Until the results from the blood test come back…I don't know."

Sensing that Bonni's silence was the beginning of the end, Stink placed his hand on her thigh and said, "Bonni, I…Love…You, and I ain't trying to lose you over this."

Bonni quickly shot him a questioning look, hearing him confess his love for her for the first time in their relationship. Noticing the sincere look in his eyes, she bit down on her lip to supress her initial reply. Speaking in a firm tone, she began, "Rahsaan, if you are the child's father, you've got to handle your responsibility, no matter what." Pausing, she became more serious, "But don't EVER, leave me in the dark about anything. EVER!" she stated threateningly. Leaning over to give him an assuring peck on the cheek, she whispered, "I love you, too."

Hearing that, mixed with her hot breathe in his ear had Stink smiling from ear to ear.

That following Monday Stink received a call from his grandfather telling him that he had a very important piece of mail there. As soon as they hung up, Stink jumped in his jeep and flew to his grandparents' house.

Arriving, Stink was slightly nervous; he knew what the letter contained and the results could very well change his life forever.

He hurried into the house, where he was promptly met by his grandfather, who pulled the letter from his suit jacket. Handing Stink the letter, his grandfather cut his eyes in Stink's grandmother's direction and winked his eye. Stink picked up on his grandfather's conspiratorial actions and whispered, "Thanks, Papa."

Tearing into the letter frantically, nearly ripping it in the process, Stink read the words.

"IN THE CASE OF RAHSAAN A. JONES vs. LATRINA M. JAMISON, IT IS HEREBY FOUND THAT RAHSAAN A. JONES IS 99.9% <u>NOT</u> THE PATERNAL PARENT OF SAID CHILD: RAHSAAN ADRIAN JAMISON."

The pounding in Stink's chest subsided, as he let out a sigh of relief. He now knew for certain that he wasn't the father.

He left his grandparents' house with the weight of the world lifted from his shoulders. However, something more dramatic was brewing as he celebrated his personal victory.

The early spring temperatures were at an all time high, as the sun began to set over downtown Newport News. Kids were out, playing in record numbers, while every corner was packed with hustlers.

Lil Man drove through the city aimlessly, dropping off drugs and picking up money, oblivious to everything except the ear shattering bass inside his jeep and the stacks of money that grew with every stop he made.

Unbeknown to Lil Man, he was being followed. Every stop he'd made on that sunny afternoon, his predators made as well.

Marco hadn't forgotten the disrespect that Lil Man had shown him so he had been plotting and scheming for three days until he could put his plan into action.

Lil Man turned left onto 24th Street and pulled in front of the Friendship House. Hopping out, he paid no attention to the blue oldsmobile that crept past him. Lee-Lee and one of her friends sat on the porch watching her kids enjoy the beautiful spring weather as Lil Man approached.

Marco and his man, Gooney, parked the battered oldsmobile down the block and hopped out, but not before double-checking their weapons of choice. With their guns snuggly tucked into their waists, they casually walked back toward where Lil Man had parked.

Lil Man stood at the bottom of the steps talking to Lee-Lee and her girl, Sabrina. With his back to the impending danger, he was an easy target for his assailants.

Marco and Gooney strolled down the block inconspicuously, then suddenly with guns drawn, they bolted toward an unsuspecting Lil Man.

Lil Man, noticing the instant fright on Lee-Lee and Sabrina's faces, quickly turned. The sight of the two men rapidly approaching caused him to instinctively reach for the gun, nestled in the small of his back.

"Boom, Boom, Boom, Boom!" Marco squeezed off numerous shots, two hitting his target.

Lil Man, unable to extract his firearm, took one of Marco's shots square in the chest. The thunderous pain he felt immediately caused him to wet his pants. Not known for being one to quit, Lil Man miraculously got his gun out and squeezed off a succession of shots, *Bop, Bop, Bop, Bop!* The retaliation backed the two men up, however, the damage had been done. Lil Man looked to his right and saw half of Lee-Lee's head stuck against the front of the house. Unable to bear the pain anymore, he faded to black.

Stink stood over the stove preparing his famous meal of country fried steak smothered in onions and gravy, green beans and mashed potatoes. He was planning on celebrating his good news. Bonni was on her way from picking Tayvia up and he wanted to have everything prepared when they arrived. He'd chosen not to tell her about the results from the blood test when he'd talked to her earlier that afternoon. He wanted it to be a surprise.

Just as he was putting the hamburger patties into the gravy, the house phone rang then simultaneously, his cell phone rang. Slightly perplexed at both phones ringing, Stink chose to answer his cell phone.

"Hello."

"Yo, Stink, Lil got shot! Stink, I don't think he gonna make it man! He got shot in the chest and Lee-Lee dead, man. Yo, where you at, man?" Dame blurted in one breath.

Unable to respond, Stink just held the phone in shock.

"You hear me, man?"

"Yeah…Yeah. What happ…I mean…" Stink stammered.

"Yo, Stink! He might die, man!" Dame concluded hysterically.

The house phone had been continuously ringing the entire time he was on the phone with Dame.

Grabbing the house phone, Stink spoke into his cell, "What hospital he at?"

"River…side," Dame answered, openly crying.

Stink pushed 'END' on his cell then put the house phone to his ear. "Hello!" he barked.

"RahSAAN! She's dead! Oh my GOD, she's dead!" Bonni wailed into the receiver.

"I know, baby, I know. Where are you now, Bonni?" he asked, attempting to console her.

"At my Momma's. Baby, she's dead. Lee-Lee's dead," Bonni sobbed.

"Baby, is Tayvia with you?"

"Yeah."

"Stay there. I'm on my way," Stink instructed.

He threw all the pots and pans, food and all, into the sink. Making sure the stove was completely off, he ran upstairs and got both his guns then quickly exited his townhouse.

Stink, Bonni, Dame and Natasha sat in the waiting room, along with Lil Man's mother and Nicole, waiting on the outcome of Lil Man's surgery. All that could be heard in the large room were the after effects of grief.

Stink stood and paced the floor, racking his brain for answers. Lil Man was somewhere in the same hospital highly sedated and heavily guarded. At that moment, Dame was just as emotional as the women in the room. Stink needed answers, fast. Not only had his man been gunned down, he also felt threatened by the unforeseen force.

Just as Stink had made up his mind to go downtown and do his own investigation, a fifty-ish white man, wearing a long, white smock entered the room, garnering everyone's immediate attention.

"Yes, which one of you is Kareem Little's parent?" the doctor asked. Standing, Lil Man's mother answered, "Me."

"Mrs. Little, if you would so kindly step into the hallway with me."

"No! Whatever you have to say, say it now!" she defiantly stated.

The doctor, apparently used to this type of reaction, replied, "Very well. Mrs. Little, your son is a very strong man, however, he has been traumatically injured. We have performed heart surgery, repairing the damage that was caused to the left ventricle by the gunshot. Nonetheless, your son is not out of harm's way yet. He is in ICU, attached to a breathing stabilizer and -"

Cutting the doctor off, Lil Man's mother asked, "Is my son going to make it, doctor?"

"That very well depends on how much *he* wants to live, Mrs. Little. It's out of our hands," he concluded.

"Doctor, I want to see my son," she stated.

"I'm afraid that won't be possible." Dropping his head, the doctor turned and walked away.

After getting Bonni and Tayvia home safely, Stink began to devise his plan. The first thing he had to do was get in contact with Cross. The second thing he needed to do was find out who was behind the shooting.

Chapter 10

Although Lil Man had made strides in his recovery, he was still hospitalized but he was alive.

Lee-Lee's funeral had come and gone. Her kids would forever be without a mother.

Stink turned down the stereo, blasting Dr. Dre's *Chronic* and looked over at Cross. "Yo, these niggas we about to see trying to get me to hit them with some work, but I don't trust them like that," Stink revealed, explicitly urging Cross to analyze the pair they were headed to meet.

Ever since Stink had sent Cross $500.00 to catch a plane to Virginia, they'd been inseparable. Their first order of business had been to find the people who'd been responsible for the attack on Lil Man, then exact proper revenge. Once Stink made the choice to vindicate Lil Man's attack, he would never be the same.

It didn't take long for Lil Man to point the finger at Marco as the person responsible for his ambush. After calling in a few favors, all the information that was needed to eliminate Marco was gathered.

Marco, once a feared hustler and head of the notorious 'Woodsong Posse,' had succumbed to the product that he'd once peddled. He was now known to frequent crack houses posing as a hustler, but would end up in a back room with the glass 'dick' in his mouth. This bit of information made Stink and Cross's mission that much easier.

Just three weeks since Cross had landed in Virginia, he and Stink were slouched in Bonni's Honda Accord. Eyeing the traffic that came and went at the crack house on 41st Steet, they both shared the same intent - murder. This was the house that Marco felt the safest practicing his hustler/smoker routine.

Patiently they waited until the old battered Oldsmobile pulled up in front of the large two-story house. Eyeing the driver, Stink announced, "That's him!" He then attempted to exit the car until Cross grabbed his arm.

"Nah, B, just chill. We got 'em now," he stated firmly.

Stink relaxed, then asked, "So how we gonna do it?"

Cross shot him a devious grin, then explained his plan.

Stink sat in the Honda alone and watched the crack head that he'd just paid walk to the door of the crack house. After a brief exchange of words, the door was closed and the crack head scampered off, one hundred dollars richer.

Stink was beginning to think Cross's plan hadn't worked, until the front door flung open and people began to run from the house, as if it was on fire.

Stink eyed the dark figures exiting the house, until he spotted their man.

Marco trotted from the house and jumped in his car. All he knew was he didn't want to go back to prison and if the tip that had been given to the house's owner was true, he was definitely dodging a free trip to the pen.

Marco jumped behind the wheel and turned the ignition, suddenly he felt the cold steel of a gun at his temple.

"Put both of your hands on the steering wheel and drive. Any false moves and I won't hesitate to murder you," Cross advised in a low tone.

Marco was immediately gripped with fear. He followed Cross's directions in hopes that his life would be spared. Marco had done a tremendous amount of dirt in his life, but never did he think that those acts would catch up to him.

"Yo, man, what you want-" Marco began, only to be abruptly cut off by the deafening sound of a gun shot. It didn't register immediately that Cross had actually shot him until the extreme burning sensation erupted near his groin. "Ahhhhh! Oh Fuck! Agggggh!" he yelled in agony.

Following closely, Stink was alerted when the Oldsmobile suddenly swerved across the center lane into on-coming traffic.

Cross forcefully pushed the gun against Marco's temple, and said, "Straighten this muthafucka up and pull over. I told yo bitch-ass to be cool, but nah…"

The chill in Cross's voice, along with gunshot wound so easily inflicted, confirmed that he was going to die. Willing to try anything at that moment, Marco stomped the gas and simultaneously snatched the wheel hard to the left.

Just as Marco attempted the desperate move, Cross began to let off: *"Bop, Bop, Bop, Bop…!"*

The majority of the shots hit Marco below the waist, instantly paralyzing him.

The old clunker slammed onto the curb then crashed into a telephone pole, bringing the car to a halt.

Stink pulled behind the car and jumped out with his gun drawn. Prepared to shoot anything that moved, he was quickly relieved when a visibly amused Cross jumped from the backseat.

"Yo, god, can you believe this nigga tried me?" he asked, mildly shocked, with a smile on his face.

As they approached one another, Stink eyed Cross closely, looking for any signs of his being hit by the gun fire that could clearly be heard as he followed.

"You alright, man?" Stink inquired with concern.

"Yeah, I'm good, but ya man's…I know I hit'em ten times," he boasted.

A slight movement behind Cross caught Stink's attention. With the speed of a cheetah, he slammed his shoulder into Cross and squeezed off four quick shots. *"Boom, Boom, Boom, Boom!"* He could see two of his shots tearing pieces of flesh from the figure that wiggled on the ground.

Once what had happened registered in Cross's mind, he quickly ran over to the still figure and emptied the remaining bullets from his clip into the body.

Stink and Cross quickly jumped into Bonni's Honda and fled the scene. One thing was sure as they made their escape: Marco would not be having an open-casket funeral.

Daz and his partner, Luck, strolled over to Stink's jeep and hopped in.

"Yo, Stink, you ready to do that thing we talked about?" Daz asked as Luck counted their money.

"Nah, I ain't ready yet. I'm a little low on this package, but I got y'all on the next one," Stink explained, as he turned around to get a better view of the treacherous pair.

Cross hadn't taken his eyes off the pair since they'd gotten into the jeep. Gripping the P-89 in his lap, he gave them both unblinking stares.

Luck finished counting the money and passed it to the front, where Cross quickly grabbed it then passed Luck a bag containing large, white chunks of crack.

Expertly fanning through the stack of money, Cross looked Luck in the eye with a murderous glare. "Check it, son. Next time, have that paper counted before we get here, a'ight?" he stated firmly, as the pair exited the jeep.

Stink instantly noticed their fear as they walked away.

"Yo, god, you should let me handle them niggas. They think they hard, but I see the bitch in 'em."

Stink inwardly smiled at what he'd just witnessed. Cross had mentally chumped two of the city's most feared niggas. It was common knowledge that neither Luck nor Daze would hesitate when it came to squeezing that steel.

"I'll tell you what," Stink began, then paused to quickly do the math in his head, "I'll give you the work for twenty-one grand and you can give it to them for whatever you want," he proposed, thinking that it may be smarter to allow Cross to handle the 'Lucks' and 'Dazs' of the city. With Cross's brash personality and aggressive demeanor, it was a no-brainer.

Tossing Stink the stack of money that they'd received from Luck and Daz, Cross said, "A'ight, bet!" signaling his acceptance.

Stink peeled off $4,000 then threw it into Cross's lap.

"What's this for?" Cross asked, confused.

With a sly grin, Stink replied, "First day on the job, nigga."

At that moment, an unbreakable bond was created.

Driving down Mercury Blvd., one of the busiest streets in Hampton, Stink noticed a 'For Lease' sign in the window of a business in a small strip mall. Making a quick u-turn, he pulled into the parking lot to check it out.

After inspecting the property through the window, he presumed that the building had been used as a barbershop or a beauty salon.

He jotted the number down, then hopped back into his jeep. As he drove away, the idea hit him plain as day. He could kill two birds with one stone by investing his money in a legitimate business and getting Bonni her own salon.

Later that night, while Stink and Bonni laid in bed, he turned to her and asked, "Bonni, how would you like to own your own salon?"

"I'd love to. Why?" she inquired.

"Oh, I checked this spot out and tomorrow I'm going to see some people about it," Stink stated nonchalantly.

Suddenly becoming interested, Bonni asked, "Are you serious?"

"Yeah, I'm serious. Why would I ask if I wasn't?"

Bonni overlooked his slick remark and continued to question him. They ended up talking nearly half the night, each building on the other's ideas.

Before they fell asleep, they'd come up with a name and a business plan.

It was only a matter of time before 'Bonni's Beauty Boutique' became a reality.

Since Stink had brought Cross in on the business side of things, he'd taken the ball and run with it. Cross was moving more drugs than Dame, Lil Man and Stink did combined. Although Lil Man was nowhere near his old self, he still tried to work himself back into the game.

Lil Man seemed to be trying to prove that the shooting hadn't changed him in any way. One change that was evident was the bullet proof vest Lil Man sported religiously.

Dame was still a key player in their crew. However, the manner in which he handled Lil Man's shooting had shed a new light on his character.

Cross, on the other hand, had proven to be an asset. Their operation had doubled in profits since his insertion. Cross hustled in overdrive, fronting the drugs out in abundance, to any and everybody. His murderous demeanor, along with his care-free spirit stood as an encouraging factor for people to pay him the money.

Lil Man hadn't said anything about Cross's constant presence, however, deep down Stink knew Lil Man envied the union that he and Cross now shared.

By the end of the summer, Stink was engrossed in bringing Bonni's Beauty Boutique into existence. He worked full time to ensure that the place would be up and running by Bonni's birthday.

He had also found a nice house in Hampton, equipped with a double car garage. It was by accident that he acquired the house.

Stink was supposed to be meeting Leaf to make a cash drop-off so pulling in front of the address that he'd been given, Stink noticed the house was for sale. Thinking that he had the wrong address, it wasn't until he noticed Leaf's car in the driveway, along with a Cadillac bearing the identical logo as the sign in the yard that he knew he was in the right place.

Walking up to the door, Stink observed Leaf and an older black man conversing in the front room.

Before Stink could knock, Leaf invited him in. "Come on in, Stink," he instructed. "Jacob, this my man, Stink. Stink, this is Jacob, my realtor," Leaf introduced.

Hearing Leaf call the conservatively-dressed, older black man his realtor, impressed Stink greatly.

Leaf and Jacob continued their conversation, as Stink wandered through the first floor of the house. After seeing the first floor, Stink was in awe of the beautifully-designed home.

He went back into the room where Leaf and Jacob were finishing their conversation, when he heard Leaf say, "Nah, Jacob, I was looking for something more…more…extravagant. Nah-mean?" Leaf turned toward Stink, who was openly gawking at the interior of the house, then continued, "But it looks like my man, Stink, is diggin' this spot, huh, Stink?" Leaf asked.

"Huh?" Stink asked confused.

"I was telling my man, Jacob, that you might be interested in this crib."

Quickly closing the distance, Jacob stepped to Stink. "Umm, Stink, would you be interested in this property?" Jacob asked with a phony smile plastered across his face.

"I mean, I like it, but I-"

"Does assuming the mortgage something you'd be interested in?" Jacob blurted, cutting Stink off.

That was all it took. Less than a week later, he and Bonni moved into their new home.

Chapter 11

September 1992

Bonni's Beauty Boutique was set to have its grand opening in less than a week and Stink spared no expense on the salon. He had had hardwood floors installed and black leather salon chairs with matching black leather sectionals in the waiting area and had even mounted a 55-inch screen from the ceiling. As a final touch, Stink had a section for kids to play in while their mothers got their hair styled. He had spent nearly $50,000 in order to make 'Bonni's' one of the premiere salons in the Tidewater area.

On September 10th, Bonni celebrated her 20th birthday with the grand opening of her own salon. There was food served while the women waited to get their hair done. Bonni could hardly believe that her dream of owning her own salon had finally come true.

She approached Stink from behind as he and Natasha conversed. Sliding her arms around his waist, she whispered into his ear, "I love you, Rahsaan."

"Just make sure you make my money back up in this bitch," Stink quipped, trying to suppress his smile.

"Mmm hmmm…what if I don't?" she asked seductively.

"Let me get out of here so ya'll women can do what ya'll do," Stink announced, pulling away from Bonni, then heading toward the door. He motioned for Cross, who was seated in the waiting area, whispering in some girl's ear, that he was ready to leave.

Stink and Cross pulled into the Charles Barker Lexus dealership on Virginia Beach Blvd. Leaf had introduced Stink to a salesman who was willing to manipulate the paperwork for a nominal fee, enabling Stink to purchase two new Lexus'.

Money had been pouring in the entire summer. The money he'd spent on the salon and what he'd spent on the house was nothing compared to what he was making. He had even put $150,000 up at his grandparents' for a rainy day.

Noticing Stink and Cross, the salesman quickly made his way outside and greeted them. "Hello, Rahsaan. How are you doing?"

"I'm good, Kevin," Stink replied, gripping his outstretched hand.

"Sooo, have you figured out what you want yet?"

"Nah, not yet, but I'm-a look around."

"Ok, I'll be in my office when you're ready," Kevin said, then turned to leave.

Casually walking around the lot, Stink and Cross inspected the luxury automobiles closely. Eyeing a silver LS 400 parked beside a forest green ES 300, Stink approached the two cars. Given silver was his favorite color and green was Bonni's, he instantly made his choice.

After brief negotiations and the exchange of $17,000, Stink and Cross drove off the lot with two new Lexus'.

Racing back to Hampton where they parked Stink's Lexus in the driveway of his house, he jumped in Bonni's smaller ES with Cross at the wheel.

Inspecting the interior of the smaller Lexus appreciatively, Stink noticed that Bonni's car came equipped with the prestigious Coach package.

"Yo, B, you know you ain't gonna be able to drive downtown in a Lexus without po-po fucking wit a nigga," Cross warned.

"Yeah, yeah, I know, that's why I kept Bonni's Honda," Stink replied nonchalantly, marveling at the interior of Bonni's new car.

After dropping Cross off at the townhouse that he'd once called home, Stink went to pick Bonni up from the salon. Intentionally pulling up to the front door, he hopped out, hoping Bonni had seen what he was driving.

As he walked in, a few of the girls still waiting to get their hair done, eyed the Lexus suspiciously, causing Bonni and a few of her employees to focus their attention toward the shiny luxury vehicle as well.

"Uh, baby, whose car are you driving?" Bonni questioned.

Grinning mischievously, he replied, "Yours."

"Baby, no you didn't! I know you...didn't!" she exclaimed, running to the door, stunned.

The entire salon exited behind Bonni, getting a closer look at the car.

"Guurl, that's a Lexus. Damn!" a large woman, with her hair still in rollers, declared.

"Bonni, this car is fly as shit! Mmmm, chile, I wish I had a man like him," the nail technician stated with a twinge of jealousy.

With her palms covering her mouth, somewhat shocked, Bonni began, "Baby, it's so, sooo, beautiful. I..." At a loss for words, she whirled around and hugged Stink tightly, as tears fell from her eyes.

"Happy Birthday, baby. Happy Birthday," Stink consoled tenderly, rubbing her back.

Bonni pulled into their driveway, then looked from Stink to the big Lexus in the driveway. "You got one, too?" she asked surprised.

Smiling broadly, Stink replied, "Yeah, you know."

"But your birthday isn't for two weeks," she jokingly whined.

Stink had planned to take Bonni to his favorite restaurant that evening, however, Bonni wanted to enjoy a movie cuddled in front of the television.

As the night wore on, the sight of Bonni's jiggling ass struggling to escape the thin fabric of her panties became too much for Stink to bear.

Easing between her legs as she focused her attention on her favorite movie, Stink flicked his tongue along the insides of her thighs.

Instantly garnering her attention, Bonni moaned, "Boy, you being bad."

Stink took that as motivation to go further. Hooking her panties with his thumb, he pulled them down her legs. As Bonni laid there naked from the waist down, Stink began to move his tongue closer to her womanhood.

Desperately trying to concentrate on the movie, Bonni felt jolts of pleasure from her center, as Stink's tongue worked its magic.

The more Stink manipulated her core, the more she relented herself to him. Ultimately, Bonni submitted herself totally to him that evening, performing oral sex for the first time in their relationship. Their lovemaking became so intense that it was more like a battle, ending with Stink releasing a powerful jet of semen into Bonni at precisely the right moment. Unbeknowst to either of them, a child had been conceived.

Stink awoke early on his 19th birthday, to a short note from Bonni:

"Happy Birthday, boo. I may not be able to buy you a Lexus, but I can give you all my love.

Forever, Love Bonni"

After wiping the smug smile from his face, Stink hopped in the shower, got dressed and headed to the townhouse to pick Cross up.

As Stink entered the townhouse, Cross passed him a perfectly-rolled Philly blunt. "Spark up, birthday boy!" Stink accepted the marijuana-stuffed cigar and lit it up. After smoking as much of the blunt as he could alone, they headed downtown to meet someone who was interested in obtaining drugs from Stink. Word had spread that Stink was the man to see if large quantities of crack were what a person desired.

Cruising the streets of Newport News in the big Lexus, Stink felt untouchable. As they turned onto Jefferson Avenue, the 18-inch chrome Anteras glistened off the Lexus's silvery body, instantly making Stink and Cross the focus of the entire block.

Reaching to turn the thunderous bass down, Cross began, "Ay, yo, Stink, you know prices uptop have gone down," he revealed, referring to drug prices in New York.

"Why you say that? You think Leaf fucking me on his prices or something?" Stink asked defensively.

"Nah, I'm not saying that. What I'm saying is a quick flip would definitely put niggas on," Cross replied in a conspiratorial tone.

Stink quickly thought, *Nigga, I'm already on.* His silence prompted Cross to continue. "See, Stink, you ain't making no money off of Lil Man or Dame. And fo'real, you only making like three Gs a joint off me. Them niggas getting they work for free. Fo'real, god, you working for Lil Man, Dame and Leaf."

Stink cut his eyes at Cross evilly, initially feeling that Cross was attempting to play him. Yet, after a second thought, Stink knew that ultimately Cross was right, however, he wasn't prepared to go against his crew that easily.

"So what are you saying? Take everybody's money to New York and cop?" Stink asked accusingly.

"That's exactly what I'm saying," he retorted, grinning slyly.

Pulling behind the purple Cherokee with the music blasting, Stink allowed what Cross said to marinate until after they had handled their business. There were at least fifteen guys milling around the short block, however, Stink and Cross were there only to see one.

Fat Shawn was a hustler who'd been getting money before Stink even moved to Virginia. His whole family hustled. They even controlled an entire block in downtown, however, Stink's connections and his intelligence caused him to be sought out by even those who had been in the drug game before him.

He knew Fat Shawn's M.O. before he'd ever laid eyes on him. He'd done his homework on Fat Shawn. Stink also knew that Fat Shawn had a habit of not paying his suppliers and that was where Cross came into play.

Stink and Cross slowly exited the car, eyeing the packs of hustlers cautiously.

Instantly, Fat Shawn's hulking 6-foot-3-inch, 300-pound figure appeared, making his way toward Stink and Cross. The crowd seemed to part as the behemoth approached with his hand held high. "What up, Stink? I'm glad you came through to holla at me," he said, gripping Stink's hand.

"Yeah, but um…this my cousin, Cross, from New York. He's basically running all my shit downtown," Stink informed, directing the focus onto Cross.

Cross stood in his best b-boy stance, giving Fat Shawn a demonic grin, before saying, "What up, B?"

Fat Shawn, initially disappointed, began to kick his game, directing it mostly toward Cross who seemed to be absorbing it like a sponge.

"Look , son, I'm-a hit you with a half a bird and we'll see how shit goes from there. Cool?" Cross announced cockily.

Smiling from ear to ear, Fat Shawn replied, "Cool."

As Stink and Cross turned to leave, Cross abruptly turned back to face Fat Shawn. "Oh, one more thing. You fuck that paper up, I swear I'll murder you," Cross stated coolly, instantly wiping the smile off Fat Shawn's face.

Stink shook his head in disbelief as they pulled off. Cross had basically promised Fat Shawn that he would kill him, yet the crazy thing was that Stink knew he meant it.

Just as they finished placing the bills into neatly stacked piles, Cross leaned back and put the lighter to the tip of the blunt. "I'm telling you, god, the only way you truly get rich in this game is to take chances," Cross said, inhaling the weed smoke.

"Hey, yo, fo'real though, that's some grimy shit, man," Stink replied, his tone immediately becoming defensive.

"Nah! What's grimy is that nigga Leaf getting rich off us! That's what's grimy!" Cross snapped.

"Sheeit! We getting rich off him too!" Stink protested with his arms held wide.

Instantly, Cross knew he had to change his approach. "Look, Stink, if we did it one time, we wouldn't have to do it anymore. Lil and Dame would get their work and Leaf would get his paper," Cross reasoned calmly.

The more Cross talked, the more Stink was feeling his idea. Even though it wasn't right, Stink felt that he needed to do it, if he ever wanted to have the riches that Leaf was enjoying.

Showing his first sign of defeat, Stink asked, "If I do it, how we gonna get the drugs back?"

Anxiously, Cross leaned over the table and began, "I know this kid uptop…" When Cross was finished presenting his scheme, Stink was completely sold.

"Surprise!" Was the first thing Stink heard when he turned the door knob. Bonni and Tayvia stood in the living room, holding a birthday cake.

"Tha…thanks," Stink managed to say, slightly startled.

Bonni and Tayvia performed the entire rendition of 'Happy Birthday.'

"Make a wish! Make a wish!" Tayvia yelled excitedly.

"You've got to help me blow the candles out first," Stink said, picking Tayvia up.

After successfully blowing out all nineteen candles, Bonni led them into the kitchen.

"What you wish for?" Tayvia asked curiously.

"I can't tell you or my wish won't come true," Stink teased.

With a strange look on her face, Bonni eyed the exchange between Stink and Tayvia.

Noticing Bonni's look, Stink put Tayvia down and went to Bonni's side. "What's wrong, baby?" he inquired with concern.

The response Stink received was a torrent of tears rolling down Bonni's cheeks.

"What's wrong, Bonni?" he repeated firmly.

Bonni raised her tear-filled eyes, and then said, "Rahsaan, I'm pregnant."

"What!" Stink asked in shock.

"I said, I'm pregnant!" she repeated firmly. "Rahsaan, I understand if you don't-"

Stink silenced her by placing his lips to hers, initiating a sensuous kiss then gently placing his palms on both sides of her cheeks. Looking her deeply in her eyes, he said, "Bonni, I love you."

The manner in which he did that left no doubt in Bonni's mind that he wanted her to become the mother of his child.

Laying in bed while Bonni and Tayvia slept, Stink eased out of the bed and began to dress.

Bonni stirred then asked through a sleep-filled haze, "You going somewhere?"

"Yeah, um, I'm-a go fuck with the fellas, you know…maybe have a birthday drink or something," Stink explained.

Sitting up and crossing her arms across her chest, visibly upset, she said, "Oh."

Sensing her displeasure with him leaving, Stink said, "Come on, baby. I'll be back in a little bit. I'm just going to holla at my niggas on my birthday." Walking over to her side of the bed, Stink attempted to plant a kiss on her lips, only to be met with her hand.

Shaking his head in disappointment, Stink headed for the door.

Loudly sucking her teeth in annoyance, Bonni quipped, "Be safe."

As Stink pulled in front of the townhouse, Cross stood out front with a freshly-rolled blunt hanging from his lips. "Let's bounce, birthday boy," Cross said, hopping into the passenger seat.

Stink navigated the Lexus through the tunnel that separated Newport News from Portsmouth. Cross turned the volume up on the radio a few decibels, leaned back and lit his blunt up. The Wu-Tang Clan was performing at David's night club so that's where they were headed.

Pulling into the parking lot of David's, Stink's eyes were tiny slits. "Man, what the fuck did we just smoke?" Stink asked through a marijuana-induced haze.

"This is that 'Black Buddah', B," Cross replied giggling.

As they exited the car, Stink absent-mindedly left the keys in the ignition. "Yo, god! You fucked up fo'real," Cross said, grabbing the keys from the ignition.

They made their way to the entrance, bypassing the long line, as they had become accustomed to doing. Cross approached the doorman and slid him a c-note then motioned for Stink to follow.

As they were ushered into the exotic club, Stink eyed the scantily-dressed women swaying erotically to the thunderous music. The dance floor, located in the middle of the club, sunk into the floor elegantly.

Cross led the way through the crowd to the bar. Slapping two bills down, immediately drawing the attention of the attractive pecan-brown bartender, Cross said, "Let me get two bottles of Mo'"

The woman quickly scampered off to retrieve the champagne. Returning, she sat the two frosted bottles of Moët on the counter, then said, "Thank you," giving Cross a seductive wink.

Stink popped the cork on his bottle and stood with his back to the bar, taking in the club's scenery.

Prompting their exit from the spot, Cross nudged Stink then led the way through the packed nightclub. Following closely, Stink gripped his bottle fashionably, while taking notice of the stares they received. Stink endured this type of observation all the time, however, attention was something Cross didn't get a lot of.

Handsome was something Cross wasn't. His dark, keen features and naturally-piercing eyes gave him an almost wicked appearance, but he was always impeccably dressed and well-groomed. He sported a short Afro with a chemical relaxer in it which made his hair look like mink. Even though he and Stink were roughly the same size in stature, Cross was a true gangster in every sense of the word; his walk, his talk and his actions confirmed it.

They found a table in the back of the club, near where pictures were being taken. As they sat back sipping their champagne and enjoying the music, a brown-skinned girl approached them.

"Excuse me, but my friend wants to meet you," she said, looking toward Stink.

Looking at the girl as if she was crazy, Stink quickly noticed that his dumbfounded gaze and prolonged silence seemed to agitate her.

"So do you have a name or what?" she snapped.

Humorously, Stink leaned over to look behind the girl, then asked, "Where your girl at? She scared to come meet me herself?"

Rolling her eyes and visibly upset, she turned on her heels and walked away.

As the girl disappeared into the crowd, the DJ began to scratch in one of the Wu-Tang Clan songs, then announced:

"ALL THE WAY FROM THE SHOALIN! IT'S THE...WU-TANG-WU-TANG-WU-TANG!" The crowd chanted along with the DJ, as waves of people rushed the stage in flocks.

Stink and Cross sat back and watched the scene unfold, sipping on their bottles of Moët.

Stink had just about forgotten about the earlier fiasco with the girl, until he noticed her nearly dragging a very attractive light-brown-skinned girl by the arm.

"Here she is!" she announced.

Stink looked the girl over, eyeing her appreciatively. She was a very pretty girl. Her hair, long and flowing, hung down her back. Her eyes were a strange color and slanted as if one of her parents was Asian. Her pouty lips begged to be kissed. The short black skirt she wore complimented her every curve.

Eyeing her hungrily, he introduced himself, "What's up, my name is Rahsaan."

"My...my name is Melody," she replied shyly, and then pointed to her friend. "This is my friend Kayla."

"Oh, hi, Kayla. It seems like I met you before," Stink said sarcastically, then motioned to Cross, "This my man, Cross."

Cross looked up from his bottle and then asked, "Why ya'll not up there enjoying the show?" The Wu-Tang Clan was in the middle of performing their hit song, *C.R.E.A.M.*

"Umm, it's too crowded up there," Melody replied.

"So why don't you ladies have a seat," Stink offered. Sipping his drink, he didn't move a muscle in assisting the ladies to a seat.

Melody took the seat nearest Stink, while Kayla moved to sit beside Cross.

Immediately spitting his New York game, Cross grilled Kayla. Stink knew it was working, because every time he glanced in their direction, she was all smiles.

Meanwhile, Stink's conversation with Melody was nowhere near as animated. He held a platonic conversation with Melody. Quickly, he found out some personal things about her. She was a student at O.D.U. and was originally from a glitzy county outside of Richmond, Virginia.

Melody seemed like a good girl, and for one quick second the image of a pregnant Bonni flashed in his head, however, Stink managed to make that image and any guilt related thereof disappear.

Once the rap group finished their performance and order was restored, Cross bought two more bottles of champagne, one for him and one for the ladies, while Stink sipped on his first bottle.

Suddenly, it seemed as if the entire club had decided to take pictures, turning their once-secluded area into a zoo.

Glancing through the long line of party-goers wishing to take pictures, Stink noticed a tall girl eyeing him suspiciously. At first glance, he shrugged it off even though the girl's face was extremely familiar. Before he could fully identify the girl, out of the corner of his eye, he noticed Trina closely following the tall girl and they were headed his way.

Trina, her hair cut excessively closer than what he had remembered, made it hard for him to positively identify her. As she approached, Stink prepared himself.

"Hi, Rahsaan," Trina beamed, cutting her eyes at Melody.

Trying hard to hide his contempt for her, Stink replied, "Whazup, Trina?"

"And who is your friend? I haven't seen you with her before," Trina said in a sarcastic manner.

Melody didn't show any reaction to her comment. Cross and Kayla were so engrossed in their own conversation, they didn't even see the spectacle playing out before them.

Stink decided to have a little fun - he was feeling nice from the weed and champagne - so he said, "Oh, well, that's because you probably can't see through the tint on my Lexus when she be pushing it."

Melody let out a slight gasp, while Trina's face became beet red. "Fuck you, Rahsaan! I hope you DIE!" she exclaimed, and then stormed off.

Before Trina got out of earshot, Stink shot back, "Bitch! You need to be trying to kill your hairdresser, not me!"

This brought a round of laughter from everyone who'd heard the comment. After Melody regained her composure from the laughter, she asked, "What was that about?"

Before Stink could answer, Cross chimed in. "Now that's an example of a good girl gone bad," he said, quoting a song by the rapper, Scarface.

As the club came to a close, Stink and Cross made their way to the exit, accompanied by Melody and Kayla. The combination of the marijuana and a whole bottle of Moët had Stink deliriously high. Using Melody as a crutch, Stink draped his arm over her shoulder and allowed her to help him to his car. From the way she kept smiling at him every time his hand would graze her behind, he could tell she was enjoying the closeness.

Stink flopped down in the driver's seat, with both doors open, and blasted one of the songs Wu-Tang had just performed. He took Melody's number with promises to call then zipped down High Street.

Chapter 12

November 1992

Everything had been carried out in order for Stink and Cross to make their move. Stink had gathered Lil Man and Dame's money, along with what he owed Leaf, while Cross contacted his connects in New York.

They gassed up Bonni's old Honda and hit the highway with a little less than $500,000; everything was set.

As they traveled through Baltimore on interstate 95, Stink began to have second thoughts about his rash decision. *What if this nigga is setting me up to rob and kill me?* Stink quickly thought, then shot a glance at Cross, who returned his look with an earnest smirk.

Stink had been the only person to show him love in Virginia, making it possible for him to 'eat.' There was no way Cross would 'cross' Stink. With that out of his mind, Stink sat back and relaxed.

Arriving in New York City, Stink and Cross put the money up in Cross's mother's house. After securing the two book bags of cash, they took the Honda to a car shop on 8th Avenue.

Cross held a brief conversation with the shop's owner, detailing exactly what he wanted done to the car. After getting his point across to the Arab, Cross hailed a cab to take them uptown.

They exited the cab on 155th and Broadway and began walking up the block. Cross claimed to know personally the guy they were off to see, however, Stink wasn't prepared for what he was about to witness.

Cross led them to a building about halfway into the block and pressed a small button on the door.

"*Quien es?*" a voice cracked from the intercom.

"*Soy yo*, Cross," Cross replied.

About twenty seconds later, the door's lock popped open.

Cross entered the building, leading the way up the stairs to the second floor.

"*Como tu esta*, Cross? What brings you this far uptown?" an older Spanish guy asked, embracing Cross in a brotherly hug.

Stink looked through disbelieving eyes at how hospitable the man was toward Cross.

"I haven't seen you in some time, my friend," the Spanish guy continued, holding Cross by his shoulders.

"Yeah, me and my man been down south doing our thang," Cross replied, motioning to Stink. "Oh, this my man, Stink. Stink, this is José, the one I've been telling you about."

"Se, se, nice to meet you...uhh, is it *Stink*?" José asked, extending his hand.

"Yeah, it's Stink," Stink said, gripping José's hand.

"Well, come on in," José said, leading them into a small, modestly-furnished apartment. Motioning for Stink and Cross to take a seat, José sat across from them, then began, "So is it *pediqua* that you all are interested in?"

"Yeah, but we trying to spend some real cash, José," Cross informed.

"How much are you talking about?"

"We got nearly a half a million dollars," Cross revealed.

José's eyes lit up in surprise. "Hmm...I see things have been going well for you and your friend," José replied, then said, "I can handle that, but it's going to be around fourteen a gram."

Stink looked to Cross quizzically, prepared to protest the number that José had quoted.

"José, that's a little high for hard, ain't it? We was thinking more like twelve a joint," Cross stated pleadingly.

Playfully hitting himself in the forehead, José said, "Oh! You guys want it hard. I'm sorry. I can do eleven-and-a-half for hard."

Stink's mind quickly calculated the numbers at eleven-and-a-half a kilo. At that price, they would make out better than either of them expected.

"So, the powder is fourteen a kilo?" Cross asked.

"*Se*. I was under the impression you wanted *polvo*," José explained.

"Well, if we buy the powder and cook it ourselves, how much crack do we get back?" Cross anxiously asked.

Hesitantly, José explained, "*Oye*, it depends on a lot of different things. You may get a lot, but your product would be *basura*. You want repeat customers so you don't want to be out there selling garbage."

Cross continued to grill José, attempting to get all the measurements and ingredients for transforming cocaine into crack.

After remaining silent throughout Cross and José's exchange, Stink finally asked, "Are you saying that we would come out better buying the powder and cooking it into crack ourselves?"

"Se. If you all could find someone to cook it for you, you would come out much better," José explained.

Stink and Cross simultaneously looked at one another intently; silently they had made their decision.

Cross turned to face José and announced, "We've got $400,000 to spend. When and where?"

"Man, I knew that nigga, Leaf, was jerking you," Cross stated in a taunting manner.

Stink sat slouched in the back seat of the cab, deep in thought. Cross's words were absolutely true; Leaf had been overcharging him the entire time. José had proven it with much cheaper prices.

As the cab driver drove down 125th Street, Cross yelled, "Pull over right here!"

The cab driver stopped in front of a large project building where a few guys were hanging out.

Cross leaned out of the cab's window, and asked, "Ay, yo! Ya'll niggas seen Blanco?"

A young Spanish guy got up off the bench and walked over to the cab. "Yo, what up, Cross? Blanco is in the spot. Want me to get 'em for you?" he offered.

Cross reached in his pocket and pulled out a few bills. "Yeah do that for me, B," he said, handing the bills to the guy.

After five minutes had passed, a skinny Puerto Rican with long curly hair fashionably styled on his head, came from the building. "My muthafuckin' nigga, Cross. What up, son?" he said, gripping Cross's hand.

"Yo, Blanco, I need your help on something. I know you got the meanest whip game in Harlem," Cross stated.

"So you ready to part with that twenty-five hun'ed to learn my craft, huh?" Blanco asked with interest.

"No question, B. I'm ready," Cross anxiously replied, removing a wad of money from his pocket and handing it to Blanco.

Stuffing the money in his pockets, Blanco said, "Yo, son, name the time and place. I'm there."

"You remember my spot on 139th? Be there in one hour. Oh, and bring ALL the utensils; you got enough paper to cover everything right there," Cross said, pointing to Blanco's pocket. "I got your twenty-five hun'ed when you get there."

Less than two hours later, Stink, Cross and Blanco were huddled over the stove in Cross's old apartment.

"See how the coke breaks down with just a little bit of water," Blanco demonstrated, intently giving a 101 lesson in cooking cocaine. He continued, "No matter what amount you cook up, the key is the water, son." Blanco lifted the pyrex pot off the stove containing the mixture of cocaine, baking soda and water, and then began to stir it furiously.

As Blanco sat the pot into a tray of ice water, Stink and Cross eyed him in amazement while the mixture instantly transformed into a rock-solid cookie.

Blanco held the cookie up for inspection and then snapped it in two. "I'm telling you, B. This shit is butter," he proclaimed boastfully.

Cross looked to Stink and then asked, "Yo, Stink. You think you got it?"

Returning his stare assuredly, Stink replied, "Yeah. I got it."

The following day, Stink and Cross were scheduled to meet with José at one of Cross's girlfriends' house, but only after they picked up the Honda.

Pulling up to the car shop, they both noticed the Honda double-parked in front of the business.

"Looks like it's ready," Cross said, exiting the cab.

The shop's owner instantly appeared in front of the building. "I see you guys made it back. Come, let me show you how everything works," he said in his Middle Eastern accent, leading them to the Honda.

Stopping at the trunk of the Honda, he explained, "I installed de compartment in de trunk, so you guys will have more room to store your, um…goods," he stated sarcastically. "Now, you must have the car in gear. Can one of you guys please help me out?" he asked, staring at Cross, who hopped in the driver's seat, turned the ignition and put the car in gear.

"Secondly, you must have de signal light on," he instructed.

Cross flipped the signal on and waited for any further directions.

"And de final thing," the repairman announced, walking around to the passenger door. He opened the glove compartment and pushed the little button to open the trunk. "Push dis button two times and..."

Suddenly a light humming sound came from the open trunk.

Stink stepped to the rear of the car and watched in astonishment as the floor of the trunk miraculously opened up, revealing a space the size of a large suitcase.

Still in the driver's seat holding the brake, Cross anxiously blurted, "Hey, yo! Can I see the shit?!"

"Yeah, yeah. Just shut de car off; it won't close," the repairman informed.

Cross quickly joined Stink, who was inspecting the compartment. Giving Stink a conspiratorial wink, Cross turned to the repairman and asked, "So, how do you close it?"

"Just as you opened it, my friend."

Stink and Cross arrived at Cross's girlfriend's building only a few minutes before they were to meet José. Each grabbed a money-filled book bag and entered the pissy-smelling stairwell.

Cross produced a key and opened the door to the small, poorly-furnished apartment. No more than five minutes after they'd arrived, there was a knock on the door. Instantly, Stink was frozen, remembering his trusted .9mm was safely put away in his house.

Cross crept over to the door. Peering through the peephole, he looked back and gave Stink a reassuring smirk.

He opened the door and allowed José and two modestly-dressed mafia goons to enter.

"*Oye*, Cross, I see you are ready for business," José said, eyeing the stacks of money on the coffee table.

"Always, José."

José motioned for his goons to place the bags that they carried onto the floor.

"Well, let's do this," José announced, pulling a money counting machine out of one of the bags.

As José and his goons left the apartment, Stink and Cross loaded the perfectly-wrapped packages into a duffel bag.

"Ay, yo, Cross. You think we should check to see if this shit straight?" Stink asked suspiciously.

"Nah, B. José's shit is straight," Cross assured, zipping the duffel bag up then standing to leave. "You'll see." With that, he led the way out the door.

Cross dozed off as Stink drove attentively, obeying all posted signs on the interstate. During the drive down 95, Stink dissected the manner in which Leaf had been doing business with him. Deep down, Stink felt betrayed. He looked up to Leaf as a mentor of sorts so the realization that Leaf had been playing him the whole time hurt deeply.

Leaf was making at least $10,000 a kilo off of Stink and from the way Blanco had shown them how to cook the drugs, maybe even more.

Stink hadn't figured out exactly how he'd handle the situation with Leaf yet but one thing was evident: he would have to do something.

Stink cut the Honda off then reached over and shook a slobbering Cross out of his deep sleep. "Wake up, nigga! We're here," he announced.

"Wha…What? We where?" he asked groggily.

"Come on man, we got work to do," Stink said, initiating the process of opening the compartment. As before, Stink heard the humming sound, signaling the compartment's opening. He retrieved the duffel bag from the trunk, then sauntered off into the townhouse, followed by a yawning Cross.

To get things in motion, Cross promptly left the townhouse to buy a Clear Vision cookware set.

Stink unpacked the kilos from the duffel bag, eyeing the logo of a bird on each package. Afterwards, he decided to call Bonni.

"Hellooo, Bonni's Beauty Boutique, Tracy speaking. May I help you?" one of Bonni's employees sang joyfully.

"Yeah, let me speak to Bonni." Stink asked dryly.

"Umm, yes. But, may I ask who's calling?"

Deciding to flex his status, Stink stated firmly, "Yeah, you could but I own that shit!"

"Oh, I'm so sorry, Rah, um, Mr. Rahsaan…please hold," she stammered apologetically.

After a brief wait, Bonni's voice came onto the line. "Hey, baby. Are you home, yet?" she asked joyfully.

"Yeah, I'm back, baby."

"I'm so glad you're home, boo, but why are you harassing our employees?"

Stink sighed, and then replied, "I ain't say nothing but I own the place. Damn."

"Ok, baby, we forgive you," Bonni joked, then continued, "But you'd better be home when I get there."

"I'll be home later, baby. I've got some business to handle," Stink informed, dreading the task at hand.

"Business! I thought that's why you just spent the last two nights out of town!" She blurted, her voice dripping with attitude.

Stink gripped the phone, clenching his teeth to suppress his remark.

His prolonged silence let Bonni know that she'd hit a sensitive nerve with him, causing her to quickly change her demeanor, "Alright, boo, I'll see you later on. I love you."

Before Stink could return the sentiment, she'd hung up, signaling Cross's entrance with a large shopping bag.

"Let's get to work, god," Cross said, suddenly feeling full of energy.

After Stink and Cross had finished cooking approximately ten of the kilos, it was nearly midnight. Transforming the kilos of powder into crack turned out to be a tedious task, however, Blanco's instructions were invaluable, making the process that much smoother.

Elated to be away from the hot stove, Stink flopped down on the couch, and then sighed, "Damn!"

"Yeah, we got it, B. Ain't no stopping us now," Cross boasted.

From Stink's view on the couch, he noticed Cross opening another of the tightly wrapped packages. "Come on, god. Ain't no time for sleep; sleep is the cousin of death, nigga," Cross stated philosophically.

Stink looked at Cross as if he was crazy, yet, somehow he mustered the energy to join him in the kitchen, once again.

When Stink finally made it home, it was daybreak. He and Cross had successfully cooked twenty of the twenty-nine kilos, into crack.

Stink entered the house and was met with the morning sounds of Bonni preparing Tayvia for school.

Dead tired, Stink slurred, "Whazup, baby?"

Eyeing Stink worriedly, Bonni replied, "Boo, you look tired."

"I am, baby," he said as he fell across the bed.

Bonni assisted him in undressing, and then asked, "Rahsaan, when are we going to start being a family?"

In an agitated tone, Stink snapped, "What 'chu mean? We are a family."

"Rahsaan! I mean when are you going to stop running around like you ain't got shit to live for! Rahsaan, I am ….pregnant, with your child!" she declared angrily.

"Baby, I'm trying to get shit together for us. I'm doing thi-"

"No, Rahsaan, you're doing this for you! We've already got everything we need!" she yelled, holding her arms wide. "What else could you possibly want?" she asked in frustration. "If you keep doing…whatever it is…you do, sooner or later…" Unable to finish through the sobs, Bonni grabbed Tayvia's bag and stormed out of the room, slamming the door as she exited.

Stink laid there, listening to the sounds of Bonni and Tayvia, until sleep engulfed him.

It was almost four o'clock that afternoon before Stink woke up. He knew there were some issues that he needed to address, however, there was business that needed to be conducted first.

He quickly jumped in the shower, grabbed his phone and pager, which read 'full', then exited.

Noticing Lil Man's number several times, Stink flipped his cellphone on and punched in his number.

"Yo, whazup, Lil?"

"What's up with you, Man? I've been waiting on you."

"Everything's straight. I'm ready when you are."

"Shit, I'm ready now!" Lil Man blurted.

"A'ight, just give me a minute. I call you in about thirty minutes."

"A'ight, peace."

Stink's pager began to vibrate. Eyeing the digits, he quickly decided not to return the familiar number, especially since he didn't have the money that he owed Leaf yet.

Entering the townhouse, Stink noticed Cross on the couch, counting stacks of money.

"Damn! What, you ain't go to sleep or something?" Stink asked.

"Nah, baby. I can't sleep broke. Besides, only dreams come to sleepers," Cross replied, once again delving into his philosophical reserve.

Stink walked into the kitchen and opened the cabinet that they had put the drugs in the night before. Unable to locate them, Stink went back into the den to ask Cross where he'd moved them.

Before he could even ask, Cross answered, "36-24-36, baby. It's in the bedroom."

After a quick search, Stink located the safe in the closet. Smiling, he thought, *This nigga too much.* Smoothly working the numbers Cross had given him, Stink heard a "Click" as the door popped open.

Cross had organized the safe, placing the crack on one shelf and the powder on the other.

Stink pulled out the drugs he planned to give Lil Man then heard Cross. "Grab five more. Luck and them ready, plus that nigga, Fat Shawn."

With a book bag containing fifteen kilos of crack cocaine, they headed out the door. The entire ride downtown, Stink thought about the warning that Bonni had given him earlier that morning. Yet, here he was, transporting enough drugs to land him in jail forever.

Stink pulled up behind Lil Man's car but before he could get out, Lil Man was making his way toward them.

"So now you two niggas are inseparable, huh?" Lil Man asked jokingly.

"What's up, *cuz*?" Cross said sarcastically.

Stink could sense the tension between the two yet he decided against getting in the middle. Reaching into the backseat, Stink grabbed the bag containing Lil Man's drugs. "Here, Lil. I just gave you an even ten, a'ight," Stink said, handing Lil Man the bag.

"Oh, word. I'll have that for you in a minute."

Stink waved him off, "Nah, nigga, it's already taken care of."

"What? The numbers changed?" Lil Man asked, baffled.

"Something like that," Stink replied. "Yo, we're out, Lil. Peace," Stink said pulling off.

Stink and Cross had made a couple of trips to the townhouse to retrieve more drugs. It seemed as if the entire city was in the market for crack and they were the only merchants.

On the third trip to the townhouse, Stink's pager went off. Quickly recognizing the number, he announced, "It's Leaf."

Entering the townhouse, Stink went directly to the telephone.

"Yo, Leaf. Whazup, this Stink."

"Son, where you been?" Leaf asked suspiciously.

"Man, I ran into a few problems but everything's good," Stink lied, looking to Cross who smiled approvingly.

"So when you gonna be ready?"

Stink had already accumulated the money he owed Leaf but he still wasn't prepared to face his mentor. "Probably tonight but I gotta set some shit straight in these streets," Stink stated in a serious tone, reinforcing his lie.

"Yo, B, if it's short paper, let it go. Just cut them niggas off," Leaf advised, sensing Stink's seriousness.

"Yeah, I got you but I'm-a handle my business tonight, then I'm-a get at you."

"A'ight, just hit me when you're ready," Leaf said, then ended the call.

As soon as Stink hung the phone up, Cross jumped up excitedly. "Yo, god, you played that shit like you was Charlie Sheen or some shit! Yo, you deserve an Oscar - at least an Emmy!"

Later that evening, Stink dialed Leaf's number, finally prepared to face him.

"What up?" Leaf answered.

"Yo, Leaf, I'm ready."

"A'ight, B. Give me an hour then meet me at Giovanni's on Holland Road in Norfolk," Leaf replied, then gave Stink the directions to the restaurant.

Stink hung up then turned toward Cross who was tucking his P89 in his waistband.

Noticing Stink's awkward glare, Cross said, "Just in case that nigga get froggy about that paper being late, I'm-a sit his ass down."

Stink giggled at Cross's remark and led the way out the door.

Stink and Cross impatiently sat in Giovanni's parking lot eyeing every car suspiciously.

"Yo, god, call that nigga again!" Cross demanded.

"Just chill, man. Give'm ten more minutes and we're out," Stink replied.

For the next ten minutes, they scanned the parking lot intently. Before Cross could say anything, Stink pulled his phone out and dialed Leaf's number.

"Yo, what up?" Leaf answered, as loud music played in the background.

Stink desperately wanted to sever ties with his once-mentor on good terms, however, Leaf was making it extremely hard. "Hey yo, Leaf! Where you at, man? I'm here!" Stink announced in a firm tone, which clearly displayed his growing agitation.

"I'm on my way now. What you driving?"

Stink's antennas immediately went up. "Um, I'm in a, umm…black Accord," he stammered.

"A'ight, sit tight, baby," Leaf instructed before hanging up.

Cross looked to Stink with a crazed look. "Why the nigga wanna know what we driving?"

Stink didn't respond. Cross's paranoia had finally rubbed off on him as he scanned the parking lot nervously. Eyeing the headlights of a red Nissan 300zx as it entered the parking lot, Stink's mind began to race in overdrive.

The car pulled up beside them and an attractive redbone exited then made her way to Stink's window.

Stink could see Cross clutching the P89 while his eyes darted around in preparation for an ambush.

Stink rolled the window down wondering why she was there, then asked, "Yeah, whazup? Can I help you?"

In an extremely proper manner, she asked, "Are you Stink?"

Mildly shocked, Stink replied, "Umm…yea…yeah. Whazup?"

"Oh, Jaleaf sent me to pick something up from you," she explained.

At hearing that, Stink was in total shock. He looked over at Cross who sat gripping his gun with a contemptuous stare.

Stink couldn't believe that Leaf had actually sent a woman to pick the money up. The act alone was a breach in the drug game.

Unable to come to grips with the situation, Stink sighed and turned his attention back to the girl. "Leaf sent *you* to get the money?" he asked unbelievingly.

"Yes, or whatever it is I'm supposed to be picking up," she retorted, showing her own impatience.

Stink shook his head then grabbed the bag containing the money. Handing it to the girl, he rolled up the window and pulled off.

The entire ride back to Hampton, Cross griped about the lack of drug dealer ethics that Leaf displayed with that act. "I told you, B, it would only be a matter of time before the nigga did some clown shit. The nigga sent a bitch! A bitch! Come on, god!" Cross ranted.

Stink knew that would be the final time he ever dealt with Leaf.

Chapter 13

<u>February 1993</u>

Stink had changed all of his numbers and concentrated on handling his business without depending on Leaf. He and Cross had finished selling all the drugs that they'd gotten from José and were planning another trip to New York.

After they paid Leaf off and had given Lil Man and Dame their drugs, they still made off with nearly $400,000 in profits.

Since their argument concerning Stink's actions, he made it home to Bonni every single night, however, with their trip to New York in the wings, Stink knew it was only a matter of time before her anger resurfaced. With this bit of knowledge, he planned to buy Bonni something that would light her eyes up and quench her anger at the same time.

Traveling north on interstate 95, Stink and Cross were each occupied with their own thoughts. With over $300,000 in the stash compartment, every ounce of the drugs they were headed to get would be theirs. Leaf was now totally out of the picture.

Arriving in New York, they went directly to Cross's girlfriend's house on Convent Avenue where they'd handled the transaction before.

Stink hadn't formally been introduced to Kamesha yet, however, when Cross opened the door to the small apartment, she stood nearly naked in the middle of the floor, with only a thin t-shirt covering her shapely thighs and hips.

"Mesha, get yo muthafuckin' ass somewhere and put some clothes on!" Cross snapped.

The brown-skinned New Yorker looked at Cross as if he'd lost his mind. "Nigga, this is my muthafuckin' house and I'll do as I damn well please! The last time I checked, there was no fucking ring on my finger and my daddy been dead, nigga!" she retorted, rolling her eyes animatedly. Prancing off to her bedroom, she slammed the door.

Laughing, Cross growled, "My man ain't trying to see your nasty ass, bitch."

José arrived a little while later, followed by the two goons, just as before. Unlike before, José chose not to use the money counting machine, which made the transaction shorter. Sliding the stacks of money into a duffel bag, José exited with the words, "You guys be careful."

Cross hid the bag containing the kilos in the spare bedroom, then they left.

They rode around New York, smoking blunts and enjoying the nightlife. After eating a late night breakfast at a diner on Lenox Avenue, they went to Cross's mom's house and crashed.

Early the next morning, Cross burst into the bedroom where Stink was asleep and announced, "Yo, get up, son! Let's go spend some of this paper!"

Stink desperately wanted to buy Bonni a nice piece of jewelry to make up for his wrongdoings. He quickly jumped up and got dressed. Each one of them strapped with an abundance of money, they headed out of the door.

Dipping the Honda in and out of the New York traffic, Cross boasted, "I'm telling you, B. This spot got all the crazy fly shit."

They parked the car on 46th and 6th Avenue, then walked inside the long block. Jewelry stores lined the block on both sides of the street.

Looking into the shop's windows, Stink was amazed by all of the sparkling jewelry. Eyeing a large diamond encrusted eagle medallion that put Lil Man's necklace to shame, Stink exclaimed, "Yo, Man, this shit is hot!"

"Come on, let's go check it out."

Stink gazed at the jewelry adorning the walls in awe. The sparkling diamonds seemed hypnotic as they glittered flawlessly.

The jeweler instantly appeared then engrossed Cross in a showing of his finest pieces. Profiling a large gold chain with a crucifix medallion that was flooded with diamonds, Cross asked, "Yo, god. You like this shit?"

Stink nodded his head approvingly. "Yeah, it's definitely you."

The jeweler, motivated by the wad of money Cross produced, began to pull out an assortment of jewelry for them to inspect.

Stink, already sold on the piece in the window, was absolutely mesmerized when the jeweler showed him an engagement ring with nearly six carats of impeccable VVS diamonds, set in white gold. Stink knew that once Bonni laid eyes on the ring, their union would be solidified.

After parting with nearly $60,000 between the two, Stink and Cross walked out of the jewelry store with enough ice to cause a winter storm.

On the drive uptown, Stink contemplated the direction in which his life was headed. Bonni's words had begun to ring true: he did have everything he wanted. After he and Cross sold the kilos that they'd bought, their proceeds would total just shy of a million dollars.

Stink wanted to get out of the game, yet, he didn't understand that the hustle was just as addictive as the drugs he sold.

Arriving at Kamesha's building, they quickly made their way up the pissy stairwell. Just as before, Cross used his key to enter the apartment, only to be met with the sounds of music.

"Hey, whazup, boo!" Mesha yelled over the music, standing near the kitchen table where two older women and an older man sat drinking beer.

Mesha promptly introduced her aunt, mother and mother's boyfriend to Stink. Everybody assembled already knew Cross.

Stink took a seat on the sofa while Cross went to the back to retrieve the drugs.

Once Cross disappeared, Stink became the object of attention, especially from Kamesha's aunt.

Taking a seat on the sofa beside Stink, she seductively asked, "Where you from, good-looking?"

"Uh, I'm from, uh, Jersey," Stink lied.

"Oh, you's a 'Joursey' boy," she replied in her thick New York accent, allowing her eyelashes to flutter invitingly.

The woman was actually old enough to be Stink's mother and there she was trying to put moves on him.

She do kind of got a phat ass, Stink thought, then quickly shook his head in an attempt to erase the thought.

Rescuing him from the flirtatious aunt, Cross called him to the bedroom.

"Excuse me," Stink said standing up.

Entering the bedroom, Stink noticed the duffel bag on the children's bed and bricks of cocaine strewn around the room. In a concerned tone, Stink asked, "What's up, Man?"

Shaking his head in disbelief, Cross disclosed, "Three joints is missing."

"What!" Stink blurted, his voice increasing a few decibels. They each eyed the bricks, mentally counting them. José had given them twenty-two kilos, yet there was only nineteen accounted for.

"Do you think Shorty took 'em?" Stink asked suspiciously, referring to Kamesha.

With a crazed, demonic look, Cross said, "I know that bitch took 'em." As he packed the drugs back up, he declared, "Don't worry, I'm-a handle that bitch. I promise."

As Cross stood to leave, Stink noticed a bead of sweat on his nose. Instantly changing his demeanor, Cross threw on a 1000-watt smile and led the way out of the bedroom. "Mesha, I'm-a call you tonight, a'ight, baby," he stated lovingly, masking any signs of anger.

"Ok, baby," Kamesha replied affectionately.

Her aunt winked her eye at Stink suggestively as they walked out of the door.

"What we gonna do, man?" Stink asked, breaking the silence. They had aimlessly been riding around New York for thirty minutes. "We just can't ride around New York with 20 keys all day!"

"I know, but we can't drive this car back," Cross advised.

"Why not?" Stink shot back.

"The bitch probably already called the police. I know the bitch took the work. That's why she had her funky ass momma an 'nem in the house, so I wouldn't murder her ass!"

Cross's mind raced frantically, trying to come up with a plan. He knew that driving the Honda back to VA wasn't an option. He'd also eliminated public transportation as a means of getting back to Virginia.

Making a quick u-turn, Cross yelled, "I got it!"

"You got what?" Stink asked confused.

"You taking a limousine back to VA."

"A what?"

"You heard me, a limo...sine," Cross repeated, deliberately emphasizing the pronunciation of limousine. "I'm-a stay here and handle that bitch," he spat.

As they pulled in front of a cab stand in St. Nicholos Avenue, Stink began to protest, "Nah, nigga. If you stay, I'm staying."

Cross shot him a look that quickly summed up what was about to go down.

Two hours later, Stink sat comfortably in the back of the plush limousine, headed south on 95. It didn't take much thought to figure out exactly what Cross was planning to do to Kamesha, yet somehow Stink found himself actually concerned about his man.

In an attempt to relax, Stink pushed 'play' on the VCR and watched the tiny screen come to life. The movie, although entertaining, did nothing but magnify exactly what Stink was living. *Marked for Death* played on the screen.

The limousine pulled up to the townhouse early the next morning. Stink gathered his bags, thanked the driver and then went inside.

The first thing he did was call Lil Man.

"Yo, Lil, whazup?"

"Ain't shit, nigga. Where you been? I've been trying to call you."

Avoiding Lil Man's prying questions, Stink replied, "I've been chillin', but uh...I need to holla at you."

"A'ight, I can come through. Where you at?"

"I'm at my old spot, out at New Hampton Townhouses."

"Ok, give me about thirty minutes. Peace," Lil Man said, hanging up.

Stink decided to jump in the shower and throw on an outfit he'd bought in New York, along with his new necklace.

While Stink waited on Lil Man, he contemplated revealing the situation with Leaf and his new arrangements to him but quickly decided against it.

Unloading bricks from the duffel bag into the safe, Stink recounted them, hoping that the missing kilos would somehow miraculously reappear.

The faint sound of bass, followed by a horn blowing caused Stink to shove the rest of the drugs into the safe and quickly exit the townhouse.

Stink slid into the passenger seat of Lil Man's Benz and noticed Lil Man eyeing him closely.

"What's up, Lil?"

"Damn, playboy! That shit is hot!" Lil Man yelled, grabbing the shiny eagle that hung from Stink's necklace.

"Yeah, you know," Stink replied nonchalantly, then said, "Take me by my crib real quick so I can get my phone and shit."

Lil Man looked at Stink suspiciously. "What? Bonni done kicked you out or something?"

Returning Lil Man's look with an incredulous look of his own, he retorted, "Come on, nigga. Get real."

Lil Man turned the bass up and pulled off, occasionally sneaking a peak at Stink's medallion.

After retrieving his sources of communication, Stink desperately wanted to call Bonni, yet her bitching cancelled the thought. Instead, he paged Cross on his skypager, putting his cellphone number in.

Quickly, Stink's phone rung. "Hello."

"What up, god?"

"Oh, shit! Whazup, nigga?" Stink replied excitedly, hearing the sounds of New York in the background.

"I see you made it back smoothly. Did you enjoy the ride, B?"

"Oh, yeah, definitely. But uh…I'm-a make a few moves."

"Do you, nigga! I'm-a handle my business up here, then I'll be on my way," Cross replied.

At hearing that, he knew for sure Kamesha was a dead woman. "A'ight, just call me."

"A'ight. Peace!" Cross said then hung up.

"That sounded like 'yo nigga'," Lil Man surmised with a twinge of jealousy.

Stink nodded his head in agreement.

Continuing his interrogation, Lil Man asked, "So, um…you got some work yet, or you waiting on 'yo nigga'?"

Stink was immediately became vexed at Lil Man's statement. He knew he couldn't keep him in the dark any longer. "Look, Lil. I ain't fucking with Leaf no more."

"Yo, man, I knew something was up, I knew it!" Lil Man exclaimed, then continued. "The coke you gave me last time had niggas going crazy. We ain't never had no crack like that!"

With his eyebrows raised in astonishment, Stink bit down on his lip to suppress the smile that had formed on his face. "Oh yeah."

"Yeah, that work was waaay better than the shit Leaf had. Who you fucking with now?" Lil Man asked.

Without going into great details, Stink made up some fictitious story to suffice Lil Man's inquisitive appetite.

"So are you straight or what?" Lil Man asked.

"Yeah, I'm straight, but I'm trying to just chill today. I got you first thing tomorrow," Stink vowed.

Somehow, Lil Man had aimlessly driven to Norfolk, prompting Stink to remember the pretty girl he'd met a few weeks back at the club in Portsmouth. "Ay, yo, Lil. Do you know where O.D.U is?"

"Yeah, I know where it's at."

"Ride through there real quick."

"Why? You've got some bitches out there or something?" Lil Man asked.

The only thing Stink remembered about the exotic looking girl was that her name was Melody. "Uh, yeah...I got some broads out there," he lied.

Lil Man quickly found the campus of Old Dominion University. Navigating the Benz through the tiny streets of the campus, he leaned extra hard. "So which dorm she stay in?" he asked.

Hunching his shoulders coolly, Stink replied, "I don't know."

"What you mean? I thought you-" Lil Man barked, before being cut off by Stink.

"Man, just pull over and ask one of these broads."

Lil Man pulled in front of a group of girls, who directed them to the girl's dorms.

As they pulled up to the first dorm, Stink rolled the window down and yelled to a girl entering the building, "Hey, Yo! Excuse me!"

The girl turned and pointed to herself.

"Yeah, you!"

Noticing her caution as she approached the car, Stink asked, "Umm, I was wondering if you knew a girl who lives in this dorm by the name of Melody?"

The girl put her hand on her hip, and looked to the sky as if she was in deep thought. "Does she have funny eyes and long hair?" she asked.

Excitedly, Stink replied, "Yeah, yeah!"

"Well, I think she's in class now, but...," she began to explain before Stink cut her off.

"Look, do me a favor and tell her to call this number as soon as you see her," Stink said, jotting down his cellphone number, then handing it to the girl. He then dug into his pocket and handed the girl two twenty dollar bills to ensure that the message got delivered.

Reaching for the money, she asked, "And your name is…?"

"Oh! Tell her to call Rahsaan."

"Ok, I'll definitely tell her to call 'Rayshawn'."

"Nah. Rah-saan," Stink corrected.

"I'm sorry, Rah-saan," she refashioned in a mocking manner.

As they pulled off, Lil Man gave Stink a patronizing smirk, then said, "Rah-saan, huh?"

Stink grinned, then responded, "Yeah, nigga, Rahsaan. 'Stink' is for the streets, and 'Rahsaan' is for the ladies."

Stink and Lil Man walked out of the mall just on the city line, separating Norfolk from Virginia Beach and jumped into Lil Man's Benz.

Stink had just about forgotten about the message he'd left with the girl from the college, when, "Blurrrrp! Blurrrp!" his phone began to ring.

"Speak," Stink answered coolly.

"Yes, is this, Rahsaan?" the girl asked.

"Yeah, this him. Who is this?"

"Oh, hi, this is Melody. I just received your message. I was beginning to think that you didn't want to talk to me," she stated in a disappointing manner.

"Nah, nah, I've just been real busy."

"I did page you several times, but you never returned my call. I thought you just didn't…," at a loss for words, her voice trailed off.

"I probably didn't recognize the number, you know," Stink offered.

"Well, I'm really glad that you came to see me. I'm just upset that I wasn't here to see you," she stated apologetically.

"Are you there now?"

"Umm, yes…but I'm not dressed and my hair's a mess."

"Shit, it don't matter. I'm trying to see you in your essence anyway," Stink replied smoothly.

"Are you serious?" Melody asked innocently.

"Yeah, I'm serious."

"Well, should I put something on, or are you going to come up?" Melody asked excitedly.

"Nah, you really ain't gotta put nothing on, if you don't want to," Stink replied, suggestively. "But, I got my man with me, so…"

Giggling, Melody instructed, "Well, just ask for Melody Jordan at the dorm office.

"A'ight, just give me about fifteen-to-twenty minutes and I'll be there," Stink said, then hung up.

Lil Man looked at Stink smirking, then said, "Her 'essence', huh?"

Thirty minutes later, Stink and Lil Man sat in the waiting area, under the watchful eye of the dorm supervisor. The suspicious glances that the fat, white woman cast in their direction gave Stink the feeling that they were visiting a prison instead of a college.

Melody rounded the corner wearing sweatpants and a t-shirt.

Standing to give her a hug, Stink was greatly impressed with her natural beauty. Her chinky eyes seemed to be a totally different color than what Stink remembered.

"It's so nice to see you again, Rahsaan," Melody stated sincerely, as they embraced.

Allowing his hands to slide down to the small of her back, he replied, "Yeah, it's nice to see you too." Turning to an openly gawking Lil Man, Stink introduced the two. "Melody, this Lil Man. Lil, this Melody."

Responding in his customary urbane manner, Lil Man said, "Yo, whazup?"

Melody extended her hand, while keeping the other securely wrapped around Stink's waist. "Nice to meet you, Lil Man," she said somewhat properly, causing Stink and Lil Man to giggle.

"Come on guys, let's go up to my floor," she announced interrupting their bout with laughter. Melody led them to an elevator then pushed the button for the second floor.

The scene that played before them as the elevator's doors slid open was something out of a Hollywood movie. Scantily dressed girls in t-shirts and panties were sitting around doing various things.

Stink looked over to Lil Man, whose eyes were wide as saucers. A devilish grin spread across his face as he soaked the scene up.

Melody led them to a couch situated near the television, where a girl stood as they approached. "Chelle, this is the guy I was telling you about. Rahsaan, Lil Man, this is my friend, Chelle."

Chelle was an attractive girl, even with her hair wrap and faded t-shirt. "Hi, nice to meet you guys," Chelle stated in a proper tone, rivaling Melody's.

Lil Man extended his hand, while eyeing her lustfully. Allowing his gaze to settle on the 'Y' of her thick thighs, where he could see her womanhood through the tight shorts, he stated in his best attempt at sounding debonair, "They call me, 'Rich Little'."

"They call me, Chelle," she replied, returning Lil Man's gaze with one of her own.

Witnessing the spectacle briefly, Stink and Melody took a seat at the opposite end of the couch. To Stink's surprise, Melody actually looked better than she did that night at the club. Her hair, pulled back in a neat ponytail, showed off her naturally beautiful features, specifically the grayish tint of her eyes, which mesmerized Stink.

"Would you like something to drink?" Melody asked, interrupting Stink's admiring stares.

"Umm, yeah. That's cool."

Melody stood and sashayed her way down the hallway. Stink's eyes were glued to her backside, marveling at the way her ass jiggled as she walked.

She returned and handed Stink a glass. "All I had was 7-up. I hope that's fine," she said biting her bottom lip nervously.

"It's cool," Stink replied gulping the beverage down. He sat the glass down and turned to Melody. Taking her hands in his, he looked into her unique eyes.

From the way she continuously averted her gaze from his, he could tell she was extremely self-conscious. Placing his forefinger on her cheek, Stink forced her to look him in the eyes.

"Why you keep doing that?" Stink asked.

Faking confusion, she asked, "Doing what?"

Stink wanted to tell her just how beautiful she actually was. Deciding to go a step further, he showed her by planting a soft kiss on her lips.

As Stink pulled away, breaking the kiss, Melody looked him straight in his eyes nervously. "Why did you...umm...stop?" she asked in a voice that cracked.

Stink looked around the room then shot her a look as if to say, *In here with all these girls?*

Melody quickly picked up on this and grabbed his hand then said, "Come on." Standing, she called out to Chelle.

"Yeah," her friend answered, breaking the trance Lil Man had her locked in.

In a conspiratorial tone, she said, "Look out for me."

"Girl, you know I got you," Chelle assured, then quickly refocused her attention back to Lil Man.

Melody led Stink down the hallway and around a corner into a small dorm room, resembling a hotel room. Melody attempted to straighten up, removing stuffed animals from one of the beds.

Stink took a seat on the tiny bed and watched Melody continue to clean up. Suddenly, Stink's mind began to stray. *I wonder what Cross is doing right now?*

Chapter 14

Meanwhile, Back in New York

Cross stood on the corner across from Kamesha's building and watched her and a male companion enter the building, groping one another.

Cross was furious, not because Kamesha was being felt up by another man, but because he knew that she thought that she had gotten away with taking the three kilos.

Moving stealthily, Cross quickly covered the distance to the entrance of the building. Carefully, he made his way up the stairwell, sure nobody could see his silhouette.

Dressed in all black, Cross carried a roll of duct tape and his P89 Ruger.

Inconspicuously, he made his way to the apartment's door and heard the faint sounds of music being played inside. Devilishly smiling to himself, Cross pressed his back flat against the door as an old lady crept by, oblivious to his presence.

Controlling his heavy breathing until the woman disappeared, Cross turned around and pulled the key out that Kamesha had given him years before. Carefully sliding the key into the lock, he didn't make a sound. As he entered the apartment, the music blasting from the bedroom would be critical in assisting him in carrying out his murderous intentions.

Quietly, he tiptoed into the bedroom, where he was met with Kamesha's cries of ecstasy. "Ah, yess! Oh, yeah! Fuck my pussy, Daddy! Fuck me!" she yelled, as her male companion frantically humped between her outstretched legs. "Hell yeah! Right there, baby! Get this pussy!" Kamesha moaned passionately.

"You like it like this, baby? Huh? Yeah, this pussy goood!" the guy between Kamesha's thighs declared passionately.

Cross tiptoed into the bedroom, undetected by either of them and gently tapped the naked man on his temple with the barrel of his gun.

In total shock, the guy froze in mid-stroke, then babbled, "Wha…What, the…man, I-."

"Don't say another muthafuckin' word," Cross's voice sliced through the air, quickly silencing the unsuspecting man.

As the guy's manhood began to shrivel inside of her, Kamesha began to plead, "Cross, it's not what you think. I…umm, I-."

"Bitch, shut up! Don't say another fuckin' word unless you're spoken to," Cross barked with pure rage in his eyes.

He pulled out the roll of duct tape and tossed it toward the guy. "Tape her wrists and ankles up good," he instructed.

The guy, who was frozen from fear, hesitated, yet the look in Cross's eyes urged him to do as he was told.

In an attempt to assist in getting the fiasco over with, Kamesha placed her hands out in front of her.

"From the back, nigga!" Cross spat.

Whimpering, Kamesha rolled over onto her stomach.

"Bitch! Didn't I tell you to shut, the, fuck, up?" Cross growled.

The guy slowly began to wrap the tape around Kamesha's wrists, occasionally glancing toward Cross.

"Tighter, muthafucka!" Cross instructed angrily.

The guy began to vigorously wind the tape around her wrists, then followed suit with her ankles.

Once Mesha was bound, he looked to Cross for further instructions.

"Turn over, nigga!" Cross yelled.

"But, man...I, just-" he began to protest.

Before he was able to finish, Cross forcefully swung the gun down across his head. "Didn't I tell you to shut, the fuck, up?" Cross commanded frustrated.

Dazed by the blow, he promptly rolled over onto his stomach. Cross gripped his wrists and roughly wound the tape around his wrists and ankles.

Once he was secured, Cross walked around the bed to face Kamesha. Tears ran freely from her eyes as she attempted to suppress her cries.

Seeing her like that only enraged Cross more. Reaching down on the floor, he snatched her ruffled panties up and stuffed them into her mouth. Grabbing the duct tape, he wound it around her head, as her eyes pleaded with him.

Watching the scene through disbelieving eyes, her male companion laid there in shock.

"Turn over. Lay on your back, muthafucka!"

Struggling, he managed to roll over to face Cross.

"Now, I'm-a ask you one time. Where my shit at?" Cross asked barely above a whisper.

Lying there naked, he didn't respond to Cross's question fast enough. Refusing to play games, Cross stormed off into the bathroom to find something that he knew would get him the answers he was in search of. Rummaging through drawers, he quickly found what he was looking for.

As he returned to the bathroom with the curling iron in his hand, he instilled immediate terror in Kamesha and her friend.

"Yo, B. I know you ain't trying to die because of this bitch, so I'm-a give you one last time to come clean," Cross reasoned.

"Word is bond, son, I'ont know what you talking ab-," the pleading man began, before having his boxers stuffed into his mouth.

"Ok. Y'all wanna play games; let's play games," Cross announced triumphantly. He plugged the curling iron into the socket and began to search the bedroom. Thinking that maybe the drugs were there, he began to fling clothes from drawers in search of the three kilos.

Unable to locate any evidence of the missing drugs, Cross walked over and picked up the burning hot curling iron.

As Cross stood over Kamesha, gripping the hot iron, she began to squirm helplessly. He gripped her duct taped ankles and flipped her over onto her back, forcing her knees to her chest. Despite her kicking, Cross placed the tip of the blistering iron at the opening of her vagina.

Menacingly, Cross asked, "Do you know where my shit is now?"

Mesha's eyes showed complete terror at Cross's question, which didn't satisfy his madness. He forcefully shoved half of the iron into her pussy, causing a sizzling sound once the fiery steel made contact with her juices.

Mesha's body bucked wildly as the iron fried her insides. The panties stuffed in her mouth muffled her cries, as she collapsed from the pain.

Cross pulled the iron from Kamesha's limp body, then turned his attention to the naked, gagged and bound man, whose eyes bugged out of his head in horror.

"Looks like you're next, playboy," Cross said, grinning devilishly.

The man began to shake his head violently.

Mimicking a line from his favorite movie, Cross said, "Well, whadda ya know, the nigga got some sense after all."

The helpless man shook his head 'yes', signaling that he was ready to cooperate.

"Just tell me where my shit at and I'll spare you," Cross offered half-heartedly.

The naked man nodded his head animatedly, prompting Cross to remove the underwear from his mouth. Breathlessly, he looked to Cross and began, "Yo, B, it was all her idea! I ain't know shit about it! I swear!" he revealed visibly sobbing.

Filling Cross in on exactly how the entire situation transpired, he gave Cross the address of the apartment where the drugs were stashed, along with the keys.

Cross made sure that both of them were securely bound and gagged, then turned the music up a few decibels and exited just as he'd come.

After Cross had retrieved the drugs, he knew he had to return to Kamesha's apartment. If he allowed them to live, only one of two things would occur, both bad.

As Cross went back into Kamesha's apartment, everything seemed to be as he'd left it. The loud music still played, however, once he entered the bedroom, he only saw Kamesha lying on the bed.

In a panic, Cross rushed around the other side of the bed and breathed a sigh of relief. Kamesha's sex partner laid there on the floor, attempting to wiggle his way out of the situation.

Cross grabbed a pillow from the bed and placed it over the squirming man's head, then fired three shots into his skull. *Pop, pop, pop!*

Moving over to Kamesha, he repeated the act. *Pop, pop, pop!* He took a moment to survey his work and quickly exited the apartment.

Stink and Melody laid across the small bed, caressing one another while embraced in a sensuous kiss.

"Rahsaan, do you have protection?" Melody asked tenderly.

In frustration, Stink replied, "Damn."

"Don't worry, I've got one somewhere," she said soothingly, as she got up from the bed and began searching through her dresser.

Tossing the condom onto the bed, Melody began to slowly undress down to her cotton panties.

Stink quickly jumped up and discarded his clothing. Seeing Melody sexily crawl onto the bed caused his manhood to become defiantly hard, making the task of rolling the rubber onto his shaft effortless.

As he crawled between Melody's legs, he could feel the heat from her smooth thighs against his own skin.

Stink felt her entire body become limp after planting a tender kiss onto her mouth. Smoothly, Stink slid her panties to the side and eased his dick in slowly.

"Oh...my...God!" Melody gasped as he entered her moist center.

Feeling the extreme tightness of her pussy engulf him urged Stink to plow into her deeper.

"You like that?" Stink asked, grinning lustfully.

Arching her back, she purred, "Yes...yess, Rahsaan! It feels soo....good!"

Stink pumped into her a few more times, before becoming frustrated with her panties. Removing himself from her center, he pulled Melody's panties down over her outstretched legs and threw them on the floor.

He now had a clear view of her pretty pussy. Once again, he took his position between her thighs, then rubbed the tip of his manhood within her fat lips and watched her shiver.

"Ooh, Rahsaan...please! Please!" she begged.

Pushing his dick into her, Stink ground his pelvic bone into her, giving her all of him.

"Rah...Rahsaan! I love...the way you feel...inside of me!" she huffed sexily, wrapping her arms around Stink's neck, she pulled him closer inviting him to a passionate kiss.

He pulled Melody's legs from around his waist. Locking her thighs with his forearms to give himself better leverage, he pounded into her.

"Ooh, Rahsaan...you're so deep in me! I'm...! Oh, my...God! I'm cumming!" Melody screeched in ecstasy.

Stink watched in awe as her face contorted and her juices freely flowed from her center, glistening on the condom.

Pulling out of her once again, he turned her over onto her stomach and quickly mounted her from the rear. Easing himself into her already drenched pussy, he took it slow, allowing her time to get used to the new position.

After a few short strokes, Stink began to pound into her once again, beating the pussy up.

Melody buried her face into the pillow to suppress her cries.

The sound of her wet pussy sloshing caused Stink to quicken his pace, building to an intense climax. "Oh, shit...I'm about to cum!" Stink announced gritting his teeth.

"Oh, yess, Rahsaan! Yess! Cum for me!" Melody coaxed, feeling her second orgasm explode.

Hearing her say those words caused an explosion from within Stink, as he grunted, "Ahh...fuck, yeah!" Instantly filling the condom, he collapsed on top of Melody breathlessly.

After a short rest, Stink hopped up and walked into the small bathroom on wobbly legs. He threw the condom in the stool, then grabbed a washcloth from the towel rack and washed himself thoroughly.

As Stink turned around, Melody was leaning against the door frame smirking. "I see you found my face cloth."

"Oh, my fault. I was coming to wash you up."

Sitting on the stool, she replied, "Thanks anyway."

Stink went into the room and began to gather his clothes.

Melody entered the room just as Stink was pulling his shirt over his head. "Rahsaan, I hope this isn't going to make you look at me like I'm a ...ho or anything," she stated worriedly.

"Nah, not at all," Stink replied, reaching out to her. "I know I've got that kind of effect on you," he stated boastfully.

"You do, Rahsaan. You really do," she revealed sincerely. "Rahsaan, I swear, I don't just do things like this."

Stink hugged her in an attempt to soothe her insecurities, he said, "I know, Melody. I know."

Eyeing the clock, Melody quickly got dressed trying to beat the 12 o'clock curfew on visitors.

She led Stink into the dayroom, looking for Chelle and Lil Man. Unable to find them, Melody impatiently asked another girl, "Lisa, have you seen Chelle and a tall..."Melody began, only to stop in mid-sentence as she noticed Chelle and Lil Man headed in their direction.

Cuddled up as if they were newlyweds, Lil Man and Chelle strolled into the dayroom. "Yo, you ready, Stink?" Lil Man asked, smiling from ear to ear.

Returning Lil Man's 'I- just-got-some-pussy-too' smile, Stink said, "Yeah, let's bounce."

After saying their goodbyes, Stink and Lil Man exited just before the 12 o'clock curfew, each wearing shit-eating grins.

Stink exited Lil Man's Benz just before one o'clock in the morning and crept into the house, trying not to wake Bonni. As he was discarding the last of his clothing, he heard Bonni stir.

"Rahsaan, is that you?" she asked sleepily.

"Yeah, baby. It's me," he said walking over planting a soft kiss on Bonni's cheek. Knowing the keen sense of smell a woman has, he knew not to get any closer.

"Baby, I'm-a hop in the shower. I've been driving all night," he lied, making a bee-line for the shower.

"Ok, boo."

While Stink showered, he was contemplating giving Bonni the ring as soon as he got out, however, once he went back into the bedroom, Bonni was sound asleep.

The following day, Stink and Bonni spent the entire day together. Stink constantly checked his pager to see if Cross had called. The only call that he'd received was from Lil Man, setting up a time when they could meet up and handle their drug transaction.

After he and Lil Man hung up, Bonni's whole attitude began to change. "I guess you gotta go now, huh?" she inquired in a voice that dripped with attitude.

"Nah, baby. That was Lil Man, I just got to meet him later on," Stink explained.

They chilled around the house until 7 o'clock when Stink jumped up. "Baby, I'll be back in a little bit."

"Mmm, hmmm, I won't wait up," she snapped sarcastically.

Stink shook his head in frustration and headed out the door. *Maybe it's the pregnancy that got her attitude fucked up*, he thought hopping into his Lexus.

Stink arrived at the townhouse and quickly set up shop. As he began the process of transforming the powder into crack, his mind shifted back to Cross. It had been twenty-four hours and he hadn't heard anything from his partner; Stink had begun to worry. After he pulled the first batch of cookies from the pot, he grabbed the phone and paged Cross.

Stink had three pots of cocaine bubbling when the phone rang. "Hello," he answered, balancing the phone on his shoulder, as he closely watched over the drugs.

"Yo, what up, god? I'm in B-more. My plane should land in Norfolk at 10:45, flight 147, American Airlines," Cross blurted in one breath. "Oh, I've got a surprise for you too. Peace," he said, hanging up.

Stink instinctively looked toward the clock, which read 9:48. He had less than an hour to finish up his business and get to Norfolk.

He promptly called Lil Man.

"Hello," Lil Man answered.

"Yo, Lil, be at the townhouse in fifteen minutes. Peace," Stink directed then quickly hung up to finish cooking the drugs.

Stink laboriously prepared the cocaine into crack, precisely weighing every ounce. He then packed them into large plastic bags.

Once the process was finished, he paced the floor, occasionally glancing out of the window in anticipation of Lil Man's arrival.

Reflecting on Cross's comment, Stink wondered what type of surprise he could possibly have for him.

At 10:03, Stink called Lil Man again. "Yo, Lil! Where you at?" he asked impatiently.

"I'm pulling up now."

Flying through the tunnel that separated Norfolk from Hampton, Stink eyed the dashboard clock. It read 10:29 which meant that if he was going to be on time, he had to put a move on. He stomped down on the accelerator, and watched as the speedometer shot past the 100mph mark.

When Stink pulled into the airport's parking lot, it was 10:50. He parked and rushed into the airport. Scanning the large monitors showing the 'Arrivals' and 'Departures', Stink noticed flight 147 had just arrived at gate 19.

Getting the attention of an elderly security guard, he asked, "Could you tell me where gate 19 is?"

"Yes, it's down that way, to your left. You can't miss it," he directed.

Rushing off in the direction that the security guard instructed, Stink was met with a flood of passengers exiting the plane. Standing off to the side, he eyed the crowd in search of Cross.

After nearly the entire plane had exited, he finally spotted Cross. Stifling laughter, Stink stared at Cross through unbelieving eyes. Cross was dressed as if he was in catholic school. He wore the whole outfit - shirt and tie, slacks and a pair of shiny, hard-bottomed shoes.

Stink walked over and embraced his man. "Whazup with the new gear?" he asked suspiciously.

Stepping back in his very best modeling pose, Cross jokingly replied, "Oh, you like my new style?"

"What, you done went schoolboy on me?" Stink questioned humorously.

Throwing the book bag over his shoulder, Cross said, "Nah, I'm just smart. Let's bounce."

They made small talk until they reached the car, once they got in, things turned deadly serious. Pulling out 2 bricks, identical to the ones they'd lost in New York, Cross tossed them to Stink. "Here. These are for you."

"How...How did you get'em back?" Stink asked mildly shocked.

"Come on, god. You know my style," Cross stated boastfully, then continued. "The other one is halfway to hell with that conniving bitch and her nigga, but I got this too." Cross pulled out a stack of money along with some jewelry. Separating the jewelry, he handed Stink a gold Rolex with tiny diamonds around the bezel.

Stink eyed the watch skeptically then asked, "Who the fuck you rob?"

"You's a funny nigga, B," Cross said laughing.

Pulling out of the parking lot, one thing was for certain, Cross was a true murderer who would kill for anything - or for nothing.

As Bonni wobbled over to the couch, Stink couldn't help but notice how much more striking her already-beautiful features had become. The pregnancy had brought a radiance out in her Stink wasn't used to seeing.

Stink had silently vowed to make Valentine's Day special for Bonni. Not only had he made reservations for that evening at one of Virginia Beach's premiere oceanfront restaurants, afterwards he planned to give her the ring he'd bought in New York.

Stink professionally cracked the king crab legs and fed them to Bonni. Their table was reminiscent of a seafood buffet. Jumbo shrimp, Maine rock lobster tails, scallops, and every other crustacean imaginable covered the table.

The candlelight flickered off Bonni's features, making her seem angelic.

Sipping his champagne, Stink envisioned what life would be if he didn't have Bonni at his side. Instantly a rush of panic flowed through him and he knew that he would have to leave the 'game' behind.

They made it to their suite overlooking the icy Atlantic and quickly settled in. Watching Bonni exit the shower with nothing but a t-shirt on and given that the seafood was like an aphrodisiac, Stink's manhood was at complete attention.

Crawling onto the bed tiger-like, Bonni huskily whispered into Stink's ear, "Baby, I love you."

Turning to face her, he returned the sentiment. "I love you too, Ma."

Bonni straddled him, then leaned in for a deep passionate kiss. Breaking the kiss, she moved to his ear, then left a hot trail down to his nipples.

She aroused sensations in Stink that forced him to bite down on his bottom lip to suppress his cries.

"Stop, baby...sto...baby, stop. Tonight's about you," he managed to say, then turned Bonni onto her back. Careful not to put too much weight on her stomach, Stink planted soft kisses from her forehead down to her protruding belly.

Stink stood at the foot of the bed and removed the rest of his clothing. Starting at Bonni's feet, he slowly and meticulously began to massage her.

Bonni threw her head back and enjoyed the attention that she was receiving from her man.

After she was totally relaxed, Stink moved upward, methodically giving each part of her body ample attention. As he massaged Bonni's creamy thighs, he felt the terrible urge to taste her.

Kissing the insides of her thighs, sending jolts of pleasure through her body, Stink leaned in giving himself full access to her womanhood. He continued to lick and kiss, concentrating on the crevice that separated her thighs from her lips.

Bonni squirmed uncontrollably once Stink's tongue made contact with her sensitive area. "Baby, stop...please, baby! It feels like I'm...about to pee," she whimpered.

Removing his tongue from her clitoris long enough to say, "Go ahead, and pee," Stink dove back into her most prized possession, continuing to make her squirm under his touch.

Unable to endure the feeling any longer, Bonni roughly grabbed the back of Stink's head and ground her pelvic into his face. "Ahh, yessss! Mmm Hmmm!" she moaned.

Stink pried himself away from Bonni's grasp after his breathing was short-circuited. "Damn, girl, you trying to kill a nigga," he gasped breathlessly.

Reaching for Stink's manhood, Bonni begged, "Please, Daddy! Please don't do me like this! I need you inside of me now!"

Teasingly, Stink asked, "But what about the baby?"

"I swear it won't hurt the baby. Please!"

Stink turned Bonni onto her side. His dick, already stiff, easily slid into her hot pussy.

"Umm, yesss, Daddy," she huffed sexily.

Stink took his time, slowly stroking in and out of Bonni until she began to get excited. She pushed her ass back onto his dick forcefully, making a clapping sound as their flesh connected.

"Work your pussy, Daddy," she crooned passionately.

Stink had heard myths about how good pregnant pussy was, however what he was experiencing at that moment was phenomenal. In an attempt to prolong his orgasm, he began to think of other things, yet nothing seemed to work.

Quickening his pace, Stink announced, "Baby, I'm…cum…cumming."

"Daddy, please don't…cum! Please!" Bonni begged to no avail.

Stink spasmed, shooting his load deep into Bonni's core.

Tangled in each other's arms, Stink eased out of bed and went to his jacket to retrieve the velvet box that contained Bonni's ring.

Bonni quickly leaned up and asked full of attitude, "Are you planning on going somewhere?"

Cuffing the tiny box in his hand, he replied, "Nah, baby. I was just looking for something."

Bonni eyed him suspiciously as he made his way back to the bed.

Kneeling down on Bonni's side of the bed, he looked directly into her eyes. "Bonni, you know I love you more than anything and I don't think I want to ever be without you." Pulling the box out and opening it, he continued, "Bonita Labelle Lawson, will you be my wife?"

Instantly a stream of tears began to flow from her eyes, as she eyed the sparkling ring in amazement. "Baby, it's, so…so beautiful," she said between light sobs.

"So, will you marry me, baby?" Stink repeated.

"Yes, Rahsaan! Yess!" she yelled, hugging him tightly.

Abruptly, Bonni pulled away and looked deep into his eyes. "But, baby, you gotta stop doing what you're doing. Please, baby! I don't want to lose you," she said firmly, allowing the tears to run freely from her eyes.

"Baby, in three months, I'm out. I swear," Stink vowed adamantly.

"I pray that you will stop. I swear I do," Bonni stated solemnly.

Chapter 15

March 1993

   Within a month after Cross had returned to Virginia from New York, things had gotten extremely hot. It was rumored that NYPD was in VA asking questions about Cross.

   Although none of these rumors were proven, Cross wasn't going anywhere near New York City. Their last shipment of drugs had been distributed long ago, prompting another trip. Cross had been urging Stink to take the trip alone, while he laid low in VA.

   Early on, Stink was reluctant, however, with the promise he'd made to Bonni, he rationalized that he needed to make this last and final trip so he promptly boarded the flight to New York.

   Arriving in New York, Stink took a cab to one of José's spots uptown in Washington Heights and handled the drug transaction. Then he hopped another cab to take him to St. Nicholos Avenue to meet the limousine driver.

   As the cab pulled onto the crowded New York City block, an eerie feeling overcame Stink. Exiting the cab, it seemed as if the entire block glared in his direction. Carrying enough drugs to realize nearly all of their hustler dreams, Stink quickly put on his unmanning ice grill and casually strolled into the cab stand.

   Sitting behind the desk with a fat cigar wedged between his lips, Louis the Limo Driver asked, "So, you ready to roll, young fella?"

   Digging into his pockets to retrieve the customary $500 fee, Stink replied, "Yeah. I'm ready."

   "Just give me a second and we're out."

Gripping the duffel bag containing twenty-five kilos, Stink took a seat.

Less than thirty minutes later, they were headed across the George Washington Bridge.

The limousine was so comfortable that Stink quickly fell asleep watching the exact same Steven Segal movie he'd watched before.

The loud static from the television, signaling the movie's ending, roused Stink to consciousness.

Looking around dazed, Stink quickly came to his senses. Feeling the deep rumbling in his stomach, he tapped the partition that separated him from the driver.

Instantly, Louis rolled the partition down and asked, "What can I do for you, young fella?"

"You think we can stop and get something to eat?"

"No problemo," Louis replied, and then rolled the partition back up.

Ten minutes later, they pulled into a Wendy's just off the interstate. Louis navigated the big Lincoln through the drive-thru, stopping so that Stink's window was at the menu board.

After ordering his food and offering to buy Louis a meal also, Louis pulled up to the cashier's window.

As Stink handed the young girl his money, he noticed the entire staff attempting to get a peek at him.

"Are you somebody famous?" the girl asked grinning foolishly, as she handed him his food.

"Yeah, you could say that," Stink teased, flashing a phony smile.

"I told y'all! I told y'all!" she yelled to her fellow employees.

Stink inwardly smiled then rolled the window up. The attention he received over the years was almost addictive. Even though leaving it all behind would be hard, Stink knew he had to do what he had to do.

\----------------------------------

Stink knocked on the door with his free hand as he held the duffel back with the other.

Swiftly, Cross snatched the door open looking disheveled. He quickly motioned for Stink to enter. "Yo, son, DT's been to my mom's crib talking about, *we just want to talk to him*. Them muthafuckas trying to lock my black-ass up," Cross stated cynically.

Shrugging his shoulders naively, Stink said, "Maybe they do just wanna talk to you."

Pacing back and forth Cross shot him a look of disbelief. "Yo, B, I gotta just lay low until shit blows over. You gotta run the show, son," he revealed in a panicky tone.

"Yo, I got it, man. Just be cool and lay low; I got it," Stink reassured calmly and then took the duffel bag containing the drugs to the safe.

After putting the drugs up, Stink called a cab then listened to Cross offer a defense on why Kamesha and her boyfriend had to die.

Hearing the horn blow outside, Stink was relieved because Cross was just about to get into the gruesome part. "Yo, Cross, just be cool, man, I got everything under control. Tomorrow I'm-a handle my business and get this money," Stink stated soothingly then walked out the door.

\----------------------------------

"Wassaan! Wassaan! You and mommy gonna be married?" Tayvia yelled animatedly, as Stink entered the bedroom.

"Yeah, me and mommy gonna be married," Stink confirmed, catching Tayvia in his arms as she leaped from the bed.

Bonni laid there with one eye on the television and one planted on the interaction between he and Tayvia.

"Yippeee!" Tayvia screamed joyously. "Do dat mean you gonna be my daddy too?" she asked curiously.

Intentionally stalling, Stink stuttered, "I, umm…I." Looking toward Bonni for some sort of help, he continued, "Uh…yeah, yeah, Tayvia. I guess I'm gonna be your daddy too," Stink finally said eyeing Bonni's heart-melting smile.

"Oh, goody!" Tayvia exclaimed happily.

Sitting Tayvia back onto the bed, Stink went into the bathroom contemplating just how he was going to break the news to Cross. He'd just made his final run.

Early the next morning, Stink was awakened by the sound of his pager dancing around on the dresser. Grabbing the pager, Stink eyed the number through sleep filled eyes: 555-2496-911-911…

Noticing Lil Man's phone, followed by 911, Stink quickly returned the call.

"Hello!" Lil Man answered in a worried tone.

"Whazup Lil?"

"Man, where the fuck you been? I've been trying to call you all muthafuckin' night!" he yelled hysterically.

"I had to handle some business, nigga! Why? Whazup?" Stink retorted defensively.

"Man, that nigga Cross got po-po coming to my mom's house looking for his ass." Pausing to judge Stink's reaction, Lil Man continued, "I told you to leave that nigga in New York," he spat accusingly.

"Look, man, he already know New York D.T.'s looking for him so he bounced this morning," Stink lied.

"So the nigga left after making shit hot for us, huh?"

Reiterating his lie, Stink replied, "Yeah, man, he's gone."

"A'ight, that's good. But, umm, you ready to do that, or what?" Lil Man said switching subjects.

"Yeah, just let me get up and I'll call you."

"A'ight just hit me when you're ready," Lil Man said, then hung up.

Stink quickly showered, got dressed and headed out the door. As Stink got into his Lexus, his pager began to vibrate. Looking down at the screen, Cross's code flooded the screen: 155-911-155-911...

Stink dialed the number to the townhouse and was met with a voice that sounded like a child. "Helloo."

Slightly confused, Stink asked, "Uh, yeah, is Cross there?"

"Ha, ha, ha! It's me, B. Where you at?"

"I'm on my way over there right now! Whazup?" Stink snapped.

"A'ight, B. Hurry up," Cross said then hung up.

Entering the townhouse, Stink was met with the strong aroma of cocaine being cooked. "What the fuck you doing up in here?" Stink asked covering his nose with his forearm.

"Yo, god, you sleep too much. Fo'real," Cross replied, standing over the oven managing four pots of cocaine.

"How much you got ready so far?" Stink asked.

"Like twenty-two," he stated.

Confused about the situation, Stink asked, "Twenty-two what? Ounces?"

"Nah, nigga! Bricks!" Cross stated triumphantly. "While you was sleeping; I was creeping, nigga!"

"Damn!" Stink replied in amazement. "I'm about to go see Lil. You want me to go see them niggas downtown, too?"

"Yeah, holla at Luck and Daz, but that nigga, Fat Shawn, playing games. He's about to make me pay him a visit," Cross responded threateningly.

Stink quickly weighed and packaged the drugs that needed to be delivered, threw them in a gym bag then looked at Cross. "Yo, I'm out. I'll call you later." With that, he walked out the door.

Riding down the interstate with enough drugs to land him in prison for life, Stink said a silent prayer and obeyed all posted signs. This was his final run.

Stink hopped out of his Lexus in front of Lil Man's house, which usually looked like a luxury used car lot but that day was seemingly empty. As he stepped up onto the porch, Lil Man snatched the door open.

"Come on in, man. Ya man got my shit hot fo'real! Muthafuckin' detectives think I'm hiding that nigga," Lil Man said looking around nervously.

Following Lil Man into the house, Stink asked, "What happened now?"

"Man, the fucking detectives told my moms what I was driving and the whole shit. Talking about, 'We've got reason to believe he's with your son'," Lil Man mimicked.

Leading Stink into a small room at the back of his house, a gust of marijuana smoke invaded Stink's nose. Dame sat on the couch with a blunt hanging from his mouth, playing a video game.

"What up, Stink?" Dame said extending his hand.

"Ain't shit, Dame," Stink replied. Ever since Stink witnessed how Dame had cracked up when Lil Man was shot, their relationship just wasn't the same.

"Shit getting crazy, Stink, man," Dame stated handing the blunt to Lil Man.

"Yeah, I know but shit's gonna blow over," Stink replied confidently.

"Blow over! Stink, man, them muthafuckas talking about a double homicide, man! I told you to leave the crazy muthafucka in New York," Lil Man ranted accusingly.

Initially Stink wanted to throw out what he and Cross had done to the person who was responsible for nearly taking his life, however, after a quick rationalization, Stink thought better of that low-blow and looked at Lil Man. "Yeah, you may be right, man," Stink stated somberly, then handed Lil Man the bag of drugs.

"A'ight, Stink, just be careful, man," Lil Man warned handing Stink a bag containing $280,000.

Walking out of the door, Stink replied, "Y'all niggas be careful too." He then exited the room.

Stink drove around the city aimlessly trying to shake the distraught feeling that came over him. In times like these, there was only one person who could put things back into perspective for him. His grandfather was his bridge over troubled waters.

Stink quickly detoured and steered the Lexus into the direction of his grandparents' house.

As Stink pulled into the driveway of his grandparents' sprawling estate, he noticed his grandfather standing out by the garage.

He hopped out of his car, and said, "Hey, whazup, Papa?" Quickly covering the distance to where his grandfather tinkered in the garage.

"The rent!" he quipped before realizing that something was bothering his grandson. "What's bothering you, son?" he inquired naturally concerned.

Stink explained the situation, filling his grandfather in on almost everything that had transpired concerning Cross and his dilemma.

After pondering on the situation for a few minutes, his grandfather looked him in the eye and said, "First of all, son, keep your promise to Bonita. She's a good girl. Secondly, if you consider this uh, Criss or Cross or Stripe or whomever he is, a friend, then you have to help him. Never

turn your back on your friends. Help him get some legal
help but don't wait until they catch up to him. That's where
black folks are always messing up. They wait until the
police get them, then they screaming for a lawyer. Let it be
a white person; they come walking in the jailhouse with
their lawyer..." his grandfather philosophized. However, his
advice had already been accepted.

Stink ran upstairs and put some money in his stash
then came back outside feeling much more enthusiastic. As
always, his grandfather had given him light when everything
was dark.

As Stink hopped into his car, his grandfather stopped
him. "Oh, yo, one more thing. You might want to make a
contribution to the police department and get you one of
those stickers that shows you support the force," he advised
motioning toward Stink's Lexus. "It's a wonder they allow
you to drive that machine without pulling you over on every
corner. How do you youngsters think that ya'll can ride
around in a car that the chief of police couldn't even afford
and not get harassed? In my day..."

Sighing heavily, Stink turned the ignition and pulled
off before his grandfather could finish his statement.

Engrossed in the movie that was playing, Cross said,
"Hold on, god. This is the best part."

Patiently, Stink sat there looking from Cross to the
big screen in disbelief. *Here this nigga is, supposedly
wanted for a double murder and he watching a movie*, Stink
thought.

"That's that Charlie Sheen shit, son. You ain't up on
that!" Cross stated emphatically. Turning the television off,
he turned to Stink. "So, whazup?"

"Look man, Lil said 5-0 been to his mom's house
looking for you. Now they think Lil is hiding you or some
shit," Stink explained.

"Yeah. So what he want me to do? Turn myself in?" Cross snapped sarcastically. Turning serious, he vowed, "Nah, son. He can forget that, I ain't going back to jail. Next time the carrier of the state sees me, it'll be in a box!"

"Ay yo, who's the best lawyer in New York City?" Stink asked.

Cross's eyes lit up as he answered, "Shit, that's easy. John Gotti's lawyer."

"What's his name?"

"Bruce Cotler. Why?"

"Cause we gonna hire him to be your lawyer," Stink replied confidently.

A devilish grin stretched across Cross's face as he lit a blunt up. "You buggin' out, god," he said inhaling deeply on the cigar.

Stink grabbed the phone and dialed 411. "Yes, can I have the number to the law offices of Bruce Cotler?" He quickly found something to write with and jotted the number down.

After being put on hold for nearly an hour, Stink finally got through to the lawyer known to have helped the 'Teflon Don' himself escape prison.

Now all they needed to do was to get five grand to his law office by twelve noon the following day and he was on the case.

Cross quickly devised a scheme to get his mother the money that evening.

When Stink headed out the door, Cross was elated. At that moment, he felt as if he was the 'Don.'

Chapter 16

<u>May 1993</u>

Stink's final month in the game and he still hadn't told Cross of his plans to exit it. Cross was in such high spirits, he wouldn't have cared.

Mr. Cotler had handled his business in New York, proving why he had been able to represent 'The Don.' The New York City police department didn't even have a warrant for Cross. Detectives only wanted to question Cross probably so they could browbeat a confession out of him. Although Cross was labeled as a suspect, Mr. Cotler had assured Cross that the NYPD wouldn't be bothering him anymore unless they were charging him.

Cross was ecstatic and ready to celebrate. It was time that everybody knew he was no longer in hiding.

Just as Stink put the final touches on his outfit, Bonni looked up from the television and eyed him slyly. "Where are you going? To kill somebody?" she asked sarcastically, referring to Stink's choice to wear the all-black Guess jean suit.

Killing being the furthest thing from Stink's mind, he laughed at her statement, then said, "Nah, baby. I just like wearing black."

Giving Bonni a quick peck on the cheek, he headed out the door.

Cross exited the townhouse as Stink pulled up. Hopping into the passenger seat with a freshly-rolled blunt in his ear, Cross said, "Let's bounce, god."

Stink promptly hit the interstate, headed to Mr. Magic's, one of the hottest clubs in the Tidewater area.

As Stink and Cross approached the entrance of "Mr. Magic's," Stink checked himself out in the large mirror, making sure that his attire was proper. As they had become accustomed to doing, they bypassed the line of party-goers with the passing of a crispy Benjamin.

Strolling into the club, all eyes were on Stink and Cross, as their jewelry sparkled flawlessly. The Rolex that Cross had given Stink was now equipped with an upgraded diamond-studded bezel that complemented his diamond-encrusted medallion to perfection.

They made their way through the crowd to the bar and ordered their drinks. Cross ordered his customary bottle of Moët while Stink chose a Heineken.

Scanning the crowd for familiar faces, they both lounged at the bar, enjoying the scenery.

A couple of cute ladies breezed by in an attempt to get noticed by Stink and Cross, however, neither of them acknowledged any of the young ladies' ploys. Stink had been tempted to give in to a caramel-complexioned cutie who'd given him a flirtatious smirk as she sashayed past him, he decided against it.

Just as Stink had made the decision to address the cutie, Cross nudged him. "Yo, son, there goes that nigga, Fat Shawn," he said pointing to a group of guys mingling with a group of females. "I'm-a go see why that nigga been playing with that money," Cross stated walking off in the direction of Fat Shawn and his crew.

Eyeing the hulking figure in the crowd, Stink quickly fell into step behind Cross.

Cross walked straight up to Fat Shawn and said, "What up, B? Why you ain't get at me, son?" in a confrontational manner.

With a look of shock on his face, Fat Shawn attempted to explain. "Oh, umm, whazup, Cross? I, uh, was trying to holla at you man," he stammered.

"You's a lying-ass nigga! You know yo ass ain't tried to get at me!" Cross snapped mockingly.

"Um…umm, I have, man. Forreal," Fat Shawn replied nervously.

Two of Fat Shawn's boys stepped up in an attempt to show support for their man. This act would only prove to be deadly on their part. Glaring in Cross's direction, one of his boys asked, "Yo, Shawn. You alright?"

Cross peered from Fat Shawn to his courageous partner with fire in his eyes.

"Uh, yeah. I'm good," Fat Shawn said, backing his boys down.

Cross smiled at Fat Shawn menacingly, then in a soothing manner said, "Look, playboy, just get at me tomorrow. I've got something real sweet for you. A'ight, son," Cross patted Fat Shawn across his back, then turned to leave.

"Um, ok, Cross. I got you, man. Tomorrow," Fat Shawn called out to Cross's back.

Cross led the way back to their spot at the bar. "That nigga will never see tomorrow! I'm-a murder that nigga! Word to mother, son!" he pledged furiously.

Stink looked at Cross in an attempt to discourage him from doing anything crazy but the murderous glare in Cross's eye instantly cancelled any thoughts of stopping him.

Fat Shawn had owed Cross $12,000 the entire time Cross was on the lam. Every time Cross paged him, in an attempt to get his money, Fat Shawn would ignore his calls.

Seeing Cross standing there fuming, Stink attempted to reason with him about doing anything stupid. "Ay, yo, Cross. Don't let that bitch-ass nigga spoil what we came to do, especially about that punk-ass twelve grand, nigga," Stink stated, attempting to calm him by down playing the situation.

"Yo, B. If you let one nigga play you, everybody's gonna think they can play you. So this ain't about money; it's about respect," Cross reasoned philosophically.

Stink gave up on trying to dissuade him from doing whatever it was he intended to do. The night was young and the fine specimen that had garnered Stink's attention earlier had suddenly reappeared.

Averting his attention from a visibly fuming Cross, Stink motioned for the young woman to come over to him.

"Hi, my name is Nataki," she said extending her hand.

Eyeing her sensuous curves, Stink coolly replied, "Rahsaan."

Stink and Nataki stood by the bar holding a seemingly-amusing conversation while Cross remained defiantly determined to make Fat Shawn a victim of his wrath.

After a few drinks and twenty minutes of small talk, Stink was certain that he could sample Nataki's goodies if he chose. The thought of Bonni at home with his child growing inside of her quickly diminished the thought.

As the club came to a close, Stink accepted Nataki's phone number with no intentions of calling, then watched her sway her shapely ass toward the exit.

Stink and Cross made their way outside with the rest of the club's party-goers. As they got settled into Stink's Lexus, Cross reached under the seat and pulled out his Taurus 9mm.

Stink looked at him and asked "What you about to do, man?"

"I'm-a see what that fat bitch gotta say now," Cross retorted.

"Come on, man. You buggin if you-," Stink began, before abruptly being stopped by Cross holding his hand up.

"Hold up. There they go right there," Cross stated in a hushed tone. Eyeing Fat Shawn and his crew like a hawk, Cross eased out of the passenger seat.

Attempting one final time to stop Cross, Stink said, "I know you ain't about to do no stupid shit with all these people out here."

Before Cross closed the door, he turned to Stink and said, "The more, the merrier."

Sighing in frustration, Stink knew he couldn't allow his man to go up against four possible gunmen. Grabbing his own 9mm, he quickly exited the car.

Stink scanned the crowd in search of Cross. He immediately noticed Cross approaching Fat Shawn and his boys who mingled around his jeep.

Stink swiftly covered the distance, dipping in and out of parked cars as if he was a professional football player. Just as he arrived on the scene, Cross was raising his gun in Fat Shawn's direction.

"Watch out Shawn!" one of his boys yelled.

Before Fat Shawn could take cover, Cross fired. *Bop-bop-bop-bop-bop...!*

Stink witnessed chunks of Fat Shawn's torso ripped from his body.

The parking lot instantly became a chaotic scene as people began to run in hopes of not becoming a victim of the gun shots.

Noticing one of Fat Shawn's boys frantically reaching under the driver's seat of the jeep, Stink raised his gun and fired two precisely aimed shots. *Bop-bop!*

Cross stood over Fat Shawn and marveled at his act of rage then turned and ran. Stink had already taken shelter among the stampeding crowd in an attempt to blend in.

Stink witnessed a young girl fall in the mayhem and nearly get trampled before he grabbed her and pulled her behind a parked car.

As Stink stood to see exactly where he was in relation to where his car was parked, he saw Cross waving him on. "Come on!" Cross yelled standing beside Stink's Lexus.

Taking one final look at the hysterical girl, Stink sprinted off toward his car and hopped in the driver's seat.

Cross looked at him smirking and calmly instructed, "Let's bounce, son."

Like the other drivers in the packed parking lot, Stink too whipped out into traffic, driving erratically.

"Yo, god. Don't panic," Cross advised coolly. "Remember, we ain't done shit," he stated with a devilish smile.

The following day, Stink stayed home and watched every newscast televised. The constant buzzing of his pager and the ringing of his phone prompted him to turn them both off.

He laid on the bed, replaying the night before until the house phone blared, jarring him out of his thoughts. Reluctantly, Stink answered, "Hello."

"Damn, baby. Why you ain't answer your phone or pager?" Bonni asked suspiciously.

"Oh. I cut'em off."

"Well, that's a first," she snapped sarcastically, then continued, "Anyway, I was wondering if you could bring me some Chik-Fil-A?" Bonni, in her third trimester had begun to use her pregnancy to get Stink to do just about anything for her.

"Uhh...yeah, I can do that. Just give me a minute to throw on some clothes," he replied, desperately dreading leaving the confines of his house, however, he didn't need to arouse Bonni's suspicions.

"Ok, that's fine, baby, but don't forget I'm eating for two," she said only half kidding.

As Stink got dressed, he wondered why the news hadn't reported the incident from the night before. There was no question that he and Cross had each murdered a man.

Stink walked into the salon carrying Bonni's food. Making his way through the sea of women waiting to get their hair fixed, he heard Bonni yell, "Hey, boo!"

As he approached her, she grabbed the bag of food then pressed her palm against his forehead. "Are you sick, baby?"

"Nah, I'm ok. Why?"

"It's just that you're acting strange, all in the house on a Saturday."

Faking a yawn, Stink replied, "I'm just a little tired."

"So you'll be home when I get there?" she asked invitingly.

"Yeah, I should be," Stink replied giving her a peck on the cheek then turning to leave.

As Stink made his way to the door, he glanced up at the television and was instantly frozen in his tracks.

"This is Maria Shaver, reporting live from Mr. Magic's nightclub here on Newtown Road in Virginia Beach. The information is scarce at this time, but apparently two men were gunned down and another critically wounded in an ambush type of shooting that took place in the parking lot behind me. Police say around 2:30 this morning, they responded to a call of shots fired. When they arrived, two men lay dead and one fighting for his life at this hour. Back to you, Ed."

Stink watched in horror as the screen switched back to the anchorman in the studio. *"Maria, do the police have any suspects and have they released the names of the victims?" he asked.*

"No, Ed, they won't release the names of the victims until the immediate family has been notified. And if police have any suspects, they haven't released that information either. This is Maria Shaver reporting to you live."

Stink peeled his eyes from the television and methodically made his way to the exit. Instinctively, he turned back to look at Bonni, only to find her eyes boring into his own accusingly.

"Deshawn Lamont Johnson and Latrell Harrison, both of Newport News, were fatally shot early Saturday morning in Virginia Beach. Police are asking anyone with information to call, 1-800-LOCK-U-UP."

Stink read the article over and over, trying to come to grips with the events of that night. It had been almost a week and he still hadn't ventured outside of the house.

Bonni had become increasingly suspicious of his actions, occasionally tossing sly remarks in his direction.

Frustrated, Stink flung the controller to his video game toward the big screen and yelled, "I stopped hustling, now you bitching about me being home too much! Damn!"

Two weeks had passed since the incident at the club. The murders had come and gone. Stink expected the police to knock on his door any day, yet it never happened. Gradually, Stink began to venture out of the house, however, only in the company of Bonni.

Lil Man had been calling Stink pressing him for some drugs. Even though Stink explained to him that he was officially out of the game, Lil Man persisted.

Finally, Stink told Lil Man that there might be some drugs left in the townhouse and if he went to get them, they were his. Refusing to go through his cousin for anything, Lil Man pleaded with Stink to get the drugs for him. After thinking it over, Stink agreed to do that for his man.

Stink opened the door of the townhouse and was immediately met with the smell of stale trash. Empty food containers, pizza boxes and beer bottles littered the floor. As he cautiously walked across the room, avoiding the debris, Cross instantly appeared, gripping a beer bottle.

Sporting a broad smile he announced, "I knew you'd come back for me."

"Man, what the fuck you been doing up in here?" Stink asked, looking around in disgust.

"Laying low, nigga!" Cross retorted, then said, "We let them bitch-ass niggas have it! Fat Boy had a heart attack before I even pulled the trigger. Ha, ha, ha, ha, ha, ha," he laughed in a sinister manner.

Stink shook his head at Cross's poor sense of humor, then walked off in the direction of the bedroom.

After he had retrieved the drugs, Cross eyed the book bag slung over his shoulder, then asked, "Who dat for?"

"It's for Lil. Why?"

"Oh, nothing. You gonna take it to him?"

"Yeah. I'm about to go meet him."

Cross began to put his boots on. "I'm-a roll with you, B. I need to see his bitch-ass anyway. My moms was telling me some shit he was saying about me being down here," Cross explained, preparing himself to leave with Stink.

Oblivious to what Cross's next move might be, Stink asked, "You gonna shoot your cousin too?"

Laughing at Stink's remark, Cross replied, "You's a funny boy. Let's roll."

Stopping Cross in his tracks, Stink said, "No guns on this trip, man."

Cross threw his hands up as if he was being searched. Exiting, they both shared a laugh.

Cruising down the interstate, Stink called Lil Man to inform him that he was on his way.

"Yo, what up?" Lil Man answered.

"A, Lil, I'm on my way, man, so be there when I get there."

"A'ight, I'm right around the corner. I'll be there," Lil Man assured.

"A'ight, peace," Stink said pressing the end button on his phone.

He popped in Mary J. Blige's, '*What's the 411? (Remix)*' and rapped along, *As I sit back and relax, steam a blunt, drink a Becks, think about the sexy singers that I wanna sex. I probably go to jail...*

Stink was so engrossed in the music that he didn't notice the unmarked police cruiser following. Once he checked his rearview mirror, he noticed a marked HPD car following a few car-lengths behind.

Smoothly, Stink turned the music down, then said, "Yo, Cross, 5-0 is right behind us. Be cool."

"Shit, we ain't speeding or nothing, are we?" Cross asked.

"Nah, we cool, but just in case, grab that backpack," Stink advised eyeing his rearview mirror closely to see what the cop car was doing.

The cops were now less than a car length behind them. Stink immediately thought about the advice his grandfather had given him and wished he'd taken it. He put his signal light on and eased the Lexus into the right lane. When he noticed the police car changing with him, he sighed in frustration.

Instantly, the blue lights on the police cruiser came to life. Stink maneuvered the car onto the shoulder about a half a mile from the exit ramp.

"I don't believe this shit!" he yelled, banging his fist on the steering wheel angrily. "Whatever you do, Cross, don't let 'em get that bag," he stated in a pleading tone.

Cross clutched the book bag and crouched down in the passenger seat as if nothing was happening.

As Stink brought the Lexus to a stop and was about to put the gear shift into park, the unmarked police cruiser that was also following, swerved in front of them, in an attempt to block them in.

Stink panicked and stomped on the gas pedal, causing the Lexus to leap forward, barely missing one of the police officers. The officer had to jump onto the hood of the unmarked car in an attempt to get out of the way of the lunging Lexus.

In no time, the car was at top speed on the shoulder. As they rapidly approached the exit ramp, Stink was unable to make the choice, whether to get off or stay on the interstate.

Instinctively, he snatched the wheel hard to the right, trying to take the deep curve at top speed.

The Lexus wasn't able to retain its traction in the tight curve, slamming into the guard rail forcefully.

Frantically, Stink reached for the door handle, trying to exit the mangled Lexus. As he bolted from the car, he stole a quick glance at Cross, who was calmly exiting the car at the same time.

The sounds of sirens instantly jolted Stink's body into a full sprint in the direction of some woods set off on the side of the interstate. The screeching tires closing in urged him on, causing his legs to pump furiously.

"Freeze, motherfucker!" A policeman yelled as Stink disappeared into the woods. "Freeze, you black motherfucker, or I'll shoot!" the cop threatened.

Ignoring the officer's threat, Stink ran even faster, as the tough tree branches tore into his skin like whips. The ground instantly became mushy, as if he was running in quicksand.   Miraculously, this only slowed him momentarily as he continued to dig.

Feeling his heart throb in his chest, Stink carefully climbed an embankment, as the sirens seemed to be coming from everywhere.   Ascending the embankment, he peered over an open parking lot, connected to a motel.

He laid flat on his stomach and scanned the area for the police.   Quickly judging that the police hadn't made it to the lot yet, he darted in the direction of an open motel door, with a maid's cart sitting in front of it.

He rushed into the motel room and noticed a middle-aged black woman with her back to him.

His heavy breathing immediately startled the woman.   "Oh, my, GOD!   Wha…what can I…um do for you?" she asked nervously, swiveling to face a visibly disoriented Stink.

Digging into his pockets, Stink pulled out all of his money and pushed it toward the woman, then said, "Ma'am, please help me!   The police are chasing me and I didn't do nothing!   Please help me!" he pleaded.

The woman stood in shock, looking Stink up and down.   Pushing his wad of money back toward him, she said, "Young man, I will help you but I don't want your money."

Stink glanced toward the door nervously and then said, "Thank you, Ma'am.   Thank you so much." Instinctively, he looked around for a place to hide.

Waking up in a state of oblivion, Stink jerked his head up, banging it on the box spring.   The blow instantly brought him back to his dreadful reality.   He slowly pushed the mattress and box spring up using his back.   Noticing the motel room was completely dark, Stink escaped the confines of his tight hiding space and eased over to the window.

Peaking through the curtains, he was shocked to see it was pitch black outside. He quickly averted his attention to the small clock on the nightstand that read '1:48'am. He had been under the bed for nearly ten hours.

Stink ran his options through his mind and quickly came to the conclusion that he had to get out of the room fast. Afraid that the police could still be lurking, he didn't have a clue as to how he was going to get out of the motel.

Throwing caution into the wind, Stink nervously picked the motel phone up, and dialed Lil Man's number.

"Hello," Lil Man answered sleepily.

"Yo, Lil, I need you to come and get me, now!" Stink blurted.

"What the Fu-" Lil Man attempted to respond, only to be silenced by Stink.

"Just fucking listen, man! I'm at the Traveler's Lodge on Mercury Blvd., room..." Stink dropped the phone, ran to the door and snatched it open. Eyeing the room number, he quickly closed it and ran back to the phone. "Room 127. Lil come get me now, man!"

"Yo, Stink, what the fuck is going on, man? You-"

"Just come get me! I'll explain everything," Stink said, hanging up.

He desperately wanted to place a call to Bonni, but his instincts told him it wouldn't be smart. One thing was evident; he had to get out of town fast.

Peering out of the window impatiently, Stink quickly closed the tiny crack in the curtain as the bright headlights appeared.

Peeking through an even smaller crack than before, he noticed Lil Man's girlfriend's car.

Stink jumped up and snatched the door open. Darting his eyes left to right, he scanned the parking lot swiftly, then bolted out the door and hopped in the passenger seat.

Lil Man backed the car up and smoothly drove out of the hotel's parking lot.

It wasn't until they were safely on the interstate that Lil Man launched his questions. "What happened? What y'all do? Why y'all on TV?" Lil Man grilled.

Stink took a deep breath, then began, "Look man, we was on the interstate, bringing you the work and they tried to pull us over. Yo, that shit was crazy. The police tried to block us in, then…"

"They got y'all niggas on TV like y'all shot the president or some shit."

"So they ain't catch Cross neither?" Stink asked.

"Nah, I don't think so," Lil Man replied, then asked, "Man, where you trying to go?"

"Huh?" Stink asked confused.

"Where you trying to go?" Lil Man repeated hastily.

Ignoring Lil Man's question, Stink thought aloud, "I wonder how they knew it was us. The car ain't in my name. So how they know it was me?"

"I don't know, but they do," Lil Man snapped, then repeated his question, "So where you trying to go?"

"Yo, I gotta call Bonni, man," Stink stated, continuing to ignore Lil Man.

"Look, Stink! First we gotta find out where the fuck you going. We'll worry about calling Bonni later!"

Looking to Lil Man as if it was the first time he'd spoken, Stink somberly said, "Take me to North Carolina, man."

"What!" Lil Man yelled, "North Carolina? You mean right now?"

"Yeah, man. I gotta get out of here."

Arriving in Greensboro, North Carolina early the next morning, Stink directed Lil Man to his cousin, Brad's house. Stink knew he couldn't possibly go to his mother's house. It would only be a matter of time before the police checked her out. Besides, Brad's was the perfect place to be on the lam, at least until Stink figured out what he wanted to do next.

His cousin Brad wasn't the street type of guy, however, he had looked up to Stink since they were kids. Brad lived alone in a modest two-story house that was willed to him when his father passed away.

Although Brad wasn't the street type, he aspired to be 'street'. With the money he received from his father's will, he acquired every imaginable accessory to seem as if he was a hustler.

Stink and Lil Man pulled behind Brad's 325i convertible BMW just before 7:00 a.m.

Brad was ecstatic to see his cousin, immediately embracing him and Lil Man.

After giving Brad the short version of why he'd shown up on his doorstep, muddy and hungry, Stink jumped in the shower.

Lil Man, tired from driving all night, went off to the guest room to get some sleep.

After Brad was sworn to secrecy about keeping Stink's whereabouts unknown, he headed off to work, giving Stink and Lil Man full reign of his house.

Unable to sleep, due to thoughts of Bonni running rampant through his mind, Stink got up and eased out of the house. He quickly found a payphone near Brad's house and called Bonni.

"Hello, Bonni's Beauty Boutique. May I help you?" a voice answered that didn't belong to Bonni.

Disguising his voice, Stink asked, "Um…yes. Is Bonita Lawson available?"

"Yes. May I ask who's calling?"

Thinking quickly, he looked up to the street sign, and then said, "Yes, I'm Mr. Lee, calling with Lee Realtors."

"Please hold, Mr. Lee."

After a brief wait, Bonni's voice came onto the phone.

"Yes, hello," she huffed, sounding irritated.

Hearing Bonni's voice welled emotions in Stink that he didn't know existed. "Baby, I love you," he blurted sincerely.

"Oh, my, God! Baby, are you alright?"

"Yeah, I'm straight. But have the police tried to talk to you?"

"No! But I saw you on TV, and they say you tried to kill a police, and they-," Bonni explained hysterically before Stink stopped her.

"Baby, I ain't do nothing! Don't worry, ok? As soon as I get shit cleared up, I'm coming home," he stated attempting to calm her.

"But where are you? The say you're armed and I don't ..." Bonni's sobs racked her.

"Listen baby. I'm ok and that's all that matters. I love you. I gotta go."

"But, baby..." Bonni's words trailed off, as Stink hung up the phone.

He quickly jumped in Lil Man's girl's car and headed back to Brad's house. When he arrived at Brad's house, Lil Man was still knocked out. The excitement of the night before had Stink high strung. Nonetheless, once the lack of sleep caught up with him, he immediately went out.

Later that afternoon, Lil Man left for Virginia, leaving Stink with all the cash he had on him and a promise that he would look out for Bonni.

Stink quickly fell into the groove of lounging around Brad's house. With the exception of going to call Bonni, he never ventured out. After he'd been in North Carolina for nearly a month, only two people knew of his whereabouts. He'd talked to Bonni on numerous occasions and still hadn't let her know where he was.

Stink knew he needed to retain a lawyer, which he'd learned from his grandfather. The next call he made to Bonni, he instructed her to visit one of the area's most prominent attorneys.

Ashton Clancy wasn't a Bruce Cotler, however, he was one of the best lawyers Virginia had to offer. Known for his brash courtroom antics and designer suits, he was dubbed 'Fancy Clancy'.

"You did what?!" Stink yelled into the receiver.

"I gave him $20,000," she revealed defiantly. "You told me to go see him, Rahsaan, and I did! He said he needed $20,000 to take your case, so I paid him!"

Stink was furious about her paying the attorney without consulting with him first.

"So, what did he say?" he inquired in a frustrated tone.

"He said that the sooner you turn yourself in, the better it will look for you in court."

Instantly astounded by Bonni's naivety, Stink hung the phone up without a response.

Although Stink hadn't talked to Bonni in two weeks, he knew the birth of his child was just weeks away. Unlike his own father, he didn't plan to miss it. With reluctance, he broke down and called Bonni.

"Hello," Bonni answered.

Attempting to sound cheerful, Stink asked, "Hey, whazup Baby?"

"Oh, Rahsaan! I've missed you sooooo much!"

"Baby, I gotta come home," Stink revealed.

There was a brief silence between them, while Bonni allowed what he'd said to sink in. "Baby, just be careful."

"I am, baby, but I gotta be there to see my child born."

"I know…but, um, I talked to the lawyer again," Bonni divulged hesitantly.

"What he say?"

"Well of course he said that it would be better if you, ummm…" her voice trailed off, not wanting to make the same mistake as she'd made the last time they'd talked. "He said that you have three warrants - one for attempted murder of a police officer, one for hit and run and one for possession of cocaine," she explained.

Stink was confused as to how he could possibly have a drug charge, if Cross had gotten away, unless…

Before they hung up, Stink advised her to be on the lookout for him. He was coming home.

Stink arrived in Virginia Beach and immediately blended in with the flocks of beach tourists. The rental car he drove with North Carolina plates, made him look even more like a tourist, enjoying the sites and scenes of Virginia Beach.

After parking the car, Stink called Bonni.

"Hello," Bonni answered.

"Baby, I'm here. I need to see you," he blurted.

"Where you at, baby?!" she asked excitedly.

"Meet me at the beach, on 21st and Atlantic in one hour," Stink said, then hung up.

After instructing Bonni where to meet him, he strolled into a souvenir shop on the strip to do a little shopping.

Stink inconspicuously sat on a bench, eyeing the traffic intently. Clad in a straw hat and a Hawaiian button-up, his disguise fit the scene perfectly.

Bonni's green Lexus came into view, as she rounded the corner onto Atlantic Avenue. Stink studied every car within ten car lengths of hers, looking for any signs of someone following her.

Unable to find a place to park, Bonni circled the block. This gave Stink another view to see if someone was tailing her.

Watching hawk-like as Bonni parked in a small parking lot on 22nd Street, he felt that the coast was clear.

Still apprehensive about their meeting, he stayed glued to the bench with a magazine in his lap, watching Bonni's every move.

Bonni wobbled across Atlantic Avenue, searching aimlessly for him. After being unsuccessful at locating him, she planted her hands on her hips, and turned around frustrated.

"Tayvia! Tayvia!" Stink yelled making his presence known.

Instinctively, Bonni turned in the direction of where her daughter's name was being called. Her expression quickly turned into a wide smile, once she noticed Stink casually disguised, sitting on the bench.

Quickly covering the distance that separated them, Bonni exclaimed, "Baby! I missed you soooo much!"

Catching Bonni in his arms, Stink hugged her, careful not to squeeze her bulging stomach. "I miss you too, baby," Stink whispered, inhaling the fragrance of her skin that he missed so much.

Even though he was only away for two months, it felt like an eternity.

Placing wet kisses all over his face, Bonni pleaded, "Rahsaan, please don't ever leave me. Baby, I don't think I could live without you," she revealed as tears of joy and pain began to cascade down her cheeks.

"I won't ever leave you, baby.   I promise," he assured her, wiping the tears from her face.

As Stink and Bonni walked hand in hand, along the sandy ocean shore, he explained his plan. Soon as she had the baby, he would promptly turn himself in. Only, until that time, he would lay low in Virginia Beach.

Before Bonni hopped in her car to leave, Stink gave her specific instructions that would enable him to stay undetected, while he was in VA. First and foremost on his list was a call to his grandfather.

Chapter 17

June 1993

Through Stink's grandfather's connections, he had acquired a small flat in the Brambleton section of Norfolk.

Lil Man occasionally made the trip to Norfolk to hang out with Stink. He also supplied Stink with a pager and untraceable cell phone, making sure Stink had safe lines of communication.

The search for the two of them had subsequently died down, however, Stink still hadn't taken the chance of venturing onto that side of the water. The last thing he wanted to do was to be apprehended before the birth of his child.

Unbeknownst to Stink, the block in which his flat was located was run by a group of knife yielding 'Yardmen'. Stink kept a low profile, however, the attraction of Lil Man's Benz and Dame's 750i BMW drew the head Jamaican's attention.

One afternoon as Stink walked from his rental car, a long dreadlock-wearing man, resembling 'Screwface' from Steven Segal's movie *Marked for Death* approached him.

"Bredren, wha yuh do bout 'ere," the Jamaican asked in an aggressive tone.

Unable to make out his foreign accent, Stink asked, "Excuse me?"

"Yuh 'ere me bredren. I-ya say wha yuh selling round 'ere? I-ya see yuh mon's big 'Benz'," he said in an intimidating demeanor, yet all Stink could do was giggle.

"Ya mon tink me-a sissy buoy! Me-a Brooklyn bad mon!" he stated defiantly.

"Nah, nah, man. I ain't selling nothing. I'm just laying low," Stink explained.

Eyeing Stink skeptically, he asked, "You-a lay low from de Babalon?"

Hesitantly, Stink nodded his head.

Suddenly, a broad smile appeared across the Jamaican's face as he extended his hand. "Bredren, dom-a call mi, Yardi."

From that day forth, Stink never had to worry about any of the Jamaican's posse, marijuana, or the police. Yardi had given his word.

Stink sat in the tiny living room of the flat, watching television through tiny slits. The marijuana that Yardi had smoked with him earlier that day had him nearly comatose.

Snapping him from his stupor, his pager began to dance across the scarred wooden table. He reached for his it and eyed the number suspiciously: '555-9018-910-911'.

He quickly jumped up searching for his cell phone so he could return Bonni's plea for help. As he searched frantically, his pager began to vibrate again.

With the pager in one hand and the cell phone in the other, he dialed the familiar number to his house.

"Hell-o," Bonni answered in a distressed tone.

"What's wrong, baby?"

"My…water just…broke. I'm on my way…to the hospital," she explained through labor sobs.

"Baby, hold on! I'm-a call Lil!"

"It's ok…Tasha's…on her way."

"Ok. Baby, just hold on. Everything's going to be fine," he said attempting to console her.

"Baby! She's here!" Bonni announced.

Confused, Stink asked, "Who's here? The baby's here?"

"Tasha's here. We're leaving…..Ahhh, Baby!" Bonni yelled in apparent pain.

"Baby, hold on! I'm on my way! What hospital you going to?"

"Ah…River…side," Bonni quickly said through gasps, before dropping the phone.

Stink was halfway across the street, heading in the direction of the rental car. Helpless, he kept the phone glued to his ear, listening intently to Bonni's moans as Natasha ushered her from the house.

There was complete silence on the other end of the phone, as Stink snatched the gear shift into drive. Stomping down on the gas, the screeching tires could be heard for blocks.

Weaving in and out of traffic, inside the tunnel that separated Norfolk from Hampton, Stink's mind was only focused on one thing - his child. Pushing the rental car to its maximum potential, he approached speeds well over 100mph. Being pulled over for speeding never crossed Stink's mind. Only the birth of his child mattered at that moment.

Riverside Regional Medical Center sat almost four miles from the interstate, however, Stink managed to travel the distance in two minutes flat, running several red lights in the process.

He found the first parking space and bolted from the car into the hospital. He didn't have the slightest clue as to where Bonni was located in the large hospital, so he stopped at the receptionist desk, and blurted, "I'm looking for Bonita Lawson? She was brought here in labor!"

The receptionist stopped tapping on the keys to her computer, and calmly looked up at Stink. "Sir, she's probably in the maternity ward. It's located adjacent to the emergency room, down that hall," she directed, pointing Stink in the right direction.

"Thanks," Stink replied, darting off in the direction that she'd given.

Coming upon the emergency room, he looked around in frustration. "Excuse me, ma'am," Stink said, stopping a nurse. "Could you tell me where the maternity ward is located?"

"Sure. It's out of those doors and to your left," she pointed.

"Thanks," he blurted over his shoulder, going through the doors.

Quickly finding the entrance to the maternity ward, he burst through the doors.

Breathlessly, with beads of sweat trickling down his forehead, Stink caused all chatter to cease in the small lobby. Wild and untamed, everyone focused their attention on him.

Running towards Stink with her tiny arms outstretched, Tayvia yelled, "Hurry, Wassaan! Wassaan! Mommy's having a baby!"

Everyone eyed Stink suspiciously as he picked Tayvia up. Turning to face Bonni's mother, he asked, "Mrs. Lawson, where's Bonni?"

Looking him up and down as if he was an intruder, she snapped, "She's in labor."

Ignoring the obvious stares, Stink made his way through the doctors and nurses until he was by Bonni's side.

Stink had taken the ultimate risk, yet seeing the birth of his child was well worth it.

After nearly three hours of labor, Bonni gave birth to a healthy, seven-pound, two-ounce baby girl. They promptly named her Rahsaanique Tatiana Jones.

Watching Bonni cradle their beautiful daughter filled Stink with enough joy to endure all the pain that life had thrown his way.

Walking through the dark hospital parking lot, Stink sported a smile that was bright as the sun. Nothing seemed out of the ordinary as he made his way to the rental car.

Hopping inside, he inserted the key in the ignition and took a moment to thank God for giving him a healthy child.

Out of nowhere, a blinding bright light took his vision. On pure instinct, he grabbed for the door handle in an attempt to escape.

As Stink's foot hit the pavement, a voice boomed, "Put your fucking hands where I can see 'em!"

He instantly froze, placing his hands above his head. Police cars came from every direction, lights flashing and tires screeching.

A police officer carefully approached Stink, with his gun aimed at his head, and then slammed him hard against the pavement. Instantly, at least five other officers joined in on the fray, jamming their knees into his back forcefully.

"Ahh! Come on, man, I ain't resisting!" Stink yelled as his face was smashed into the asphalt.

"You want to try and kill one of our fellow officers, huh?" one of the officers spat through clenched teeth. Ignoring his pleas, the officers applied more pressure onto his back, using their knees.

Unable to bear the pain any longer, Stink allowed his body to go limp under the officers' unnecessary brutality. No longer feeling the pain, his only thoughts were of his beautiful baby girl.

Stink was transported to the Hampton City Jail, where he was formally charged with numerous felonies.

After being stripped and searched, he was escorted to a cell block, where eleven other criminals lived. The cell block was an exact replica of the one he'd spent six months in, years before. Feeling drained, Stink found his bunk and slept.

Stink woke up to the sounds of men scurrying in preparation for the morning meal. Lying there, he allowed the events of the last twenty-four hours to replay in his mind.

Staring at the ceiling, he noticed the numerous markings that had been left there by the many criminals who had been there before him.

Snapping Stink out of his daze, a deputy yelled, "Jones! Jones! Attorney visit."

Quickly jumping from the top bunk, he went straight to the cell's door, neglecting to wash his face or brush his teeth.

Peeking through the tiny window in the door, the deputy asked, "You Jones?"

After nodding his head, Stink heard the loud sound of the key opening the door.

The deputy led him to a small room on the first floor of the jail, containing a small table and two chairs.

As the deputy locked the door behind Stink, he took a seat in one of the chairs, and waited.

He had never met his lawyer personally, yet, Mr. Clancy's reputation preceded him. As the door swung open, he wondered what Mr. Clancy could possibly look like to have a nickname like 'Fancy Clancy.'

In walked a silver-haired older white man, wearing an immaculately fitting suit. "Mr. Jones, I'm pleased to finally meet you," he said, extending his hand toward Stink. "I've been retained by a..." he paused to check the file on the table, then continued, "Mrs. Bonita Lawson. She's your wife, right?"

Stink nodded in agreement.

"I see you've finally managed to get yourself caught," Mr. Clancy remarked chuckling.

Unable to find the humor in his remark, Stink tossed him a menacing glare.

"Well, I'm pretty sure you've been informed of the charges against you. If not, here's a copy," Mr. Clancy said, handing Stink an identical set of the charges he'd received the night before. "As I told your wife, Mr. Jones, I'm pretty sure I can get the drug offense nolle prossed on illegal search and seizure. As for the attempted capital murder, well, let's just say you really lit fire to their asses with that one," he explained giggling. "I should be able to plea down on that charge as well."

Stink sat dumbfounded at all the unfamiliar terms his attorney used. The one term he was familiar with, he hadn't heard his lawyer use.

"So, what's up with a bond?" he asked.

"A bond?! Are you serious?" the lawyer exclaimed sarcastically, then continued. "You took half the police department on a high-speed chase then managed to escape. And you want a bond?" he asked openly laughing. "There's no way that any judge in this state would consider giving you a bond. Just sit tight and allow me to do my job," he concluded.

That's easy for you to say, Stink thought.

Without the chance of receiving bail, Stink quickly fell into the jailhouse routine. After Bonni and the baby were released from the hospital and Bonni was able to get around, she brought him all of the necessities needed to make jail bearable. Sneakers, t-shirts, underwear, and socks were a definite luxury in jail.

After being in jail just over a week, Stink sat at the steel picnic table playing a game that he'd learned on his previous skid behind bars - chess. Just as Stink had decided to make a move attacking his older competitor's king, he heard, "Jones! You have an attorney's visit! Let's go!"

Having just talked to his lawyer, Stink was baffled as to why he would be popping up now.

Quickly getting himself together, he walked out of the cell block and into the hallway, where another deputy stood as well.

"Put your hands on the wall!" one of the deputies ordered.

Complying with them, Stink dismissed it as just another case of a police doing his job. It wasn't until he was ordered to place his hands behind his back, that an alarm went off in his head.

While one of the deputies slapped handcuffs on him, he asked confused, "Um…deputy, where am I going?"

"You'll see," one of them snapped.

As two of the deputies guided Stink to an elevator, he had already succumbed to the fact that they were about to beat his ass.

"How are you doing, *Stink*?" a plain-clothes officer asked sarcastically. Pointing to his partner, he continued, "You should remember my partner, he's the guy you tried to run over in your Lexus," he snickered. "I'm Detective Salanski, and this gentleman here is Detective Turner."

Skeptically, Stink eyed both officers. Salinski, a short, fat, balding white man, seemed to be the brains of the duo. While Turner, a guy who looked like a professional wrestler, was left to be the brawn.

As they ushered him outside to an awaiting car, Stink's mind vividly replayed the night at Mr. Magic's and he knew that things were about to get hectic.

The detectives drove him to the detectives' bureau in Virginia Beach, where they placed him in a small interrogation room.

As Stink had seen in movies, a large two-way mirror covered one side of the room where officers could inspect a suspect's movements while the detectives browbeat information from them. What he had witnessed on television was about to happen to him.

Both detectives Salinski and Turner entered the tiny room and threw a pack of Marlboros on the table.

"Have a smoke?" Salinski asked.

Stink shook his head 'no,' thinking, *These cops must be crazy. Niggas smoke Newports, not Marlboros.*

"You and your buddy, Cross, really pulled a fast one on us out there on that interstate," Salinski said, with a phony smile plastered across his face.

"Damn near ran me over," Turner added angrily.

Stink sat there, motionless at the mentioning of the car chase.

"So, why'd you all kill Latrell Harrison and Deshawn Johnson?" Turner grilled accusingly.

Instinctively, Stink wanted to launch a defense, however, he managed to maintain his stone face. He knew any statement he made would only get twisted up.

Getting directly in Stink's face, Turner spat, "Was it over drugs?"

Salinski grabbed his partner's arm, pulling him back in a restraining fashion.

Instantly Stink realized what was taking place. They were playing the oldest game in the book - good cop, bad cop.

Salinski walked over and gently placed his hand on Stink's shoulder. "Listen Stink, you need to do what's right, and just tell us exactly what happened the night you and Cross murdered 'Trell' and 'Fat Shawn.' See, we've got witnesses that place you on the scene. Now the question is, are you going to go down with Cross?" he asked casually then continued, "Now, if you tell us what happened we can help you. If you don't, you're looking at life," he advised.

Stink wanted to burst out laughing at their weak attempt to get him to snitch his man out. Apparently a slight trace of a smile crept up on his face, causing Turner to explode.

"You think this is a fucking joke? You think it's funny! I promise you your ass will be making license plates for the next twenty fucking years!" Detective Turner yelled venomously.

No longer smiling, Stink didn't move a muscle. He was absolutely stunned by the detective's outburst.

Once more, Salinski attempted his 'good cop' routine. "Stink, do everybody a favor and simply tell us the truth. You're a good kid with a good family. Once we catch Cross, he's going to sing like a bird. He'll surely put everything on you."

Stink's silence had ultimately proved to both detectives that he was not falling for either of their shenanigans.

Throwing his 'good cop' persona out the window, Salinski angrily spat, "Ok, Mr. Jones, have it your way. Just remember: you're going to burn for this!"

Chapter 18

August 1993

Over the next few weeks, Stink's attorney visited him numerous times. Mr. Clancy had assured him that he wouldn't be subjected to anymore Salinski and Turner visits unless he was actually charged. He'd also kept his word and gotten the drug charge against him dismissed. The more serious offense of attempted capital murder would be dropped to a felonious assault if Stink pled guilty.

Stink was more concerned about being charged with murder, however, once he asked Mr. Clancy about the chances, he explained it in a matter-of-fact manner. "If they had *any* evidence on you, you'd already be charged with murder so don't even sweat it."

Stink was due to appear in court in two weeks to plead guilty to attempting to run detective Turner over. Mr. Clancy had promised him that he would receive no more than a five-year sentence. After serving twelve months, he would be eligible for parole.

During a visit at the jail, he and Bonni discussed his dilemma.

"Baby, I think you should take their deal," Bonni advised. "I'm going to be there every step of the way. I ain't going nowhere, baby," she stated sincerely. On the verge of crying, she continued, "If you go to trial you might get twenty years."

Knowing Bonni had his back gave Stink the strength he needed to go into the courtroom and place his life at the mercy of the court.

Chapter 19

September 1993

Just a few days shy of his 20th birthday, Stink was sentenced to five years in the Virginia State Penitentiary. Having previously served three months, he would be incarcerated for the next nine months before he was eligible for parole.

The long bus ride to Haynesville Correctional Center gave him plenty of time to reflect. Unable to touch his daughter since the day she was born weighed heavily on his mind.

As the bus pulled up to the prison's gates, Stink knew that life as he knew it was about to take a drastic change for the worst. The guards quickly shuffled the prisoners through an assortment of tests as if they were herding cattle then sent them to their respective units.

Walking down the long sidewalk, Stink looked on in awe at the large warehouse-type of buildings that sat on both sides of the sidewalk.

As he approached the entrance to the building he was assigned to a sense of nervousness fluttered through his body. Packs of young men stood in the entrance way shooting ice grills in his direction.

Stink had been in some adverse situations before, however, none compared to the magnitude of the one he now found himself in.

Instantly overcoming any fear, he took a deep breath, held his head high and walked through the packs of young men, returning their glares with a mean mug of his own.

The C.O.,as Stink quickly learned they were called, in charge of his unit directed him to his assigned bunk in the large warehouse. As he began to get himself situated, a light-skinned guy with long French braids casually strolled over to him.

"Yo, whazup? Where're you from?" he asked in a deep, raspy voice.

Slightly startled, Stink turned around. "Oh, um, I'm from Newport News."

Extending his hand toward Stink, he said, "Oh yeah. I'm from Norfolk. They call me E.T."

As E.T. gripped his hand firmly, Stink replied, "They call me Stink."

"It's a lot of niggas up here from *Bad News*," E.T. said, using the moniker 'Bad News' in reference to the city of Newport News. This was Stink's first time ever hearing Newport News referred to as such, however, the nickname for the city rang true in numerous ways.

"Yo, when you get yourself together, we can hit the yard and I'll introduce you to some of your homies," he said, then walked away.

Stink was slightly apprehensive about going out to the yard to meet some of the other prisoners from 'Bad News.' He wasn't the most liked person in the city and he'd done his share of dirt.

Just as he'd finished putting the remainder of his belongings away, E.T. reappeared. "You ready to roll, yo?"

"Yeah, I'm ready," Stink announced.

Word had spread of Stink's arrival, prompting everybody from Newport News to come out. As Stink and E.T. approached a group of guys mingling around a bench, one face in particular looked extremely familiar to Stink.

A broad smile appeared on Jamal's face as he stepped from the crowd, giving Stink a brotherly hug. "My, muthafuckin' nigga, Stink!" Jamal exclaimed.

"What's up, Jamal? It's been a minute, man."

Actually, Stink hadn't seen Jamal since the night that he'd shot Supreme. Some of the other guys looked familiar, yet none knew him as Jamal did. Surely, they'd all heard of Stink in one way or another. His name had been the topic of many discussions in the prison, provoking some of the men to claim that they knew him when in fact they didn't.

Now that he was present, they could only stand and wait on their chance to meet him.

Sensing everyone watching he and Stink hold their own conversation, Jamal began to introduce him to the rest of the guys. "Yo! This is Tim, Fat Cat, D.J., Pen…"

Stink gave each man a pound, until he'd been introduced to them all. After enduring the questions of 'Do you know…?' and 'What is so and so doing?' Stink turned his attention back to Jamal.

"Yeah, Jamal, the last time I saw you, I-" Stink began, before being cut off by Jamal.

"Man, don't even remind me. You's definitely a wild nigga," Jamal replied. "But I've been hearing about you out there, pushing the big-boy Lexus and shit."

"Yeah, I was trying to do my thang, but hey," Stink said, holding his arms wide.

They continued to have their own reunion of sorts until the yard was closed.

As soon as Stink was cleared to have visits, Bonni made the two hour trip alone. She desperately wanted to bring Rahsaanique and Tayvia, but Stink was adamant about them not seeing him under such oppressive conditions. Although Stink wanted nothing more than to see his daughter, he'd made the choice to prolong their reunion until he was freed.

As soon as the C.O. called Stink's name for a visit, he bolted from his unit and quickly made his way to the visiting room.

After being frisked, he was allowed to enter the humungous room and search the sea of people for Bonni.

Eyeing the entrance way nervously, his heart nearly skipped a beat as he saw Bonni walk in. Looking even more beautiful than he remembered, Stink quickly closed the distance between them. He noticed that she had shed the weight from the pregnancy, and now donned a more curvaceous shape. Her flaring hips, along with her more-shapely behind, gave her a perfect heart-shaped ass.

As Bonni drew closer, Stink saw that her bright complexion was flawless. Eyeing her appreciatively, he silently cursed himself.

Seeing her man in such a vulnerable position, Bonni's defense instantly caved in as they embraced.

Stink held her tight as her body convulsed with each sob. Attempting to console her, he said, "Baby, it's gonna be ok. I promise."

After a short time, Bonni regained her composure and they took a seat. As Stink looked deep into her eyes, he could tell that the entire situation weighed heavily on her. He could see the stress etched into her face as he leaned over to wipe a tear away.

Her voice filled with emotion, she said, "Rahsaan, I miss you soooo much."

"I miss you too, baby," he confessed, then asked, "How's everything going?"

Bonni filled him in on everything that was going on with the kids, the shop and the gossip. "Oh, before I forget. I received a call at the shop the other day from some girl claiming that she was calling for Cross. Anyway, she knew who I was and everything, but she said to tell you that Cross said, 'He loves you and he'll see you when he gets there.' Whatever that means," she surmised sarcastically.

Stink desperately wanted to grill her with a zillion questions, yet, he narrowed them down to one. "Is he locked up?"

"I don't know," she responded flatly.

The remainder of their visit was marvelous. They laughed, joked and even flirted sensuously, until the issue of money was brought up.

"Baby, I've only got around twenty thousand at the house. And with the house, the shop and both our cars, I...," she revealed in a distressing tone, before sighing in frustration.

Gripping both of her hands, Stink said, "Listen, baby, don't worry about nothing. I've got some money put away, ok. All you need to worry about is you and the kids. I got us," he stated assuredly.

Before she left, Stink had instructed her to allow Lil Man to sell her car. The loans on both their cars were fabricated, making it impossible to trace. He'd also assured her that she'd have twenty thousand dollars by the end of the week.

With everything handled, Stink stood and planted a long passionate kiss on Bonni's lips, ending their visit.

Chapter 20

<u>November 1993</u>

As the holidays rolled around, Stink had fallen into the pattern of prison life. Bonni had already visited him three times, putting plenty of miles on her new minivan. She still respected Stink's wishes not to bring the kids to see him, however, hearing Rahsaanique baby talk on the phone just wasn't enough.

When Stink wasn't on the yard swapping stories with the homeboys, he was in the dorm riding the telephone. Up until then, he'd only call Bonni, his mother, his grandmother and Lil Man.

One evening while he was on the phone with Lil Man, out of the blue, Lil Man asked, "Yo! Do you remember them girls from O.D.U. that we fucked that night?"

Remembering the night vividly, Stink said, "You talking about Melody and her girl, um…"

"Yeah! Chelle! But anyway, from time to time, I still be fucking with Chelle, and every time I see Melody, she asking about you."

Slightly shocked, Stink replied, "Oh, yeah."

Lil Man continued, "I told her you was doing a bid but she begged me to give you her number, so…"

Stink was surprised that Melody had inquired about him. Seeing as how he'd hit it and never called, he figured that she probably simply wanted to curse him out. Nonetheless, he took the number anyway, at Lil Man's urging.

Stink waited a few weeks before he decided to give Melody a call. His very first time calling her, he was surprised that she was genuinely happy to hear from him, practically begging him to call her back.

He began to call Melody whenever he wasn't calling Bonni. Every time he'd call Melody, their conversations seemed to become more and more geared toward sex. Until one night, Stink called Melody and in the middle of their conversation, Melody blurted, "Rahsaan, I want to have phone sex with you."

Stink couldn't believe his ears, he'd heard of guys getting their girlfriends to play with themselves on the phone, however, he'd never experienced it.

The time left on their call negated any chance of negotiating her request so throwing caution into the wind, Stink announced, "When I call back, be ready."

Stink left the phone dangling, signaling the other prisoners that the phone was taken. He hurriedly went to his bed area and gathered the necessary utensils for masturbation.

Sitting comfortably on the floor with a blanket covering him, Stink held the phone to his ear and listened as Melody pressed one, accepting his call.

"Hellooo," Melody softly crooned.

"Wazup, baby, are you ready?" Stink asked, maneuvering a sock over his manhood.

"Mmm, hmmm," she replied sensuously.

"So, tell me, what are you wearing?"

"My birthday suit."

"Damn! I wish I could crawl between your legs and plant kisses from your pussy lips to your mouth," he said, slowly stroking himself.

His sexy voice instantly caused Melody's pussy to become moist. "Mmm hmmm, I can feel your lips on me, baby."

"What are you doing now?" he asked excited.

"I'm gently rubbing my pussy lips," Melody moaned.

"Damn, baby. I can taste your juices."

"You have me soooo wet right now. I can feel my pussy juice running down my thighs," she revealed in a raspy tone.

"Put your finger in it, baby," Stink urged.

"Ooooh, yes, baby! I can feel you inside me! Oh, yes, I'm so tight!"

"You feel me baby? I'm deep inside of you!" he hissed, stroking his defiantly hard shaft like a piston.

"Yes, boo! Give it to me!" Melody hissed in a quivering voice.

Now oblivious to his surroundings, Stink nearly yelled, "You like it, baby!"

"Yes, baby! Please fuck me good! Please!" Melody huffed in ecstasy, feeling her orgasm rise deep from her center.

The mental picture had been painted for Stink, he was already spasming like a fish out of water. "Agh! Fuck!" he gasped into the phone.

"Cum for me, baby. Cum inside of my pussy! Yesss!" Melody panted, experiencing the sharp waves of her own orgasm racking through her body.

After the unforgettable experience with Melody on the phone, Stink and Melody began to talk everyday. The time was flying by for Stink. The unit counselor had informed him that he would be going up for parole in four months. He was ecstatic about the news, yet most of the prisoners he shared the information with weren't as enthusiastic.

Apparently parole wasn't something that was so easily given. Most of the guys tried to prepare Stink for his first *hit*, which is what they called parole denial.

However, Stink remained optimistic about his chances and was reinforced by only one other person - E.T.

"Don't worry, you gonna make it Lil bro, fo'real yo."

Chapter 21

Christmastime 1993

Christmas in prison was a totally different time than any other during the year. Tensions were extremely high as prisoners reflected on the joyous season that they *wouldn't* be spending with their families.

This time of year affected Stink just as it did any other prisoner. As Christmas approached, the raw irony of his situation set in: it was his daughter's first Christmas and he wouldn't be able to spend it with her.

Bonni continuously asked him if he wanted the kids to come along and after a quick contemplation he relented.

On Christmas morning, Stink got up and went straight to the weight pile in the blistering cold. He had implemented a vicious workout routine into his daily plan. He'd turned his naturally wide frame into a sculpture that would cause some professional weight trainers to be envious.

Curling the 45lb plates exerted Stink's muscles to their max. With each breath, a cloud of brisk wintry air escaped his mouth, as Nas's 'Illmatic' boomed through his headphones, pushing him harder.

After he felt that he'd completed his workout, he headed back to his unit to prepare for his visit.

"Aww, shit! Why the fuck you gotta pull so hard?" Stink asked grimacing.

"Boy, I thought you were tough," Ronald, aka Rhonda, stated in a girlish voice, lacing French braid after French braid into Stink's head.

This was the only part about getting his hair braided that Stink hated. Having a homosexual doing his hair was a new experience. Stink was definitely *all* man, however, sometimes even the slightest line of communication with *gumps* opened doors that needn't be opened. The sly advances and slick remarks were sometimes downright repulsive.

"Don't worry, baby, this is the last braid," *Rhonda* said, attempting to sound sexy.

Once his hair was finished, Stink headed for the showers, eyeing the clock. He knew he had to be quick; Bonni and the kids would be there any minute.

"Jones! Visit!" The C.O. yelled just as Stink was pulling his shoes on. He quickly tied them up and headed out the door.

As Stink entered the visiting room, butterflies fluttered through his stomach.

Scanning the visiting room intently, he heard, "Wasaan! Wasaan!" Instinctively looking in that direction, he knew it was Tayvia, pretty as ever, running his way.

Stink scooped her up and twirled her tiny body in the air. "Where's mommy?" he asked, planting kisses on her face.

"Over dere," she said, pointing to where Bonni stood, holding Rahsaanique. He quickly walked over with Tayvia in his arms.

As he approached Bonni, he allowed Tayvia to slide down onto her feet and then gave Bonni and Rahsaanique a warm hug and kiss.

Looking into Rahsaanique's pretty eyes for the first time since she was born, emotions welled up inside of him, nearly bringing him to tears.

"Nique-Nique, meet your Da-Da," Bonni said, handing her tiny body over to Stink. Cradling her in his arms, he planted soft kisses all over her tiny face, instantly irritating her.

"She's just hungry," Bonni said, handing him her bottle.

Although he didn't want Tayvia or Rahsaanique to see him in jail, the happiness he felt in his heart was well worth it.

For the entire visit, Stink held Rahsaanique while giving Tayvia his undivided attention.

That is until Bonni blurted, "They caught Cross."

Eyeing her in disbelief, he asked, "When?"

"It must have been earlier this week or last," she surmised, then continued, "I heard some girls in the shop talking about it, but-"

"Visitations are over! All visitors, please exit immediately!" the C.O. yelled.

While Bonni began to pack everything into the baby's bag, Tayvia looked up to Stink, and asked, "Wasaan, when you coming home to live wit me, mommy, and my new sister?"

Stink stood speechless, as the hurt in Tayvia's voice slammed into his chest like a bullet. He looked to Bonni who offered him no help. He then handed Rahsaanique to Bonni, and kneeled so he and Tayvia were face to face.

Taking a deep breath, he began, "Tayvia, I'm coming home with y'all soon, ok, but I've been bad and this is my punishment. You know how mommy puts you on punishment?"

Tayvia nodded her head innocently. "Well this is my punishment. So until my punishment is over, I've got to stay here, ok," he explained, and then gave her one last peck.

He kissed Bonni and Rahsaanique then headed to the exit. Unable to take one final look before they exited, Stink looked straight ahead as the tears flowed freely from his eyes.

Stink threw himself into doing everything humanly possible to increase his chances for parole. He attended NA, AA, victim's impact, anger management and any other program he felt would improve his chances.

After speaking with Lil Man, he'd learned that Cross had in fact been caught in New York. They'd finally gathered enough evidence to charge him for the murders of Kamesha and her boyfriend.

In some strange, twisted way, Stink felt partly responsible for Cross's situation.

Stink still talked to Melody regularly. Lately, she'd been pressuring him to allow her to visit. Initially, Stink was hesitant due to the chances of her and Bonni bumping into each other, however, after being assured that Bonni wasn't planning on making the trip until Valentine's Day, he gave Melody the green light.

The last thing Stink needed was to be caught by Bonni sitting in the visiting room with Melody. Therefore, everyday leading up to the planned visit, he called Bonni trying to get a feel for her schedule.

After being assured then reassured that it would be virtually impossible for Bonni to pop up, Stink relaxed a little.

He went about his visiting day ritual as normal - workout, hair, etc. - except for a quick call to Bonni just to be safe.

"Jones! Jones! Visit!" The C.O. yelled just as Stink was hanging the phone up. He quickly dressed then headed to the visiting room.

When he entered the visiting room, he spotted Melody with ease. Not only was she the most beautiful girl in the room, her hot pink outfit separated her even further from the crowd.

As she stood awaiting Stink's embrace, he noticed that her body had filled out to perfection.

Stink wrapped his arms around her slender waist, and gave her an innocent peck on the cheek. "Damn, Melody, you looking good," he said, eyeing her figure appreciatively in the form-fitting outfit.

"Thank you and you're still looking handsome as ever. Oh and I love the hair," she grinned lustfully.

They sat down and began to discuss what was going on in Melody's life with school, work, etc.

Melody finally got around to asking Stink the question that he most dreaded hearing.

"Rahsaan, why didn't you call me after the night we shared? Truthfully?" she asked sincerely.

"Truthfully?" he asked in a teasing manner.

Melody nodded her head disappointingly.

"A'ight, fo'real, Melody, I ain't call because I just didn't have the time. Then about a week after we were together, I went on the run. That's why," he explained in half truth.

Grinning, Melody soaked it up like a sponge and then asked, "Why is everybody going into that door over there?"

Without turning around, Stink knew that she was referring to the small utility closet that guys were taking their girls into and having sex. "Um, dudes taking their girls in there for a little fun," he explained, giving her a sly grin.

"So, um, are you taking me in there also?" she asked, naively.

Stink inwardly smiled at her innocence then replied, "Nah, Melody. I've got more respect for you than to take you into a closet and have sex with you," he replied sincerely.

Melody smiled, then reached over and pinched Stink's cheek tenderly.

After a few hours, the visitation ended. He stood and gave Melody a peck, promising to call her later and then she exited.

Eyeing her from the rear, Stink shook his head in frustration and then turned to leave.

Just as he was putting his clothes on after being stripped searched, the C.O. handed him a money receipt. Eyeing the small piece of paper suspiciously, it read, *Melody Jordan: 500 dollars and 00 cents.* He immediately assumed that Lil Man had given her the money for him. However, once he talked to Melody later that evening, his assumptions were cleared up.

"So, what was that money for?" he asked.

"Oh, I thought you could use it in there," she replied nonchalantly.

"So you gave me that money?"

"Yeah. Why?"

"Girl, where you get money like that?"

"You'd be surprised, Rahsaan," she replied slyly.

Chapter 22

<u>April 1994</u>

Stink's big day had finally arrived.   He was scheduled to see the parole board the following morning. He had taken advice from just about everyone - how to talk, what to say, and even how to wear his clothes. His mind was filled with all of these thoughts as he tossed and turned in his tiny bunk, contemplating his fate.

Just as he fell off to sleep, the bright lights were turned on. Instead of forcing sleep, Stink dressed, brushed his teeth and hit the weight pile.

As Stink entered the large office, he expected to see a group of older white people assembled to choose his fate. However, he only saw one middle-aged white man, sitting behind a large wooden desk, shuffling through a stack of papers.

Motioning for Stink to have a seat, the man asked, "Uh, Jones? Rahsaan Abdul Jones?"

Stink nodded agreeably then took a seat and patiently waited for him to arrange his paperwork.

"Mr. Jones, I see you've been participating in numerous programs since you've been here. That's good and the board will take that into consideration. However, the question I'd like to ask is why should the parole commission grant you parole?" he abruptly asked.

Stink sat there speechless, unable to conjure up the speech that he had prepared.

Instead of the preplanned speech, he quickly came from the heart. "Sir, I don't feel that the parole board should give me anything," he began, closely judging the man's reaction before continuing. "I feel that I should have to earn parole by programming, staying out of trouble, and accepting responsibility for my actions. I'm extremely apologetic to the victims in this situation and given the chance, I would personally apologize," Stink stated sincerely.

Looking at Stink as if he'd heard the exact same speech before, he extended his hand and said, "Good luck, Mr. Jones. Have a nice day."

Exiting the office, Stink mumbled, "Good luck. Luck is for gamblers and suckers and I'm neither," he concluded, remembering what an old timer had told him.

Things quickly went back to normal for Stink. It had been nearly a month and he still hadn't received a response from the parole board.

Bonni had begun to worry Stink so much that he gave her the phone number to the parole officer, hoping that she would stop pressing him.

After six weeks and still no answer, Stink had nearly given up on any chance of being released.

One evening Stink called home and as soon as the call was accepted, he was met with, "Baby! You got it! You got it!" Bonni yelled hysterically.

"I got what, Bonni?" he asked confused.

"You got parole! You coming home!" she announced.

"How you know that?" he asked with a hint of irritation.

"I called the number you gave me and they put me through to a computer. It said that you were granted parole," she explained.

"So you ain't talk to nobody? A computer told you I got parole?" he asked incredulously.

"Look, Rahsaan, they have a computer system that you must give your name, number and date of fucking birth," she snapped heatedly.

Stink decided not to press any further; he knew she was on the verge of flipping.

For the remainder of their conversation, Bonni's answers were short and curt.

Two days later, Stink was summoned to his counselor's office where Bonni's revelation was confirmed. He was scheduled to be released in less than a month - eight days before his daughter's first birthday.

A few days before Stink was to be released from Haynesville Correctional Center, he and Jamal were walking the track, just kicking it.

"Yo, Stink, I'm-a miss you, my man," Jamal stated sentimentally.

"It won't be long before you hit the streets," Stink replied.

"Yeah, I know, but..." Jamal's words trailed off in deep thought.

After walking half the track in silence, Jamal asked, "Didn't Trina name her son after you, or something?"

"Man, go on with that bullshit," Stink said, playfully punching Jamal in the arm.

Abruptly, Jamal turned to Stink with a serious look etched across his face. "Man, I ain't tell you this before because it was just a lot of talk but since you about to hit the bricks, I gotta tell you."

Stink looked at Jamal, silently urging him to reveal whatever had him so serious.

"Look man, Fat Shawn's brother, Kay-Kay, went home from here about four months before you came. Before he left, he vowed to murder you and Cross for killing his little brother," Jamal revealed earnestly.

Stink eyed Jamal intently, allowing the enormity of what he'd just divulged to sink in.

"Stink, I know you ain't soft or nothing. I'm just telling you 'cause I fuck with you, man."

Stink's mind was recalling all the information that he could remember on Fat Shawn's brother. If he remembered correctly, Kay-Kay was supposed to be a wild nigga known for busting his gun. He never thought that his actions on that night would continue to haunt him as it had.

Before Jamal had revealed that piece of information, Stink's concerns only involved staying free. Now he had the pressures of staying alive to worry about also.

Stink stood inside the sally port waiting for the electronic gate to open. He could already see Bonni in the parking lot, waving frantically.

As the gate swung open, Stink stepped out into freedom. Kneeling down in a prostrating position, he kissed the ground.

Bonni broke out in a full sprint and covering the distance quickly, she jumped in his arms as he stood.

Planting kisses over his lips, she panted, "Baby, I missed you sooo much!"

"I missed you too, baby," he replied, carrying Bonni to her minivan.

As they drove away from the prison, Stink took one final look and said a silent prayer.

"Baby, you've got some clothes in the back. I hope you can fit them," she said, eyeing him hungrily.

Stink reached in the back a grabbed the bag Bonni had brought along. Quickly shedding the prison blues, he aimlessly threw them out of the window. He pulled on the Guess jean shorts, oblivious to the lustful stares Bonni cast in his direction.

Catching her seductively biting her bottom lip, Stink knew he had his work cut out for him later that night.

As Bonni pulled into their driveway, Stink noticed the cars lined in front of their house.

Turning the ignition off, Bonni leaned over and slipped her tongue into Stink's mouth. "Welcome home, Daddy," she announced sexily.

As they walked into the house hand-in-wand like high school sweethearts, they were met with a chorus of 'welcome home' shouts from everyone present.

Looking around the room at all of his closest family members and friends, Stink could only smile.

Holding Rahsaanique in her arms, Stink's mother walked over to him and planted a kiss on his cheek. "Boy, you can't keep going to jail. You're a father now," she said, handing Rahsaanique over to him.

Stink tenderly took Rahsaanique in his arms and made his way around the room, distributing hugs to the men and kisses to the women.

After formally greeting everybody, Stink went into the den where his entire crew was assembled.

Lil Man, Dame, and even PJ sat in the den, talking among themselves.

"If it ain't the man of the hour," Lil Man announced as Stink entered the room carrying Rahsaanique. "How does it feel to be out of the pen?"

"Man, it feels good," Stink replied modestly.

"Yeah, I know it was rough up in that joint," Dame said.

"Man, y'all know lil cuz held it down in there," PJ chimed in boastfully.

"Yeah, I tried to," Stink replied nonchalantly.

"Ay, yo, you know they trying to give your boy twenty-five to life?" Lil Man blurted.

Unable to respond, Stink shook his head in despair.

One by one, they each filled Stink in on the happenings in the streets. Although he wasn't planning on becoming a part of the streets, he still listened intently. He wanted to ask them about Fat Shawn's brother, Kay-Kay. Deciding that Rahsaanique had heard enough 'gangsta' talk for one day, he excused himself and took her back into the living room.

As he entered the living room, his grandmother said, "Speaking of the devil."

"Y'all in here talking about me?" he asked accusingly as he handed Rahsaanique to his grandmother.

"We was just talking about the time when you…" his mother began, detailing an embarrassing story about him as a child.

"Aww man, let me get out of here," he said, quickly making an escape, before his mother's story got to the humiliating part.

He went back into the den and took a seat. Eyeing his boys intently, he asked, "So what's this about Fat Shawn's brother, Kay-Kay, supposedly doing something to me?"

Dame was the first to speak. "Yeah, I heard something like that. But it was some lil niggas downtown just talking."

"I ain't heard shit about the nigga but I know his peoples, so I can just holler at them," Lil Man said.

"Nah, Lil. Don't holla at nobody. Just keep your ears open and if y'all hear something, let me know," Stink advised.

They all nodded in agreement.

"But if the nigga wants it, I'm-a give it to him," Stink said with a hint of malice.

Attempting to lighten the mood, jokingly PJ asked, "So, Stink, since you ain't got no whip, what you gonna be driving? Bonni's minivan?"

"Nah, I'm-a get another Lexus, nigga," Stink replied triumphantly. "I still got a little paper."

At the mentioning of money, Stink automatically thought about the cash he had put away at his grandparent's house.

Once the homecoming began to wind down, Stink accompanied his boys outside as they filed out. Eyeing Lil Man's white Acura Legend coupe, Stink asked, "What year is this?"

"A brand new ninety-four, nigga," Lil Man snapped defensively.

"Oh, my fault, nigga."

"You might need to get one."

"Nah, I'm a Lexus nigga," Stink threw over his shoulder, walking back toward the house.

Just as he got to the porch, his mother and grandparents exited with Tayvia and Rahsaanique.

"Where y'all taking my babies?" Stink asked playfully.

"Oh, we thought maybe you love birds needed some time alone," his grandmother stated suggestively, winking her eye.

Stink and Bonni walked them to the car and exchanged hugs. Before his grandfather got into the car, Stink pulled him to the side.

"What's on your mind, son?" his grandfather asked in a hushed tone.

"Um, I know I told you to give Bonni that money but if you needed to use some too, I-."

"Boy, all your money is exactly where you left it except what you told me to give your lady," his grandfather blurted, cutting him off in mid-sentence.

"Oh, ok, that's cool. I was just asking cause I'm-a need a little of it to get a few things," Stink explained.

"Well, just drop by; it's exactly where you left it," his grandfather said, getting into his car.

Before he was able to close the door, Stink said, "Pa-Pa, thanks."

Stink was going from room to room, reacquainting himself with the house that he hadn't slept in in over a year. His and Bonni's bedroom was exactly as he'd remembered. Tayvia's room had been altered, only by the replacement of her small bed for a much larger one. When Stink walked into the room that was now Rahsaanique's bedroom, he was shocked to see that Bonni had turned the one-time junk room into a small sanctuary.

In the middle of the room, there was a baby bed surrounded by a lily white leather sectional sofa. Scented candles, soft music, along with other therapeutically relaxing paraphernalia, sat on white stands in each corner.

Stink moved in closer, inspecting the shrine-like decorations, when Bonni said, "I spend most of my time in here with the girls."

Slightly startled, Stink spun around to see Bonni leaning against the door in a revealing lingerie set.

"I see you didn't hold back," he said sarcastically rubbing his fingertips along the soft Italian leather sofa.

"Boy, I still got some of that money, so don't even trip," she snapped.

Stink raised his eyebrows in surprise. He eyed her hungrily. Seeing her creamy thighs uncovered caused a rumbling in his groin.

"I'm about to take a shower, care to join me?" she asked seductively, spinning on her heels and sashayed her partially-covered cheeks out of the room.

Stink quickly followed, leaving a trail of clothing along the way.

Just as he entered the bathroom, Bonni stepped her naked figure into the steaming shower, then turned and teasingly signaled him with her forefinger to join.

Disregarding his freshly done cornrows, he stepped into the hot shower, and grabbed Bonni around her waist. Pulling her body to his, he slipped his tongue into her mouth. It had been a long time since he'd held her in his arms, and his manhood showed this by instantly becoming rock hard. As their kissing became more passionate, the harder he became, subsequently poking Bonni in her midsection with his erection.

Breaking their kiss, Bonni stepped back and allowed him to soak in the breath-taking sight of her curvaceous body, glistening under the spray of water.

She gently grabbed his shaft and began to slowly stroke him. "I love you, Rahsaan," she said as her eyes bored into his. Her strokes became more intense as she placed her lips back on his.

Not wanting his first orgasm to literally go down the drain, he turned Bonni around and positioned his head at her opening, and then he slowly eased into her soaking wet pussy.

"Hmmm, Daddy, I missed my dick for sooo long," Bonni moaned, instantly grinding back.

"Damn, Baby, this shit feels sooo fucking good," Stink growled, throwing his head back in ecstasy.

"Baby, it's yours! It's all yours, baby!" she confessed, bracing herself against the shower door. "Oh, baby, I missed you sooo fucking much!" she exclaimed through clenched teeth, as Stink began to pump all of him into her.

"You miss this dick, baby?"

"Yess…yess, Rah…Rahsaan. Ooh shit!" she cried out.

Stink could feel his orgasm bubbling in his loins. "Baby, I'm…about…to cum," he crooned as the orgasm ripped through his body.

"Oh, yess, baby! I…I feel you, baby! Cum in me! Cum in me!" Bonni coaxed, feeling the jets of Stink's semen shooting deep into her core.

Reluctantly, he slipped from Bonni's folds and instantly found it hard to stand.

Bonni quickly washed him from head to toe and allowed him to exit the shower. Drained, he laid across the bed, dripping water.

Seconds later, Bonni stood over him and began to dry him off, raking her nails lightly over his nipples and down to his chiseled abdomen, causing him to shiver.

Once she came face to face with his deflated member, she began to lick the underside as if it was a lollipop.

Stroking him gently, she began to talk to his dick, "I see you miss momma, hmm mmm, momma misses you too."

Slowly, she took him into her warm mouth, causing him to arch his back in delight.

Bonni took him so deep into her mouth, the head of his dick nearly caused her to convulse, yet, she continued to suck and stroke his jewels simultaneously.

Stink placed his hand on the back of her head, urging her on. He could feel his second orgasm seconds away as he panted, "Baby…I'm-a…bout to…cum!" he warned.

Bonni responded by sucking even harder, causing slurping sounds to escape her mouth. Once she felt his hips buck, she prepared herself as the thick load of cum flooded her mouth. Instantly, Bonni jumped up and ran into the bathroom.

Stink lay there in a state of paralysis, listening to the sounds of her running water and Bonni brushing her teeth.

She walked back into the bedroom and stood over Stink once again. With her hands on her hips, she said, "I may suck but I refuse to swallow."

Stink reached out to her and cradled her in his arms. Finally in his own house, in his own bed, he drifted off to sleep.

Chapter 23

<u>July 1994</u>

Cruising down Jefferson Avenue in his brand new Lexus GS 300, Stink laid back in the driver's seat, nodding his head to the loud bass coming from the two 10-inch woofers.

The avenue was packed as the temperatures reached up into the nineties. The shiny new Lexus, sitting on 20-inch Anteras, garnered everyone's attention.

Although Stink wasn't involved in hustling, he was shining like he was. Once the light turned green, he turned the volume up a few decibels and allowed the crowd assembled on 18th Street to hear every word of the Biggie Smalls hit that he was playing.

As he pulled into the convenience store beside Lil Man's Acura coupe, he looked around for his man. Unable to pinpoint him in the sea of people, he patiently waited. Noticing a few hungry glares being cast in his direction, Stink prepared to leave until he saw Lil Man hop out of a parked car and make his way over to him.

Lil Man jumped into the passenger seat and began meddling with buttons on the console. "Yo, Stink, this joint hot!"

"Man, stop fucking with shit!" he said, fanning Lil Man's hand away from the console. "I see you still out here slangin' all on the ave," Stink commented.

"Yeah. Baby gotta eat, nigga," Lil Man quipped.

"I feel you dawg, but be careful."

"Oh, yeah, I got a message for you. As a matter of fact, I got two messages for you. The first is from your boy. He called my mom's house the other day, trying to get your number. I told him I needed to holla at you first. You know he was heated," Lil Man stated in an animated tone and then continued, "The second is from Melody. Yo man, she fucking buggin' the shit out of me. Please call that girl, man."

"A'ight, but give Cross my number," Stink advised.

"Ok. But yo, please get at shorty; she starting to get worrisome and shit!" Lil Man said then hopped out of the car, slamming the door a little too hard for Stink's taste.

Stink pulled out of the parking lot and turned the volume back up on his stereo. Riding through downtown 'Bad News,' he gave every block a glimpse of his new whip.

As he pulled up to the stoplight at 35th and Marshall Avenue, Stink bobbed his head and eyed the packs of niggas on each corner. There was a different type of vibe that he received sitting at the light. Some envious and some wishful, however, one face in the crowd grilled Stink menacingly. Upon further scrutiny, he knew why. Fat Shawn's brother, Kay-Kay, stood in the middle of the crowd with a murderous glare aimed toward Stink.

Instinctively, Stink reached for his gun, yet he quickly remembered that he didn't have a gun on him.

As he and Kay-Kay locked eyes in a silent battle, he slowly pulled away from the light. Taking one final look at his newfound nemesis, he witnessed Kay-Kay aim his forefinger at him as if it was a gun, solidifying their beef.

The lure of selling drugs was strong as Stink witnessed his stacks dwindle. The money from the salon barely covered its expenses and this caused Stink to seriously contemplate taking a trip to see José.

The constant ringing of his cell phone snapped him out of his daze. "Hello," he answered in an irritated tone.

"Um, yess, is this Stink?" a girl asked with a thick New York accent.

"Yeah, this is him. Who is this?" he asked suspiciously.

"I'm calling for Cross."

"A'ight, put him on the phone," he blurted, forgetting that there was no way to just put him on the phone.

"Uh, I'm going to call you back and he'll be on the phone then. I just wanted to make sure you were going to be available," she explained.

"Yeah, just call me," he said, and then hung up.

Thirty minutes later, his cell phone rang again. "Hello," he answered.

"Yo, what up, B?" Cross asked in an excited tone.

"Ain't shit. Wazup with you, man?" Stink asked, naturally happy to hear from his man.

"Yo, Stink, I love you, nigga," Cross blurted sincerely.

"Yeah, I love you too, nigga. But what's up with you, man?" he repeated.

Reluctantly, Cross filled Stink in on everything that was going on in his case. Although he'd been in jail for nearly a year, they still hadn't brought him to trial. The same detectives that had harassed Stink had made the trip to New York, attempting to fool Cross into thinking that Stink was going to rat him out. Cross instantly dismissed their attempt and sent them back to Virginia frustrated.

Changing subjects, Cross asked, "You been up top, yet?"

"Nah, man. I've just been chillin'."

"Come on, B! I know I taught you better than that!" Cross scolded. "Get that muthafuckin paper, B!" he advised emphatically.

Stink immediately felt that the conversation was headed in the wrong direction. "Nah, I'm just chillin', man," he replied dryly.

"You need to go holla at José. You know he'll look out for you," Cross advised, oblivious that he was talking on the jail phone.

"Nah, I'm good. But I'm about to go handle something so hit me back later, a'ight," Stink said, feeling it was time to end Cross's reckless conversation.

"A'ight, B, I'm-a get at you later. Peace," Cross said, his voice laced with disappointment.

After they hung up, Stink replayed the entire conversation over in his head. *Maybe I should go holla at José*, he reasoned. Stink felt that the least he could do would be to hook up Lil Man with José.

Stink quickly got Rahsaanique prepared to leave, so that he could make his monthly appointment with his parole officer. He'd almost forgotten about the monthly visit until he noticed that it was the 5th of the month.

"Damn!" Stink barked, walking out of the door with Rahsaanique in his arms. Not only was he rushing, he'd also have to drive straight through police headquarters in his thirty-five- thousand-dollar car, with his fourteen-month-old daughter riding without a car seat. The day was starting out horribly.

Sitting in the waiting room of the probation and parole office, Stink bounced Rahsaanique on his knee playfully.

"Jones! Please come with me," his probation officer announced, leading the way to his office.

"Have a seat, Mr. Jones. I see you're babysitting today," the probation officer stated jokingly, once they reached his small office.

"Yeah. Her mother had to work, so…"

"Well, it does show that you're a family man," he commented.

After covering the basics, Stink was allowed to exit. On his way out of the door, he mistakenly bumped into somebody, while looking down at Rahsaanique.

"Oh, excuse me," he apologized without looking up.

Once he looked up and saw who he'd bumped into, his breathing instantly became labored. As he and his newfound enemy's eyes locked in a silent battle, Stink's heart pounded in his chest.

Kay-Kay's eyes narrowed into evil slits as he spat, "You better watch yourself, nigga, 'cause I'm-a see you for what y'all did to my brother!" Then walked off.

Stink quickly made it to his car as the rage inside of him continued to rise. He knew there was no way he could allow Kay-Kay to get away with threatening him in front of Rahsaanique. He had to die.

Stink promptly dropped Rahsaanique off at Bonni's mother's house and then called Lil Man.

"Who dis?" Lil Man answered.

"Yo, Lil! I need to holla at you!" Stink exclaimed in a worried tone.

"Holla, nigga!"

"Not over the phone! Meet me somewhere!"

"Oh, a'ight. Meet me at my spot out Hampton in twenty minutes," he responded, feeling Stink's urgency.

"A'ight," Stink said, hanging up. He began to cruise the city aimlessly, trying to regain control of his anger.

Stink ended up sitting in front of Lil Man's condo before he arrived. Hearing the bass from Lil Man's jeep, Stink hopped out and approached him before he could get out. "Lil, that nigga Kay-Kay threatened me in front of my fucking daughter, man. That nigga is dead!" Stink vowed.

"Yo! Calm down, man! I feel you on what you're saying, but you gots to calm the fuck down or you gonna do some dumb shit!"

"Yeah, yeah, you right but I gotta handle my business, dawg," Stink said.

"Whatever you do, man, I'm with you."

"I gotta be smooth, man. I ain't going back to prison for no dumb-ass nigga."

"Yeah, you gotta be smart about it," Lil Man advised.

They stood on the sidewalk in front of Lil Man's condo and discussed Stink's plight, until he abruptly revealed, "I've been thinking about making a move, man."

Lil Man eyed Stink surprisingly. He knew that the game would eventually lure him back but not that soon.

"Yeah, we would definitely blow if you could get them numbers you use to get," Lil Man replied, attempting to hide his excitement.

"Man, if I don't go I'm-a at least introduce you to José."

Lil Man's eyes lit up at the mentioning of being plugged in with one of the largest cocaine distributors o the eastern seaboard. "Just let me know when you're ready man and I'm down."

"A'ight, I'm-a let you know but first I gotta handle this problem," Stink said.

"Look, man, why don't you just chill? Maybe go over to Norfolk and holla at Melody. Get your mind right, then…," Lil Man stated, without saying the obvious.

"Yeah, I just might do that," Stink said, walking toward his car. As he pulled off, he dialed Melody's number for the first time since he'd been home.

"Hello," she answered in her naturally sexy voice.

"May I speak to Melody?"

"This is she. Who's calling?"

"Oh, yeah. Let me find out you got niggas crawling behind you," Stink joked.

"I know this ain't...Rahsaan!" she screamed, then quickly changed her tone and asked, "Why haven't you called me?"

"I've been trying to adjust back into society," he replied coolly.

"Mmm hmm, I bet," she said sarcastically, then asked, "So when am I going to see you?"

"Shit, right now," Stink replied, already driving through the tunnel headed to Norfolk.

As Stink pulled up to the modest two-story house, he thought that maybe Melody had given him the wrong address. He pulled his phone out and dialed her number.

"Hello," she quickly answered.

"Yo, Melody. I'm outside," he announced.

"Oh, ok. Come on inside then."

Stink hopped out of his Lexus and walked up the driveway. Suspiciously, he glared at the drop top 325i BMW and the Mitsubishi Montero that were parked in the driveway.

Just as he stepped onto the porch, the door swung open and Melody ran out and jumped into his arms.

"Rahsaan! Why'd you do me like that?" she asked whining and hugging him tightly.

Allowing her to slide to her feet, Stink explained, "I'm sorry, Melody. But I've just been trying to settle in."

Leading him into the house, she turned to face him. "Rahsaan, please promise me you won't just leave me in the dark like that again?"

Stink didn't want to intentionally lie, therefore he contemplated her request. "I promise," he finally replied, halfheartedly.

Melody leaned in and planted a sensuous kiss on his lips.

Stink gripped her voluptuous ass and allowed her tongue to lead the way.

Once the kiss subsided, Stink looked around the room appreciatively, eyeing the immaculately decorated house. The cream-colored, leather sectional sofa was wrapped nearly around the entire room, leaving just enough space for the exceptionally large big screen and matching cream-colored marble bar.

"You like?" Melody asked child-like, leading him around the first floor of the house.

"Yeah. This shit is a'ight," he replied casually, "But, um, whose is it?" he asked suspiciously.

"Me and Chelle are roommates," she revealed, leading him up the stairs by his hand. As she opened the door to her bedroom, the elaborately decorated room instantly impressed Stink. The room's soft hues of lavender immediately set the mood as she closed the door behind them and slid her arms around Stink's waist.

Swaying her body as if there was soft music playing, she looked deep into his eyes. Slowly, she moved her glossed lips toward his, slipping her tongue into his mouth.

Locked in the passionate kiss, Stink backed her up to the bed and gently laid on top of her. Groping her firm body, he pulled her flimsy shorts down around her thighs.

Standing, he pulled his shirt over his head and dropped his pants in one motion.

Melody followed suit and pulled her tank top over her head, revealing her perky breasts. She stared up to Stink with a vulnerable look of lust etched across her face.

Stink stood in awe, analyzing Melody's flawless body; she was like a goddess.

Melody leaned up and ran her hands up and down Stink's rippled chest and stomach. "Rahsaan, your body is so beautiful," she said, kneading the knots in his abs.

He pushed Melody back onto the bed and laid between her thighs. Instantly, he could feel the heat from her vagina on the tip of his dick. Planting soft kisses on her forehead, he slowly made his way down to her perfect mouth-sized titties.

As he gingerly suckled each nipple, he could feel Melody's body respond. She gripped the back of Stink's head, urging him on.

"Ahhh! Rahsaan...yes...suck...mmm!" she hissed.

Stink nibbled on each nipple, causing them to stand erect. Moving down her stomach, he left a hot trail that stopped at the soft petals of her womanhood. Stink ran his tongue across her lips, sampling her juices.

"Ooh...Rahsaan...please!" she begged as his tongue made contact with her lips.

He ran his tongue across her exposed clitoris, causing her to arch her back in anticipation. Seeing how sensitive she was, Stink latched on to her clitoris, sucking it vigorously.

Once Melody's body began to jerk uncontrollably, he placed two fingers at her entrance, and slowly inserted them into her slick tunnel.

"Oh my...God! Rah...saan, please...stop!" Melody gasped passionately.

Stink continued to pump his fingers into her, while he had her clitoris wrapped in his tongue. His probing fingers had located the spongy flesh of her G-spot as he manipulated her body.

"Rah...saan, I'm...cum...ming!" she announced, gripping his head as her body contorted under the spasms of ecstasy.

Her body jerked with every tender lick Stink placed on her clitoris.

Once her body recovered from the intense orgasm, Stink repositioned himself between her thighs, with his defiantly hard manhood aimed directly at her quivering pussy.

Stink rubbed his head between her glistening lips teasingly, then pushed himself deep inside of her. He instantly felt her muscles contract around his dick.

"Rahsaan…you feel…so good…inside of me!"

Savoring each stroke, Stink took his time and made love to Melody.

She began to gyrate her hips rhythmically, then said, "Rahsaan…please…don't move."

Stink froze, allowing Melody to do her thing. He could feel something foreign inside of her pussy that she was manipulating with her motions.

After several minutes of this, Melody's insides exploded as her pussy literally spit juices from her.

Stink watched in shock as Melody's body twisted and turned, while her mouth gulped for air. Instinctively, he stopped and asked, "You alright, Melody?"

She managed to nod her head.

Stink turned her over onto her stomach and entered her from the rear, easing himself into her. Once he was coated with her juices, he gripped her ass cheeks firmly and drove his entire length into her.

"Oh, yes, Rahsaan! Fuck me! Yess!" she screamed, urging him on.

He pounded Melody's pussy with long forceful strokes, eyeing the creamy juices that oozed down her thighs.

"Ooh, yess! Work your pussy, daddy!" she yelled, looking back to Stink with a crazed look on her face.

Stink couldn't take the tightness of her pussy any longer, as his body jerked as if he was in cardiac arrest.

"Yess! Cum in me, baby! Cum in my pussy!" Melody responded, feeling his seed flood her center.

"Rahsaan, this pussy is yours, baby. It's yours," she announced earnestly.

Still inside of her, Stink collapsed on her back breathlessly.

After showering, Melody and Stink laid cuddled in her king-size bed, enjoying pillow talk. He and Melody talked about everything, from his contempt for Kay-Kay, to his relationship with Bonni. Melody soaked up everything he said, not once interrupting. When she did respond, Stink was shocked.

"Rahsaan, I know we haven't been together that long but ever since I saw you, I knew I loved you. I mean when I'm with you, I feel special...like a queen," she said with sincere eyes. Turning over to straddle him, she said, "Rahsaan, I love you. And for you, I would do anything. *Anything*," she repeated.

Stink was speechless. He pulled her into his arms lovingly and planted a sweet kiss on her forehead.

Chapter 24

September 1994

Stink hadn't been to New York in nearly two years and things had definitely changed. Before he went to prison, José had been giving him kilos of cocaine for a little over fourteen thousand. Now, he was forced to get at least twenty thousand a kilo. Although prices had gone up everywhere, the profit was the same. With nearly $400,000, Stink made the trip alone.

José was ecstatic to see Stink, treating him like family as soon as he arrived in New York. Instead of giving Stink fifteen kilos, José gave him an even twenty, allowing him to owe the remainder.

With the whip game that Stink had mastered, he could easily turn the twenty kilos of cocaine into thirty kilos of crack.

After making the transaction, Stink quickly escaped New York in the same limousine he'd vowed never to ride in again.

Bonni's birthday was less than a week away. Stink was planning to throw her a party that she'd never forget. He'd already rented the hottest nightclub in the tidewater area, Harlem Nights, and was working on getting somebody to perform.

Since Stink had been home, he had talked to Yardi a few times. Before Stink had made his move to New York, Yardi desperately tried to put Stink down with his crew.

Yardi was running nearly the entire Norfolk and Portsmouth. Though Stink had politely turned him down, they remained cool.

Yardi had often proclaimed to Stink that he was the most known and feared 'bredren' to walk the streets of Brooklyn. Just to see how much notoriety he actually had, Stink called him up.

"Whappen, bredren?" Yardi answered in his deep raspy Caribbean accent.

"Yo, wazup, Yardi? I need a favor, man."

"Speak pon'it, bredren."

"I need you to get a rapper to perform at my girl's party. You know, like Method Man or Biggie Smalls or some shit," Stink explained.

"Yuh, mon, mi can link up wit di mon Biggie," he replied cockily.

"Ok, nigga! Hit me back and let me know wazup," Stink said excitedly.

"A'ight, mi ah work pon dat an'a link yuh back, bredren. Easy now," Yardi said, then hung up.

After a few phone calls and the exchange of five grand, Biggie Smalls was set to perform at Bonni's party.

As Stink kept one eye on the video game that played on the sixty-inch television and the other on a busy Rahsaanique, his cell phone rang. Quickly snatching it up before Rahsaanique could get to it, Stink pushed talk. "Hello."

"What up, god?" Cross asked hyped up.

"Just chillin'. Babysitting."

"That's cool. Oh yeah, good looking on that paper, B" Cross said, confirming that he'd received the money Stink had sent.

"No problem. You's my nigga."

"So when you coming back up top?" Cross asked.

"Um...I don't know. Why?" Stink asked suspiciously.

Immediately sensing Stink's hesitancy to answer his question, Cross tried to clear up Stink's assumptions. "See, there you go with that bullshit. I ain't even talking crazy, I'm on some other shit," he explained, knowing that Stink had warned him before about his reckless conversations, then continued, "Yo, B, I got this crazy fly Dominican bitch uptown. She thinks I'm-a sucker or something," he explained.

"A bitch, huh?" Stink asked in a voice laced with trepidation.

"Yeah, a bitch. I already told her about my lil bro down south. So as soon as she sees you, she gonna be fucked up," Cross said laughing.

"What 'chu mean, 'fucked up'?"

"Nigga, you's a pretty boy! Plus, shorty got something for you," he slyly threw in.

"I won't even ask what she could possibly have for me," Stink replied.

"You's a funny boy, forreal," Cross said laughing.

They talked for a while longer before Stink hung up but not before he jotted down the number of the New York girl.

Stink talked Lil Man into waiting until after Bonni's party before they returned to New York. Stink had promised Lil Man that after this trip, it was all his; he'd already dropped Lil Man's name to José.

Lil Man and Dame had literally run through the twenty kilos, doubling their money.

After spending nearly ten thousand dollars to make this evening come true, Stink wanted things to be perfect. He constantly made calls to the club, Yardi and to Lil Man.

Bonni was still unaware that she was having the most anticipated party of the year.

She casually slid the Coogi dress over her curvaceous frame as Stink eyed her hungrily.

He knew that his lady would be the center attraction in more ways than one. Stink peeled his eyes from Bonni and began to dress. He pulled on the short-sleeved Coogi sweater that closely resembled the color pattern as Bonni's. He then slipped on his jewelry. The Rolex that Cross had given him years before had been redesigned with so many diamonds it was hard to tell the time on it. He still had his eagle medallion which sparkled flawlessly from his neck.

Bonni's bright red gator boots complemented her outfit perfectly while the rock that Stink had given her twinkled with every move she made.

Stink pulled his blue, low cut ostrich shoes from the box, and looked to Bonni. "Baby, you ready to roll?" he asked.

"Yeah, but where are we going so dressed up?" she inquired.

"You'll see. Let's go," he replied, leading her out the door.

As Stink pulled in front of the Harlem Nights night club, party goers could be seen as far as the eye could see.

Bonni eyed the crowd, then looked over at Stink. "Boo, there's no way we can get in there. Look at all of those people."

Stink grabbed the door handle and said, "Watch." He jumped out of the car and walked around to Bonni's side. "Come on, baby. Tonight is all about you," he announced, gracefully helping Bonni from the car.

Gripping her tightly around the waist, Stink led her straight to the entrance of the club. Stink winked at the doorman who quickly cleared the way for them to enter.

As they made their way through the corridor into the club, the crowd roared, "HAPPY BIRTHDAY!"

Bonni froze in shock, with her hands glued to her face, as the DJ dropped an old birthday tune. All of Bonni's friends and employees quickly rushed over to her, prying her away from Stink. They ushered her to the table set up for her. Before she got out of earshot, she turned and mouthed, 'I love you.'

Stink casually strolled over to where Lil Man, PJ, Dame and a few others stood talking.

"What up, Stink?" Lil Man said, holding his hand high in preparation to give Stink some dap.

"Ain't shit, Lil. Wazup, P? Wazup, Dame?"

Giving Stink a brotherly hug, PJ looked Stink up and down, and then said, "I see y'all doing the Coogi thang."

"And look at the 'Rolly' wit all that ice. My nigga doing it!" Lil Man added emphatically.

Stink smiled, and grabbed a bottle of Dom from the table. Taking his place beside Bonni at their table, he tapped two champagne flutes together, garnering everyone's attention.

"I'd like to propose a toast," he announced, mimicking a scene from an old gangster movie.

Everyone quickly followed suit and grabbed their champagne glasses, as Stink continued, "To the love of my life, the mother of my children, my wife. Happy Birthday, Bonni!" Stink held his glass high, with his eyes locked on Bonni. Just as he turned his glass up, he witnessed a tear roll down her cheek.

Lil Man had pulled out a freshly rolled blunt and lit it up. Stink, Lil Man, Dame and PJ passed the cigar amongst themselves until the weed took its hypnotic affect.

As the women held their own conversation and the fellas laughed and joked while sipping their champagne, the DJ abruptly stopped the music.

"Hold up! Hold up! We gotta special guest in the house tonight, Reppin' B.K. to the fullest! Please allow me to introduce…Biggie Smalls!"

The gigantic rapper sauntered onto the stage just as the DJ dropped the Isley Brothers hit *Between the Sheets*.

I love it when they call me Big Poppa!Tthrow yo hands in the air if you's a true player…

The crowd went crazy, immediately rushing the stage.

"Come on, baby," Stink said, leading Bonni toward the dance floor. The burly bouncer cleared the way as they walked onto the dance floor and the crowd parted in front of them like the Red Sea.

He and Bonni danced through a couple of the rapper's hits until sweat trickled down their foreheads. The bouncer promptly reappeared to let he and Bonni through the crowd.

As they exited the dance floor, Stink heard someone yell, "Yed mon! Bo! Bo! Bo! Bo! Bo!"

He glanced in the direction and witnessed Yardi and his entire crew throwing their hands up gesturing gun shots. Stink smiled and threw his hand up. As he quickly scanned the area, Stink saw something that nearly knocked the wind out of him.

Dressed in a revealing black mini, Melody stood giggling as some dude put his mack down on her.

Stink eyed the pair, shooting daggers in their direction, until Bonni asked, "What's wrong, baby? Why you looking like that?"

"Huh? Oh, nothing," Stink replied witnessing Melody's eyes lock with his. Stink shot her one last menacing glare, then turned his head.

"Who was that bitch, Rahsaan?" Bonni snapped accusingly.

"Who? What girl?" he asked confused.

Rolling her eyes animatedly, she said, "Mmm, hmmm."

"Girl, if I asked you about every nigga in here looking at you, we'd be here til tomorrow," he said smiling.

The party turned out to be a success. The only downside was Stink nearly being busted grilling Melody. Just as Stink had figured, Melody blew his pager and cell phone up. Nonetheless, he ignored every call. The more he thought about it, the more he softened up. Although he was there with his woman, in some strange twisted way, he looked at Melody like she was his also.

After he got himself together from all the drinking the night before, he went to the carwash.

As Stink stood in front of the carwash watching as the attendant laced his 20-inch Pirellis with black magic, his cell phone rang.

Snatching the phone from his waist, he answered, "Yo, what up?"

"Rahsaan, please don't hang up!" Melody blurted. "Last night it wasn't what you thought, I swear!" she stated in a pleading voice.

"Last night? Oh, that wasn't nothing," he replied nonchalantly.

"The way you looked at me Rahsaan, I knew you were pissed. Please don't be mad at me! Please, I'll do anything!" she begged.

"Come on Melody, it was nothing. Forreal," Stink said, enjoying the way Melody was breaking.

"See, Rahsaan, you're acting as if you're not mad, but I know…you're not going to be with me anymore," she stated in a voice dripping with pain.

"Nah, Melody, it ain't like that. I just-" Stink replied, stopping in mid-sentence, suppressing his true feelings.

"Rahsaan, that guy was trying to talk to me all night, and I swear I didn't do ANYTHING!" she disclosed, openly crying.

"Look, Melody, I'm on my way over there, a'ight," Stink said, pushing end on his cell phone.

Twenty minutes later, Stink pulled into Melody's driveway and hopped out. As he walked up onto the porch, the door slowly crept open. Melody stood behind the door inviting him in.

Stink stepped in and looked Melody up and down with a mixture of pity and anger. Her eyes were bloodshot red, apparently from crying all night. Shyly, she stood there with his shirt on and a pair of thongs. As she looked up at him with tears of despair welling up in her eyes, Stink's heart melted.

Taking her into his arms, Melody wrapped herself around him and began to sob uncontrollably.

"What's wrong, Melody?" he asked tenderly.

"I don't...wanna...lose you...Rahsaan," she said through sniffles, then continued, "The way you...looked at...me..." Unable to finish she cried hysterically.

"Don't worry, you ain't gonna lose me," he assured, tilting her head up to meet his gaze. He then began to plant soft kisses over her tear-stained face, until he reached her lips.

Embraced in the passionate kiss, they stumbled up the stairs to her bedroom. Backing her onto the bed, he stood over her eyeing her silky thighs hungrily.

Looking into Stink's eyes lustfully, Melody began to quickly undo his pants. As his pants dropped to his ankles, she began to sensuously run her tongue around his navel. As she moved downward, she roughly ran her tongue through his pubic hairs, causing a sensation that he'd never experienced. Just when he thought the chills from the strange sensation had subsided, he felt Melody's warm mouth engulf him.

"Oh! Shit...Mel...Melody! Damn!" Stink hissed, holding on to Melody's shoulder as his knees gave way.

Taking his entire length into her mouth, Stink felt as if Melody had taken over him. And that was exactly what was about to happen, for in no time flat, he gasped, "Melody...I'm...cuummming," as his seed spurted down her throat.

Lying in Melody's bed dazed from the earth shattering sex, Stink's cell phone rang, snapping him from his stupor.

"Hel-lo," he answered.

"What up?" Lil Man asked, full of energy.

"Nuf..fin."

"Nigga! Get up! You said after the party you'd be ready, so nigga, let's rock!" Lil Man yelled.

"What time is it?"

"Showtime, nigga! Let's go!"

"Give me thirty minutes and I'm-a call you back," Stink said, pulling himself up.

"Thirty minutes, nigga! Peace!"

Stink hung up and made his way to the shower.

Five hours later after a slight change of plans, Stink and Melody were passing through Maryland with a little over a half of a million dollars in the rental car.

Lil Man was upset about the change of plans and his not being able to meet José but he was happy that Stink was making the trip.

Stink laid back and allowed Melody to drive the entire way. She was more than happy just to be in Stink's presence.

Melody pulled into the Holiday Inn in Fort Lee, New Jersey, just across the bridge from New York.

After they checked into their room and secured the money, they hit the city.

"Where do I get off?" Melody asked, just as they crossed the George Washington Bridge.

"Take the Westside Highway downstate," Stink advised with the expertise of a native New Yorker.

Melody veered onto the exit, then asked in astonishment, "You really know your way around here, huh?"

"Yeah. I've been coming up here for a while," he revealed nonchalantly.

"So, where are we going?"

"You'll see."

As they approached the exit for 125th Street, Stink said, "We're getting off on the next exit, so get over."

She followed his instructions precisely, exiting on 125th Street, in the heart of Harlem.

As they drove down 125th, Melody was in awe at how lively the city was. Even though it was nearly midnight, the city still bustled as if it was midday.

As they passed the Apollo Theater, Melody eyed the monumental building in shock, nearly side-swiping a parked car.

"Oh, my God! It's really the Apollo," she said amazed.

"Yeah. It's really the Apollo. Now watch where you're going before you kill somebody," Stink snapped, inwardly smiling.

After finding a parking spot, they walked down 125th Street hand–in-hand, taking in the scenes of the city.

Just as Stink and Melody exited Saks Fifth Avenue, his cell phone rang.

"Hello," he answered.

"Rahsaan, will you be home tonight?" Bonni asked in a voice dripping with attitude.

"Um…I'm out of town right now, so…" he replied, stuffing bags into the trunk.

"What could you possibly be handling out of town, Rahsaan?" she snapped.

"Look, Bonni, if I tell you I'm out of town handling shit, then don't fucking question me!" Stink stated firmly.

"Nah! Your ass is out there in them streets with that same bullshit and I ain't going for it!" she barked angrily. "You've got a choice. Me and your child, or the streets! Now you make the call!" she threatened, slamming the phone down in his ear.

Instantly, he began to call her back but he had business to handle and there was no time for drama.

That's how niggas get knocked, he thought as he hopped into the driver's seat and pulled off.

Melody gave him an understanding look and rubbed his shoulders in an attempt to soothe him.

Later that afternoon, Stink met José at an apartment in Teaneck, New Jersey.

After the drugs and money had been exchanged, José said, "Oye, the next time I promise you better prices."

"José, as I said before, I want to introduce you to my friend. Hopefully you will allow him to come alone," Stink explained, setting the stage for Lil Man to meet José. Unbeknownst to José, Stink planned to exit the game, once and for all.

"Oye, any friend of yours, is a friend of mine."

Stink followed Melody into the house, carrying a half a million dollars worth of cocaine.

Melody immediately went into Chelle's room showing all of the clothes she'd gotten in New York.

Stink went into the bedroom and called Lil Man.

As Stink and Lil Man rode through the tunnel, Lil Man looked over to Stink, and casually said, "I found out your boy lives in Harbor Homes with some bitch."

Confused, Stink asked, "What?"

"Kay-Kay. He lives in Harbor Homes," he repeated.

"How you find out?"

"I've got my ways, nigga," he replied, smugly.

During the remainder of the drive, Lil Man filled him in on the information he'd gathered on Kay-Kay.

"So, don't nobody know this but me and you?" Stink asked incredulously.

"Nah. Nobody," he replied calmly.

"Nobody?" Stink repeated more firmly.

Lil Man looked to him with a reassuring look, then replied, "Nobody."

The entire time Stink had been laboriously slaving over the hot stove, his mind had been consumed with how he was going to eliminate his enemy and get away with it.

"So, how many more you gonna cook up?" Lil Man asked.

"Huh?" Stink asked, still processing a way to kill.

"I said, how many more…you…gonna…cook?" he repeated sarcastically.

"Oh. I'll do like five more. The rest I'll do later."

Stink and Lil Man strolled out of Lil Man's modest home, carrying enough freshly cooked crack to get them both life sentences.

As Stink walked toward Lil Man's jeep, he shook his head in disbelief, noticing all the luxury cars and trucks that sat in the driveway. Lil Man was screaming to anyone who cared to listen: "I'm-a drug dealer!"

As Stink noticed the partially covered motorcycle also sitting in the driveway, a bright light went off in his head.

"Come on, Stink. Let's bounce," Lil Man said getting into his jeep.

Once Lil Man pulled away, Stink's mind intently formulated his plan. Now, all he had to do was talk Lil Man out of his motorcycle.

"Yo, I'm-a holla at you tomorrow," Lil Man said just before Stink closed the door.

Dreading what was about to go down, Stink replied, "One." Then turned and walked up his driveway.

Stink eased into the house where everything was quiet besides the faint sounds of the upstairs' television.

He tip-toed up the stairs and went into the bedroom where Tayvia, Rahsaanique and Bonni lay sound asleep. Stink treaded, feather-like, over to the bed and scooped Rahsaanique up. Careful not to wake her, he whisked her off to her room. Returning, he did the same with Tayvia.

Once he'd put Tayvia and Rahsaanique into their respective rooms, he quietly undressed and eased into bed, snuggling up behind Bonni.

Apparently faking her deep slumber, she hissed, "Rahsaan, don't fucking touch me!"

"Come on Bonni. Why you acting like this?" he asked in a whining tone.

"Rahsaan, wherever you were last night...go back!" she said angrily.

"I told you, I was handling some business out of town."

"Business my ass!" she retorted heatedly, jumping from the bed.

Stink laid there in frustration until Bonni emerged from the bathroom and stood defiantly at the foot of the bed.

"Rahsaan, I am not going to be a part of your games! And I am serious!" she stated in a matter of fact tone. "If them nosy-ass bitches that come in that shop know your business, then what makes you think the police don't know?" She questioned angrily.

Stink began to protest, but was unable to find the correct words to extract a defense.

"You keep doing what you're doing, and you're going back to jail. And, Rahsaan, I'm not going to be there," she confessed earnestly, storming from the room in tears.

Stink wanted to run behind her and say all the right words, however, his mind shifted to a more pressing issue - murder.

Stink awoke early the next morning and put his plan into action. Grabbing the phone and punching numbers, he figured that the first order of business was to call Lil Man.

"Hell-o," Lil Man answered sleepily.

"Wazup, nigga?" Stink said full of energy.

"I'm glad you called. I need you to come on and get the rest of them thangs cooked up. It seems like we the only mazurkas that got work. Niggas is going crazy!" Lil Man explained.

"A'ight, I'm on my way but later, you gotta show me that spot ole boy be at," Stink said slyly, referring to Kay-Kay's whereabouts.

"Soon as you get them birds ready," Lil Man replied, then hung up.

"Yo! Niggas is paying thirty grand for a bird of crack!" Lil Man said excitedly, hovering over Stink's shoulder. "I'm telling you, if you can turn one to two, we gonna be some rich niggas!"

"Oh, I can do it," Stink snapped assuredly. "The question is, can you sell 'em?" he quipped in a challenging manner.

"Nigga, I can sell 'em! Don't even worry about that!" Lil Man replied emphatically.

Stink went to work preparing the cocaine to be cooked into crack. He'd gotten better and better at manipulating the measurements so the 1:2 ratio wouldn't be a problem.

Stink leaned back in the passenger seat of Lil Man's Benz as they rode past the project building where Kay-Kay was supposedly living. After Lil Man pointed the exact apartment out, they hopped on the interstate, headed back to Lil Man's house.

"So what you gonna do, man?" Lil Man inquired.

"I don't know yet," Stink lied. He'd already calculated his plan, all that was missing was the keys to the motorcycle in Lil Man's driveway.

As they pulled up to Lil Man's house, Stink asked, "What you doing with that bike?"

"Shit, nigga, I ride it, that's what," Lil Man retorted.

"I was just asking, damn! I ain't never seen you ride," Stink replied, in a cunning fashion, drawing Lil Man into his trap.

"Just cause you ain't seen me ride, don't mean I can't," Lil Man stated defensively. I bet I out ride you!" he challenged.

Lil Man had fallen right into Stink's snare. "Oh yeah, so what you willing to bet?" Stink challenged.

"Whatever, nigga!"

"I'll tell you what," Stink began coolly, "If you can ride better than me, I'll give you five gees. If I ride better than you, give me the keys to the bike." He knew Lil Man wouldn't back down, however, Lil Man had basically given

Stink the motorcycle. Growing up in North Carolina, Stink had been riding bikes since he was a kid.

Lil Man uncovered the green Kawasaki Ninja and put the key in the ignition. After going through the preliminaries of allowing the bike to warm up, Lil Man took off down the block.

Watching Lil Man aimlessly speed up and down the block, Stink inwardly smiled. Taking the motorcycle from him was going to be like taking candy from a baby.

Lil Man rolled the motorcycle to a stop near Stink and said, "Yeah nigga, you see how I change them gears." Holding the bike up for Stink he said, "Be careful, nigga!"

As Stink pulled off, he gradually pulled the motorcycle to one wheel and gunned the engine. He stopped at the end of the block and turned around. Revving the engine while holding the brake, he caused the motorcycle's rear wheel to spin feverishly. A cloud of smoke instantly engulfed Stink and the motorcycle.

Lil Man stood in awe, as the cloud consumed Stink. Suddenly the motorcycle burst from the cloud at top speed.

Slowing the motorcycle in front of a visibly sulking Lil Man, Stink shut the bike off.

"You tricked me, nigga!" Lil Man spat.

"Nah, nigga. You tricked yourself," Stink replied, removing the motorcycle's key from Lil Man's key ring, then asked, "Where's the helmet?"

Stink shut the motorcycle off in front of Melody's house. He knew Melody wasn't home yet; this was another piece of his plan coming together.

He rang the doorbell and waited patiently for Chelle to answer the door.

"Hi, Rahsaan. Melody hasn't gotten in yet, but you're welcome to wait," she said in her customary, prissy manner.

Stink followed her into the house and then asked, "Chelle, can I use the phone to call Melody real quick?"

"Sure, go ahead. You know where it is," she said as she disappeared up the stairs.

Stink quickly dialed the number to Melody's cell phone.

"Hello," she answered.

"Wazup, baby? I'm at your house right now," Stink announced.

"Oh, goody," she replied, child-like, then said, "I'll be home in a minute. Don't leave; I'll be home in a few minutes."

"Hold up. I need you to stop and grab a few things on the way."

"What do you need?"

Stink paused for a second, trying to think of the best way to give her his strange request. Finally, he just blurted it out, "I need you to stop by a hardware store and buy five cans of black spray paint. Then I need you to buy a dreadlocked wig from a beauty store or something."

There was a long pause as Melody processed his unusual request.

"You hear me, Melody?" Stink asked in an irritated tone.

"You're serious, aren't you?" she asked skeptically.

"Yeah, I'm serious!" he snapped.

"Ok, ok, I'll be there in a little while. Just don't leave."

Almost an hour later, Melody arrived carrying a large shopping bag. Instantly, Stink prepared to curse Melody out if any of the items he'd instructed her to get weren't in the bag.

"Hey, baby!" Melody yelled, rushing to give him a hug. "Is that your motorcycle out front?" she inquired.

"Yeah," he replied, eyeing the bag.

Noticing Stink's lingering glare, he walked over to the bag. "I got your things," she said, handing him the bag. "Oh yeah, while I was at the hardware store, I bought you these," she said, pulling an oversized set of black coveralls from the bags.

Inwardly smiling, Stink gave her a peck on the lips and said, "Thanks, baby." Grabbing the bags and heading for the door, he threw over his shoulder, "I'll be in the garage if you need me."

The once-green motorcycle was now a glossy black. Stink meticulously painted every inch of the bike, using nearly all of the cans of paint.

The door leading into the kitchen eased open as Melody appeared carrying a glass of juice. "I thought you might need something to drink," she said, offering Stink the glass.

He grabbed the glass and gulped it down in one motion, then said, "Thanks, baby."

"Rahsaan, you did a good job," she complimented, eyeing the motorcycle's new black finish. "But why didn't you take it to a professional?"

Stink cut his eyes at Melody piercingly, instantly silencing her inquisitiveness. She smiled naively and went back inside.

Stink went over the motorcycle one final time and then rolled it out into the night air to dry.

He turned and went into Melody's house and made his way to her bedroom. As he entered the room, Melody laid across the bed in a short t-shirt and a hot pink thong. Instantly, he felt the familiar rumblings in his groin. Nonetheless, he ignored the rumblings and Melody and headed into the adjoining bathroom.

Stink placed the Taurus 9mm on the stool, stripped down and hopped in the shower, allowing the steaming hot water to run over his body. Stink replayed his plan of action in his head until he felt a breeze from the shower curtain being moved.

Melody eased into the shower and stared up at Stink as if she was waiting to be ordered to move. Without any words being spoken, she began to slide down to her knees. Before Stink could stop her, he felt her mouth encircle him totally.

Stink rode past the apartment that Lil Man had pointed out earlier. Intently eyeing the building, he didn't see anything that would suggest that Kay-Kay was there. He'd planned on this and was willing to be patient and wait.

He parked the motorcycle in the parking lot adjacent to the apartment building, which gave him a clear view of the front and the rear entrances of the building.

In an attempt not to draw any attention, Stink casually got off of the motorcycle and walked across the parking lot. On the opposite side of the lot, there were numerous trees that shielded him from the bright streetlights.

Stink blended in with the darkness, patiently eyeing the building for any signs of his sworn nemesis.

After nearly two hours of surveillance, there was no sign of Kay-Kay. Stink had begun to second-guess Lil Man's information and was just about to abort his mission.

When he began to walk out of the shadows toward the motorcycle, he heard loud laughter coming from the rear of the building.

Unable to make out the figures headed his way, Stink coolly slipped the helmet over the wig and mounted the bike.

Eyeing the two figures coming from the darkness, oblivious to him sitting on the bike, Stink's heart began to pound thunderously.

There he was, right before him, Kay-Kay and one of his boys casually walking past him.

Stink couldn't believe his luck as he gripped his gun tucked in his waist and dismounted the motorcycle. He hurriedly approached the unsuspecting pair as they approached a parked car.

Quickly covering the distance, Stink garnered their attention. "Beg yuh pardon, bredren," he said in the deepest Jamaican accent he could muster. As both of them stopped and turned toward Stink, he continued, "Mi-a look fi-." It was all he managed to say before he squeezed the trigger.

"Bop! Bop! Bop! Bop! Bop!..." He unloaded round after round into each man's torso.

As their bodies crumbled to the concrete, Stink stood over them, listening to the gurgling sounds each man made on their own blood. Instinctively, he raised the gun and fired two well-placed shots to each of the dying men's heads.

As chunks of brain, mixed with blood oozed down the sidewalk, Stink quickly jumped on the bike and gunned the engine, causing the dreadlocks to swing in the wind.

Stink made it to Norfolk, without incident. He parked the motorcycle in one of Norfolk's most notorious housing projects and casually walked away, leaving the keys and helmet intact. He knew in less than thirty minutes the entire project would be joyriding through Norfolk.

After tossing the sweaty wig into the trash, Stink called Melody. "Yo, Melody. I'm at the 7-Eleven on Princess Avenue. Come and get me," he stated, walking into the convenience store.

"Where?" Melody asked.

"The 7-Eleven across the street from Robert's Park on Princess Ave!" Stink barked.

"Ok, I'm on my way," she said hurriedly, sensing the urgency in Stink's voice.

Once again, Stink was greatly impressed by the sense of loyalty Melody possessed when it came to him. *If only Bonni had the same quality*, Stink thought to himself.

Chapter 25

November 1994

The murders of Kay-Kay and his man had been pinned on a wild Jamaican that Kay-Kay supposedly owed money to. Only one person knew who that Jamaican was and he wasn't Jamaican at all. Stink suspected that Lil Man knew he was the culprit, however, if asked to be truthful, he couldn't even put Stink with the double homicide.

On one occasion, Lil Man commented on the situation, by saying, "Yeah. Your boy Kay-Kay finally got it, huh?" sporting a smug grin.

Without showing an inkling of emotion, Stink replied, "Yeah, I heard about that."

Lil Man eyed him closely, looking for any kind of reaction but didn't receive anything.

Inwardly, Stink smiled. Not only had he executed his enemy, he'd done it and gotten away with it.

Stink, Lil Man, and Dame counted $765,000 in Lil Man's basement. After splitting the money, they each had a little over a quarter of a million.

The following week, Stink planned to take Lil Man to meet José, officially making it his final trip. He was only going to reinvest $100,000 and receive a kick back every so often from Lil Man and Dame.

Since he and Bonni had argued, they hadn't spoken even ten words to one another. Stink had never seen her act in such a way. He'd made reservations for the two of them on a twelve-day cruise to the Caribbean in hopes that it would rekindle their once-perfect union.

Melody drove Stink and Lil Man to Norfolk International Airport as they prepared to catch a one-way flight to New York City. They each carried $225,000 in their suitcases.

Stink was anxious to bring this chapter of his life to an end. He still had over $150,000 at his grandparents' and another $50,000 at his house.

He gave Melody a quick peck and exited the car. Stink caught up with Lil Man at the ticket counter who was purchasing their tickets.

As they casually strolled to the loading gate, they blended in perfectly with the business commuters dressed in slacks, button-up oxford shirts, and silk ties. Neither of them sported their usual flashy clothes or extravagant jewelry. This too was a lesson that Stink had learned from Cross.

Once they reached their flight's loading gate, Stink instantly noticed quite a few people milling around the entrance aimlessly.

Suddenly, an eerie feeling arose from the pit of his stomach as he placed the suitcase on the conveyor belt to be x-rayed.

Stink looked back at Lil Man who followed closely then stepped through the metal detector.

Just as he reached for the suitcase, he heard, "DEA! Don't move! Place your hands where I can see them!" Gripping a chrome gun in one hand and a small badge in the other, the frail looking white man approached Stink cautiously.

Stink was frozen in shock, as everything seemed to be moving in slow motion.

Lil Man, in an attempt to flee, was roughly slammed to the ground. "Why y'all fucking wit me? I ain't do shit!" he yelled in protest as his hands were tightly cuffed behind his back.

The agent who'd first approached Stink now had him securely handcuffed. "Rahsaan Jones, you are under arrest for federal drug trafficking and conspiracy to distribute. You have the right to remain silent, you have the right to…" As the agent rambled Stink's rights off, the words faded from his consciousness. Never would he have guessed in a million years that the Feds would get him.

As the agent tossed Stink in the back of the unmarked car beside a visibly distraught Lil Man, Stink's body was totally numb.

Stink and Lil Man were transported to the Federal Courthouse in Norfolk, where they were photographed, fingerprinted, and formally given a copy of the official indictment.

They sat in the small holding cell, inspecting the document that was charging them and twelve others with numerous counts, the most serious of them being conspiracy.

As Stink scrolled down the list of names, he was shocked when he read, 'Jaleaf Shaw, aka Leaf' and 'George Scott, aka Cross.'

After reading those two names, none of the others mattered. Stink looked over to Lil Man who was breezing through the document and asked, "Yo, you see this shit?"

"See what?" he replied without looking up.

"They got Leaf and Cross in this shit, too," Stink revealed.

"What?!" Lil Man replied, walking over to inspect Stink's as if his was different.

Pointing to Leaf and Cross's names, Stink said, "Right there, man."

"I knew it, man! I knew that nigga had something to do with this shit! I knew it!" Lil Man surmised angrily.

Stink dropped his head in frustration and said, "Man, I don't believe this shit!"

A week before the Thanksgiving holiday and Stink was caged in a tiny jail cell in Suffolk, Virginia. Facing multiple life sentences behind bars, he could only think about Bonni, Rahsaanique and Tayvia as he laid in the tiny bunk. In a split second, Stink's entire life played in his mind, abruptly ending at the present. Sleep came like death - quick.

"Chow time! Chow time!" a loud voice boomed, instantly jarring Stink from his sleep. Looking at his surroundings confused, in his half-conscious state, Stink quickly remembered his real life nightmare from the day before.

"Chow time! Get up! Chow's here!" the voice repeatedly yelled.

Stink hopped up and walked over to the bars. Noticing the jail's trustees passing out trays of food, he suddenly became extremely hungry.

Quickly snatching the tray through the slot, Stink sat down on the bunk and began to devour the tasteless food.

Apparently not happy with the effects of their yelling, the trustees then switched the television on, turning the volume up to ear shattering decibels.

Stink tried to block out the familiar sounds of jail and force the disgusting food down his throat. Suddenly, the morning newscast caught his attention.

"Yesterday, Federal, State and local authorities arrested eleven of fourteen suspected drug dealers from the Tidewater area and as far as New York. In a sting that authorities have dubbed Operation Green Leaf, agents seized more than one million dollars in cash, several homes and vehicles that were valued at over two million, along

with several businesses. More on this story later. Back to you Ed."

Stink had made it to the bars just as the screen was showing a Lexus closely resembling his own being towed away.

"Yo, Stink! Stink!" Lil Man yelled from his cell next door.

"Yeah. Wazup?" he replied dazed.

"That was Yo shit, man!" Lil Man stated in a matter of fact tone.

Defeated, Stink replied, "I know, man. I know."

After two days of solitary confinement, Stink and Lil Man were moved into population. Desperately wanting to use the phone, Stink dropped his mattress at the door and rushed over to the phone. Snatching the phone out of its cradle, he frantically punched the number to his house. After being met with a succession of rings, he hung up and tried again only to be met with the same outcome. He then tried the salon's number. Once again, he held the receiver to his ear as the phone continuously rang.

Frustrated, Stink dialed his grandparents' house. After a brief wait, his grandfather's voice came on the line.

"Hello," his grandfather answered casually.

"Pa-pa, I'm in jail! Where's Bonni?" Stink blurted.

"Well hello to you too, son," his grandfather snapped sarcastically, then said, "I know you're in jail, boy. It's all over the television. And if by chance I missed the television, the lady on the phone just made it clear that you were in jail. Now, the answer to your question, 'Where's Bonni?' Hold on."

Suddenly, Bonni's voice came on the line. "Rahsaan, what did you do?" she asked crying. "What is going on, Rahsaan? They took everything! Ev-ery-thing, Rahsaan!" she yelled hysterically.

Attempting to seem as if he was still in control, Stink coolly said, "Baby, first you gotta calm down."

"Calm down? Calm down? How can I calm down when my man's face is on every channel in Virginia, huh? How can I calm down when the police just took everything we owned then put me and my kids in the streets?! Answer me, Rahsaan!" she revealed in an irrate manner.

"Bonni! Calm the fuck down, and listen!" he demanded then continued, "I want you to call my lawyer as soon as we hang up and give him whatever he wants. Then-"

"With what, Rahsaan?" she blurted, "I don't have anything. No money! No nothing!"

"A'ight, look. I still got some money, just call my lawyer," he advised, hearing Bonni cry uncontrollably. "Baby, you've got to pull yourself together! Everything is going to be ok. I promise!" Stink vowed assuredly then hung up.

"Jones! Jones! Get ready for court!" a deputy yelled through the bars, startling Stink from his sleep.

Unaware that he even had a court appearance, Stink slid from the bunk and prepared for court. Bonni had visited him the day before after leaving $40,000 with his attorney which instantly put him on the case.

As Stink was brushing his teeth, the cell's door electronically slid open. He exited the cell and walked down to Lil Man's cell. Noticing that Lil Man's cell was still closed, Stink rattled the bars and then asked, "Yo! Lil! Lil!" he called, ignoring Lil Man's cellmate.

Lil Man quickly hopped off the bunk and stepped over to the bars. "What are you doing out, man?"

"They say I gotta go to court. They ain't say nothing to you?" Stink asked concerned.

"Nah, but I must gotta go too, right?" he inquired.

"I don't know, but listen, if they try some slick shit, call Bonni," Stink instructed, rattling off Bonni's number.

"A'ight, I got you, but see if I'm supposed to be going too."

"Jones! Let's go!" the deputy yelled, instantly appearing in the doorway.

Walking toward the door, Stink asked, "Do you have a Kareem Little on that list for court?"

Before looking down on the paper bearing the names of the prisoners scheduled for court, the deputy looked at Stink questioningly.

Quickly adding in a cordial manner, Stink said, "Um, sir, he's my co-defendant."

"Little? Nah, ain't no Little on here. Now let's go," he snapped.

Once everyone had been taken to court, Stink still sat in the bullpen.

"Excuse me, sir. Am I supposed to be going to court?" he asked a passing deputy in a worried tone.

Without breaking stride, the deputy glanced at Stink and kept going.

Furious, Stink sat in the bullpen for thirty more minutes until the same deputy that had ignored him earlier returned. "You're Jones, right?"

Stink nodded his head.

"Ok, the U.S. Marshals will be here any minute to get you," he advised, then disappeared.

Patiently Stink sat in the bullpen until two casually dressed white men appeared in front of the cell.

"Rahsaan Jones, how are you doing this morning? I'm agent Michael Perry with the D.E.A. and this here is agent David Young with the I.R.S."

"Are you hungry, Rahsaan?" agent Young asked, maneuvering the federally issued Crown Victoria in and out of the early morning rush hour traffic.

"Nah. I'm good," Stink replied flatly.

The agents drove him to F.B.I. Headquarters in Norfolk then escorted him to a large boardroom-style room. Once they seated him at the head of the long table in the middle of the room, agent Perry turned to Stink and asked, "Those shackles aren't too tight, are they?" Without waiting for a reply, agent Perry looked to the other agent and said, "Um, Dave, go ahead and take 'em off."

"Now Rahsaan, we brought you here to give you a chance to help yourself. Out of all of your co-defendants, you seem to be the brightest," agent Perry concluded, then said, "We're giving you a chance to help us help you."

Help you, help me? Stink thought, nearly busting out laughing. *These were the same people who'd kicked my eighteen-month-old daughter out in the cold.*

As if he was reading Stink's mind, agent Young firmly added, "Now, Mr. Jones, if you don't cooperate with us you will receive at least twenty years in a Federal penitentiary.

Noticing that their ploys weren't working, both agents looked to one another conspiratorially. Agent Perry walked over to a stand holding a board and began to write. Stink strained his neck to see what the agent was writing.

Because the agent's body was in Stink's line of vision, he was unable to see what Perry was writing. Patiently, Stink waited until he stepped away from the front of the board.

What he read nearly made his jaw drop in shock. Agent Perry had drawn a makeshift diagram that detailed the conspiracy's hierarchy. At the top of the diagram was José Rodriguez/Drug Lord.

"I see agent Perry's diagram has gotten your attention," agent Young stated, eyeing Stink's reaction closely.

Stink's mind began to work in overdrive, trying to figure out how they could possibly know about José. The more he racked his brain he continued to come up with one name. Stink tried to shake the thought from his mind, yet all the evidence pointed directly to Cross.

"Looks familiar, huh?" Agent Perry asked, snapping Stink out of his daze. "Especially since Rodriguez was expecting you and Kareem Little to have landed in New York with the $584,000 we took off you all in the airport."

Stink sat there completely relaxed, prompting Agent Young to add, "Rahsaan, we're not going to play any games here. You give us José Rodriguez and we can promise that you won't spend a day in federal prison."

Still unfazed, Stink coolly replied, "I want to talk to my lawyer."

"Rahsaan, all we need is a thumbs-up from you and we can begin to process right now. Just give us the thumbs-up," Agent Young urged.

A devilish grin formed across Stink's face as he maneuvered his handcuffed wrist to give the agents an awkward thumbs-down.

Both of the agents looked at Stink dumbfounded at his act of rejection.

"Ok, Mr. Jones, have it your way. But don't expect a deal once all of your buddies have turned on you," Agent Perry concluded.

The thought of being sentenced to prison for the remainder of his short life in prison weighed heavily on Stink's mind. In the weeks leading up to the trial, Stink's lawyer was doing all he could to get him out of the situation. He'd filed every motion imaginable, trying to get the government to disclose their evidence.

After finally receiving the startling information, Mr. Clancy visited Stink. "Rahsaan, you've got two co-defendants and an unidentified informer who are scheduled to testify against you," he disclosed, and then asked, "Do you have any idea who these people may be or what they might say?"

Stink only knew three people on the entire indictment. Leaf, who hadn't been caught yet, Lil Man and Cross.

Bonni had faithfully visited Stink every weekend. However, he could tell the enormity of his situation had taken its toll on her. All she would do is sit through the fifteen-minute visit crying uncontrollably.

"Rahsaan, I don't think I can make it without you out here," she surmised, tearfully.

"What do you mean, Bonni?"

"I'm trying…but…I," her voice trailed off unable to finish.

"But what, Bonni?" Stink barked.

"I…don't…know, Rahsaan," she replied softly.

Eyeing her through the thick glass, Stink knew that Bonni had reached a crossroads and the decision she made would be one that she would have to live with for the remainder of her life.

"Jones! Visit's up!" the deputy yelled.

He looked Bonni deep in her eyes, and then in a voice filled with emotion, he said, "I'll always love you, Bonni." Not waiting for a response, he replaced the receiver and walked out of the visiting booth, signaling that it was the end.

Chapter 26

December 1994

As the trial rapidly approached, rumors began to fly. There was a rumor that Leaf's body had been found in East St. Louis, Illinois with the fingers cut off and the teeth extracted from the corpse. The only way the body was identified was a driver's license that was conveniently found next to the body.

Out of the initial twelve people that the government had indicted, only four were prepared to go to trial. The remainder had pled guilty in return for lighter sentences. Stink was continuously trying to be optimistic about who was going to testify against him, yet deep down he'd already accepted the facts.

On the eve of the trial, Stink sat in the jail's dayroom, numbly watching the evening news. Every story that was broadcast, he incorporated into his plight.

Just as Stink had succumbed to the fact that all of America was involved in an extremely large conspiracy, the deputy called his name.

"Jones! Attorney's visit!"

Stink quickly pulled his bright orange jumpsuit up around his waist and exited the door.

Once he arrived at the lawyer's panel, his lawyer was already seated shuffling through papers.

"Sooo, Rahsaan, are you ready for our big day tomorrow?" Mr. Clancy asked full of optimism.

"Yeah, I guess so," Stink responded in a defeated tone.

"Now, Rahsaan, I have to inform you that the government has offered you another plea agreement," Mr.

Clancy stated, judging Stink's reaction, then continued. "They've agreed to drop counts 2,3, and 4 if you agree to plead guilty to count 1," he explained.

Stink was aware that the feds used this ploy to persuade defendants to plead guilty. Their plan was to fool a defendant into thinking that they were receiving some type of deal, when in fact, they would still be held responsible for the dismissed counts. In Stink's case, count 1, conspiracy, would easily swallow the ousted counts, still holding him responsible for each count.

"Nah. I'm-a take my chances with a jury," he concluded, only after a few minutes of thought.

"Well, however it goes, I'm going to fight diligently for a not-guilty verdict. Now, let's go over the testimonies of…" Mr. Clancy began, pausing to shuffle through his briefcase, he continued, "…A Miss Kendra Cox. In your own words, what could she possibly be testifying to concerning yourself?" he asked, grabbing his pen in preparation to take notes.

In deep contemplation, Stink tried to put a face with the name, yet he continued to come up with a blank. "I don't know who she is," he replied.

"Are you sure about that, Rahsaan? Think hard."

Stink nodded his head reassuringly.

"Ok, so what about Mr. George Scott, aka Cross?" Mr. Clancy asked, shattering Stink's hopes in the process.

Stink had been holding on to the faintest hope that Cross wouldn't be the one responsible for destroying his life. Nonetheless, his lawyer's question had brought everything to light: Cross was going to ruin him.

Stink placed his head in his palms and thought of all that he and Cross had been through. He couldn't bring himself to tell his lawyer about the murders that he and Cross had committed.

"Rahsaan, we don't need any surprises tomorrow. You are going to have to give me everything on this guy so I can build a defense for you," Mr. Clancy explained earnestly.

Stink slowly raised his head, then said, "I don't know him."

In the middle of the night, Stink was abruptly awakened by the violent screams that seemed to be stuck in his throat. Profusely sweating, Stink tried to shake the visions that vividly played in his mind. Pictures of Kay-Kay's gruesomely bloodied body lingered in his mind. Instantly, Stink felt that the visions were some sort of sign.

Instead of returning to his nightmare, he began to prepare for the most important day since his conception.

At 4:30 am, Stink's door was electronically opened,signaling that it was indeed show-time.

Once Stink arrived at the Federal Courthouse, he was happy to see Lil Man sitting on the steel bench, carrying on a conversation with two other prisoners.

Stink, already deeply troubled by Cross's desertion, would have been crushed if Lil Man had done the same.

"Yo, Stink! What up, my nigga?" Lil Man asked excitedly, as soon as he noticed Stink. Motioning to the other two men in the cell, he said, "This is Neek'o and this is Supreme, Leaf's brother."

Instantly, Stink noticed the strong resemblance between Leaf and Supreme. Extending his hand, he gripped Supreme's hand.

"Yo, what up, son? I've heard mad shit about you from my peeps," Supreme stated in his customary New York accent. Motioning to the other guy, he said, "This is my man, Neek'o."

After exchanging pleasantries with Neek'o, they all sat down and conversed until their moment of truth arrived.

As the four men sat in the holding cell dressed in the finest garments from Italian designers, they each silently contemplated their own fate.

Stink looked around at the somber faces that each man sported and instantly compared their situation with that of a funeral. Each man was facing his demise.

"Gentlemen, are you ready?" a sharp-dressed marshal asked, breaking the stressful silence.

Instantly, three other dapperly dressed marshals appeared, holding sets of handcuffs.

As the marshals properly handcuffed each man, Stink felt his stomach flip and flutter nervously while being led down a long corridor into the courtroom.

Stink had been in courtrooms before, yet the seriousness of the situation magnified the entire scene. The judge's bench seemed to be much higher than he'd ever remembered. Everything in the courtroom seemed to be magnified in presence.

The courtroom was filled with onlookers. Stink attempted to scan the sea of people, before being seated at the defense table. He managed to spot Bonni, his mother and grandmother seated on the front row. However, it was a face in the rear of the courtroom that caught his attention. With tear-filled eyes locked onto his, Melody mouthed, 'I love you.'

Inwardly smiling, Stink turned to face his fate.

Stink's lawyer, accompanied by the other men's lawyers, promptly appeared. Huddled around the defense table, they began to outline the strategy for the trial.

"Here ye! Here ye! All rise for the Honorable Henry L. Jackson presiding!" the bailiff yelled, bringing everyone in the courtroom to their feet.

Shockingly, a middle-aged black man entered the courtroom in the customary black garb. "You may now be seated," he instructed, as he took his seat behind the bench. "Counselors, are you ready to proceed with trial?"

"Yes, Your Honor," they all mumbled in unison.

"Any pretrial motions?" the judge asked.

Stink's attorney stepped up. "Um, yes Your Honor. I'd like the court to reconsider my motion for a separation of trial?" Mr. Clancy asked.

Without any thought, the judge replied, "Denied!"

Unaware that his attorney had filed the motion, Stink eyed the defeated look plastered across Mr. Clancy's face and wondered what the motion was all about.

The judge turned toward the prosecution and went through the same formalities. After being assured that both sides were prepared, he turned to the bailiff. "Please bring the jury in, Deputy."

The bailiff quickly exited a door near the judge's bench and promptly reappeared leading a succession of twelve diverse people to the jury box.

The attorneys had chosen the jury weeks before the trial. According to Mr. Clancy, they had chosen a 'good' panel of jurors.

As the judge was instructing the jury on what and what not to do, Stink's mind began to wonder what Cross would actually say once he was on the stand. He immediately thought about the phone conversations and even the mystery woman in New York; they all could have been tools of deceit.

All of these things ran across Stink's mind as the United States Attorney delivered his opening statements to the jury. "Ladies and gentlemen of the jury, the government will prove far beyond a reasonable doubt that Jaquan Shaw, Kareem Little, Nicholas Hayes and Rahsaan Jones all conspired to traffic, distribute and manufacture at least one hundred kilos of cocaine and cocaine base…" U.S. Attorney Alberto Hernandez, went on and on for at least an hour, before allowing the defense to respond.

After a quick huddle, the defense lawyers agreed that Supreme's smooth-talking New York attorney would present their opening arguments. The young Italian-looking lawyer got straight to the point, wasting no more than twenty minutes before he closed.

Immediately following opening arguments, the judge looked to the U.S. Attorney and said, "The government may call their first witness." This was the signal that it was officially 'show-time'.

"The Government calls Ms. Kendra Cox to the stand."

A bailiff promptly entered, escorting a young woman who Stink didn't immediately recognize. After further inspection of the light-skinned girl, it hit him.

'Are you Stink?'

'Umm…yea…yeah. Wazup?'

'Oh, Jaleaf sent me to pick something up from you.'

Sitting there replaying the incident in his head, Stink somehow knew that night would come back to haunt him.

Once she was sworn in, the U.S. Attorney began his interrogations.

"Could you please state your full name for the record?"

"Yes. Kendra Malika Cox," she replied, nervously.

"Ms. Cox, you've been found guilty of money laundering. Correct?"

"Yes."

"Can you explain to the court what you did to be charged with money laundering?"

Kendra went into some long, drawn out story of how she was attending college and somehow fell in love with an abusive Leaf, leading her to launder money for him, blah, blah, blah, blah…

As Kendra poured her heart and guts out to the jury, the courtroom remained silent.

"Ms. Cox, do you know Jaquan Shaw?

"Yes."

"And how do you know him?"

"He's my boyfriend's brother, well, my *deceased* boyfriend's brother," she replied, confirming Leaf's brutal death.

"What else do you know Jaquan as?"

"Um, Supreme or Premo."

"Ok. Have you ever witnessed Jaquan Shaw, aka Supreme, aka Premo, involved in any illicit activities?"

"You mean like drug activity?" she inquired.

"Yes, like drug activity," the U.S. Attorney agreed.

"Objection! Counsel is leading the witness," Supreme's lawyer yelled.

"Sustained! Counsel, please watch your line of questioning," the judge instructed.

"Ok, yes, Your Honor. Ms. Cox, in your own words, what kind of illegal activities did you see Mr. Shaw involved in?"

"Ummm, I traveled to New York to take him money several times," Kendra disclosed.

"Were you aware of what the money was for?"

"Objection! Your Honor, now counsel is asking the witness to speculate," Supreme's attorney argued.

"Sustained! Mr. Hernandez, I will not tolerate these types of shenanigans in my courtroom. Do I make myself clear?" the judge asked in a threatening tone.

Mr. Hernandez continued questioning Kendra, until he manipulated his way into getting her to say she was transporting cocaine back from New York.

Kendra's testimony had made Supreme look just like the 'Drug Lord' Mr. Hernandez vowed to prove he was, in his opening statements. Now it was time she did the same to Stink.

"During your time of running drugs for your boyfriend and his brother, did you ever meet Stink?" he inquired cockily.

"Um, yes. My boyfriend sent me to pick up some money from him at a restaurant in Norfolk."

"Do you remember what that money was for?" he asked slyly.

"Uh, yeah. It was for drugs," she answered, getting the hang of what she was supposed to be doing.

Stink's heart sank as the words escaped her mouth yet outwardly, he didn't twitch a muscle.

Mr. Clancy stood slowly. "Your Honor. This is pure speculation on the witness's part. I object," he stated coolly.

The judge took his glasses off and eyed Kendra suspiciously. He then asked, "Ms. Cox, how did you know the money was for drugs?"

Kendra looked from the judge to U.S. Attorney Hernandez nervously, and then blurted, "'Cause I took them."

"You may continue, Mr. Hernandez," the judge instructed.

Stink sat at the table fuming. He could feel his entire face becoming blistering hot. He desperately wanted to jump up and yell, 'You lying BITCH!' Yet somehow, he kept his cool.

"Ms. Cox, when you went to the restaurant to get the money for the drugs from Rahsaan Jones, aka Stink, did-"

"I object Your Honor!" Mr. Clancy yelled at the top of his lungs. "The U.S. Attorney has given this, this moniker a person's name without any positive identification!" Mr. Clancy barked angrily.

"Mr. Hernandez, please have the witness identify which defendant she knows as 'Stink,'" the judge instructed.

"Alright, Your Honor. Ms. Cox would you please point to the man seated at the defense table that you know as Stink?"

Kendra eyed the foursome intently, and then looked them over a second time before pointing. "Him," she said assuredly.

"What is he wearing, Ms. Cox?" the judge asked.

"The one in the blue suit and silver tie," she said.

Instantly, there was a loud gasp from the courtroom, followed by loud chatter.

"Order! Order!" the judge barked.

Stink looked down at himself, then over to Lil Man who was wearing a blue suit and a silver tie. Stink wore a gray suit and a white tie.

U.S. Attorney Alberto Hernandez had a look of total disbelief on his face.

Mr. Clancy stood and triumphantly announced, "I'd like to move to strike all testimony given by this witness against my client."

"Sustained! All testimony by Ms. Cox given on Rahsaan Jones is to be stricken from the record," the judge said, instructing the jury. Turning his attention back to a visibly distraught Mr. Hernandez, he asked, "Mr. Hernandez, are there anymore questions for this witness?"

"No, Your Honor," he replied, flatly.

"Ms. Cox, you may step down," the judge instructed.

After Kendra was escorted from the courtroom, the judge recessed until after lunch.

As Stink stood to be handcuffed, he turned toward the courtroom full of onlookers and noticed Bonni beaming in his direction. He returned her bright smile with an expressionless glare, then turned and allowed the Marshal to escort him from the courtroom.

Chapter 27

<u>After Recess</u>

As the Marshals led the foursome back into the courtroom, Stink's stomach once again fluttered nervously. Once their handcuffs were off and they were seated, the bailiff stood.

"Here Ye! Here Ye!" signaling the judge's entrance.

As before, the judge promptly summoned the jury. After the jury was seated, the judge instructed the U.S. Attorney to call their next witness.

Staring directly toward Stink, Mr. Hernandez announced, "The government calls George Scott to the stand."

Stink's heart pounded thunderously in his chest, as he witnessed the bailiff escorting Cross to the witness stand. Instantly, Stink felt as if his tie was choking him as beads of sweat popped up on his forehead.

As Cross sauntered to the witness stand, not even shackles and handcuffs could hinder his bouncy swagger.

Cross carefully stepped onto the stand and fixed his eyes on Stink. Allowing a devilish grin to etch into his features, he winked at Stink. Leaning in a slouched manner, Cross raised his right hand high and continued to stare in Stink's direction.

Unable to put his finger on it, this wasn't the reaction he was expecting from Cross.

Shuffling through a stack of papers, Mr. Hernandez looked at Cross and asked, "Mr. Scott, you've been found guilty of drug trafficking and murder, correct?"

Nonchalantly, Cross replied, "Yeah."

"And you're here today to testify on your own free will?"

"Yeah."

"Were you promised anything from the Government for your testimony?"

Hesitantly, Cross replied with a slight chuckle, "Nah."

"Ok, Mr. Scott. Do you know Rahsaan Jones?"

"You mean Stink, right?" Cross asked snickering.

"Uh, yes. Could you point out the defendant that you know to be Stink?"

"Yeah, he's the one in the gray suit, sitting beside Lil Man," Cross replied, casually.

"Please allow the record to show that the witness positively identified Rahsaan Jones as Stink," Mr. Hernandez announced triumphantly. "Now, Mr. Scott, you have transported drugs from New York to Virginia, correct?"

"Yeah, I did that," Cross answered coolly, garnering a slight chuckle from the courtroom.

"Mr. Scott, did you ever transport drugs with or for Rahsaan Jones, aka Stink, from New York to Virginia?"

Cross's eyes became evil slits as he glared toward Mr. Hernandez with a murderous scowl etched across his face. This was the first time Cross had shown any type of emotion. The piercing gaze and prolonged silence caused Mr. Hernandez to fidget nervously.

Breaking the monotonous silence that engulfed the courtroom, the judge firmly instructed, "Mr. Scott, answer the question."

Cross looked toward the judge briefly then turned his attention back to Mr. Hernandez, who stood nervously awaiting a reply.

With his features transforming into a contemptuous grin, Cross casually said, "Sti…"

Find out the rest of the story when ***Deceived Again*** comes out **August 30th, 2011**

Sample Chapters

From Hoodfellas

By
Richard Jeanty

Chapter 1
The Natural Course

"Mr. Brown, we're not really here to negotiate with you. It's more like a demand, or whatever you wanna call it," said Crazy D.

"What makes you think I'm gonna do what you're telling me to do?" Mr. Brown asked. "Yo, Short Dawg, bring her out," Crazy D ordered.

Short Dawg appeared from behind Mr. Brown's storage area with a knife to Mr. Brown's wife's neck while her left hand is covered in blood. "She still has nine good fingers left, but next time we won't be cutting off fingers, oh no, we ain't interested in the same body part twice. Next time it might be one of her eyeballs hanging out the socket," Crazy D said as he signaled for Short Dawg to bring the knife to Mrs. Brown's eyes. "Tell me what you want and I'll do it, just don't hurt her," said Mr. Brown. "We've been watching you for a while now and my guesstimation is that you make about fifty to a hundred thousand dollars a month. Forty percent of that is ours and we're gonna collect it on every first of the month," he said. "How we supposed to survive? The shop doesn't even make that kind of money," Mr. Brown pleaded. "Do you need motivation to make that kind of money?" Crazy D asked as he raised his hand to Short Dawg, ordering him to start taking out one of Mrs. Brown's eyes. Before he could stick the knife in, Mr. Brown chimed in and said, "Okay, I'll do it. I'll give you forty percent of what we make." Crazy D smiled and said, "No, you'll give me forty percent of a hundred thousand dollars every month. He ordered Short Dawg to drop the knife with a swift movement of his head.

As Crazy D and Short Dawg were making their way out of the shop, Mr. Brown reached for his shotgun. However, before he could cock it back, Crazy D had his .45 Lugar in his face saying, "It's your choice, old man, you can die a hero or you can become a zero." Mr. Brown wisely placed his shotgun down, and then apologized to Crazy D. What Crazy D did to the Browns was routine since he came out of the State Pen. Crazy D walked out of jail wearing some donated clothes that were twenty years out of style and fit a little too snug around his six foot-plus frame. The difference this time was the tightness of the fit. He had gained a considerable amount of weight in muscle. The shirt was tight around his arms and his pants barely made it past his thighs. He was ridiculed as he rode the bus back to his old neighborhood. The kids were pointing at him, adults shook their heads at him and women just laughed at him. Crazy D was fed up with the treatment he received his first day out of jail. He looked like a buff homo. With no money and no skills to get a job, Crazy D had no choice but to turn back to a life of crime. After serving a twenty-year sentence for robbery and second-degree murder, the system failed him miserably, but even worse, they failed the rest of society by letting a loose canon out of jail without the proper rehabilitation.

While in jail, Crazy D's mom only visited him the first few months. She soon fell victim to the crack epidemic and ultimately had to turn her back on her son at his request. There came a time when she could hardly remember that she had a son. While constantly under the influence of crack cocaine, his mother did her own stint in prison for prostitution and other petty crimes only to get out and start using again.

Crazy D went to jail at the young age of seventeen and it was there that he learned his survival tactics. Wreaking havoc on people before they got to him was what he learned when he was in prison. The attempted rape on him the first week after he arrived at the Walpole facility in Massachusetts brought his awareness to a level he never knew existed. He was lucky that one of the toughest inmates in that prison was a friend of his father's. Word had gotten out that Crazy D was being shipped to Walpole and his father's best friend made a promise to his mother to look after him. Crazy D's dad, Deon Sr., and Mean T were best friends before his dad got killed, and Mean T was sent to prison for thirty years after a botched armed robbery against a store owner.

Chapter 2

Mean T and Sticky Fingers

Mean T and Sticky Fingers aka Deon Campbell Sr. were best friends throughout their entire lives. They were more like vagrants from the time their mother decided to allow them to walk to school by themselves. In fact, the very first day that they walked to school without any supervision, they decided to make a detour to the corner store. Mean T was the lookout while Sticky Fingers robbed the store of candy, potato chips, juices and other valuables that matter to kids. It was a little distance from Evans Street to Morton Street in Dorchester, Massachusetts, but their parents trusted that they would walk directly to school everyday. The Taylor Elementary School was where most of the kids who lived on the Dorchester side of Morton Street went to school. Stealing became a fun habit for the duo and every morning they found themselves down the block at the corner store stealing more items than their pockets could afford. Mean T was the bigger of the two, but Sticky Fingers was the conniving thief. He could steal the bible from a preacher, and Mean T would knock the daylights out of a pregnant woman.

Over the years, the duo broaden their horizons from stealing candy to stealing sneakers and clothes out of a store called 42nd Street located in Mattapan Square. By then, they were in high school being promoted because of their age and not the work that they did. The two were dumb as a doorknob, but one was an expert thief and the other an enforcer. The two friends were the best young hustlers from their block. The Korean owner of the store was forced to install cameras because Sticky Fingers and Mean T kept robbing the store and there was never any proof to prosecute them. Usually, the cops didn't respond on time and by then the two had made it home safely with their stolen goods. The shop owner was growing tired of this and decided to arm himself in order to keep from getting robbed.

Mean T and Sticky Fingers wore the freshest gear to school. Everything was brand name because they stole the best of everything from the different stores downtown Boston. Their favorite stores were Filene's, Jordan Marsh, Filene's Basement and of course, 42nd Street in Mattapan Square. On top of that, the two of them sold some of the stolen merchandise to some of the kids at the high school when they needed money. Their bad habit became an enterprise. The two thieves outfitted their bedrooms with stolen goods from stores all over the Boston area. They had enough merchandise to supply a whole high school of kids with clothes, shoes and other clothing items such as socks, t-shirts, underwear and long johns needed for at least a month. However, Mean T and Sticky Fingers would run into some difficulty when they decided to rob the 42nd Street store once more. The Korean owner had had enough and he felt he needed to protect his livelihood, so he bought a gun.

By this time, Mean T and Sticky Fingers were pretty known to the entire Korean family who worked as a unit in the store. While Sticky Fingers walked around and stuffed his bag with stolen items, so he could dash out of the store using the same tactics they had used in the past with Mean T knocking out the father who stood guard at the entrance, the father looked on. However, on this day, they would meet their fate. As Sticky Fingers rushed towards the exit, all he felt was a hot bullet piercing through his heart. Mean T didn't even have time to react as the small Korean man raised his gun and stuck it in Mean T's mouth. Pandemonium rang out in the store as everyone tried to make it to the exit. Meanwhile, Sticky Finger's lifeless body lay on the ground with his hands clutched around a duffle bag filled with stolen items. The cops arrived in no time. Someone's life had to be taken in order for the cops to respond in a timely manner.

Mr. Chang, as the community later found out the store owner's name, had to defend himself against the whole community. No one came to his defense when he was being robbed blindly, but everyone was angry because another young black life had been taken. Sticky Finger's mom came out shedding tears as if she didn't know what her son was doing in the street. A search of the victim's home revealed about fifty thousand dollars worth of stolen items from different stores, including Mr. Chang's 42nd Street. Sticky Finger's mom had to have known that her son was hawking stolen merchandise because the officers could barely take a step into his room without stepping over stolen clothes while serving the search warrant. The whole place was cluttered with clothes scattered all over the room.

To top off an already insane situation, the cops found a loaded gun on Mean T after searching him at the scene. Mean T aka Tony Gonsalves, an American born Cape Verde heritage young man was handcuffed and taken to jail where he faced aggravated robbery, illegal possession of a handgun, first degree armed robbery and a list of other charges concocted by the district attorney to ensure his proper place away from society for the next thirty years. It didn't help that Tony and Deon weren't in good standing at school. No teachers, counselor or principal would vouch for them as good people. The media smeared their names even further and there was no way that Tony was going to walk even though his friend was killed.

A few months after Deon's murder, the media revealed that he had left behind a pregnant woman with an unborn child. That child would be named Deon after his father. Mean T would receive a thirty-year sentence, the maximum allowed under

Massachusetts law. He was transferred from the correctional facility in Concord to the facility in Walpole after his sentence. As a young man, Mean T didn't really understand the extent of his sentence, so he chose to act in a machismo way and accepted his fate. On the van ride from Concord to Walpole, while shackled to other hardcore criminals, reality started to set in for Mean T and he understood clearly that his life had taken a drastic turn for the worst and he had better start thinking about his survival tactics. Mean T rose to prominence very quickly at the prison as he engaged some of the tougher inmates in fights and defeated quite a few of them while earning their respect.

Mean T was tested the very day he was headed to Walpole to start his sentence. One repeated offender wanted to impress all the impressionable first timers in the van, and he made the unthinkable mistake of picking on Meant T.

"You're gonna be my bitch when we touch down," he said to Mean T with a tempted grin. The whole van was laughing except Meant T. He was sitting in the row in front of Mean T and had to turn his neck around to talk to him. Before he could turn around to say something else, Mean T threw his handcuffed hands around his neck and choked him until he passed out. Words had gotten around about the incident and Mean T was given his props for almost killing a man who was known as Nutty Harold in prison. Nutty Harold was released on a technicality and he unfortunately had a confrontation with Mean T on his way back to prison after killing a man six months out of prison.

It was almost eighteen years later, a few months short of his eighteenth birthday, when Crazy D aka Deon Campbell Jr. would walk into the prison in Walpole to meet the guardian angel known to him as Abdul Mustafa Muhammad. Mean T had converted to Islam while serving his sentence. He had gotten into many fights after arriving at the prison, including one that involved sending a prison guard to the emergency room, which earned him an additional ten years to his sentence. Mean T was casually walking to his cell after code red was called. This one particular guard, who hated him for garnering the respect of his fellow inmates, felt Mean T was not walking fast enough. He used his stick to rush Mean T back to his cell thinking that the other two guards behind him provided a safe haven from an asswhip. Mean T was much too quick and strong for the guard as he found his neck wrapped inside Mean T's massive biceps. The two guards stood back as Mean T threatened to choke the life out of the guard who unjustly pushed and hit him with the stick. The white guard started turning pink and his eyes bulging out of their sockets as he fainted from the chokehold feeling that life itself was about to end. The other two guards could only watch in horror before stepping in to provide some relief for the guard using their night stick. He became a lifer. Abdul, formerly known as Tony Gonsalves also formerly known as Mean T on the streets, was a highly respected man in prison. As a lifer, he had earned the reputation of a tough, intelligent and manipulating leader. He protected those close to him and destroyed those who went against him.

RJ PUBLICATIONS
INTRODUCE

Stick &
MOVE III

No Way Out...

A Different Kind of Street Tale

a novel by
SHAWN BLACK

Serosa becomes the subject to information that could financially ruin and possibly destroy the lives and careers of many prominent people involved in the government if this data is exposed. As this intricate plot thickens, speculations start mounting and a whirlwind of death, deceit, and betrayal finds its way into the ranks of a once impenetrable core of the government. Will Serosa fall victim to the genetic structure that indirectly binds her to her parents causing her to realize there s NO WAY OUT!

In Stores!!!

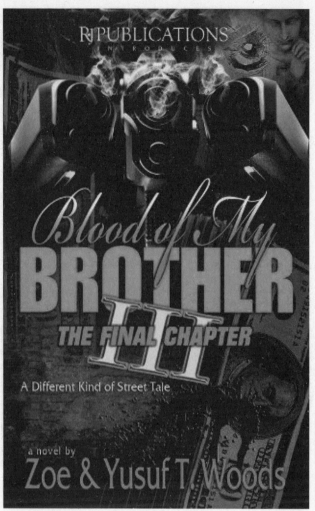

Retiring is no longer an option for Roc, who is now forced to restudy Philly's vicious streets through blood filled eyes. He realizes that his brother's killer is none other than his mentor, Mr. Holmes. With this knowledge, the strategic game of chess that began with the pushing of a pawn in the Blood of My Brother series, symbolizes one of love, loyalty, blood, mayhem, and death. In the end, the streets of Philadelphia will never be the same...

In Stores!!!

RICHARD JEANTY

Authors of Neglected Soul's, Meeting Miss Right & Sexual Exploits of A Nympho

INTRODUCES

Miami
NOIRE

"The sequel to *Chasin' Satisfaction*"

WARNING
HIGHLY
ADDICTIVE
READING MATERIAL

A NOVEL BY
W.S. BURRETT

After Chasin' Satisfaction, Julius finds that satisfaction is not all that it's cracked up to be. It left nothing but death in its aftermath. Now living the glamorous life in Miami while putting the finishing touches on his hybrid condo hotel, he realizes with newfound success he's now become the hunted. Julian's success is threatened as someone from his past vows revenge on him.

In Stores!!!

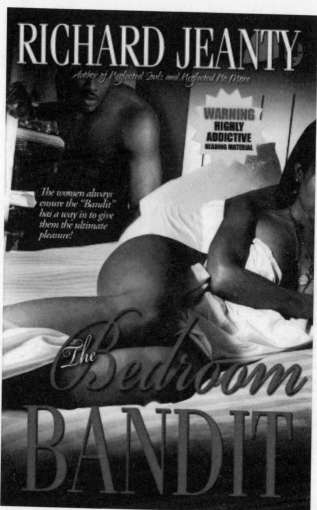

A NOVEL FROM THE BESTSELLING AUTHOR OF "MEETING MISS RIGHT" AND "SEXUAL EXPLOITS OF A NYMPHO"

REVISED EDITION

Neglected SOULS

"Dark alleys, cold and lonely nights just trying to survive... Who can you run to? Neglected Souls made me gasp and grip my heart."
—Rashamba Williams, Best Selling Author of Driven and At The Court's Mercy.

RICHARD JEANTY

NEGLECTED SOULS

Motherhood and the trials of loving too hard and not enough frame this story...The realism of these characters will bring tears to your spirit as you discover the hero in the villain you never saw coming...

In Stores!!!

Jimmy and Nina continue to feel a void in their lives because they haven't a clue about their genealogical make-up. Jimmy falls victims to a life threatening illness and only the right organ donor can save his life. Will the donor be the bridge to reconnect Jimmy and Nina to their biological family? Will Nina be the strength for her brother in his time of need? Will they ever find out what really happened to their mother?

In Stores!!!

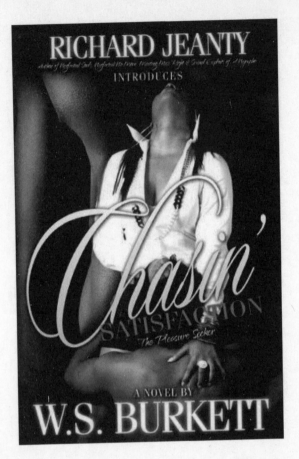

Betrayal, lust, lies, murder, deception, sex and tainted love frame this story... Julian Stevens lacks the ambition and freak ability that Miko looks for in a man, but she married him despite his flaws to spite an ex-boyfriend. When Miko least expects it, the old boyfriend shows up and ready to sweep her off her feet again. She wants to have her cake and eat it too. While Miko's doing her own thing, Julian is determined to become everything Miko ever wanted in a man and more, but will he go to extreme lengths to prove he's worthy of Miko's love? Julian Stevens soon finds out that he's capable of being more than he could ever imagine as he embarks on a journey that will change his life forever.

In Stores!!!

The police in New York and other major cities around the country are increasingly victimizing black men. The violence has escalated to deadly force, most of the time without justification. In this controversial book, noted author Richard Jeanty, tackles the problem of police brutality and the unfair treatment of Black men at the hands of police in New York City and the rest of the country.

In Stores!!!

Just when Darren thinks his relationship with Tina is flourishing, there
is yet another hurdle on the road hindering their bliss. Tina saw a
therapist for months to deal with her sexual addiction, but now Darren is
wondering if she was ever treated completely. Darren has not been
taking care of home and Tina's frustrated and agrees to a break-up with
Darren. Will Darren lose Tina for good? Will Tina ever realize that
Darren is the best man for her?

In Stores!!

Ronald Murphy was a player all his life until he and his best friend, Myles, met the women of their dreams during a brief vacation in South Beach, Florida. Sexual Jeopardy is story of trust, betrayal, forgiveness, friendship and hope.

In Stores!!!

A NEW NOVEL FROM THE AUTHOR OF "NEGLECTED SOULS" AND "MEETING MS. JulIE"

RICHARD JEANTY

SEXUAL
exploits of a
NYMPHO

" The book is hotter, steamier and sexier
than the title suggests. Jeanty has done it again."
–Treasure E. Blue Essence best selling author of
Harlem Girl Lost

Tina develops an insatiable sexual appetite very early in life. She only
loves her boyfriend, Darren, but he's too far away in college to satisfy
her sexual needs.
Tina decides to get buck wild away in college
Will her sexual trysts jeopardize the lives of the men in her life?

In Stores!!!

Faith Jones, a woman in her mid-thirties, has given up on ever finding love again until she met her son's best friend, Darius. Faith Jones is walking a thin line of betrayal against her son for the love of Darius. Will Faith allow her emotions to outweigh her common sense?

In Stores!!!

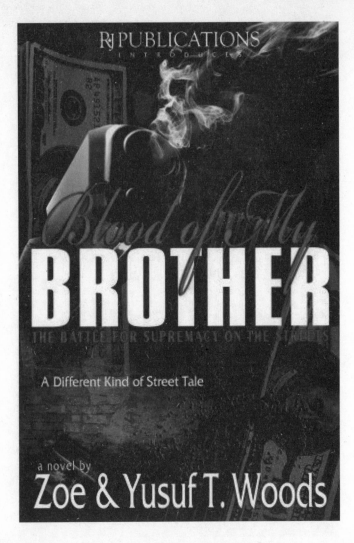

Roc was the man on the streets of Philadelphia, until his younger brother decided it was time to become his own man by wreaking havoc on Roc's crew without any regards for the blood relation they share. Drug, murder, mayhem and the pursuit of happiness can lead to deadly consequences. This story can only be told by a person who has lived it.

In Stores!!!

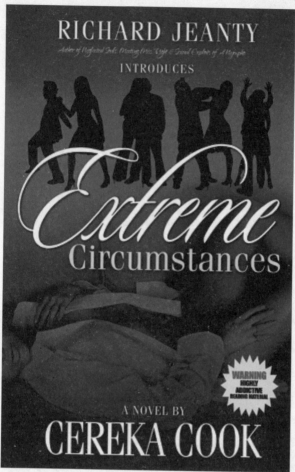

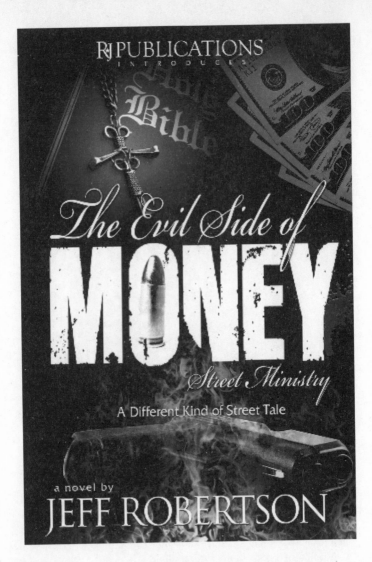

Violence, Intimidation and carnage are the order as Nathan and his brother set out to build the most powerful drug empires in Chicago. However, when God comes knocking, Nathan's conscience starts to surface. Will his haunted criminal past get the best of him?

In Stores!!

RJ PUBLICATIONS
I N T R O D U C E S

Stick & MOVE

A Different Kind of Street Tale

a novel by
SHAWN BLACK

Yasmina witnessed the brutal murder of her parents at a young age at the hand of a drug dealer. This event stained her mind and upbringing as a result. Will Yamina's life come full circle with her past? Find out as Yasmina's crew, The Platinum Chicks, set out to make a name for themselves on the street.

In stores!!

RICHARD JEANTY

Author of Neglected Souls, Hunting Miss Kayla & Sexual Exploits of A Nympho

INTRODUCES

Too Many

SECRETS

& Too Many Lies

**WARNING
HIGHLY
ADDICTIVE
READING MATERIAL**

A NOVEL BY

SONYA SPARKS

Ashland's mother, Bianca, fights hard to suppress the truth from her daughter because she doesn't want her to marry Jordan, the grandson of an ex-lover she loathes. Ashland soon finds out how cruel and vengeful her mother can be, but what price will Bianca pay for redemption?

In stores!!

Malcolm is a wealthy virgin who decides to conceal his wealth From the world until he meets the right woman. His wealthy best friend, Dexter, hides his wealth from no one. Malcolm struggles to find love in an environment where vanity and materialism are rampant, while Dexter is getting more than enough of his share of women. Malcolm needs develop self-esteem and confidence to meet the right woman and Dexter's confidence is borderline arrogance.

Will bad boys like Dexter continue to take women for a ride?

Or will nice guys like Malcolm continue to finish last?

In Stores!!!

RICHARD JEANTY

Author of Rejected Girls and Rejected No More

INTRODUCES

WARNING
HIGHLY
ADDICTIVE
FEATURE PARALLEL

Cater to Her

A NOVEL BY
SEAN MITCHELL

What happens when a woman's devotion to her fiancee is tested weeks before she gets married? What if her fiancee is just hiding behind the veil of ministry to deceive her? Find out as Sean Mitchell takes you on a journey you'll never forget into the lives of Angelica, Titus and Aurelius.

In Stores!!

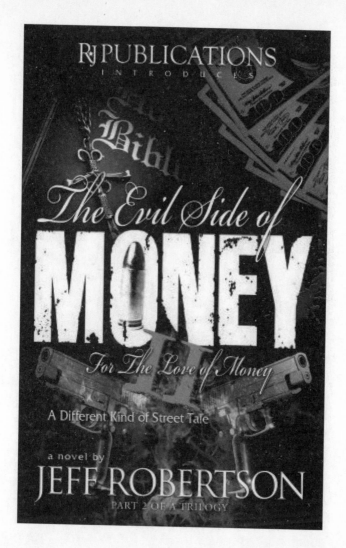

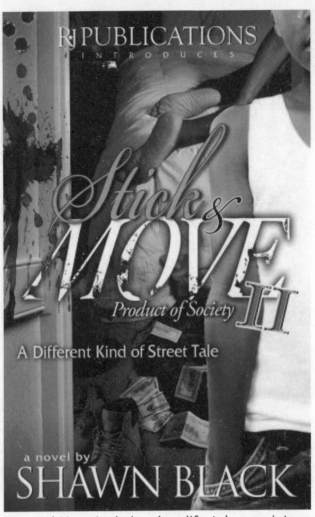

An ex-drug dealer finds himself in a bind after he's caught by the Feds. He has to decide which is more important, his family or his loyalty to the game. As he fights hard to make a decision, those who helped him to the top fear the worse from him. Will he get the chance to tell the govt. whole story, or will someone get to him before he becomes a snitch?

In Stores!!!

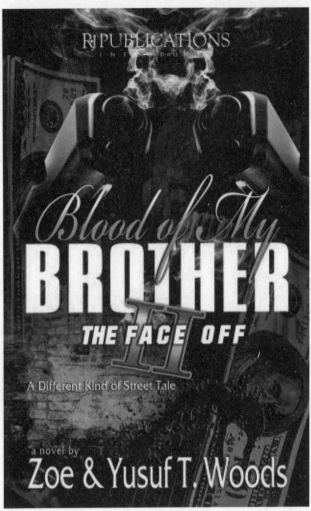

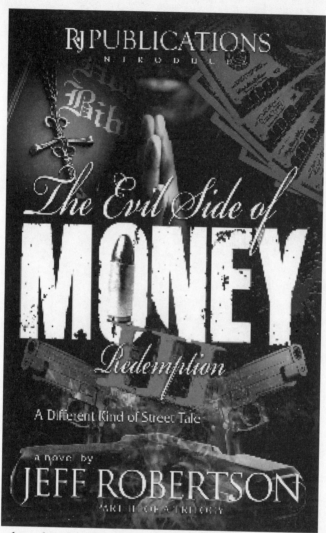

RJ PUBLICATIONS INTRODUCE

The Evil Side of
MONEY
Redemption

A Different Kind of Street Tale

a novel by
JEFF ROBERTSON
PART II OF A TRILOGY

Forced to abandon the drug world for good, Nathan and G
attempt to change their lives and move forward, but will
their past come back to haunt them? This final installment
will leave you speechless.

In Stores!!!

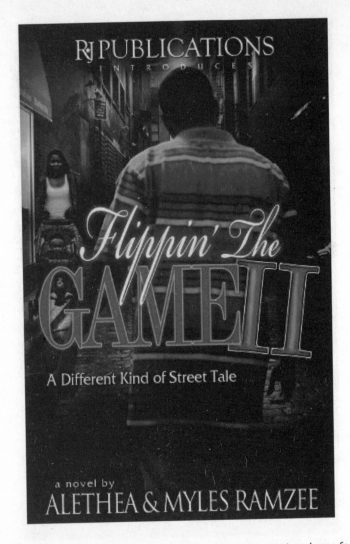

RJ PUBLICATIONS
INTRODUCES

Flippin' The
GAME II

A Different Kind of Street Tale

a novel by
ALETHEA & MYLES RAMZEE

Nafiys Muhammad managed to beat the charges in court and was found innocent as a result. However, his criminal involvement is far from over. While Jerry Class Classon is feeling safe in the witness protection program, his family continues to endure even more pain. There will be many revelations as betrayal, sex scandal, corruption, and murder shape this story. No one will be left unscathed and everyone will pay the price for his/her involvement. Get ready for a rough ride as we revisit the Black Top Crew.

In Stores!!

RICHARD JEANTY

Author of Neglected Souls and Neglected No More

Mr. Erotica

Jealousy can be a dangerous game for anyone...

WARNING HIGHLY ADDICTIVE READING MATERIAL

Dave Richardson is enjoying success as his second book became a New York Times best-seller. He left the life of The Bedroom behind to settle with his family, but an obsessed fan has not had enough of Dave and she will go to great length to get a piece of him. How far will a woman go to get a man that doesn't belong to her?

In Stores!!!

Deon is at the mercy of a ruthless gang that kidnapped him. In a foreign land where he knows nothing about the culture, he has to use his survival instincts and his wit to outsmart his captors. Will the Hoodfellas show up in time to rescue Deon, or will Crazy D take over once again and fight an all out war by himself?

In Stores!!!

RICHARD JEANT

INTRODUCE

Too Many
SECRETS
& Too Many Lies II
NEVER GONNA LET YOU GO

WARNING
HIGHLY
ADDICTIVE
READING MATERIAL

A NOVEL BY

SONYA SPARKS

The drama continues as Deshun is hunted by Angela who still feels that ex-girlfriend Kayla is still trying to win his heart, though he brutally raped her. Angela will kill anyone who gets in her way, but is DeShun worth all the aggravation?

In Stores!!!

Buck Johnson was forced to make the best out of worst situation. He has witnessed the most cruel events in his life and it is those events who the man that he has become. Was the Johnson family ignorant souls through no fault of their own?

In Stores!!!

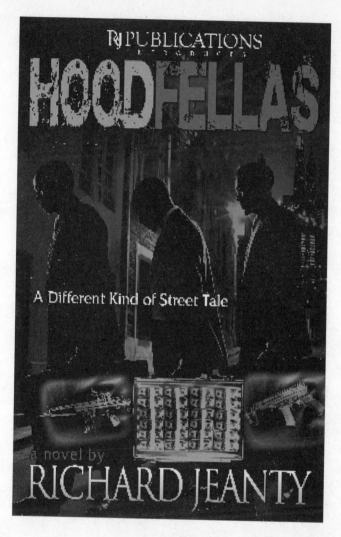

When an Ex-con finds himself destitute and in dire need of the basic necessities after he's released from prison, he turns to what he knows best, crime, but at what cost? Extortion, murder and mayhem drives him back to the top, but will he stay there?

In Stores !!!

RICHARD JEANTY
Author of Neglected Souls, Neurotic Erica & Sexual Exploits of A Nympho
INTRODUCES

Insanely IN Love

WARNING HIGHLY ADDICTIVE READING MATERIAL

A NOVEL BY
CEREKA COOK
Author of *Extreme Circumstances*

What happens when someone falls insanely in love? Stalking is just the beginning.

In Stores!!!

PUBLICATIONS
BRINGING EXCITEMENT, FUN AND JOY TO READING

Use this coupon to order by mail

1. Neglected Souls, Richard Jeanty $14.95 Available
2. Neglected No More, Richard Jeanty $14.95 Available
3. Ignorant Souls, Richard Jeanty $15.00, Available
4. Sexual Exploits of Nympho, Richard Jeanty $14.95 Available
5. Meeting Ms. Right's Whip Appeal, Richard Jeanty $14.95 Available
6. Me and Mrs. Jones, K.M Thompson $14.95 Available
7. Chasin' Satisfaction, W.S Burkett $14.95 Available
8. Extreme Circumstances, Cereka Cook $14.95 Available
9. The Most Dangerous Gang In America, R. Jeanty $15.00 Available
10. Sexual Exploits of a Nympho II, Richard Jeanty $15.00 Available
11. Sexual Jeopardy, Richard Jeanty $14.95 Available
12. Too Many Secrets, Too Many Lies, Sonya Sparks $15.00 Available
13. Stick And Move, Shawn Black $15.00 Available
14. Evil Side Of Money, Jeff Robertson $15.00 Available
15. Evil Side Of Money II, Jeff Robertson $15.00 Available
16. Evil Side Of Money III, Jeff Robertson $15.00 Available
17. Flippin' The Game, Alethea and M. Ramzee, $15.00 Available
18. Flippin' The Game II, Alethea and M. Ramzee, $15.00 Available
19. Cater To Her, W.S Burkett $15.00 Available
20. Blood of My Brother I, Zoe & Yusuf Woods $15.00 Available
21. Blood of my Brother II, Zoe & Ysuf Woods $15.00 Available
22. Hoodfellas, Richard Jeanty $15.00 available
23. Hoodfellas II, Richard Jeanty, $15.00 03/30/2010
24. The Bedroom Bandit, Richard Jeanty $15.00 Available
25. Mr. Erotica, Richard Jeanty, $15.00, Sept 2010
26. Stick N Move II, Shawn Black $15.00 Available
27. Stick N Move III, Shawn Black $15.00 Available
28. Miami Noire, W.S. Burkett $15.00 Available
29. Insanely In Love, Cereka Cook $15.00 Available
30. Blood of My Brother III, Zoe & Yusuf Woods Available
31. Mr. Erotica
32. My Partner's Wife
33. Deceived 1/15/2011
34. Going All Out 2/15/2011

Name_____

Address_____

City_____State_____Zip Code_____

Please send the novels that I have circled above.
Shipping and Handling: Free
Total Number of Books_____Total Amount Due_____
Buy 3 books and get 1 free. This offer is subject to change without notice.
Send institution check or money order (no cash or CODs) to:
RJ Publications
PO Box 300771
Jamaica, NY 11434
For more information please call 718-471-2926, or visit www.rjpublications.com
Please allow 2-3 weeks for delivery.

PUBLICATIONS
BRINGING EXCITEMENT, FUN AND JOY TO READING

Use this coupon to order by mail

35. Neglected Souls, Richard Jeanty $14.95 Available
36. Neglected No More, Richard Jeanty $14.95 Available
37. Ignorant Souls, Richard Jeanty $15.00, Available
38. Sexual Exploits of Nympho, Richard Jeanty $14.95 Available
39. Meeting Ms. Right's Whip Appeal, Richard Jeanty $14.95 Available
40. Me and Mrs. Jones, K.M Thompson $14.95 Available
41. Chasin' Satisfaction, W.S Burkett $14.95 Available
42. Extreme Circumstances, Cereka Cook $14.95 Available
43. The Most Dangerous Gang In America, R. Jeanty $15.00 Available
44. Sexual Exploits of a Nympho II, Richard Jeanty $15.00 Available
45. Sexual Jeopardy, Richard Jeanty $14.95 Available
46. Too Many Secrets, Too Many Lies, Sonya Sparks $15.00 Available
47. Stick And Move, Shawn Black $15.00 Available
48. Evil Side Of Money, Jeff Robertson $15.00 Available
49. Evil Side Of Money II, Jeff Robertson $15.00 Available
50. Evil Side Of Money III, Jeff Robertson $15.00 Available
51. Flippin' The Game, Alethea and M. Ramzee, $15.00 Available
52. Flippin' The Game II, Alethea and M. Ramzee, $15.00 Available
53. Cater To Her, W.S Burkett $15.00 Available
54. Blood of My Brother I, Zoe & Yusuf Woods $15.00 Available
55. Blood of my Brother II, Zoe & Ysuf Woods $15.00 Available
56. Hoodfellas, Richard Jeanty $15.00 available
57. Hoodfellas II, Richard Jeanty, $15.00 03/30/2010
58. The Bedroom Bandit, Richard Jeanty $15.00 Available
59. Mr. Erotica, Richard Jeanty, $15.00, Sept 2010
60. Stick N Move II, Shawn Black $15.00 Available
61. Stick N Move III, Shawn Black $15.00 Available
62. Miami Noire, W.S. Burkett $15.00 Available
63. Insanely In Love, Cereka Cook $15.00 Available
64. Blood of My Brother III, Zoe & Yusuf Woods Available
65. Mr. Erotica
66. My Partner's Wife
67. Deceived 1/15/2011
68. Going All Out 2/15/2011

Name_____

Address_____

City_____State_____Zip Code_____

Please send the novels that I have circled above.

Shipping and Handling: Free

Total Number of Books_____Total Amount Due_____

Buy 3 books and get 1 free. This offer is subject to change without notice.

Send institution check or money order (no cash or CODs) to:

RJ Publications

PO Box 300771

Jamaica, NY 11434

For more information please call 718-471-2926, or visit www.rjpublications.com

Please allow 2-3 weeks for delivery.